HER FATHER'S DAUGHTER

By

Patricia E. Walker

Copyright © Patricia E. Walker 2020
This book is sold subject to the condition that it shall not, by way of trade or otherwise, be lent, resold, hired out, or otherwise circulated without the publisher's prior consent in any form of binding or cover other than that in which it is published and without a similar condition including this condition being imposed on the subsequent publisher.
The moral right of Patricia E. Walker has been asserted.
ISBN: 9798647445919

This is a work of fiction. Names, characters, businesses, organizations, places, events and incidents either are the product of the author's imagination or are used fictitiously. Any resemblance to actual persons, living or dead, events, or locales is entirely coincidental.

With thanks to my husband Andrew for all his on-going support.

AUTHOR'S NOTE

The main problem in writing a historical novel is language. Every generation has had its own individual words and phrases which, over time, have mainly disappeared from daily use even though some of them can still be found in the dictionary. As an author, I must bear in mind that the last thing the reader wants to do is to pause to clarify a word in the dictionary, at the same time however, I need to bear in mind that the story must be as realistic as can be told, which means using some period words or phrases within the text.

CONTENTS

Chapter One *1*
Chapter Two *13*
Chapter Three *24*
Chapter Four *34*
Chapter Five *53*
Chapter Six *73*
Chapter Seven *92*
Chapter Eight *105*
Chapter Nine *119*
Chapter Ten *133*
Chapter Eleven *142*
Chapter Twelve *152*
Chapter Thirteen *164*
Chapter Fourteen *177*
Chapter Fifteen *189*
Chapter Sixteen *201*
Chapter Seventeen *212*
Chapter Eighteen *228*
Chapter Nineteen *241*
Chapter Twenty *256*
Chapter Twenty-One *267*
Chapter Twenty-Two *282*
Chapter Twenty-Three *294*
Chapter Twenty-Four *306*
ABOUT THE AUTHOR 319

Chapter One

FEBRUARY, 1785

The marriage of Maxwell Giles Alexander Seer, The Most Noble the Marquis of Deerham to the Lady Louisa Markham, only daughter of the Earl and Countess of Markmoor, had not been a love match. Arranged by their respective fathers when Seer was thirteen and Louisa barely out of the cradle, both parties concerned had accepted their parents' wishes; the gentleman because, not to have done so would have been dishonouring his late father, and the lady, thanks to her late parent's chaotic lifestyle and reckless spending, had been given no choice.

The late Earl of Markmoor may have been the possessor of a proud and honoured name but his estates were heavily mortgaged, placing an unbearable strain on his son and heir, due, in the main, to his predilection for all games of chance.

The late Marquis of Deerham, as his son knew very well, had been the first to deprecate the late Earl of Markmoor's behaviour, but his reasons for entering into that betrothal agreement had stemmed from reasons which Markmoor had never understood. Louisa's mother had been the youngest daughter of the Earl of Halford, an old and dear friend of Seer's father, a man he had held in great respect. It had been Halford's dying wish that the two families should be united by marriage, and since Markmoor had neither the time nor the inclination to set aside a moment's thought for his family's welfare or future, he had readily acquiesced in his father-in-law's plans for the betrothal of his daughter to Deerham's only son.

With his son's education already prescribed from the date of his birth, running true to form in typical Markham tradition as well as entering his name in various clubs for future membership, and his daughter's future was secured, the late Earl of Markmoor, deeming he had fulfilled his duty as a parent by doing everything that was required of him for his children, shelved any further responsibility for their welfare, happily leaving anything else pertinent to their needs and interests in the hands of his wife and Stringer. He had no doubt at all that these two most capable individuals would do a far better job than himself, and since he had more pleasurable calls upon his time awaiting him in town, he said goodbye to his wife and family without a twinge of conscience or backward glance. Over the ensuing years he had gone full tilt down his hedonistic path pursuing his pleasures at will, and apart from the odd visit to his ancestral home and the occasional trip to town by the countess, Stringer, his long-suffering man of business, was firmly of the belief that if he ran plump into his wife and children in the street, he would not know them from Adam!

His lordship, who had much preferred to remain uninhibited by his man of business, a circumstance that would have been unavoidable had he conducted his affairs in Cavendish Square, had therefore ordered him to remain at Markmoor Manor to transact his business from his ancestral home. Consequently, keeping track of his lordship's movements had been almost a full-time occupation for Stringer, as this erratic peer never seemed to remain in one place for long enough to pin him down to either discuss his affairs or consult him over his offspring. On the occasions when he had been fortunate enough to find him at home in Cavendish Square, he had more often than not found him to be either on the point of attending a race meeting somewhere or preparing to visit friends out of town or, which was by no means unusual, he had been still abed recovering from his potations the night before, declaring belligerently that he was in no mood to discuss estate business or anything else, and therefore he was to do as he saw fit.

Stringer had done so, as far as he was able, but not even his excellent management and organizational skills could perform miracles and, despite his many warnings and sound advice, verbal and written, his lordship, much preferring the company of his cronies at the gaming table or the attentions of the lady currently enjoying his protection, could not be brought to see that affairs were reaching crisis point, and that the mortgages held on three-quarters of the estate were in danger of being called in. Having reluctantly been forced to give his man of business a few moments of his time, Markmoor had briefly scanned the papers held out to him, the startling truth which met his eyes coming as a reeling blow. Stringer, who had strenuously argued against taking out the mortgages in the first place had been shocked to discover that his employer had gone ahead and handled the transaction himself behind his back, told his lordship that his affairs needed immediate attention and that if he was to avoid complete and utter financial ruin his signature was required in order to extend their terms for a further six months, when, hopefully, a mutual agreement could be drawn up for the redemption of them. Markmoor had duly signed the papers, but although he had been stunned at discovering the true state of his affairs he nevertheless refused to consult any further with Stringer until his return from Leicestershire the following week, stating that he could not at this late stage disappoint his friend Miles Carew by failing to join his party. As far as Stringer was concerned the condition of his estates and the need to salvage what he could was far more important than keeping a social obligation, but as he could see his lordship would not be turned from this he had merely nodded his head, relieved to know that he had at least got Markmoor's attention if nothing else after years of striving to bring his business dealings to his notice. He had left Cavendish Square in a hopeful if not entirely confident frame of mind, never for one moment suspecting that it would be the last time he would set eyes on his lordship.

It had come as a terrible shock when informed that he had broken his neck following a fall from his horse during his stay with Miles Carew at his hunting box in Leicestershire, and Stringer, whose emotions upon hearing this were somewhat mixed, could only now look hopefully at his lordship's son, Christopher Viscount Chedworth, who, thank God, had inherited none of his father's financially ruinous habits.

As far as the Countess of Markmoor was concerned, she had never entered into her husband's business affairs nor he discussed them with her, and as there had always seemed to be sufficient monies for her needs there had been no call to enquire. The death of her regularly absent husband had come as rather a shock, but it had come as even more of a shock when Stringer had been forced to tell her that the coffers, if not actually bare, would certainly not support too heavy a strain on their meagre resources. He had tried his best over the years to hide the truth from her, but when faced with all the demands the estate would be called upon to support in the immediate future, not merely the mountain of debt her late husband had accrued, which was crushingly burdensome, or his obsequies, but the pending emergence into society of the Lady Louisa, a heavy financial outlay for any parent who wanted their daughter's launch to be a success, not to mention her marriage to Deerham, providing of course, he did not renege on it, it was impossible to conceal the realities of their monetary situation. Upon discovering the truth about her late husband's gambling debts she had looked in horror at Stringer, the total sum quite staggering, but since he could not provide her with even a modicum of good news to relieve her despair, and his late patron had continually disregarded his warnings and advice, that was when he could be brought to spare a moment for something other than his own pleasures, he could only offer her ineffectual sympathies, which clearly did nothing to help.

It was bad enough to learn of her husband's enormous gambling debts, but for her to learn that there were also numerous bills from coachmakers, the finest modistes in town as well as a hefty account from one of the most fashionable and expensive jewellers in Bond Street for an emerald and diamond necklace, a ruby and diamond bracelet and other expensive pieces, made her feel quite sick. Anger and humiliation quickly followed, and it was therefore with considerable difficulty that she remained in her seat, listening to Stringer's explanations and apologies with as much dignity as she could muster. Christopher, of course, must have known all about the claims being made on the estate and the true extent of his father's embarrassments and, like Stringer, the countess, who, apart from being extremely relieved to know that her son had no turn for gambling or showed the least inclination to follow in his father's wayward footsteps, was nevertheless angry to know that through no fault of his own it was now his task to try to bring back into order what his father had thoughtlessly squandered.

Their marriage, like so many others, had been arranged to suit their parents' wishes, but, even so, they had rubbed along together remarkably well. It would be an exaggeration to say that they had eventually tumbled headlong into love, but they had nevertheless grown to be very fond of each other. The countess knew that her husband much preferred the gay life in town to the quiet of his estates, nevertheless the full sum of his activities caused her profound shock and pain. She could not understand how her late husband could have possibly gambled away over three-quarters of his entire fortune at the tables or on the turf; never having taken part in anything more dangerous than whist herself. Since his death, she had come to know that her husband, apart from his gaming and expensive stable of hunters, had also enjoyed the more pleasurable but ruinously costly times he had spent with his mistresses, maintaining them in luxurious style while the connection had lasted, which, had she but known it, was even now the talk of the ton. Being tucked away at Markmoor Manor in Gloucestershire for most of the time raising her children, having no desire to participate in the hectic whirl of London social life, she had been kept away from the gossip and scandal which followed her husband's reckless gambling and amatory affairs, and if, on the occasions she did go to town and felt the eyes of her acquaintance closely regarding her, she easily put this down to the fact that they were sorry she was not in town more often.

She had never for one moment believed that her husband had remained faithful during the twenty-seven years of their marriage, but that there had been so many fair dashers under his protection profoundly shocked her. It seemed the whole of London knew what she had only recently discovered; discretion, it seemed, holding no place in her late husband's thoughts as he openly flaunted his latest flirt about town. It was long before she could banish the mental images of all those women who had shared her husband's life as well as the family box at the theatre and the opera, realizing with sickening disgust the meaning of those stares and shakes of the head from all her friends and acquaintances on the few occasions she had visited town and decided, after many tears had been shed, that her only course now was to look to the future and ensure that her daughter was creditably established in the world.

Christopher, of course, had the unenviable task of stepping into his father's shoes, and she could only be thankful that he had not inherited any of the late earl's tendencies. On the contrary, he was a quiet and rather reserved young man who much preferred the country life and its pursuits, the very thought of being in town for very long was something he could not contemplate without a shudder. He took no pleasure from the giddy world of ton parties and social engagements any more than he did in the risks which surrounded the laying of bets either on the turf or at the tables, where thousands of guineas were won or lost on the turn of a card and, far from wanting to spend time with the kind of women his father had often kept company with, he looked forward to the day when Miss Charlotte Laid became his wife. The life of a country gentleman suited him very well, indeed, he had almost sanctioned his mamma's suggestion to sell the house in Cavendish Square, considering its enormous upkeep, even when unoccupied, to be ruinously expensive, but only a very little thought was enough to convince him that to have done so would merely confirm the financial necessity for such an action. There was still too much gossip in town about his father without adding to it by advertising their circumstances as being every bit as dire as they believed, but, not only this, there was his sister's launch into society as well as her forthcoming betrothal and eventual marriage to Deerham to consider. For such events to be inaugurated from under a roof other than their own could not be contemplated, and therefore the imposing mansion would remain in the Markham family. Even taking into account those crippling mortgages, which, thanks to Stringer's strenuous efforts, a mutually satisfactory agreement had been drawn up with the mortgagees, there were still enough funds to allow this, but even though Christopher was prepared to keep the house in town, his father's stable would have to be sold. He knew he could not expect such prime specimens to sell for anywhere near the exorbitant sums his father must have paid for them, but they were nevertheless blood cattle and should therefore realize good prices and, since he was not a spendthrift, saw that this much-needed revenue, together with a little extra economy and common sense, would enable him to slowly salvage what his father had casually and, all too frequently, gambled away.

Stringer had had no intention of enlightening the young viscount as to the extent of his father's debts and the damage he was doing to the estate, still hopeful that, even now, he could bring Markmoor to a sense of his responsibilities and get him to curtail his heavy spending. However, upon returning to Markmoor Manor following a fruitless meeting in Cavendish Square, failing yet again to bring that erratic earl to give him his attention regarding his worsening affairs as well as persuading him that it would be better if he conducted his patron's affairs in Cavendish Square and not miles away in Gloucestershire, to find even more bills awaiting him for payment upon his return to Markmoor Manor, he would not have done so. His frustration had been such that it had taken all his resolution to remain in his unenviable office and not leave Markmoor's employ on the instant, and had it not have been for Christopher entering his room at that moment to ask how he had found his father he would not have a breathed a word, but this quiet and solicitous enquiry, perfectly natural of course, somehow had the effect of pushing his patience to the limit, causing him to momentarily forget what he owed his patron, by angrily disclosing the true state of affairs. It may have relieved his feelings by getting his grievances off his chest but there was no denying the profound shock his revelation had had upon the young man staring incredulously at him, and he was immediately vexed that he had allowed his anger and frustration to lead him into such an utterance.

As only to be expected, it was several horrifying moments before Christopher recovered sufficiently from the reeling blow of discovering the full extent of his father's dealings, and although his numerous amatory affairs, all of which appeared to be conducted under the amused and interested glare of the ton without a thought to his own or his wife's dignity, was bad enough, it was nothing compared to the enormity of the sums he owed his creditors and the amounts he had lost at play. He may have been totally at a loss to understand such recklessness, but he had nevertheless fully agreed with Stringer that his mother must be shielded from the truth unless it was absolutely necessary to tell her. Like his father's man of business, Christopher could only view such a lifestyle as the one his father engaged in as ruinous, but since it was not his place to caution his father about his way of life, he had hoped, though not very confidently, that he would eventually call a halt before it was too late. He had not done so, for which Christopher did not blame Stringer. That harassed man of business had, over the years, gone to desperate lengths to try to get his father to attend to his warnings and advice as well as trying to persuade him to tend to estate business and, only at the very end, was he able to gain his attention, but whilst his father had made a move to remedy the situation by signing the documents presented to him, he still preferred to put a pleasurable engagement before his commitment to his estates and family.

But although a few inroads had now been made to revert matters, Christopher's overriding concern was the betrothal of his sister to Deerham who, as he knew only too well, was not legally bound to honour that verbal agreement which had been made between his late father and his own grandfather, and could, if he so wished, renege on it. He had only met Deerham a few times, and then only over the last six months or so during his visits to town on business, but although they had exchanged polite courtesies, no mention of the betrothal had been made. This was not surprising given the circumstances of his father's recent death and the fact that, because his sister had only just turned eighteen and the betrothal, should it come to pass, would not take place until she was nineteen, there had been no reason for either of them to touch upon it.

At the time the agreement was made the Markham estates were hale and hearty, but, over time, tremendous damage had been done, rendering any assets practically worthless, and Deerham, more than anyone, would know this only too well. He would know too that should he make an offer for his sister he would have to pay through the nose for her, and whilst this would be a heavy weight off Christopher's mind there was every possibility that Deerham may consider marrying into the Markham family not worth the extortionate price he would have to pay for the privilege.

It was only natural that the couple would wish to meet one another prior to any offer being made, but even if Deerham liked what he saw he may still consider the settlements far too high to bestow his name upon her. The world and his wife knew that the Seers were as wealthy as they were proud, and although Deerham was perfectly amiable there was a certain reserve about him which made it difficult for one to read his mind. It could well be that he resented the idea of having to rescue an estate from the verge of bankruptcy brought about through the excessive and ruinous behaviour of one whose selfish pursuit of pleasure had brought a once thriving estate to its knees. Not only that, but Deerham could look as high as he chose for a wife. There had been, and still were if the rumours were true, mammas aplenty looking hopefully in his direction for their daughters, on top of which he could well have someone else in mind other than his sister, a woman for whom he would not be expected to hand over anywhere near the amount of settlements as he would for Louisa. Should he decide to offer for his sister after all, then Christopher could not deny that such a timely boost to the family coffers would go a long way to reclaiming his estates, should Deerham determine not to do so however, then the future looked extremely bleak to say the least.

Christopher could only admit to heartfelt relief in that his parents had only been blessed with two children. The way things were, he failed to see how the estate could possibly have supported younger siblings at Eton and Oxford, and whilst he loved his sister, he could not fail to own that it would be a relief to see her off his hands and to know that as the Marchioness of Deerham her future security would be assured. This, of course, was by no means certain, but Deerham, like his father, was a man of honour and integrity and it could well be that he would much rather agree to the settlements than bring his father's word into disrepute. But this possibility as well as Louisa's *entrée* into society could not, of course, be contemplated until a decent interval had elapsed following his father's death, but as his sister had only just turned eighteen and nothing could be done for another year about her betrothal to Deerham, assuming of course he did come up to scratch, and neither he nor his mother were in any hurry to see her enter an alien world just yet, it would do her no harm to remain here in Gloucestershire for a while longer.

*

Louisa had naturally been informed of the betrothal agreement from a very early age, and whilst as a child she had not given any thought to it, indeed there had been no reason why she should, after all it was common practice for parents to arrange the marriages of their offspring, especially daughters, but as she had grown older it had gradually intruded in her thoughts more and more. She had never met Deerham nor, for that matter, any man other than members of her family or the parson and those neighbours her father had not ostracized in one way or another, for which living quietly at Markmoor Manor was responsible.

As far as her father was concerned, she could only recollect seeing him half a dozen or so times in her life, when he had seen fit, for whatever reason, to visit his home, and then for only half an hour at most before dinner. She remembered him as being a tall man, a little thick around the waist with a florid face and accentuated lines around the eyes and mouth, but there had still been traces to suggest that he must have been a very handsome man when young. She had had no idea of the profligate life he had led in London or the disastrous path he had blithely trod, but now, since his death, she had learned a little of what had been kept well hidden, and since Christopher was not a man prone to exaggeration or telling lies she had no reason to doubt him or question the desperate straits in which her father had left his wife and children.

Christopher, who was six years older than his sister, his mother having lost three children in between them, had always been very protective of Louisa and therefore upon being faced with the task of explaining their situation to her, he had, strangely enough, found it easier to apprise her of their dire financial circumstances than talking to her about her marriage. He knew she was aware of the betrothal agreement and that she had accepted it well enough, but as he explained matters in greater detail, his mother by far too distressed by everything which had fallen upon her of late to discuss it with her daughter herself, he discovered it was by far the hardest thing he had yet to do. As gently as he could he acquainted her with the unpalatable fact that as their circumstances were now common knowledge, she could not expect too many, if any, offers for her hand if Deerham did not honour the betrothal as no prospective suitor wanted to marry a virtually portionless bride any more than he would want to be saddled with hefty settlements, and therefore it was vitally important that when she did eventually meet Deerham she do nothing to give him a disgust of her which would make him cry off. Christopher refrained from telling her that should he do so then their case would be desperate indeed because no amount of optimism could lead him into thinking that they would come about without the marriage taking place and the finalizing of those all-important settlements.

Louisa had been deeply shocked by all she had learned about her father's activities when away from his family, which was often, and could not understand why Deerham, who could not fail to be aware of her father's way of life, would want to even consider offering for her. Marriages of convenience may be a way of life in her social circle, but even so she found it hard to believe that a man would want to offer marriage to a lady he had never laid eyes on before, particularly one who was the daughter of the Earl of Markmoor, and if Deerham was as proud as she had been led to believe by the Reverend Berry when he had called to see her mamma two days ago, then she failed to see why he would want to.

But Mamma, far from pleased to learn that the Reverend Berry had dared to make such a comment to her daughter, told her that Deerham, like any man, had his faults, but he was, nevertheless, everything she could wish for in a husband for her. But although she accepted that a thirteen-year age difference may be considered by some as being a little too wide between them, she maintained that Louisa could only benefit from it, and therefore with her husband's experience to help and guide her she foresaw a most agreeable future for her. What she wisely did not tell her daughter was that Deerham, a connoisseur when it came to women, would certainly be disappointed in Louisa, who, apart from being no beauty, possessed none of the accomplishments which were considered indispensable for a young lady on the verge of entering society. Her sewing and embroidery left a lot to be desired, her drawing and water-colouring were something to be ashamed of and her skill on any musical instrument, not to mention her singing, were alike painful to the ear, and no amount of tuition had succeeded in getting her to speak one sentence in French or Italian which was even halfway intelligible, and all of this in spite of the very expensive governess employed to teach her these arts. However, she told herself that all was not lost because Louisa, whilst finding sewing and all the rest a dead bore, was an avid reader, indeed the information she had crammed into her head from the hundreds of books in the library was astounding, then, of course, she enjoyed dancing, walking and no one, thank goodness, could find fault with her seat on a horse, but the one thing she excelled at, though heaven forbid it ever became known, was mathematics. Why the child should find working out a numerical problem exciting she had no idea, and whether Deerham offered for her or another, no husband wanted a bluestocking for a wife!

Thankfully though, no one could dispute the fact that, despite her youth, she had excellent taste, knowing precisely what became her and what did not, and this alone gave her hope. With close on a year to further instruct her daughter as to what would be expected of her when she entered society as well as preparing for her marriage, assuming it came off that was, it was to her immense relief that Louisa, who was blessed with a quick and lively mind, as well as being naturally excited about going to London, proved herself eager to learn all she could.

Like her brother, Louisa had inherited none of her father's profligacy, for which her mamma was devoutly thankful. She was a very well brought up young lady and, like her maternal grandfather the late Earl of Halford, she was genuine and honest and fiercely loyal. She had a friendly and open disposition and seldom sank into a fit of sullenness or lost her temper, possessing an impish sense of humour which was as mischievous as it was infectious and really quite irresistible but, and this was by no means a criticism by her mamma, she did have a tendency to say the first thing which came into her head without giving herself time to pause to consider. She may have no cause to blush for her daughter's manners, but her mamma could not deny that lurking just beneath the surface of her many endearing qualities was an unexpected streak of tenacity which had more than once raised its head, proving that once her mind was made up to something she was not easily diverted.

Having only a month ago attained her nineteenth birthday, she was old enough to realize the practicalities which surrounded her marriage and the importance of making a good match, if not with Deerham then someone equally as wealthy, but she was also young enough and woman enough to want to be courted for herself and not because it was required of the gentleman to pay conventional court to her. She had often, in the quietness of her room, imagined the kind of man she would marry and, of course, he was very handsome and loved and adored her, ending in a walk down the aisle to live happily ever after, but, in the real world, she knew such dreams held no place and, like so many before her, she was on the point of being given in marriage to a man she had never laid eyes on. She had no reason to doubt her mamma's assurances that Deerham had all the necessary qualities which went to make up an eligible husband, but the thought that he was marrying her for reasons other than love made her wonder what their future together would be like, assuming of course he did not renege on the agreement, but as she tumbled into bed her first night in Cavendish Square she was not entirely certain whether to hope he would or not.

*

Her mother, who had endeavoured to present herself and her daughter creditably dressed, had to own that without the help and support of her only surviving brother, it would have been quite impossible. Indeed, there were times when she had despaired of their circumstances, so much so that she could not help reiterating her earnest recommendation that her son sell the town house in Cavendish Square for a smaller and far more economical establishment, but due to his representations, reinforced by those of her brother, that such an action was out of the question, particularly if Deerham did not come up to scratch, it could so easily jeopardize Louisa's chances of contracting another suitable marriage as it would only advertise their straitened circumstances even more. She had allowed the matter to drop, but she could not help wondering what was to become of them and could therefore only hope and pray that Deerham did not intend to renege on his late father's promise and would in time become her son-in-law, eventually bearing the brunt of what she could only describe as a mountain of debt but since he had as yet to approach Christopher on this all-important matter, her mind could not be entirely relieved of care.

Her brother, who really did have a fondness for her, had never liked his brother-in-law. A staid, quiet man himself, he had deprecated the late earl's disastrous way of life, and on the one and only occasion he had dared to remonstrate with him he had been told in no uncertain terms that he was neither his man of business nor the keeper of his morals and he would thank him to mind his own business in future. He had done so, but not without an effort. He had not mentioned this conversation to his sister or even attempted to hint as to his lordship's activities when away from the family home, and therefore he had no idea whether she knew of his reckless spending or the women who frequently shared her husband's life or not, but he could not find it in him to enlighten her. The late earl had made no effort to either curb his spending or to conduct his amatory affairs with even a modicum of discretion, but when he actually flaunted them at the opera and the theatre, in the family box for all to see, even his closest friends believed he had gone too far.

Christopher had wanted to provide his sister with all the finery a young lady deemed essential for her *entrée* into society, but thanks to the late earl's chaotic lifestyle and reckless spending it had been impossible for him to meet all the demands alone. He had every intention at some future date of repaying his Uncle Julian every penny he had expended on his mother and sister, but when he told his uncle this, he had merely shaken his head, saying, "Forget it boy! 'Sides," he nodded, "you'll be wanting all the money you can get your hands on to put this place in order." Then, upon seeing the look of chagrin which crossed his nephew's face, he patted him fondly on the shoulder, saying, "Don't think I don't honour you for wanting to pay it back, but I don't want it. I'm rich enough to stand the nonsense!" Be this as it may, Christopher was nevertheless determined to repay his every kindness.

From what Christopher had been privileged to see of Deerham on the few occasions they had met and from all he had heard his grandfather say of him, he was confident enough to know that he was an honourable man and one, moreover, rich enough to buy an abbey as the saying went, and if his sister was to be sold into matrimony to save the family from ruin, then he would much rather it be Deerham than anyone else. He was pleased that his relationship with Louisa was a close one and that she trusted him enough to talk and confide in him and, because of this, he had gleaned from her that whilst she was prepared to honour the betrothal which had been made for her all those years ago she would, given the opportunity, prefer to choose her own husband.

He could well understand this, after all he had chosen Charlotte himself and was therefore perfectly aware of the unfairness of it, but since he was himself, like Deerham and his own grandfather, an honourable man, he could not now withdraw from the proposal in order to afford his sister the luxury of looking about her a little to allow her to meet and fall in love with a man she would like to be her husband. Even if that betrothal agreement had not been drawn up between the late Marquis of Deerham and his grandfather, the truth was that the damage done to the estate by his father's reckless spending would have rendered it essential that Louisa contract an advantageous marriage in any case.

"I shall, of course, try to be a conformable wife," Louisa told her brother seriously, "but, Christopher," she shook her head, a slight crease furrowing her forehead, "do you think that Deerham really *wants* to marry me?"

Christopher certainly hoped so, but when, within five days of their arrival in town he received a note from Deerham informing him that, if it was convenient, he would do himself the honour of calling in Cavendish Square at eleven o'clock the following morning in order to discuss the question of the betrothal, he was not at all sure whether to feel relieved or anxious as Deerham had given not the slightest indication as to his decision.

Had Christopher but known it, his future brother-in-law had thought long and hard before arranging that morning call in Cavendish Square because whilst he had no desire to bring the name he bore into disrepute by giving the lie to his father's word, he could not deny that a connection with the Markham family held no appeal for him whatsoever. It was perhaps fortunate for his prospective bride-to-be that she had not been privileged to have seen him a few days before he returned to town, seriously debating the wisdom of offering for her, or that she had not the least idea of how close she had come to being rejected as a far from suitable wife. Hurtful though such knowledge would have been to a young lady who was merely doing as she was bidden, her potential husband, by no means a callous or unfeeling man, had nevertheless given very deep thought to the step he was about to take.

Chapter Two

Worleigh, Deerham's principal seat in Hampshire, was a most imposing residence. There had been a house of one kind or another on this site for centuries, but due to either the prevailing mode or the whims of each succeeding Marquis of Deerham, it had gone through many changes until it had finally developed into one of the most beautiful stately homes in the country. The visitor, having travelled over a mile from the gatehouse, could only look in awe at the north front, a Palladian principal edifice with colonnades of iconic columns either side, the northern ends of which were linked to screen-walls containing gateways, the one leading into the stable court and the other to the kitchen court. The south front, which had also undergone many changes during the past fifty years or so, was a magnificent example of neo-classical architecture stretching for over four hundred and sixty feet in length and thought by many, including its present owner, to be even more stunning than the north front, particularly as it overlooked the landscape gardens which stretched for as far as the eye could see, with a lake and the deer park beyond. The interior, boasting a domed hall of fifty-six feet in height, which was regarded as one of the finest in England, as well as numerous saloons and two dining rooms in addition to a state dining room, was equally as impressive, but it was the library where Deerham relaxed and spent most of his time when at Worleigh.

Although it spanned fifty feet in length, it was a most comfortable apartment, with chairs and sofas sitting at angles on a red patterned carpet. Reaching out on either side of the central marble fireplace, old and rare volumes lined the walls continuing over the double mahogany doors at each end of the room and the far end east wall, whilst on its opposite counterpart hung a map depicting the changes in the Worleigh estate since its beginnings. Two huge desks rested against the walls between the long south facing windows which gave an uninterrupted view of the lake and landscape gardens and to the deer park beyond, but on a late and rather cold evening in mid-February the heavy brocade curtains were drawn, shutting out what normally was a commanding prospect. Above the fireplace hung a portrait of the first Marquis of Deerham dated 1485 by an unknown artist.

Very little resemblance could be detected in the face looking unconcernedly down upon the library's only occupant, who, for the past three hours and more, had been sprawled in a winged chair in front of the roaring fire, one booted leg flung negligently over its left arm and the other stretched out in front of him, staring blindly ahead at nothing in particular. Leaning back with his left arm raised to support his head and the other resting carelessly along the well-worn arm, abstractedly twirling a wine glass between his strong fingers and thumb, he was not only wholly impervious to the time but also to the fact that he had consumed over half the decanter's contents, reposing on a small side table next to him.

Unlike his forebear, he was tall and loose-limbed with a dark, swarthy complexion and clear dark grey eyes set under heavy lids, which, at the moment, were narrowed in thought. He was considered to be striking rather than handsome, for which his aquiline nose and the deep cleft in his square and purposeful chin were largely responsible, but his well-shaped lips could, on occasion, break into a smile which was really quite irresistible. Right now though, lost in deep and not very edifying thought, they were compressed into a thin uncompromising line, and the deep frown which creased his forehead made him look rather unapproachable, indeed he appeared at his most forbidding. His dark hair, which, in general, was neatly tied with a black bow in the nape of his neck, was, at the moment, looking somewhat dishevelled, the direct result of dragging his fingers heedlessly through it. The lawn cravat, which he always wore when riding round his estates, was slightly askew, and the top buttons of his shirt were unfastened, exposing his tanned neck and throat, giving the impression that he was far from sober, but even though he had consumed a deal of wine he was by no means drunk. Apart from the gold pin in the slackened folds around his neck, the only other adornment was the plain gold signet ring he always wore on the little finger of his left hand.

When he was on his own at Worleigh with only his secretary for company at the table, he never changed for dinner and therefore he had entered the house following an afternoon spent in visiting some of his tenants with the intention of going over some estate business with William, but the letter he had been handed by Clifton, not long having been brought up from the receiving office, drove any desire to work out of his head. Having briefly perused the contents, a deep frown descending onto his forehead, he issued rather curt instructions that he did not want to be disturbed and that dinner was to be set back a couple of hours, then, dismissing Clifton, he shut himself up in the library with only the decanters and glasses for company. The order that dinner was to be set back was carried out, but Jules, his artistic culinary sensibilities offended, had raised his arms in exasperation, exclaiming his talents were wasted in such a household; threatening to leave on the instant, but, instead, had given vent to his feelings by gesticulating and issuing oaths in a way which Clifton described to his spouse as very French.

His lordship, meanwhile, had known for some time that he could not shelve the question of his betrothal indefinitely, not only that, but courtesy demanded he inform Markham of his intentions regarding his sister. Louisa now must be almost nineteen, the age stipulated by her grandfather, the late Earl of Halford, as being appropriate for her marriage. The brief conversations Deerham had had with Christopher Markham whenever they had met in town over recent months, had not encompassed this delicate question, but considering the age of his sister at the time and the recent death of his father, it had not only been inappropriate but he had by no means settled it in his own mind. Now though, according to the society page in *The London Gazette*, the Markhams, after twelve months of mourning the late earl's death at Markmoor Manor, were returning to their London home and fixed to remain there for the season. It followed therefore, that not only was the family ready to take up their place in society again but Christopher Markham would certainly be expecting a visit from him regarding the betrothal.

Deerham knew that his father had held the Earl of Halford in the greatest esteem, in fact they had been friends for many years, but as far as his friend's son-in-law was concerned his father had had nothing but contempt for him. The truth was the late Marquis of Deerham had been one of the first to shun that noble peer, not only for the disgraceful and shameful way he had flaunted his mistresses in public without any pretence of discretion or common decency but had recklessly gambled away almost his entire fortune without a thought for his estates and the son who would one day inherit.

Markmoor had been a hardened gamester and one who had favoured deep play. Deerham himself had seen Markmoor at the tables gambling away thousands in a night's sitting. Deerham doubted there was a man in London who had not received, indeed still held, the late earl's vowels to pay the sum he had lost to them, and seriously questioned the estate's resources in being able to settle the half of them, much less accounts and demands for payment from his creditors. But it was not only the tables which had drawn Markmoor; the turf too had held equal appeal for him, his tall figure being a familiar sight at any meeting. He had been known to lay hundreds on a long-odds horse for no other reason than a laughingly offered wager by a friend, only to see, more often than not, the animal come in way behind the field. Society may look askance, perhaps even indulgently, at such irresponsible behaviour, but when it came to flaunting one of his mistresses at the Duchess of Devonshire's town house ball or escorting one or the other of them to the opera or theatre, decked out in clothes and jewels he had lavishly bestowed on them, and in the Markham box under the very noses of the ton who knew the countess well, he had gone his length. But Markmoor, impervious to snubs or being given the cut direct by certain members of the ton, had gone on his reckless way without even a modicum of discretion; only his oldest and most intimate of cronies supporting him. Nevertheless, he had been Markham of Markmoor, and although he had alienated most of his acquaintance as well as everyone else in society by his blatant disregard of the rules governing gentlemanly conduct, the name he bore still counted for something, but although doors had continued to be opened to him for that reason only, there were those who were very much offended by having to do so, his fatal, and most unexpected, accident, twelve months ago by no means making him any more acceptable to them.

*

Deerham and Christopher Markham may move in the same circles but as this young man had no taste for the life his father had enjoyed, he seldom showed himself in society other than putting in an occasional appearance at one of the clubs for which his father had put his name forward for membership, magnanimously doing one final and indispensable office for his son. It was only to be expected that Deerham would run across Christopher at one or other of these various gentlemen's establishments, but mostly at White's, but it had been apparent from the outset that the son was a very different kettle of fish altogether to the father. From the conversations Deerham had had with him it was clear that he preferred the quiet of Gloucestershire to the entertainments on offer in town, and not until his father's death a year ago had he come to town so often. Christopher's reception by the ton had been warm and friendly with no mention made of his father other than a natural expression of condolence, and if there were those whose memories still recalled the late earl's antics or those whose sensibilities were still deeply offended by them, they had at least the good sense and decency not to touch upon them.

Deerham was not overly surprised to discover that Christopher was keeping the house in Cavendish Square in the family, any more than he was to see the late earl's stable go under the hammer at Tattersall's; prime cattle which he had paid a fortune for, but Deerham would own himself astonished if they realized the price Markham had paid for them. Nevertheless, the revenue from the sale must have brought in much-needed funds to the virtually bankrupt Markham estate but he doubted it would defray even a fraction of the late earl's debts. Deerham applauded

Christopher for his efforts in trying to salvage the wreckage wreaked from his father's reckless spending and could well understand his desperation to finalize the betrothal agreement, dreading the thought that he might renege at the last minute, necessitating finding another and equally rich husband for his sister to boost their almost dwindled funds!

Considering it was in Christopher's best interests to see his sister safely established as soon as possible and to have the settlements securely deposited in the Markham coffers, he could so easily have found it worthwhile during their conversations to have extolled at length on her virtues and qualities, but he had not done so, for which Deerham was not at all sure whether to be glad or sorry. Had Christopher done so however, it would be only natural for a brother to speak well of his sister, especially to her prospective bridegroom, and a bridegroom, moreover, who was rich enough to pay handsomely for her. Nevertheless, Louisa Markham was an unknown quantity to him, and whilst Deerham supposed, in fairness to her, he should reserve judgement, or, at least, his decision, until he had met her, after all he would like to see what he would be getting for his money, he could not deny that the thought of marrying a woman about whom he knew nothing and the late Earl of Markmoor's daughter to boot, was something he could not contemplate without misgiving.

Should he honour his father's promise, then he could expect to pay dearly for the privilege of marrying the Lady Louisa Markham, a young lady, a *very* young lady in fact, who could, for all he knew, be a replica of her father. From what he could see Christopher was not tainted with his father's vices and it was reasonable to suppose that his sister was not either. Of course, being tucked away in the heart of Gloucestershire all her life, it was fair to say that she had had no opportunity to display such inherited traits but, once in town, adorning society and attending numerous balls and card parties, coupled with her youth and inexperience, could be just the catalyst to spark off what had so far remained dormant. It seemed unlikely, but, even so, it was just as possible for a daughter to inherit her father's traits as it was for a son. If gaming was in her blood then nothing would remove it and having all too often seen the lengths hardened gamesters would go to indulge their obsession as well as the results accruing from it, then the last thing he wanted was to be bled dry by a wife whose wayward tendencies would prove to be equally as ruinous as her father's, especially having paid through the nose for her already! But the late Earl of Markmoor's decadence was not only a passion for gaming, it incorporated other and more self-indulgent pastimes which…!

A ground out expletive left Deerham's lips, banishing such a ridiculous notion, and pouring himself another glass of wine he decided that, whatever Louisa Markham may or may not be, he doubted very much that her faults included the taking of countless lovers and flaunting them in front of him.

Anger, frustration and mounting uncertainty had him in their grip, so much so that he could not help but retrieve the letter he had stuffed into his waistcoat pocket, reading the warning again:

'*Deerham,*

Now that Christopher Markham has taken up residence in Cavendish Square and it is almost a year since the death of his father, I believe the time is almost upon you when you will be approaching him regarding the betrothal agreement made by your father and his grandfather many years ago. You will, of course, dictate your own affairs, but, from one who wishes you well, I would strongly recommend caution in your dealings. I trust I have no need to remind you of the adage, 'like father like son', or, in this case, 'like daughter.'

A well-wisher.'

He had no idea who had sent him this *communiqué*, the handwriting clearly disguised, the author obviously preferring to remain anonymous, but whilst Deerham had never been one to hang a father's mantle around the necks of his children, it could not be denied that, in this case, the mantle could very well fit. No matter how unpalatable the thought, he knew that whoever had taken the trouble to write to him either had his best interests at heart or had hidden motives of their own, in either case, it had done nothing to make his decision any easier.

Unlike the late Earl of Markmoor, his own amatory affairs had been conducted with the utmost discretion, and although he had thoroughly enjoyed the pleasurable hours he had spent with the lady currently enjoying his patronage, he was perfectly aware that, at thirty-two and with no brother or male relative to succeed him, he would have to marry eventually, and although he had never turned his back on matrimony, it had to be said that there had been no one for whom he had felt even remotely like endowing his name. There were any number of eligible young ladies in society who were not unattractive, indeed there were some real diamonds of the first water, and from most exceptional families, none of whom would be averse to receiving an offer from him and, certainly, not their mammas, but, unfortunately, not one of them had sparked anything remotely resembling love inside him, and whilst he knew that for one in his position love had very little if anything to do with marriage, he would like to think that he would at least have a liking for the lady with whom he would spend the rest of his life.

Upon reflection however, he was compelled to admit that it was perhaps as well that not one of them had touched his heart, because whilst that betrothal agreement had no basis in law, a mere gentlemen's agreement in fact, as far as he was concerned it may as well have been carved in stone, and for him to renege on his father's word, something he regarded as being just as binding as any legal document, would be an act of unspeakable dishonour. He could, if he so wished, inform Christopher Markham that he was unwilling to uphold the betrothal agreement, and there would really be nothing that young man could do about it, but for a man of Deerham's integrity he knew he could not do it as not only would it be an insult to his father but to Louisa Markham as well, and as this would be just as ungentlemanly as anything her father had ever done, he knew he had little choice but to go through with it.

It soon became apparent to every member of the household that his lordship was in no very good humour, but only the initiated had the least idea why. The under-servants, who seldom set eyes on him, were nevertheless agog to hear the smallest piece of news regarding his lordship, but since Clifton maintained a very strict household and an even stricter guard on his tongue, they had to console themselves with speculation. Clifton, who had been butler in his lordship's father's time, prided himself on holding a privileged position within the household as well as possessing a unique knowledge of affairs, but even he would have been astonished had he known the content of that letter, which, at this very moment, was occupying his lordship's mind.

Deerham's parents had enjoyed an exceptionally happy marriage. Beginning with nothing more than a slight acquaintance it had gradually grown into a love which had endured until his father's death four years ago. His mother, now living quietly in Bath, was still very much in love with her late husband and, on his regular visits to see her, Deerham often sat listening to her recounting instances which, however small, meant so much to her.

His mother may live quietly in Bath but she knew all about the late Earl of Markmoor's activities. Whilst she had never believed in interfering in her son's affairs any more than she had in questioning her husband's dealings, she could claim no liking for the match her son was now contemplating, indeed, should he honour the agreement his father had made, then as far as she could see the future for her only son looked extremely bleak. She admitted freely that she knew nothing of Markham's daughter, in fact she had never once laid eyes on the girl, but, for all that, she was most disinclined to welcome the match.

It was in the middle of these deliberations that William, having learned from Clifton that he had, on two separate occasions, attempted to inform his lordship that dinner, having been put back as he requested, was, if not ruined, seriously impaired, only to retire without him being aware of it, unobtrusively entered the library. After silently closing the door behind him, he trod softly over to where Deerham was lounging in the winged chair beside the fire in profound and not very edifying thought.

"My lord," he said quietly, inclining his head.

At the sound of William's voice, the frown lifted and the slightest of smiles touched Deerham's lips and, looking up into the serious face of his secretary, asked quietly, though not without a touch of amusement, "Well, and what crisis demands my attention?"

William smiled. "No crisis, my lord. It is merely that Clifton asked me to inform you that dinner was ready some twenty minutes ago, having been put back as you requested."

"Since when have you been employed as my butler?" Deerham enquired.

Ignoring this, William said calmly, "Clifton has twice attempted to apprise your lordship of it."

Deerham raised an eyebrow. "Has he? I was not aware of it."

"No, my lord," William confirmed.

William Forman had been in Deerham's employment for four years, ever since he had come into the title, and although he was by no means inundated with work he had more than sufficient to keep him continually occupied, taking great pride in managing all his lordship's business affairs which also encompassed his other residences and properties as well as Worleigh. He was of no more than middle height, a slightly built and unprepossessing young man of nondescript appearance, only his light brown eyes giving any indication that a keen sense of humour lay hidden beneath his staid exterior, but he had proved himself an admirable secretary and one Deerham would be loath to lose. His hopes, of course, lay in becoming a member of parliament one day, and upon coming down from Cambridge armed with a well-earned degree and full of eagerness to set his plans for his future career in motion, it had been at his cousin's suggestion that he would find his aspirations could best be served if he first found employment as a secretary to some peer in order to not only gain valuable experience but who could possibly be persuaded into acting as his sponsor. It was therefore through his cousin's agency that William had found his present post, and although Deerham seldom presented himself in the House of Lords he was nevertheless known, on occasion, to take his seat and, even, to make a speech, which, although it met with William's approval, he did wish that his lordship would be a little more impassioned. He would also like to see his noble employer take a more active role in the Lords than he did, nevertheless, it had to be said that when his lordship did rouse himself to attend, those of his fellow peers privileged to hear him make his speech were not disappointed.

Over time he had come to know Deerham very well and, despite his own somewhat serious turn of mind and strict views, he had nevertheless grown to like his lordship more than he would ever have thought possible.

His employer had, upon discovering his political aspirations, raised an amused eyebrow, saying, not unkindly, "My dear boy, what on earth for?" But, for all that, he had happily offered his sponsorship to assist his ambitions when the day came for him to make his political debut. When this would be precisely William was not very sure, but until an opening to put himself forward as a candidate in the right constituency in which he felt he could be most beneficial presented itself, he was perfectly content to serve Deerham in any way he could.

Like Clifton, he was well acquainted with the dilemma which faced his employer. He had seen that letter which had been handed to him, and although he was not conversant with its contents, being marked 'private', in view of Deerham abandoning the work he had intended to go through with him to shut himself away for the last two hours and more instead, he had a rather shrewd idea what message it conveyed. He could not pretend to having a liking, much less approval, for the kind of life the late Earl of Markmoor had led, whose antics, even now, were the talk of the ton, and whilst he could not claim to knowing anything about his offspring, if it were at all his place to do so he would have strenuously cautioned his lordship about becoming tied to any member of that disgraceful peer's family. From the looks of it though, Deerham was by no means enamoured of the idea himself, because whilst he too had enjoyed the company of more than one fair dasher, William had never heard it said of Deerham that he was a care-for-nobody or a man without honour and integrity, on the contrary he was a man of the highest principles who upheld the name he bore with dignity and he would therefore shrink from bringing it into disrepute.

William eyed Deerham now with a knowledgeable eye and sincerely wished there was something constructive he could do regarding his predicament, but as he was not employed as an adviser and Deerham would neither welcome nor want his input unless he specifically asked for it, especially on something he was by no means certain of himself, William kept his own counsel even though it was his firmly held belief that Deerham, if he had any sense, would do well to steer clear of the Markham marriage.

With the sole exception of William, who naturally knew of the betrothal agreement his late father had bestowed his approval on and would, should the agreement be honoured, oversee the question of settlements, Deerham, apart from lightly touching upon it, had never discussed it in any detail with him and certainly had no intention of doing so now. He had a very shrewd idea of William's thoughts on the subject, and whilst these clearly ran parallel to his own, he was really in no frame of mine to have his own feelings confirmed.

"Why don't you tell me I'm as sulky as a bear and be done with it?"

Deerham smiled, showing an excellent set of strong white teeth, struggling to ease his loose-limbed body out of the winged chair, placing his empty glass down onto the side table.

"Not that, my lord," William shook his head. "A little blue devilled, perhaps."

"Yes," Deerham acknowledged, almost to himself, tucking the letter into his waistcoat pocket, "a little blue devilled."

"If there is anything I can do, my lord," William offered.

"Thank you, William," Deerham smiled, "but that won't be necessary. You must not be thinking however, that I do not appreciate all the time and effort you expend on my behalf," he smiled, attempting to tidy himself up, "I do, but I doubt even *your* excellent qualities can find the answer I seek."

William said nothing more, but as he followed Deerham out of the library and across the marble domed hall to the smaller of the three dining rooms, he could not help but wonder if there *was* an answer to be found for his predicament. He knew his employer to be a generous and tolerant man and, like his father before him, he was a good landowner who cared passionately for his estates and his people. Liked and well respected by all who came into contact with him, except for those who had tried to flatter or toad eat him and got short shrift for their pains, he could be relied upon to stand as a very good friend. He was proud without being arrogant, rendering him insufferable, and it was seldom he lost his temper, but there was a quiet strength of purpose and determination beneath that agreeable, if often reserved, manner, which was as inflexible as it was inherent.

Keeping these reflections to himself he sat through dinner conversing on a number of topics; laughing over something he had heard in the village, then spent some time in listening to Deerham's ideas for the Long Bottom Field and, following his lead, William entered into lengthy discussions about this tract of land ending by saying, "I will speak to Higgins tomorrow, my lord."

Deerham nodded his silent agreement, after which he considerably surprised his industrious companion by saying, "By the by, William, I shall be returning to town tomorrow. Will you please ask Trench to come and see me after dinner? I shall be in the library."

"Yes, of course, my lord," William nodded, surprised, "but I thought you were established here for another few days?"

"Yes," Deerham sighed, "so did I," rising to his feet and throwing his napkin down onto the table. "I think, William," he nodded, laying a hand on his shoulder as he walked past his chair, "that very soon now you will be able to wish me happy."

So, he was going to honour his father's word after all! William had no liking for it, but Deerham was not asking for either his opinion or advice and therefore said resignedly, "Yes, of course, my lord; very happy."

"You might at least look it," Deerham smiled.

"I beg pardon, my lord," he shook his head, "it is just that…"

"Well?" Deerham enquired amusingly.

"You do not think that Markmoor…?"

"My dear William," Deerham cried in mock surprise, raising a sceptical eyebrow, "are you *daring* to suggest that Markmoor will turn down my offer for his sister's hand! No, no, my dear boy," he shook his head, a wry smile twisting his lips, "I shall be welcomed with open arms in Cavendish Square, I assure you!"

Chapter Three

Deerham's well-wishers, and there were many, may advise caution in his dealings with the Markham family, even going so far as to strenuously recommending him to steer clear of the marriage with the late earl's daughter, but in one quarter at least it was devoutly trusted that he would honour his father's promise and, hopefully, bring himself to ruin in the process.

Digby Singleton had never met the late Earl of Markmoor's offspring, much less heard him speak of them, although considering he hardly ever laid eyes on them it was not really surprising, but it stood to reason that one or the other of them would inherit their father's traits, possibly both; he hoped so. Yes, he devoutly hoped so! He hoped too that Deerham would marry Edmund Markham's daughter and that she would lead him a merry dance or, if not her, then her brother; better still, both of them, either way Deerham would be bled dry!

They may move in the same circles and know the same people but they had never been friends, even less so since Deerham had twice spoiled his game; the first being that ill-fated game of cards with young Lord Finchley, a plump bird ripe for plucking, fresh from Cambridge with more money than experience. Having cleverly manoeuvred him into visiting that gaming hell, it had been Singleton's intention to empty his fat purse, but no one, not even Deerham, could accuse him of being a card cheat, his skill far surpassing the need to resort to such tactics, especially on so naïve and callow a youth, but, somehow, Deerham had learned of the deception which had been perpetrated on his trusting young friend and had determined to put a stop to it. Then there had been the Dalby chit! How Deerham had got wind of what he had planned for her he would never know, but that he had done so and thwarted his schemes, rankled to this day.

There had never been any love lost between them, which had nothing whatever to do with their difference in age, and Singleton could not see this changing, but he was honest enough to admit that if he could bring about Deerham's downfall he would gladly do so, and therefore he had known no compunction in sending him that letter. He knew Deerham to be a man of integrity and one who had pride in the name he bore and would, for that reason, shrink from bringing it into disrepute, which, failing to uphold his father's promise, would surely do. But there was that in Deerham which could not be pushed, but, hopefully, a little nudge urging him not to do what he had no mind for, could just well prove the mechanism which would see him doing precisely the opposite! Singleton could hazard a pretty good guess in what state his old friend's affairs had been left, and if he needed further confirmation he had only to think of his prime cattle coming under auction at Tattersalls, and therefore it did not take much to know that Deerham, should he decide to offer for the girl after all, would have to pay dearly for her; Christopher Markham would have to be a fool to let him off lightly!

No one was more interested in Deerham's decision than Singleton, but since they only exchanged a civil nod in passing it was hardly likely that he would acquaint him with his intentions, and, consequently, he could only wait in eager expectation to learn his decision. In the meantime, however, there was his own pressing affairs to occupy his mind, which, unfortunately, must, for now at least, take precedence over Seer's matrimonial uncertainties.

Digby Singleton may be related to any number of the most distinguished and wealthiest families in society, but, unlike his relatives, he lived a somewhat precarious and impecunious existence from his lodgings in Half Moon Street, relieved only by his winnings at the table or on the turf. His paternal antecedents were unquestionable, but, like his late mother, whom his paternal grandparents had strongly disapproved of and tried by all means possible to prevent her marrying their son, had a most undesirable reputation.

*

His father, who had fallen in love with the beautiful Patricia Saltry the moment he had first laid eyes on her, had married the wayward beauty without a moment's thought to what he owed to his name or what could result from such a *mésalliance*. Her parents, the proud owners of a small but thriving hop garden in Kent, though not wealthy, had certainly been respectable, but with five daughters to marry off they had not allowed the disparity between the Honourable Anthony Singleton, youngest son of James Anthony Digby Singleton the seventh Earl of Wynchcombe and their eldest daughter to worry them over much; consoling themselves with the thought that Patricia, once married and moving in the first circles, would, in time, find suitable husbands for her sisters.

The Earl of Wynchcombe, having taken one look at the dark eyed beauty, who had made no secret of the fact that she was eager to leave her lowly origins behind her and marry into one of the most wealthy and respected families in society as well as enjoying its benefits, strongly disapproved of the connection. He had strictly forbidden his son to take any steps whatsoever in order to try and bring about a union between them, but heedless of the warnings and deeply in love, the Honourable Anthony Singleton had, by special licence and in complete secrecy, married the woman for whom he was running the very great risk of being cut off without a penny. His father had certainly threatened this dire action, but mainly due to the earnest representations of the countess, he had not done so; reluctantly granting his son a quarterly allowance as well as bestowing on the young couple a stylish but modest house in a quiet part of town where, it was fervently hoped, they would pass the notice of the ton. Regrettably, they had not done so; for which the Honourable Mrs. Anthony Singleton's craving for the life she had long desired, was responsible.

She had no intention of finding husbands for her sisters, being far too taken up in her own new and exciting life to give them a second's thought. She had no more love for her husband than she had had for any of her other numerous admirers who had hung around her ever since she was thirteen, in fact, for all she cared he could have been seventy with one foot in the grave; all that concerned her was that he was a passport to the life she had always yearned for, providing the long-awaited escape from the unbearable necessity of having to live within their limited financial sphere and the suffocating confines of respectability.

Patricia's marriage to the Honourable Anthony Singleton may have been regarded by a good many as being nothing more than a hole-in-the-corner affair when it eventually became known that not one member of his family was in attendance or one notable personage he called friend to give it the least semblance of propriety or validity, much less dignity, nevertheless she had finally achieved her ambition. She had no qualms and certainly no regrets about being the cause of bringing disgrace on her husband's name by permitting him to marry far beneath him, indeed she had accepted his offer of marriage without a blink, but now that she was his wife she was determined that, despite her father-in-law's hope of them living quietly, she was going to take her place in society where she belonged, as well as being equally determined not to go about in rags, and she had therefore chosen the most expensive modiste in town to deck her out in the first style of fashion. Her marriage to Singleton may not have met with his family's approval, indeed her own parents were suffering belated doubts as to the wisdom of it, but she cared not the snap of her fingers for any of them nor, for that matter, the eyebrows raised in shock which her antics, even in the early days, were beginning to generate.

Patricia, within months of her marriage, had already shaken off her husband's escort, enjoying the many compliments and attentions she received from those who saw at a glance she was not averse to accepting them, neither afraid nor hesitant in embarking on flirtations which, although they had not yet developed into affairs, were conducted, if not with remorse, then at least with some semblance of discretion. But whatever pretence she had perpetrated in the beginning, her husband, realizing too late that he had mistaken his emotions and acknowledging the gross error he had made in marrying her, had now completely disappeared. Careless of the glances cast in her direction as well as impervious to the gossip which abruptly ceased at her entrance, the Honourable Mrs. Anthony Singleton treated both with contempt. She would not allow narrow-minded matrons to dictate her behaviour and the sooner they realized that, the better. A passion for cards also meant she was often to be found at the table, fast acquiring the reputation of favouring deep play. Sometimes she rose a winner, but, more often than not, she lost heavily, requiring her to hand over a written promise to pay, a circumstance which made the gentlemen, far more tolerant of her antecedents as well as her actions than the ladies, smile, but which made those same ladies shake their heads in horror. No lady handed over a vowel, but Patricia, having neither the time nor the patience to pander to society's rules, frequently flouted them, and enjoyed doing so. Once, at Lady Cheston's sedate card party, she had staked her ruby earrings, a wedding gift from her husband, handing them over without a blink and then, at the Duchess of Ayrburgh's drum ball, she had been found in one of the smaller saloons playing with a recklessness which had seen her pulling the bracelets from her wrists and throwing them onto the table to cover her wager. The action had brought a moment's stunned silence, but she had merely flung back her head and laughed; the game had continued but there were those who considered such conduct as deplorable and wondered what Singleton had done to deserve such a wife. In the eyes of the censorious her youth did not excuse her and, for the well-informed, they knew precisely where to place the blame for such behaviour. Without doubt, her appallingly common background!

The bracelets as well as the earrings had been redeemed for her, but when Singleton had handed them back to his wife, he had made his displeasure known. Patricia had listened to his strictures with impatience, and when he warned her that he would not tolerate his wife making herself the talk of the town by such behaviour, she had merely shrugged her shoulders.

"I promise you, Patricia," he had said quietly, "I will not tolerate such conduct. I do not ask much of you, but I demand you comport yourself with some semblance of dignity."

She had not done so. Indeed, she saw no reason why she should. She would not be dictated to like a nobody and, totally ignoring everything but her own pleasure, had continued to create gossip, her utter disregard for propriety propelling her to do precisely as she wished. Her attendance at the card tables did not abate nor did her growing delight in admirers who were perfectly willing to show their appreciation of her beauty as well as her unconventional behaviour. She made no attempt to hide the enjoyment she derived from their company and the fulsome compliments they bestowed upon her, and certainly never gave a moment's thought to her husband's feelings or the fact that, whilst his father was a rich man, he himself had only a quarterly allowance.

If some gentleman found it necessary to express his ardour by devoting the entire evening to her, flirting outrageously with her, then so be it. She saw no reason to try to prevent him from doing so, after all, what did the old tabbies think he could do to her in the middle of a crowded saloon or ballroom? The thought made her laugh. She was young, beautiful and ready to be pleased, and did not regard a husband as an adequate enough reason to curb her behaviour. A wedding ring should have afforded her protection from the men who openly dangled after her, but she did not want or need protecting. Their attentions excited and exhilarated her and she had no intention of ceasing a pastime which gave her far more pleasure than any husband possibly could, and whose feelings and wishes neither troubled nor concerned her.

Nearly twelve months into her marriage only went to confirm, if it needed confirming, that that institution, although giving one extreme licence also gave one immediate respectability, something which she did not hesitate to take full advantage of. But, of late, her behaviour was beginning to be noticed even more, lacking the judgement she had previously shown, even her mother, living quietly in Kent since the unexpected death of her husband, had become uncomfortably aware of Patricia's conduct and, upon a discreet visit to town to see her daughter, found herself quite incapable of stemming that young lady's exuberance. Remonstrate with her daughter though she did, the only effect it had on her was a defiant toss of her head and a shrug of her pretty shoulders, saying airily, "Let them say what they will."

"You do not care what people may say of you?" asked her mother, surprised.

Patricia shrugged. "It matters not to me!"

"And your husband?" her mother had asked.

"What of him?" she had thrown over her shoulder.

"You do not think he cares about what you do, or what is said of you?" asked her mother, sadly.

"Why should I?" she shrugged.

Her mother had looked closely at the young woman she was fast coming to realize she did not know at all. "Have a care, Patricia," she had warned, glad that her husband was no longer alive to witness their daughter's antics; at a loss to understand from whom she could possibly have inherited such ways and traits.

Patricia was about to argue the point but thinking better of it she stormed out of the room, leaving her mother to sink despairingly onto a chair, wondering, and not for the first time, how to curb her daughter's wilful behaviour. From childhood, Patricia had always liked her own way, displaying flashes of temper if something was denied her, but with the optimism of a loving mother she had believed it was something she would grow out of. She had not done so. To discover that her daughter was the talk of the town shocked and saddened her, and since her own efforts had failed to instil some kind of awareness in her and, to date, Anthony, for whom she had a sincere liking, seemed to be equally unsuccessful, she could only hope and pray that her son-in-law would eventually find a way of bringing her to her senses.

Anthony's marriage to Patricia had given him much food for thought, so much so that he had, within a very short space of time following their marriage, come to regret his recklessness in allowing himself to believe that he could have been fool enough to think he had been in love with her, but upon being informed by his wayward wife that she was going to have a child he had been filled with the hope that with motherhood would come moderation. He would never know; Patricia succumbing to the hazards of childbirth.

The Earl of Wynchcombe, knowing of his daughter-in-law's antics, had, unlike his son, who harboured no misgivings that he was the child's father, doubted the paternity of the child even before it was born, refusing outright to either acknowledge or provide for its future in any way, announcing to his son that his allowance, now his wife was no longer around to squander it, should be more than sufficient to ensure the child's care as well as enabling them both to live comfortably enough. The Honourable Anthony Singleton, with no prospects of ever becoming the next Earl of Wynchombe being as he was the youngest son with older brothers and their male offspring to secure the line, naturally wanted the best for his only son but the allowance from his father, though generous, would not cover a fraction of the costs to cover his son's education. He had therefore been forced into entering the hazardous world of speculation; considerably relieved when good fortune smiled upon him and his financial investments paid dividends, ensuring his son's financial future and relieving him of the worry of funding Digby's education at Harrow and Cambridge.

The Honourable Anthony Singleton, despite the fact that any number of eligible ladies had indicated they would in no way be averse to accepting an offer of marriage from him, after all he was still a most eligible and not unhandsome man, was by no means tempted into matrimony for a second time but had instead continued to live in the house his father had so generously bestowed upon him in comparative peace and quiet. Safe in the knowledge that his son's education and future, thanks in part to the sum bequeathed to him by his grandmother who, over time, had softened towards him, if not huge, was certainly respectable, were secured. Having no desire to experience again the turbulent upheavals his late wife's conduct had generated, Anthony had been perfectly content to enjoy the convivial company of his long-standing circle of friends, engaging in nothing more dangerous than a game of piquet or faro at one or other of his various clubs or discussing shared interests over a glass of wine.

With the exception of the worrying time he had had over funds until his financial transactions had paid dividends, the years following Patricia's death had been the happiest he had known, and with the improved relationship between himself and his father he found that life, at long last, was beginning to take on some meaning again. To those who had his best interests at heart, having shaken their heads in dismay upon witnessing his travesty of a marriage, did not blame him for steering clear of becoming leg-shackled again any more than they did in knowing that he took his pleasures outside of wedlock in the arms of a lady who had for long been very much attached to him. Not even his wife's harshest critics wished ill on him, on the contrary they believed he was rid of a bad bargain, firmly convinced that now his life would be rendered less harrowing by not having to continually excuse or shield her behaviour, accepting his enduring and discreet affair with such a charming widow without a blink. As far as society was concerned, his life, having now settled into an established and conventional mode, caused no one to raise their eyes in shock or outrage, but when, within three years of his father's death, he unexpectedly succumbed to an inflammation of the lung, the ton was genuinely grieved.

Digby, being fifteen years old upon the death of his father, had continued his education with the same lack of industry and commitment as he had always done and because of his separations from his father during term times at Harrow, such a tragic loss had affected him hardly at all, and since he had never known his mother he saw no reason why suddenly finding himself without either parent should worry him in the least. Having never met his maternal grandmother her death, several years earlier, had touched him not at all and, as far as his maternal aunts were concerned, he gave them no more thought than they apparently gave him, but with the death of his paternal grandmother twelve months later, any link he had had with his father's relations, effectively ceased. His impeccable family connections through his paternal grandmother included the Dowager

Duchess of Caitheswaite, the Earl of Morney and Viscount Tunbridge and, through his paternal grandfather, to His Grace the Duke of Calden and the Dowager Countess of Crosswold, none of whom so much as accorded him a bow in passing.

His father may have left him the legacy of an impressive lineage as well as a proud and honoured name, both of which would ensure all doors in society would be open to him but that of his mother, whose traits and outrageous behaviour had shocked and outraged society and which he had all too evidently inherited, would also ensure that any number of them would remain closed against him. His love of rich living as well as a predilection for all games of chance came to the fore even before he had left Harrow, and by the time he had said a premature and heartfelt goodbye to those hallowed walls of Cambridge his debts had already accumulated to quite an astonishing sum, a circumstance which seemed to concern him not at all. His decision to sell the house he had inherited from his father caused him not one pang of remorse, as not only was it inconveniently situated but it would mean keeping old Barnett on to take care of it, an expense he could well do without, but the sale would provide much-needed revenue; especially as the money he had been bequeathed by his father and grandmother, if not entirely frittered away, would certainly not support him for much longer, already having to rely heavily on his winnings.

At first, he had been content to share lodgings in Clarges Street with a friend and like-minded spirit who, like himself, had neither the inclination nor the interest in furthering his education, but upon his crony's reluctant entry into matrimony, forced upon him by his exasperated father, Digby elected to move into bigger and more comfortable lodgings in Half Moon Street. As the son and grandson of men with impeccable credentials he had adorned the society into which he had been born, and if there were some who found his presence objectionable, mainly those who remembered his mother, they certainly did not have far to look to apportion blame for his reckless lifestyle.

To the few who wished him well, they could prophesy no good ensuing from his hedonistic way of life, and when he became a bosom crony of the late Earl of Markmoor, despite the ten years or so which separated them, not even his most devoted friends could look upon it without misgiving. For two such compatible spirits whose licentious inclinations and outrageous pursuits provided gossip for the ton and for whom the table and the turf were the Mecca of their lives, it was not long after making one another's acquaintance before their friendship was well and truly cemented. Considering Edmund Markham had a wife and family as well as working his way through his fortune just as fast as he possibly could and Singleton, who was neither acknowledged by his relatives nor those high sticklers who regarded his antics, as they had those of his mother, in abhorrence, as well as having no fortune at all but solely reliant upon his winnings, seemed to bother neither man at all.

Singleton, no more than Markham, rose from the table a winner as often as he would have liked any more than he saw the nag on which he had laid a heavy wager beat the field as frequently as he would have wished, but with the optimism which characterized him he had not allowed it to weigh with him, going on his untrammelled path without hindrance or pause. This untrammelled path however, may have afforded the interested food for gossip and even amusement, but there were those, such as his irate landlord and numerous creditors, who failed to share such a blasé attitude regarding his circumstances, and it was therefore in a mood of considerable exasperation that they presented him with their final demands; threatening him with all manner of dire consequences if the rent was not paid and a substantial sum offered to reduce his escalating accounts with his creditors. Since it seemed that they had all had the same idea at precisely the same time by deciding to converge on him *en mass*, he had found himself in the undignified position of having to try to dissuade these vulgar individuals from carrying out their threats, but although he had eventually managed to persuade them into staying their hand for the time being it had nevertheless left him with the urgent need to come up with the funds in which to make good his promises.

His luck had been out for weeks and, from the looks of it, Providence was in no hurry to smile upon him in the foreseeable future, and he was therefore obliged to look about him for other means of filling his purse, but just when he had come to think that there was nothing left but the ignominious prospect of being clapped up for debt or even fleeing the country, Providence it seemed had not turned her back on him after all, showing him a way which was guaranteed to solve his monetary difficulties. He was no stranger to living almost continually on the brink of financial ruin, but the devil was in it that he had not enjoyed such a long run of the most infernal bad luck for a long time, in fact he was fast approaching the point where he would very soon be unable to place so much as a guinea on the table let alone writing and honouring an IOU. He may be denied the acknowledgement of certain hostesses by their refusal to send him cards of invitation but he had never yet been barred from his clubs, but if he failed in this latest venture to replenish his fast dwindling resources, then there was a very real chance of that happening.

Having discovered very early on in his reckless career that there was always more than one way out of a dire situation, Singleton had seen at the outset that in the Honourable Letitia Rawnsley he had the perfect means to save himself from such a humiliation as well as filling his purse. Of course, it would mean being saddled with a wife, a circumstance which by no means suited him, but the chit was young enough to be schooled into learning what he would expect from her. He was perfectly well aware that she loathed him as well as doing everything possible to avoid being in his company, but this, nor the fact that she was twenty-four years his junior, necessary evils if he was to save himself from being clapped up for debt, failed to deter him. Society would doubtless be shocked to hear of such a marriage, but her aunt, who was as wealthy as she was proud, would be only too relieved to accept him as her niece's husband, especially when she knew that if she did not then the girl would be ruined. Like him, her aunt would know that no decent man would ever come forward with an honourable proposal of marriage when it became known that Letitia had spent an entire night in his company without even a maid to save her reputation.

Being leg-shackled held no appeal for him whatsoever, but once his ring was on her finger then what belonged to the Honourable Letitia Rawnsley belonged to him, and since she was a considerable heiress he was quite prepared to make such a sacrifice. If he were honest very young ladies held no appeal for him, but he could not deny that the Honourable Letitia Rawnsley was quite a taking little thing and, despite her abhorrence of him, which he had to admit he found strangely exciting and would no doubt add something of a spice to their forthcoming relationship, he could not afford to be selective, especially as heiresses were a little thin on the ground. Once his creditors knew that his prospects were about to undergo a dramatic change for the better they would soon stay their hand and, even, extend him credit until he could dictate the direction of his wife's fortune.

That it was considerable he knew from her brother, Algernon, a young man whose pockets were as full as they could hold. Of course, he could not expect to take possession of her fortune straightaway, but once the knot was tied and the legal preliminaries were out of the way it would not be long before he was beforehand with the world again, something that would afford him considerable relief. He may be used to continually living on the brink, indeed it had become almost second nature to him, but he had to own that it would be good to know that he no longer had any need to worry over money.

It was indeed most fortunate that her brother's ill-advised but well-timed actions had provided him with the perfect opportunity to put his plans into execution and, of course, the beauty of it all was that there would be no Deerham to intervene! Had he but known that the man he regarded as his enemy had taken it into his head to return to town several days ahead of time and would, by the merest chance, once again thwart his schemes to extricate himself from his financial embarrassments, he would not have been so confident.

Chapter Four

Had it not have been for one of his leaders unfortunately casting a shoe, Deerham would not have had to break his journey to make use of the coffee room at *'The Angel Inn'*, thereby inadvertently stumbling upon Singleton's attempt to abduct the Honourable Letitia Rawnsley. The landlord, Porstow, knew his lordship well, being a familiar figure on the road, assuring him as well as his head groom, Trench, that the blacksmith would be with them directly. Calling for a tankard of Porstow's best ale, Deerham sat in a chair beside the fire, quite unperturbed by the delay to his journey back to town, a circumstance which, had Trench been asked to give an opinion on, he would have said that his lordship was by no means in any hurry to return to town at all and that was most probably the reason why he did not leave Worleigh until well after three o'clock.

'The Angel Inn', situated halfway between Wokingham and Maidenhead, was a busy posting inn, but this early in the year, the season not having yet quite begun, Porstow's hostelry was by no means the hive of activity it normally was, but since his lordship was in no mood for company Porstow's unusually quiet hostelry suited him very well. Mrs. Porstow, well-known for her excellent home cooking and who had more than once had the honour of placing a well-dressed dinner before him, endeavoured to tempt his lordship into partaking of something to eat while he waited. Since it was by now after five o'clock and darkness had long since set in, she, like her spouse, was hopeful of him selecting a number of dishes as well as bespeaking a room for the night, but as he was not especially hungry and experienced no qualms about travelling in darkness, he politely declined both stating that his tankard of home brewed was all he needed.

Had they have known it, Deerham, being in no particular hurry to return to town to carry out a task he was still by no means certain was the right thing to do, had been sorely tempted, but, of course, he could not. He realized only too well that to postpone his meeting with Christopher

Markham was not only discourteous but it cast an unforgivable slight on his sister, and it was therefore with mixed feelings that he decided against delaying his journey, settling himself down to wait for however long it took the blacksmith to shoe his leader.

Porstow, who by no means liked the idea of Deerham partaking of refreshment in the coffee room, offered profuse apologies for being unable to show him into the private parlour due to it being momentarily occupied, was rather relieved when his lordship had made no demur, stating that he was quite comfortable where he was. No one shared this snug apartment with him, which was perhaps just as well since the frown which had suddenly descended onto his forehead made him look rather forbidding.

From the busy taproom a little further down the passageway the sound of muted voices and laughter filtered in to him through the half open door of the coffee room, but quite undisturbed by this he continued to leisurely drink his ale while waiting for Trench to inform him that the blacksmith had finished and his horses had been poled-up, but, gradually, voices other than those in the taproom began to obtrude on his consciousness. He could make out very little of what was being said but from the sound of things it seemed as though a lively exchange was in progress in the private parlour just across the passageway, and from the rather raised and agitated voice which was growing ever louder it was clear that one of its occupants was a lady. As the argument grew steadily more heated, intruding more and more on his awareness, he began to wonder more particularly about the customers in Porstow's private parlour, especially as the lady appeared to be not only rather young but extremely frightened. Curiosity tinged with the distinct feeling that something untoward was going forward, to which the lady was clearly taking great exception, he put his tankard down on the table next to him and turned his head slightly in order to try to hear better, but when, almost immediately, he heard the sound of breaking china, he rose to his feet and crossed over to the door, pulling it open a little more. A string of low-voiced but fierce warnings to be quiet unless she wanted the landlord to come in on them followed by a determined but somewhat tremulous reply that she hoped the whole inn would walk in on them, Deerham stepped out of the coffee room into the stone-flagged passageway in order to hear better. He had at first wondered if the young lady had run away from some select seminary or other and was being taken back by an exasperated parent, but as soon as he heard the man's voice more distinctly, he knew precisely who her companion was and the reason for their presence in Porstow's hostelry. Instinctively Deerham's hands formed into two purposeful fists as it was clear that Singleton, yet again, was attempting an abduction, but unlike the time before his victim was proving to be a most unwilling travelling companion.

It was just as Deerham was about to go in search of Trench when he saw him stroll in to the inn via the back door with his bow-legged gait, coming to tell him that the blacksmith had finished shoeing his leader, but upon setting eyes on his stalwart Deerham strode towards him, putting a finger to his lips.

"Shh."

"My lord?" Trench queried, his wizened and weather-beaten face echoing his surprise.

Ignoring this, Deerham whispered, "I take it there is another carriage in the stables?"

"Yes, my lord," Trench confirmed, bewildered. "Ired from the looks of it. Been there about 'alf an 'our, or so I'm told, but…"

Deerham nodded. "Have my horses been harnessed?"

"Yes, my lord," Trench confirmed. "The carriage is ready when you are."

"I am afraid that won't be quite yet, Trench," Deerham whispered.

"But I don't understand, my lord…" Trench began.

"There's nothing *to* understand," he smiled, "except we are going to help a lady in distress."

Upon being briefly told the gist of things, Trench eyed his lordship aghast. *"Hm,"* he snorted disgustedly, "it's about time somebody drew 'is cork!"

"My sentiments exactly!" Deerham said firmly. "Now, off with you," he nodded, pushing him irresistibly towards the rear door, "and be ready when I say."

Trench, who had been with the Seer family well before his lordship was breeched; had, like his father before him, been born on the Worleigh estate, and not only had he watched his lordship grow up but had put him on his first pony as well as teaching him how to tool a vehicle, guiding him through his mistakes, not failing to berate him for any mishandling of the ribbons. He was, perhaps, with the sole exception of Thomas, his lordship's long-serving valet, the only person who dared to question him, and whilst he knew Deerham to be the best of masters and the kindest of men, he also knew that he had no intention of allowing either himself or anyone else to question his orders.

After seeing Trench off the premises, Deerham retraced his steps and again stood listening outside the parlour door, which still remained slightly ajar. What he heard only served to reinforce his belief that the lady was being carried off against her will and having a natural aversion to abduction as well as nothing but contempt for Singleton and men of his calibre he never questioned the rights or wrongs of coming to her aid especially when he considered who her companion was. His lips compressed as he continued to listen, but as now was not the right time to show himself he nevertheless looked forward to thwarting yet again the disreputable ambition of Digby Singleton.

From the sound of it, it was clear that the lady was not going to be easily persuaded into continuing the rest of their journey, and Deerham, who had to strenuously resist the overwhelming urge to enter the private parlour and knock the lady's abductor senseless there and then, knew a moment of satisfaction as he pictured the impecunious Singleton trying to deal with his troublesome and reluctant captive as he attempted to drive her through the night to some unknown destination.

"You *fiend!*" Deerham heard the lady cry. "How *dare* you treat me in this fashion! Do you *really* believe that I would have gone anywhere with you voluntarily?"

"But you did," Singleton reminded her softly, the lines of dissipation around his eyes and mouth more accentuated than usual.

"Yes," she flashed, "because you tricked me!"

"Devious, perhaps," Singleton nodded, totally unperturbed by practising such a deceit, "but very necessary."

"I *hate* you!" she panted. "I *demand* that you return me to my aunt's house immediately."

"I am afraid," he told her, without the least semblance of regret, "that I cannot oblige you," his thin lips parting into a smile which made her shudder. "Oh, fear not," he assured her, "I shall return you to Cavendish Square, but not tonight."

She made an attempt to escape but he was too quick for her, and grabbing hold of her arm said softly, "You hate me, yes, but when it becomes known, and it will, I promise you," he said menacingly, "that you have spent an entire night in my company without even your maid, your reputation will be ruined beyond repair. You will even be glad to receive an offer of marriage from me."

She eyed him aghast. *"Never!"* she cried repulsively. "If you were the last man on earth I should *never* accept you!"

"Keep your voice down," he warned her again, surprised that the smashing of the china vase had gone unheard. "Do you want the landlord coming in on us?"

"Yes!" she exclaimed. *"Anything* is preferable than having to endure *your* company!" she threw at him, drawing her cloak closer around her. "And as for marrying you," she scorned, "I would *die* rather!"

Singleton seemed to consider this, saying at length, and with a confidence which made her want to cry, "Your aunt, believe me, will see it quite differently, I assure you. She will, make no mistake about it," he told her softly, the satisfaction in his voice filling her with dread, "be only too relieved to welcome me as your husband. She will know," he nodded, "if you do not, that unless she does so then you will never be creditably established. In truth," he told her, seeming to take a perverse pleasure from it, "your reputation will be ruined."

She knew he was right, but she would rather die or go home in disgrace than marry him. Despite her fear her pansy brown eyes flashed and her face became flushed with angry colour as she faced him. Had she but known it, Singleton had never found her more desirable than he did at this moment and dared to attempt pulling her into his arms. She tried to back away from him but soon found herself with nowhere to retreat to, the look in his eyes, a strange and frightening look, bringing a sob to her throat. He reached for her but somehow managing to evade him she raised her right hand and gave him a resounding slap across his painted face.

"How *dare* you!" she panted. "You are no *gentleman*, sir!"

He rubbed his cheek, a low rumble of laughter leaving his throat, but he said, quite quietly, "Very well, but I promise you I shall return this compliment. *Now,*" he said firmly, "we must go."

"I am not going anywhere with you!" she declared. "I would rather walk every inch of the way back than endure your company a moment longer!"

The painted lips thinned, but managing to control his temper, said, with a calmness which totally belied the fact that it would have given him tremendous satisfaction to have slapped her, "By all means do so," he shrugged, "but even if you set out now it will take you hours to arrive back in Cavendish Square, by which time," he smiled chillingly, "your disappearance will have been discovered. So, you see, my dear," he said with pleasurable satisfaction, "either way, your reputation will be in shreds."

Something like a sob left her lips, but determined to uphold some semblance of pride and dignity, she demanded coldly, "Where are you taking me?"

He made no answer to this but merely took hold of her arm, pulling her towards the door of the private parlour, but in spite of her strenuous efforts to resist him she found herself being easily propelled out of the room.

Deerham, quickly stepping back into the coffee room, waited only until he heard their footsteps retreat down the passageway and the opening and closing of the rear door before following them outside, watching from his concealed vantage point as Singleton gave brief instructions to the man on the box of the coach before pushing her unceremoniously inside and climbing in after her. The door was shut with a snap and instantly the equipage was seen moving out of the stable yard, and Deerham, waiting only until he had seen them round the corner of the inn out of sight he immediately signalled to Trench who brought his coach out of the dark recesses of the stable courtyard, giving the horses the office to move off as soon as his lordship had jumped inside and closed the door behind him.

By now it was almost half past six, and the light flurry of snow, which had gradually turned to rain, was beginning to fall in a light but steady drizzle rendering the air damp and chill. Even though the moon was intermittently obscured by clouds, Trench, who knew this road like the back of his hand, experienced neither concern nor difficulty in negotiating it, keeping a discreet distance from the carriage in front, never once losing sight of his quarry, knowing precisely the point where to overtake Singleton's coach.

Trench was not at all surprised to find himself embroiled in something of this nature, and although he had not even tried to remonstrate with his lordship, he knew that even if he had nothing would have changed his mind; not that he could blame him. There was a strong sense of chivalry in Deerham which, coupled with his innate sense of honour and duty, could not ignore such ungentlemanly conduct as Single was currently exhibiting, indeed continually exhibited, and Trench, although thoroughly deprecating men of Singleton's stamp was nevertheless aware of what could result from tonight's escapade should it ever become known, but this possibility apart, he would never have dreamed of leaving his lordship's side, much less abandon a lady to the likes of Singleton.

Having followed the road for over two miles in a south-westerly direction they were now approaching an elongated bend which narrowed on the other side before broadening out onto a straight stretch for several miles, and Trench, gently easing his team out into the middle of the road at least a quarter of a mile before the curve came into view, gradually spurred them on, passing Singleton's coach without mishap. Having lost sight of the coach, Trench steadily slowed his team, gradually bringing them to a halt, whereupon he skilfully manoeuvred them until the whole equipage was pulled up across the whole width of the road preventing traffic in either direction passing them, but being as it was so early in the year and the weather being most uncertain, it was most unlikely that other road users, other than Singleton, would be impeded.

Singleton, unaware that his illicit journey had been discovered, much less that he was being pursued, especially by the man he not only disliked intensely but would dearly love to pay back for his impertinence, sat comfortably back against the squabs contemplating a far more comfortable future than he had so far enjoyed, watching the mutinous face opposite in quiet satisfaction. However, his captive's demeanour was such that not even his most devoted friends and well-wishers could view his future with her with the least semblance of optimism. Sitting bolt upright, her back ramrod straight and her eyes, when they were not looking daggers at him, were staring unseeing out of the window at the wet and darkened landscape wondering if it would be at all possible to make her escape should the coach slow down sufficiently. She knew perfectly well that she had only herself to blame for the position she was in, after all she should have known Singleton could not be trusted. She hated him more than anyone, and what her brother Algernon saw in him was beyond her comprehension, nevertheless, the mere thought that he was injured and needed her help had been enough to cast her dislike aside. Upon discovering the truth, she had been horrified but fear of what lay in store for her had soon been put to flight by anger, which had momentarily taken Singleton by surprise.

However, it was not long before he recovered from this and consoled himself with the knowledge that, although his captive may despise him with every fibre of her being, her aunt did not want for sense and would instantly see that marriage between them would be her niece's only salvation and, as for her brother, he too would soon be brought to see the truth of this, and that, short of calling him out and creating the devil of a scandal therefore bringing his sister's reputation into disrepute, his hands were tied. Singleton, nothing if not an optimist, seemed impervious to the looks of pure loathing she constantly threw at him and her attitude, far from instilling in him any desire to make protestations of love to her, filled him with the earnest desire to slap her. His cheek may still smart from that resounding slap but he consoled himself with the pleasing thought that once his ring was on her finger he would take great pleasure in bringing her to bridle. He had a very shrewd idea of the thoughts she was entertaining in that pretty head of hers about trying to escape, but since it was not in his interests to either indulge or comment upon them, not that she would get far if she did manage to run away, apart from which she would have no idea in which direction she ought to go, he remained perfectly content to sit and watch the beautiful but mutinous face sitting in the opposite corner, as far away from him as she possibly could.

He could not deny that his tastes did not run to very young ladies, and if his case were not so desperate she would not be here now, but, even so, the Honourable Letitia Rawnsley was quite a tempting little thing, and whilst he envisaged his future marital state as being anything other than harmonious, her fortune would more than compensate for this. He knew beyond any doubt that once the novelty and excitement of her rejection of him had worn off he will be wishing himself well rid of her, but as that was for the future his sole aim now was to ensure his ring was on her finger and her money in his pockets as soon as he possibly could.

It was just as he was on the point of passing an idle remark to the unresponsive figure who showed not the slightest sign of relenting towards him, when the sound of horses' hooves and carriage wheels coming up behind them assailed his ears. At first, he took no notice, merely accepting it as another late traveller, and watched unconcernedly as the noble equipage sped past his vehicle, but within minutes he felt the slackening in speed of his own coach until, much to his surprise, it eventually came to a halt. Leaning his head out of the window he called to Grimshaw demanding to know what the devil was going on and why he had stopped, but there was no need for Grimshaw to say anything as Singleton saw to his astonishment a coach pulled straight across the road, preventing traffic from passing in either direction. Initially, he thought they were being held up by highwaymen, but only a moment's thought was enough to tell him that no highwayman carried out his nefarious trade in such a noble equipage, and he therefore could not help wondering what was happening.

Trench, sitting calmly on the box, had pulled out a serviceable blunderbuss from a convenient holder next to him and was, to Singleton's shocked gaze, pointing it suggestively at Grimshaw who, much to his annoyance, merely sat staring at it with his eyes wide open and his hands held up in the air. As far as Grimshaw was concerned, whatever his master had got himself into then he could get himself out of, he was not paid enough for such hazards as this nor, now he came to think of it, abducting young ladies.

Deerham, meanwhile, had alighted from the coach, having donned a drab driving coat which had been casually lying on the seat next to him and a black tricorne, now pulled rather low over his forehead, with his lawn cravat pulled up to cover the lower half of his face. Within a few strides he came up to Singleton's coach, whereupon he flung open the door and let down the steps to be met with an angry demand to know what he meant by such an outrage, while the lady, taking advantage of this unlooked-for occurrence, was already on the point of descending onto the road.

"My apologies for frightening you," Deerham bowed, taking her hand and assisting her to alight, "but unless I mistake the case, I believe you stand in need of some assistance."

"Will you help me, sir?" she cried, pulling her fur lined cloak closer about her against the cold and damp, her eyes looking up into the half-covered face with heartfelt relief.

"It will be my very great pleasure to do so," Deerham told her, his cultured voice allaying her initial worry. "If you will please make yourself comfortable in my coach," inclining his head and sweeping a hand in that direction, "I shall convey you to wherever you wish to go."

She was about to say something but thinking better of it did as she was bidden, raising her skirts and hurrying towards the coach, and Deerham, waiting only until she was safely inside did he turn his attention back to Singleton, whose eyes mirrored his shock and disbelief.

"Out!" Deerham ordered in a very different tone of voice. "Or do I have to drag you out like the villain you are?"

Singleton did not lack courage but considering the embarrassing position in which he found himself, not to mention Grimshaw periodically turning round in their direction to see what was going on, he decided to step out onto the road. He may not be able to identify the crest on the door panel of the coach in the darkness but he had no difficulty whatsoever in recognizing Trench sitting on the box in the light given off from the carriage lamps, but even before he identified the man who was holding Grimshaw almost immobile with fright he knew Deerham's voice when he heard it, and although he was consumed with anger to know that yet again his plans had been foiled by this man, he retained enough pride and dignity to say, quite quietly, eyeing his Nemesis through narrowed eyes,

"'Twould seem, would it not, Deerham, that you are making a habit of interfering in my affairs?"

"Perhaps if you desisted the habit of plucking callow youths and abducting young females," Deerham told him coldly, lowering his cravat, "there would be no need for me to do so."

Taking a moment to get his temper under control, Singleton pulled out a gold snuff-box from the capacious pocket of his velvet coat, flicking the lid with a deft thumb with a casualness he was far from feeling, before slowly raising a pinch to each nostril in turn, glancing towards Deerham's coach from under his lids as he did so then back again, saying smoothly, "'Twould seem, Deerham, that the honours go to you," inclining his head. "I can, of course," he shrugged, returning the box to his pocket, "only hazard a guess as to what brings you into this, but suffice it to say," he said with contrived politeness, "I am growing weary of your meddlesome interference in my affairs."

"Perhaps if you conducted your affairs in the manner befitting a gentleman," Deerham told him unequivocally, "there would be no need for me to do so."

"And what am I to understand from that, my lord?" Singleton raised an enquiring eyebrow, his eyes narrowing.

"I thought my meaning was plain enough," Deerham told him.

Instinctively Singleton's hand went to his left side, but upon discovering that, like Deerham, he was not wearing his small sword, dropped it, raising cold eyes to the man he silently vowed to repay handsomely. "The time *will* come, Deerham," he warned softly, his painted lips thinning, "when you and I will settle our affairs."

"I shall look forward to it," Deerham promised him.

"You are not alone in that, I assure you. And now, with your permission," he bowed mockingly, "I should be obliged if you would allow me to continue on my journey – unmolested."

"Certainly," Deerham inclined his head, "but *without* the lady."

Singleton gazed in the direction of Deerham's coach, a twisted little smile touching his lips. "Pity," he mused, heaving a deep sigh. "She is, do you not agree," raising a pencilled eyebrow, "just a little out of the common?" Then, just as he was about to step up into the coach he paused, and looking back at Deerham said, with calculated provocation, "You know, Seer, you really must let me know if the extent of her gratitude was worth your intervention."

For one awful moment Deerham knew an overwhelming impulse to send him sprawling, but as this was precisely what Singleton wanted, he managed, by a superhuman effort, to control it. "You know, Singleton," he warned, holding onto his temper with difficulty, "the next time you find yourself rolled up, you really must try to seek out less adventurous measures of saving yourself from ruin other than plucking those who have not outgrown the schoolboy or running off with heiresses young enough to be your daughter!" Beneath Singleton's powder and rouge the pallid face coloured slightly at this home truth. "You deserve to be horsewhipped for this night's work, but however difficult I find it, I shall refrain from giving you the thrashing of your life. I would strongly recommend you, Singleton," he advised, "to think twice in future before you embark on any more such feats again."

"We *will* meet again, Deerham," Singleton vowed softly, his eyes glinting. "I promise you," he warned, "this is the last time you meddle in what is no concern of yours!" Then, after impatiently ordering Grimshaw to get a move on and be quick about it, he stepped into the coach without a backward glance, taking his seat with a leisurely unconcern which totally belied the anxiety which enveloped him as he considered what tonight's failed venture to repair his ever-worsening finances signified.

Grimshaw meanwhile, was not at all motivated with the desire to go to Singleton's help. In truth, he took so much satisfaction from seeing him in the undignified position of being called to account for his actions that were it all possible he would have shaken his employer's adversary by the hand, continued to sit on the box until he was angrily told to get a move on. By the time Deerham returned to his coach Trench had returned the blunderbuss to its holder and turned the equipage round facing in the direction of London, making no effort to give his team the office to move off until he had seen Grimshaw tool the coach, with its furiously angry occupant, away in front of them.

Having been Deerham's groom ever since he was a boy, Trench, with perhaps the single exception of Thomas, could proudly boast of knowing him better than most, and knew that even if the gentleman who had absconded with the young lady had not been Singleton, his actions would have been precisely the same. Indeed, he would have expected nothing less from a man whose code of honour was such that any ungentlemanly conduct was repugnant to him. Trench may not know the precise circumstances surrounding the mutual dislike between his lordship and Singleton, but that it went deep he was in no doubt. He had spoken no less than the truth when he had told Deerham that it was about time someone drew that rasher of wind's cork, and therefore he was a little at a loss to understand Deerham's restraint when he had had the chance to do exactly that.

However, only a moment's thought was sufficient for him to realize that it was perhaps as well his lordship had not engaged in a bout of fisticuffs on the King's high road or, even worse, a duelling match, as both would have been bound to cause a deal of talk. Like Deerham, Trench knew that however much Singleton may have disliked being caught in the act of something so despicable as abduction, there was not the slightest chance of him repeating what had passed between them as not only would he be made to look ridiculous but he would be faced with utter condemnation for his actions, but his man on the box may not have been so circumspect. He may not have been able to identify Deerham or the crest on his coach, but, nevertheless, it could have created the devil of a scandal, and no reliance could be placed on people not putting two and two together especially when it became known that Deerham had returned to town early and would, out of necessity, have to travel this stretch of road.

In the meantime, the Honourable Letitia Rawnsley, still in disbelief at the unexpected turn of events, never so much as considered the fact that in this unknown and masked stranger she could so easily have exchanged one villain for another. Such a consideration never even entered her head, in fact, she instinctively knew that she was safe in this man's hands and, whoever he may be, he had miraculously saved her from a fate worse than death.

Hardly giving him time to close the door behind him, she learned forward, laying a cold and trembling hand on his arm, saying a little breathlessly, "Oh, sir, thank you for coming to my rescue."

Seating himself opposite her, Deerham merely inclined his head, patting her cold hand and saying, "My dear child, it is a very great pleasure to serve you."

"But who are you?" she asked curiously, pushing her hands back into the warmth of her fur muff, Deerham having pulled the cravat back over the lower half of his face before entering the coach.

"Who I am is not important," he told her, making no attempt to remove it or his tricorne.

"I thought at first you were a highwayman," she confided, not at all discomfited by this idea, "but then I heard you speak and knew you could not be."

"No," he said slowly, shaking his head, "I am not a highwayman."

"Well," she conceded, not at all perturbed, "if you won't tell me your name, will you not at least let me see your face?"

Like Trench, he had no fear of Singleton relating this evening's events, but he had no wish to let his identity be known to this young lady as she could so easily, from excitement or reaction, blurt out the truth and the part he had played in her rescue, but, more than this, there was no telling what Singleton, because it was useless to suppose he would not hear of it, may add to it. It was not his own reputation that concerned Deerham but that of the young lady who was looking trustingly at him, because he would not put it past Singleton to take advantage of this evening's events to either force her aunt in to agreeing to the marriage, which he had threatened her with in the private parlour of *The Angel Inn* or forcing a quarrel upon himself and should either happen the truth was bound to come out, and then nothing could prevent the scandal which followed.

"No," he said gently, shaking his head, "I won't do that, but suffice it to say you are quite safe in my hands."

By now the rain had ceased and, every so often, the moon appeared momentarily from behind the clouds filling the coach with an intermittent silvery light allowing him to see the young lady to whom he was tendering his protection and escort. It struck him that she was far younger than he had at first thought, surely no more than eighteen years of age, but the elfin face which peeped out from the fur-lined hood of her velvet cloak was as pretty as a picture, dominated by a pair of huge pansy brown eyes which looked at him without guile or fear. Her little nose, though somewhat on the short side, was flawlessly straight, beneath which was the most adorable mouth he had ever beheld and, when she smiled, it could be seen she had a perfect set of small even white teeth. He watched her consider his refusal to identify himself with interest and admitted to feeling a little relieved when she made no effort to try and press the point but, on the contrary, appeared to accept it without any kind of alarm or concern.

He had no need to be told that she was clearly a young lady of birth and fortune, and as he was no stranger to the apparel ladies deemed essential to their requirements, even having paid for them, he saw at a glance that her clothes were unquestionably fashioned by a most expensive modiste. Having gleaned from her conversation with Singleton in the private parlour at *The Angel Inn* that she was residing with an aunt in Cavendish Square, he had rapidly scanned his memory as to his acquaintance living in that fashionable part of town other than the Markhams to suggest the possible identity of this woman. This mental review had brought to mind only one possible candidate, an old friend of his mother, the formidable Dowager Countess of Pitlone. If this young lady accepting his protection was indeed the niece of this remarkable and forthright dame, then he knew that the sooner she was returned to her home without the slightest breath of suspicion or scandal, the better.

"It is very good of you to help me, sir," she told him, breaking into his thoughts, "but how did you learn of my plight? Are you a friend of Algernon's?"

He looked an enquiry. "Algernon?"

"My brother," she supplied.

"No," Deerham shook his head, "I am afraid I have not that pleasure."

"Well," she said candidly, "I did not think you were. You are not at all the kind of person he usually associates with."

He refrained from asking about the kind of people Algernon usually associated with but could not resist saying, "That sounds like a compliment, if not very flattering to your brother."

She failed to detect the amusement in his voice but sat considering her sibling dispassionately. "You see," she told him ingenuously, "you are far too old for one thing, besides being very sensible."

Deerham's shoulders shook, but his voice was perfectly controlled. "Do I seem old to you?"

She tilted her head slightly, her little nose crinkling as she considered the dark outline sitting opposite her. It was, of course, impossible for her to see whether he was handsome or not with half his face covered, but after scrutinizing him for a few moments she gave it as her opinion that he was probably not as old as she had at first thought.

He laughed at that and inclined his head in mock thanks, but once again he found himself being asked how he had discovered her plight. "I eavesdropped," he confessed.

Her eyes widened at this. "You did!"

He nodded, admitting, "You see, I was in the coffee room over the way from the private parlour when I heard raised voices. Upon discovering an altercation in progress, I listened at the door and soon discovered that you were there not of your own free will." Her eyes sparkled at the recollection. "I could not allow Singleton to abduct you," he told her reasonably, "so I had my coach made ready and followed you."

She clapped her hands and laughed. "Oh, sir, but how clever of you!"

"I am happy to have been of service," inclining his head. He regarded her for several moments before asking gently, "Tell me, are you perchance related to the Dowager Countess of Pitlone?"

She nodded, one dusky ringlet escaping the confines of her hood. "Yes.

She is my aunt. I am residing with her for the season in Cavendish Square."

"I take it she knows nothing of you being in Singleton's company?" he said gently. Upon shaking her head and biting down on her bottom lip, he asked, "Would it be impertinent of me to ask your name and how you came to be travelling with Singleton?"

Without knowing why, she knew she could trust him; she may not be able to see his face but those steady grey eyes told her all she needed to know, and it was therefore without any further prompting or hesitation that she said, in a gruff little voice, "My name is Letitia Rawnsley, and, sir, I was *duped!*" He had no difficulty in believing this. He knew Singleton too well to doubt the veracity of her statement. "Do you know him?" she asked, her large pansy eyes looking questioningly at him.

"Yes," he nodded, "I know him, but we are not friends, you understand."

"Then you will know that he is the lowest beast in nature!" she exclaimed with feeling. "I have never liked him, even though my brother tells me is a 'right one'," she sniffed. "Well, I am not quite sure what that means precisely," she confided, "but he makes me feel as though he can see right through me."

Deerham knew exactly what she meant. Singleton, although some years younger than the late Earl of Markmoor, had nevertheless been one of his bosom cronies, and, like his recently deceased friend, his unsavoury reputation was certainly earned, and even though his latest victim may hear certain stories circulating about him, Deerham doubted she knew the precise truth regarding some of his more disreputable activities, indeed, he failed to see how she possibly could.

"He and Algernon became great friends when they met at a fight," she explained, shuddering, "and although I cannot see what there is about him to like, their friendship has continued."

From the intermittent moonlight entering the coach Deerham could see the various expressions which flitted across her face and knew that she had told him no less than the truth in that she hated Singleton. It was only due to the deference and respect in which his late father and grandfather were still held which made him acceptable to the ton but not even this or his impeccable paternal lineage could prise open the doors to those real high sticklers like Deerham's own mother or his companion's aunt, the Dowager Countess of Pitlone. He had not heard it said that Singleton was on the look-out for a wife, but were he ever to do so then, having lost every penny he had been bequeathed by his father and grandmother at the gaming tables or on the turf, not to mention maintaining those fair dashers he had at one time or another had in his keeping, leaving him solely reliant upon his winnings, he could not afford to marry a portionless bride, on the contrary nothing but an heiress would do, but that he would actually go so far as to abducting one, especially after his last failed attempt, surprised even him. If Deerham's memory served him correctly, the Honourable Letitia Rawnsley would inherit a sizeable fortune on reaching her majority or if she should marry instead, which meant Singleton's affairs must be worse than he had thought.

Deerham doubted very much if she knew the full extent of her abductor's dealings, but her aunt certainly did and made no secret of her feelings. She might be forced into accepting the fact that, unless she kept her niece locked in her room, there was nothing she could do to prevent the two of them from meeting at various soirées and the like, but he could not see her sitting idly by in order for Singleton to further his acquaintance with her. For a man of his reputation, especially where women were concerned, it would surely be enough for that formidable lady to make strenuous efforts to keep her niece well away from him. As far as her brother was concerned, while Deerham could claim only a slight recognition of him in passing, and his knowledge of the family, with the single exception of the dowager countess, was scant, he could not help owning to some surprise in that he had become associated with such a man, but since he had he could only hazard a guess as to whether his aunt knew of it or not. Nevertheless, he felt reasonably certain that such a friendship would not escape her notice for very long, apart from which, if he was being drawn in with Singleton and his set, then it would not be long before he too was forced into hanging out for a rich wife!

Listening to the impassioned outpourings of his companion, Deerham soon discovered that she was the youngest of three children, Algernon, aged twenty-four, being six years her senior. Since their father's death fifteen months ago he was now the fifth Viscount Dunstan residing at the family's town house in Berkeley Square, and since her mother suffered from some unspecified but seemingly afflicting nervous disorder, preferring to remain quietly secluded at the family home in Wiltshire with Letitia's older sister, she had packed her youngest child off to London for her entrée into society under the protection and auspices of her late husband's widowed sister. Clearly, Letitia had not long commenced her first London season, and since he had been staying with a friend in Leicestershire for a few weeks prior to his visit to Worleigh, it was not surprising that Deerham had not before run across her. From her artless confidences, he learned that her sister, Jane, who, it seemed, had 'not taken' despite enjoying several seasons, had therefore decided, at the age of twenty-two, to devote herself entirely to her mamma's welfare, and that her aunt, who was really the sweetest creature imaginable, did indeed know of her nephew's predilection for the company of a man she adamantly refused to even acknowledge, and took great exception to it, rendering relations between the two residences somewhat fraught.

Naturally, Letitia had met Singleton in her brother's company at any number of parties and such like, and, on occasion, she had run across him when out shopping with her maid, but whilst she could not tell Deerham why she disliked him she only knew she did. Algernon it seemed, saw nothing wrong with his newly-acquired friend, and whilst he would not go so far as to welcome a match between them, he saw nothing wrong with his sister being in his company. Her aunt however, had other ideas, stating unequivocally that the only way he would get to know her niece better would be over her dead body, and Letitia, who had no intention of seeking his company either now or in the future, had no need to hear her aunt's warnings about a man she utterly disliked and secretly feared.

Deerham listened to her confidences without a word, and not until she paused to control her emotions did he say gently, "You have indeed endured much today, but I feel you will not be troubled further by him."

Her huge eyes looked hopefully at him and her lips trembled. "Oh, sir, do you think so indeed?"

"I do," he confirmed.

"You do not think he will try to run off with me again?" she cried, shuddering.

"I think it most unlikely," he assured her.

"But how can I be sure?" she demanded, the fight she had displayed in the private parlour at *The Angel Inn* having long since deserted her, the inevitable reaction by now having set in. Covering her face with her hands, she cried, "I am aghast when I consider how easily he duped me!"

Deerham hesitated before asking gently, "Would you care to tell me how he induced you to leave your home?"

It was several moments before she spoke and, when she did, it was noticeable that she was gradually becoming calmer. "I discovered, quite by chance, that Algernon had become involved in a dispute with some gentleman over a game of cards, and that as a result he found himself pledged to embark on a duel. His friend, Barnaby Drew, and another, were to act as seconds. I learned that the duel was to take place this morning and, last night, I urged Algernon to withdraw but he would not. He was horrified at the thought of such a suggestion, demanding to know what fool told me. He was very angry over the affair being made known to me, but I tried very hard to persuade him that it was silly to take part in a duel because you lost at play. He said the cards were marked and could not in honour cry off." She paused momentarily, her little hands clenching inside her muff. "I tried to put it out of my head by telling myself that it was something gentlemen did for some unknown reason, and that he would come out of it all right. I was terribly worried, but I decided not to confide the whole to my aunt, so I tried to put it out of my mind, only I found I could not." She took a moment to swallow the small lump which had appeared in her throat, then, taking a deep breath, said, "About two o'clock this afternoon, I received a visit from Singleton. My aunt was out having gone to visit her invalid sister in Wimbledon. She will not be back until late this evening. At first, I considered refusing to see him, but then I thought that he perhaps had news of my brother. When I spoke to him he informed me that Algernon had been seriously wounded and he wanted me to go to him." She swallowed. "I suppose I should have realized it was all a hum, but I was so frantic with worry, and I agreed to accompany him to join my brother. He advised me not to leave a note for my aunt as Algernon had expressly forbidden it, so I merely put on my cloak and went with him."

Deerham, who had listened to this in angry silence, promised himself the pleasure of dealing adequately with the enterprising Singleton before very long, but, right now, his main concern was trying to allay her fears. He saw no good in telling her that had her brother indeed been seriously wounded as a result of the duel, then one of his seconds would have apprised her of it and not Singleton, but asked instead, very gently, "When did you realize that he was lying to you?"

"A little way before we arrived at that inn. You see," she confessed in a small voice, "I began to think that it was taking a very long time to arrive at the place where he said Algernon was, and when I questioned him he merely smiled and said that it would not be much farther. I began to feel uneasy and when I asked him again he looked at me in such a way that I recoiled. I knew then he was not taking me to Algernon at all. Once inside the inn he told me that my brother was perfectly safe; both parties having deloped – whatever that means," she shook her head, "and that Algernon had then gone off with his friends."

It came as no surprise to Deerham that Singleton had stooped to such despicable lengths, his knowledge of him was enough to prove that he had merely run true to form. It also informed him that Singleton's affairs were in more desperate straits that he had thought.

He looked compassionately at his companion who could not fail to be aware that had Singleton succeeded in his endeavours then her future would have looked bleak indeed. None knew his own world better than he did and that had it ever become known that she had spent the night in Singleton's company unchaperoned, whether of her own volition or not, then nothing could have prevented the ultimate scandal which out of necessity would have forced her aunt to relent to their marriage. Deerham could think of nothing worse than a man like that being married to this lovely creature, but although he had assured her that Singleton would not make another such attempt, he would not by any means put it beyond him, but as they were by now approaching Cavendish Square and his companion seemed a little more calm, he kept these reflections to himself.

Trench, having been informed of the young lady's direction, made his way carefully through the streets, eventually pulling up outside the impressive portals of the dowager's town residence, his face totally impassive as he jumped down from the box to open the door of the coach, waiting for the occupants to alight.

Although it was a tremendous relief for her to discover that she had arrived home safely one nagging doubt continued to plague her, and turned a tired and strained face towards Deerham, who knew instinctively what was going through her mind.

"My dear child," he said soothingly, "do not trouble your head with thoughts of Singleton and what he may say. I promise you he will tell no one."

"If only I could be sure of that!" she cried earnestly.

He took hold of one agitated little hand. "You can be. He will do or say nothing which could possibly distress you further. To do so," he told her, "would merely open him up to well-deserved criticism and ridicule."

She considered this for a moment. "Yes, of course, I see you are right." She paused, saying at length, "Oh, dear sir, how can I *ever* thank you?"

"You have already done so, very prettily," he told her.

"But won't you at least tell me your name?" she pleaded. He shook his head, and she smiled as a thought suddenly occurred to her. "Well, it does not matter in the least. I know precisely who you are."

"You do?" he raised an amusing eyebrow.

"Yes," she smiled, not a little tiredly. "You are my knight errant!"

He laughed. "I am hardly that. Can you contrive to enter the house without being seen?"

"Oh yes," she assured him confidently. "My aunt won't be back for hours, she never is when she visits her sister and, besides," she smiled mischievously, "Turnbridge is a particular friend of mine."

"Turnbridge?" he raised an enquiring eyebrow.

She laughed. "My aunt's butler. We are on the most excellent terms."

He did not doubt it. She was the most adorable little creature imaginable, and he could well imagine her twisting this faithful retainer round her finger. Having stepped down onto the pavement he held his hand out to her whereupon she placed her own into it and descended onto the flagway. She barely reached his shoulder and, as she looked up into his covered face, he could see the sparkle in those large brown eyes and although he knew she wanted none of her day's adventures to be known, he nevertheless felt it was incumbent upon him to stress the need for discretion.

"It would, perhaps, be wise," he advised gently, "if you told no one of this adventure; not even your friend Turnbridge."

"Oh no!" she promised. "I won't."

He raised her hands to his lips. "Goodnight, my lady in distress," he said softly.

"Goodnight, my knight errant," she smiled.

Not until he had seen her safely enter the house did he step back into the coach, his thoughts far from elevating as Trench closed the door upon him before climbing up onto the box and making his way to Grosvenor Square.

Chapter Five

It would be untrue to say that the Honourable Letitia Rawnsley had taken Deerham's breath away, but however loath he was to find himself with a single thought in common with Singleton he had to admit that he had spoken no less than the truth when he had said she was just a little out of the common. Deerham had no doubt that one mischievous look from out of those pansy brown eyes or the merest hint of a smile from those adorably entrancing lips would be the undoing of more than one impressionable young man, but since he was no callow youth the vision which had peeped out at him from under her fur lined hood, enchantingly lovely though it was, had by no means filled him with the desire to pay court to her. Nevertheless, he did feel in some sort responsible for the young lady who had unhesitatingly placed herself into his care and protection.

He may have been only a short time in her company but it had been enough to tell him that beneath that delightful face and spirited disposition she was extremely trusting, were it otherwise she would never have accompanied Singleton on his scurrilously supposed errand to her brother or exchanged his company for that of one she had never before laid eyes on. Added to this, she would inherit a sizeable fortune when she came of age or married before then, an irresistible combination to men like Singleton who continually lived on the brink of a financial precipice, and since her brother appeared to have no qualms about the company in which his sister may well find herself, and there was no guarantee that Singleton would not make a further attempt to abduct her despite his own assurances to the contrary, he was therefore more than prepared to continue to discreetly adopt the role of knight errant which she had so readily bestowed upon him.

He knew there was no fear of him succumbing to Letitia Rawnsley, but apart from the fact that Singleton was old enough to be her father, the very thought of such an adorable little innocent or, indeed, any lady, being forced into matrimony with the likes of him, particularly through guile and deceit, was really quite repugnant to him. Under no stretch of the imagination could a libertine and hardened gamester such as Singleton be considered as being even remotely suitable as a husband let alone holding appeal to a young lady who hated him and could not bear to be near him and, like his bosom crony the late Earl of Markmoor, Singleton fell very far short of the dashing and romantic figure Deerham felt sure Letitia Rawnsley had in mind. There was, of course, plenty of time for her to look about her and fall in love, the danger being however, that she may, out of relief at being rescued, have read more into his actions other than a genuine concern for her safety and well-being, and whilst it would be no great matter for a man of his experience to nip her misplaced feelings in the bud, he could not help owning to some relief in that he had not revealed his identity to her.

To date, Deerham's amorous affairs had been mostly with married ladies from the highest echelons of society, whose husbands, enjoying an equally pleasurable extramarital affair of their own, happily turned blind eyes to their wives' liaisons acknowledging, even accepting, their lovers with every semblance of bonhomie provided of course that all-important element of discretion, that vital rule of the game, was observed, eliminating the dreadful prospect of gossip and bringing one's name into disrepute. Occasionally though, he had enjoyed more than one pleasurable liaison with certain ladies whose husbands, whilst having left them financially independent widows together with a neat and not undesirable house in such refined places as Hertford Street, had, by virtue of acquiring their wealth in trade, also ensured they remained on the periphery of fashionable society, except by those hostesses whose views were not quite so rigid. But no one could say of Deerham that he was either a seducer or a libertine or that he either broke or bent the rules, indeed the very thought of either was so repugnant to him that he had nothing but contempt for men like Singleton and the late Earl of Markmoor, whose customary unconcern for consideration and discretion as well as their total disregard for the names they bore, had earned them both well-deserved criticism.

But it was not only their libertine tendencies which had cemented their friendship, but a predilection for all games of chance, and whilst Deerham exonerated Singleton of the need to cheat, indeed his skill at the cards was too well-known to be questioned, he nevertheless lost as much as he won, and it was this circumstance which rendered him a continued danger to Letitia Rawnsley. In Deerham's estimation it was a pretty foregone conclusion that residing in Cavendish Square and attending the same ton parties she would, at some point, become friends with Louisa Markham, after all they were the same age, and since his future with her also seemed to be a foregone conclusion, it would, if nothing else, give him the opportunity to keep his eyes on the young lady he could not in all honesty believe safe from Singleton's scurrilous scheming.

*

Within two days of arriving in town, Deerham presented himself in Cavendish Square, his predictions to William being proved correct; his presence being welcomed with pleasure as well as relief. After exchanging polite courtesies with the Countess and Christopher, they were then left alone in his book room. Following a number of inconsequential pleasantries on a number of topics there then followed a brief discussion on the betrothal, throughout which Deerham by no means committed himself, tactfully suggesting to Christopher that he be permitted to speak with his sister. It was a perfectly natural request and one which her brother had no hesitation in granting, but as he tugged on the bell pull he could only hope that Louisa would find favour with him, at least sufficiently for him to honour his father's promise.

Since their arrival in town five days ago, Louisa, who had been recovering from a severe cold which she had contracted some days before they left Markmoor Manor, had not so far had the opportunity to see anything of London as she had really been in no fit condition to leave the house. Her mamma, who had no wish to see her daughter's first season get off to a bad start by such a thing as a cold, had deemed it wise for her to remain indoors until she was clear of it, because it really would not do for her to be seen in society with flushed cheeks and streaming eyes. As she was unsure of what her own reception in town would be, especially as she had not been quite able to disabuse her mind that every eye would be turned upon her the moment she stepped through the front door to escort her daughter on an exploratory expedition of the town, it was therefore with a mixture of delight and relief that she saw the numerous cards of invitation awaiting her on the spindle-legged table in the hall. These, of course, naturally included Louisa, but since she was, for the moment at least, unfit to be seen, she was not at all certain whether to be glad or not that her daughter's indisposition had delayed her own re-emergence into society, keeping her on tenterhooks as to what her reception would be, but taking comfort from Christopher's assurances in that whatever the ton's thoughts and opinions were about his father, she and his sister were above reproach, and it was therefore in a calmer frame of mind that she responded to the invitations. Her only concern now being that Louisa would hopefully be rid of her cold before coming face to face with Deerham because it could not be denied that her daughter, who had not been attacked by such a virulent chill since childhood, was in no fit condition to be seen.

She knew that Christopher had told Louisa something of her father's way of life, not everything of course, but whilst she had been clearly shocked by it she accepted it as well as a daughter could, but in spite of the many invitations which had awaited them on their arrival in Cavendish Square, her worry was that some tittle-tattling busybody could see fit to either enlighten her daughter further – quite innocently, of course! – about her father's wayward career or go so far as to directly comment upon it. No one looking at Louisa would so much as suspect she was Markham's daughter as there was nothing in her face remotely resembling his features, but the moment she said her name or was seen with her brother or mamma, no one would be left in any doubt as to who her father was.

No one knew society better than the Countess of Markmoor, and although by and large the ton had a short memory there were certain things it was not likely to forget; such as her husband's activities and his blatant disregard for convention. There was little doubt that no snide comments would be made to Louisa or knowing glances cast in her direction when in the company of her mamma or her brother, but if she were perhaps to make friends with young ladies of her own age and accompany them to some party or ball in the presence of their mammas, there was no saying what she may be subjected to. She knew she could not keep Louisa secluded in Gloucestershire for the rest of her life, but the thought that her daughter could be made to suffer such indignities caused her more concern that what may be said or done to herself.

If only Deerham would offer for her, then she could lay her worries to one side because no matter how reserved a man he was there was not a soul in society who did not respect him; his name and connections, not to mention his enormous wealth, were such that no door would ever be closed to him, and if he decided to walk down the street wearing a cherry red hat with blue feathers, no one would dare question it. Should he renege on the betrothal after all, which, of course, he was quite at liberty to do, it could do untold damage to Louisa's future because no matter how one looked at it his refusal to offer for her would soon spread, and if it was seen that Deerham had no desire to marry her in the end, then her chances of finding a husband as wealthy as Deerham, or one who could at least stand the heavy cost of the settlements, was remote. Not only would his walking away from the betrothal leave it virtually impossible to find another candidate for her hand, irrespective of his financial circumstances, but it would leave her open prey to vicious gossip and tale bearing, even direct insults to her face about her father, none of which Louisa deserved. Her husband may have trod heedlessly down a pleasurable path without a care for convention or the cost to his family and estates, but it could well be that the price of his hedonistic life may yet still have to be paid, proving to be more expensive and ruinous than even he had been finally brought to realize.

It was therefore with a sigh of relief when she learned Deerham had in fact kept the appointment, indeed so pleased was she that she could barely face him without revealing her hopes, and that he was now at this very moment in the book room talking to Christopher, and since there was every possibility that Louisa would be summoned downstairs, she entered her bedroom to apprise her of it. Of course, it did not automatically mean that he was going to offer for her, but she nevertheless felt it behoved her to ensure her daughter was ready just in case she was sent for because although Louisa knew of the importance attached to his visit, upon being told that Deerham had in fact arrived and was at this very moment talking to her brother, she had detected no signs of excitement or expectation on her daughter's face upon receiving the news.

While her mamma was rapidly scanning her wardrobe, Louisa mentally prepared herself for the summons to go downstairs, not at all sure whether to be glad or not that she had recovered from her cold. In the privacy of her room at Markmoor Manor, it had been so easy to dream of the handsome young man who would carry her off to live happily ever after, but in the cold light of day in Cavendish Square, with her prospective bridegroom downstairs talking to her brother, a man she had never laid eyes on in her life before, those daydreams crumbled to ashes. Whatever her feelings or wishes, she knew that should Deerham propose to her she had no choice but to accept his most obliging offer and, as she sat in front of her mirror as her mamma's fingers flicked or teased a curl here and there, she could not prevent the frisson of apprehension which flitted through her.

Her mamma, taking a quick and appraising look at her daughter, nodded her head satisfyingly, persuaded that Louisa, having shaken off the last vestiges of cold, was quite looking her best. But Louisa, as she well knew, was no beauty. However disheartening, she had to acknowledge that there were any number of young ladies on the town who far outshone her daughter; Melissa Cuthburtson for one, the Honourable Cybil Robards for another, then there was Lady Sutton's daughter, Imogen, not to mention Lady Diana Alexander and, even, the young Letitia Rawnsley! The list, sadly, was endless, but in one respect at least, Louisa had the advantage. Her hair, like her late maternal grandmother, the Countess of Halford, was a rich vibrant copper with natural curls which required no aid from curling papers or hot irons to make it spiral around her face and down her back. Her eyes, wide and expressive, were dark green without any contrasting flecks, which could light up on the instant, and even taking into account a mamma's bias, she had to admit that it was a truly startling combination, added to which, she had a complexion miraculously free of any freckle or blemish which normally accompanied such a colouring. Surely, this would make up for any lack of facial beauty!

Having been shown into a small sitting room at the front of the house,

Deerham conversed easily with her brother as they waited for Louisa and her mamma, listening to his ideas for the reclamation of his estates. It was clear that this young man, whilst obviously daunted by such a task, was by no means afraid of tackling the mammoth undertaking facing him, and since he had no taste for the kind of life his father had all too obviously enjoyed, Deerham envisaged that in time he would eventually bring his estates into order. But although it remained unsaid, Deerham knew that a huge financial input was required if Christopher was to succeed, and should he refuse to offer for his sister, then Deerham failed to see where that monetary contribution was to come from, since there would be no settlements from him to enter the Markham coffers. Indeed, it was extremely unlikely that such revenue would be forthcoming from anyone, especially as the Markham name was looked upon by many as not being worth the paper it was written on. Not many would be prepared to pay what in all likelihood was going to be a pretty hefty settlement directly resulting from the waste and squander of what had once been a valuable estate by a man who had had neither the time nor the inclination to worry about anything but his own pleasures.

Having come to know the new Earl of Markmoor reasonably well over recent months, Deerham found himself feeling angry on his behalf, not only because his father had given no more thought to him and his future than he did to anyone else, but that his activities had placed him and his sister in a situation which was by no means enviable and, through no fault of their own, both were most probably going to have to reap the rewards of his sowing as well as being far from viable where marriage was concerned. Having learned from Christopher that he hoped one day to marry Charlotte Laid, Deerham had commented suitably, but he knew Sir Michael Laid very well and although he had never discussed Christopher or his affairs with him, Deerham could not see this man, who, like his own father, had been one of the first to shun the late earl, relinquishing his daughter until he was satisfied that Christopher was indeed bringing his estates into some kind of order.

Deerham easily acquitted Christopher of attempting to manoeuvre him into honouring the betrothal, but he could well imagine his earnest desire to see the deed safely sealed. Although he had neither by word nor deed indicated his shock and dismay over his father's way of life any more than he had made any comment about it, he must nevertheless dislike being in the undesirable position in which he found himself; a position which meant that his sister had to be used if he was to salvage what the late earl had so casually thrown away.

Twenty minutes later, entering the sitting room beside her mamma, Louisa and Deerham came face to face with another for the first time in their lives. She was neither pert nor forward any more than she adopted a sophistication she did not possess to try to impress him, quite the contrary in fact, she was unaffected and well-mannered and her reception of him was precisely what it should have been; polite and civil. Most young ladies who had been introduced to him over the years by their hopeful mammas had either blushed and stammered and lowered their eyes or attempted to feign complete indifference, but not this young lady. Those wide green eyes neither lowered nor looked at an invisible point behind his head, on the contrary they eyed him openly without a blink.

As Louisa had not yet left the house since her arrival in town, she had had no opportunity to either see or meet other men but one look at that tall and rather imposing figure standing beside her brother in front of the fireplace, convinced her that there could not be a better dressed man in London. That coat of dark green worsted with the turn down collar, which, as Christopher later told her, was very fashionable and accepted daytime wear for gentlemen, made by the finest tailor in town, fitted flawlessly across his broad shoulders, and without a crease to be seen. His single-breasted waistcoat, short to the waist and the very height of fashion, was of cream coloured silk with an embroidered pattern interwoven in a deeper coloured thread, and his fawn stockinet breeches, accentuating his powerful thighs, and a gleaming pair of top boots covering his legs to just below the knee, completed his toilet. His only adornments were the gold signet ring on the little finger of his left hand, the fob hanging from the pocket of his waistcoat and a diamond pin tucked into the delicate folds of lawn at his throat.

Her mother may have later commented sadly on the fact about how times had changed and that, in her day, no gentleman would call upon a lady dressed in what she could only describe as clothes fit for the stables and, worse, without a hint of powder to his face, but, also, that he had not seen fit to wear a wig. But not only was this addition to a gentleman's apparel not as fashionable as it had once been, except by elderly gentlemen who refused to be seen without one, Louisa thought his own dark hair, neatly tied in the nape of his neck with a black bow, needed no covering or his face any cosmetic aid. Even though his physique was excellent, she could not call him handsome precisely; whether this was due to that aquiline nose or the deep cleft in his rather square chin she was not entirely certain, but what she did know, very much to her surprise, was that she liked what she saw. Lurking somewhere at the back of those dark grey eyes she detected a sense of humour which instantly struck a responsive chord somewhere deep inside her, having the immediate effect of putting her at her ease as well as banishing whatever apprehensions she had, which, considering the reason for his visit this morning and the fact that they had never before met, she found rather extraordinary. What was even more extraordinary, even inexplicable, was that should this man, who was looking closely at her from under his heavy-lidded eyes, not offer for her after all, then she would feel quite disappointed.

Louisa may not be a beauty, but her mother was quite right about her colouring; that thick and luxuriant copper hair, curling riotously round her face and spiralling down her back, adorned by nothing more than a narrow band of pale green ribbon threaded through it, and those huge green eyes, were indeed remarkably striking, and certainly made up for the lack of any facial perfections. Her dress was in pale green muslin and softly pleated with an increased fullness at the back with a cream sash around her waist which matched the softly arranged collar round the neck of her bodice. She was of no more than medium height, the top of her head just reaching Deerham's chest, but her figure was excellent, emphasized by the narrow waist which could have been easily spanned by the two hands of the man looking at her. She had a forehead which was just above being narrow and a nose which was really quite unremarkable, but whilst her lips may be thought by some to be a little too full and her mouth a little too wide, her chin, although softly rounded, held a distinct firmness, telling the man closely regarding her that she had decided opinions of her own.

"So, you are Louisa!" Deerham mused when her mother and brother eventually left them alone for a little while. "Forgive me," he smiled, not unkindly, "but you are not quite what I expected."

To his surprise he saw those incredible green eyes light up with barely concealed amusement and her lips break into a smile, not a nervous or embarrassed smile but one of pure mischief, showing a perfect set of even white teeth and, for one moment, but *only* a moment mind you, he felt something stir inside him, as surprising as it was unexpected, but as it disappeared as swiftly as it had materialized, he easily dismissed it.

"I had a feeling I would not be," she told him with characteristic honesty. "You see," she confessed, "I know I am not beautiful," accepting this fact without resentment, "but I really cannot be held responsible for the way I look!"

"No," Deerham said slowly, fast coming to the conclusion that her looks really did not matter in the least, "you cannot." Then, giving himself a mental shake, said, "I realize that there is always a little awkwardness attached to occasions such as this, even more so when the prospective bride and groom have never before met."

"Yes, I suppose there must," she nodded, giving no sign of any.

"What do you say we sit down," he suggested thoughtfully, "and make ourselves comfortable?"

"Oh, yes, of course! I'm sorry," she smiled contritely. "Forgive me, I am forgetting my manners."

No one looking at him sitting perfectly at his ease on the opposite end of the sofa would have had the slightest guess that he was on the point of proposing to a young lady who was quite unknown to him and one, moreover, he had not many days before, seriously contemplated rejecting as his prospective bride. Turning sideways, crossing one long booted leg over the other and resting his left arm casually along the back of the sofa in order for him to look at her, he observed that, although she was sitting bolt upright with her hands folded on her lap, she at no time tried to evade his eye or encourage his attentions by behaving coyly. Indeed, those wide green eyes looked openly at him and, not for the first time during the past few minutes, he was acutely conscious of their brilliance and, more to the point, their lack of guile.

"You know, Louisa," he said gently, "I see no reason why this situation in which we now find ourselves should cause either of us the least embarrassment by following the prescribed formalities."

"Oh, no!" she cried spontaneously. "I should dislike that very much."

"So would I," he agreed. "Indeed, I see little need to adopt such a conventional ritual, and would, instead, much prefer it if we talked a little."

"Oh yes," she smiled, "that would be far more comfortable."

"Yes, I think so," he said gently. "So, tell me, Louisa," he encouraged, "what do you think of this first visit of yours to town?"

Her eyes lit up at this. "Well, sir," she told him on a barely stifled choke of laughter, "I can't tell you." He raised an enquiring eyebrow at this, to which she easily responded. "You see," she shook her head, her thick curls dancing, "I have not yet been outside the front door since my arrival!" Another raised eyebrow produced another little choking sound deep within her throat and, turning to look at him, her eyes brimful with laughter, she said as steadily as she could, "A cold, sir!"

"A cold?" he repeated, strenuously trying to suppress the smile that twitched at the corner of his mouth. She nodded. "I am sorry to hear that."

"Yes, so am I," she confided impishly, her eyes twinkling across at him. "It could not have come at a more inconvenient moment!"

"I can imagine," he said without a tremor, having by now come to the conclusion that her nature was not only friendly and open but extremely confiding, so much so that no lady on the verge of entering society as well as a betrothal would dare admit, especially to her prospective bridegroom, to succumbing to such a thing as a cold and that her sense of the ridiculous was as delightful as it was infectious.

"Yes," she nodded, "because you see, I do so want to visit all the places I have heard of: The Pantheon, Vauxhall Gardens and Ranelagh," her eyes lighting up at the thought. "Then there is the theatre and the opera and – oh, so many other places!" she smiled excitedly, her face becoming quite animated, "- and although I know we are fixed here for several months, I did so want to begin visiting the attractions straightaway!"

"Most understandable," he acknowledged, yet again finding it necessary to firmly suppress the twitch at the corner of his mouth.

"Yes," she agreed, "and, of course, we have received numerous invitations!" she told him ingenuously.

"Which, naturally, you are eager to attend," he said with perfect gravity.

"Yes," she nodded vigorously. "Shall we see you at these parties, sir?" she asked, raising a hopeful eyebrow.

"I think it very probable," he nodded, refraining from informing her that most of them were nothing but a dead bore as well as the fact that, once he offered for her, it would create a very odd appearance if he did not accompany his betrothed.

"Oh, I am so glad!" she cried, her eyes widening.

"Are you?" he enquired, trying to ignore the resurgence of that unfamiliar stirring. "Why is that?"

"Well, you must know," she confided, "that I have not been in the way of going to parties and such like, and although I shall not be attending them alone, it will be so nice to know at least one person there other than Mamma and Christopher."

"Even though that other person," he reminded her gently, "is one you have never met before today?"

She gave this a little thought, saying at length, "Yes, but I do not feel as though I have only just met you."

To his surprise he owned to feeling precisely the same, but deeming it prudent to not only keep this to himself but to suppress the sentiment, said noncommittally, "I agree it is most pleasant to call acquaintanceship with at least one person in a room full of strangers."

"Yes," she nodded, "I think so too."

Banishing the image which had unexpectedly darted into his mind of being greeted by this unaffected young lady, whether in a room full of people or not, Deerham decided it was time to remind her, as well as himself, of the reason for his visit, but before he could do so he saw a gleam enter her eyes and instinctively knew that something was going around in her head. Experience had taught him that when a woman looked in a particular way it generally betokened a request for something, usually money, but the look in this young lady's eyes was so far removed from enticement that he easily acquitted her of ulterior motives. His acquaintanceship with her may be of extremely short duration, but he believed he had assessed her character accurately enough to feel quite certain that the impish gleam in those wide green eyes signified she was about to say something quite outrageous, and whilst he was seldom, if ever, shocked or surprised, nothing quite prepared him for what she confided.

"May I ask you something, sir?" she said eagerly, leaning forward a little towards him, conscious of no hesitation or nervousness, but perfectly at her ease in his company the same as when she was with Reverend Berry discussing a mathematical problem or hypothesis.

"Yes, of course," he nodded, wondering what was coming

"Is it true that ladies are not allowed into The Royal Academy? I mean," she hastily corrected herself, "to hear lectures and such like."

"The Royal Academy?" he repeated surprised, looking curiously at her.

She nodded her head vigorously, but although a slight tinge of colour flooded her cheeks, she looked expectantly at him. "Yes."

"I believe not," he confirmed.

"Oh," she pulled a face, disheartened.

"Does that disappoint you?" he enquired.

"Well, yes, it does actually," she confessed. "The thing is, you see," she told him, almost conspiratorially, knowing perfectly well that her mamma would be most displeased, but since there was no one else she could ask decided that if anyone should know it would be Deerham, "according to Reverend Berry," a questioning eyebrow making her break off to say, "oh, of course, you don't know him; he is our parson at Markmoor, but never mind that," to which he shook his head in silent agreement, his face perfectly grave, "he was telling me before we left home," she continued as though there had been no digression, "that on Friday next there is to be a lecture at The Royal Academy about Sir Isaac Newton and his discovery of gravity." Whatever Deerham had expected it was certainly not this, but before he could comment she said excitedly, "Do you know, sir," her excitement rendering her forgetful of the fact that she was supposed to be trying to sway her prospective bridegroom's decision in her favour, "he formulated three forms of motions?" nodding the truth of this, her eyes lighting up, overlooking her mamma's earnest entreaty that she keep this most peculiar interest a secret, "- the third of which he stated that 'to every action there is always opposed an equal reaction'. He did other things too," she explained helpfully, "to do with light and telescopes, but he was a most modest man," she enlightened him, "and I daresay that we shall never know the half of what he achieved! But the thing is, sir," she told him earnestly, "I should very much like to attend, but Reverend Berry said females were not allowed in, which I think is most unfair, don't you?" she demanded.

Having been subjected to every ploy at their disposal to make a man accede to their wishes, Deerham had thought there was nothing a member of her sex could say or do which could possibly surprise him. Even if the ladies with whom he had enjoyed some very pleasurable interludes had ever heard of Sir Isaac Newton, which he doubted, they would rather die than confess it or, indeed, admit to anything which could even remotely liken her to a blue stocking and, for one cautious moment, it occurred to him that this young lady could well be employing a completely new, though novel, tack to entrap him into declaring himself. But as he searched the face looking innocently at him, those wide green eyes free of any deceit, awaiting his reply to her question, he knew he had grossly misjudged her and that she was perfectly serious and not attempting to force his hand or merely trying to impress him. "Yes, most unfair," he replied.

"Well, I think so too," she agreed firmly. Then, as if recalling something to mind, said, not a little hopefully, "You… you will not tell Mamma I have mentioned this, will you?" to which he shook his head. "Thank you," she said relieved. "You see, she would be quite cross if she knew I had because she says that it is most unnatural for women to be interested in such things, and that if anyone were to discover it, I should be looked upon as odd. Do you think I would be?" she asked, raising an eyebrow.

"Only by those who need not concern you," he smiled. "Tell me," he raised an eyebrow, already knowing the answer, "are you, by any chance, wondering whether I could assist you in your ambition?"

"Oh, sir!" she cried impulsively, the flush of colour in her cheeks and the light in her eyes confirming her delight at such a prospect, arousing in him a pang of remorse at misjudging her, "do you think you could?"

He thought a moment. "I will speak to William," he promised her. "My secretary," he told her in answer to her raised eyebrow, "a most industrious and studious young man."

No lady of his acquaintance had ever expressed so much fervent and genuine gratitude even when he had presented her with the most exquisite and expensive item of jewellery as this young lady had over something which required no more from him than a word to William. He could well imagine what life must have been like for her shut away at Markmoor Manor in Gloucestershire, most probably meeting no one other than the parson or the local magistrate, and although she wanted to attend all the parties and routs and visit the many attractions on offer the same as every other young lady, he doubted they would even think of attending a lecture at Burlington house much less looking upon it with so much pleasure.

Having assured her that William would be delighted to do all in his power to assist her, suppressing the twitch at the corner of his mouth as he thought of his reaction to such a request, Deerham waved aside her renewed thanks before returning to the reason he was here, asking, "I trust that you are now fully recovered from your most inconvenient indisposition?"

"Oh yes, thank you," she assured him.

"I am relieved to hear it." He paused a moment, looking closely at her. "Are you, I wonder," he asked thoughtfully, "recovered sufficiently for us to discuss our situation a little?"

She looked directly at him, nodding her head. "Yes, quite recovered, but even if I were not," she told him practically, "it has to be discussed, does it not?"

"Yes," he said gently, "I am afraid it does." His eyes searched her face, hesitating before asking gently, "Tell me, Louisa, do you *really* want to marry me?"

Her brow puckered in thought for a moment but at no time did she avoid his eye, saying carefully, "Well, you see, sir, I do not mean to offend you but… well, you see, it is not really a question of whether I want to but of having to, or, if not you," she told him reasonably, "then another."

He nodded, quite unperturbed by this somewhat unorthodox reply. "And how do you feel about that?" he asked considerately.

"Well, I own it is not what I had expected," she confessed. "I mean, when I was in the schoolroom and daydreamed a little," a tinge of colour creeping into her cheeks, "but, you see… well…" she sighed, her eyes clouding slightly, "you must know, sir, that my papa left things just a little awkward for Christopher."

"Yes, I know," he said sensitively. "Tell me, Louisa," he asked gently, not unmindful of her feelings, "what has your brother told you about your father?"

"Oh, not everything I suspect," she shook her head. "I daresay he considered the half of it not suitable for his sister's ears, but at least enough for me to understand what renders my marriage essential. I'm sorry," she blushed, hastily apologizing, "I should not have said that; Mamma would not like it. She is forever telling me I must guard my tongue."

"There is not the least need to do so on my account, I assure you," he smiled.

"And you, sir," she asked, "do *you* want to marry *me*?"

Prior to entering the portals of Markham House in Cavendish Square he would have said no, and that the only reason he was going to honour his father's agreement was purely for his sake and no other, but, now, having made the acquaintance of the Lady Louisa Markham, he was not at all sure this was the only reason. No one looking at this unaffected young woman would ever guess that she was her father's daughter, and immediately he experienced a twinge of guilt to think that he had actually gone as far as to liken her to him as well as suspecting her motives. She was clearly intelligent and certainly no fool, and she was undoubtedly under no illusions about her situation either concerning her marriage or herself; indeed, she had been extremely candid about her looks, but in one respect she had grossly erred. No, she was certainly no beauty, and he should know! Nor could he deny that the Lady Louisa Markham stood very much in the shade of the young lady to whom he had offered his protection and escort the other evening as, indeed, she did to most other young ladies in town, but there was something oddly attractive about her all the same; a subtle, almost elusive quality which would intrude on the memory long after one had left her; a quality that had nothing whatsoever to do with that hair and those eyes!

"I'm sorry," she said contritely, breaking into his thoughts, "I should not have said it; it was impertinent."

"Not at all," he assured her, "after all, the question of our betrothal concerns you equally as much as it does me."

"Yes, I know," she nodded, a crease furrowing her forehead, "but you see... well," she faltered, "it is just that I thought... well... you... you may not wish to marry me because of my father."

Deerham's feelings towards the late earl could, at no time, be termed complimentary, but, now, having met Christopher and his sister as well as witnessing first-hand the true cost of their father's reckless lifestyle, these feelings underwent no change which could possibly raise that self-interested peer in his esteem. Through a selfish pursuit of his own pleasure he had rendered life extremely difficult for his children; for Christopher certainly. Not only had he left him a mountain of debt as well as the wreckage of what had once been a thriving estate to try to bring back into order, but he had seriously weakened any hope he had of marrying Miss Charlotte Laid as her father, by no means an admirer of the late earl, would not be any too eager to relinquish his daughter to a man who was very far from being in a financial position to take care of her.

As far as Markham's daughter was concerned, although all the signs pointed to the fact that she was prepared to accept an offer from him, her father had rendered it virtually impossible for her to do anything other but enter into a marriage which she may well have no liking for. It was obvious that Christopher had not told Louisa the full sum of their father's dealings but she at least knew enough for her to realize that her marriage, if not to him then to another equally as affluent who could afford to pay for her, was imperative if her brother was to come about. Deerham doubted she had laid eyes on her father more than half a dozen times in her life but whatever his faults he *was* her father, and whilst neither she nor Christopher had expressed the slightest degree of anger or resentment for the fix in which they found themselves due to his reckless spending, it would be quite wrong for him now to tell her what had obviously been kept from her.

"If you dislike the idea of marrying me because of my father," she told him with that incurable honesty her mother had strenuously tried to curb, breaking into his thoughts, "then I quite understand if you do not wish to honour your father's word and that of my grandfather, but, you see, sir," she told him, not flinching from such a painful issue, "I *am* my father's daughter, and whilst I know that this makes me a far from attractive proposition when it comes to marriage in the eyes of many, I cannot change who I am."

Had her mamma been privileged to have heard this she would have been acutely embarrassed as well as extremely vexed, especially having impressed upon her daughter the need for caution as well as guarding her tongue, especially to her prospective bridegroom, a man who held Christopher's future in the palm of his hand. To the man sitting beside her however, her openness neither offended nor shocked him, on the contrary it merely served to confirm that this young lady was definitely under no illusions and, should he offer for her after all, then it would not be because he was in love with her but purely to honour an agreement made years ago by his father and her grandfather as well as being a most timely financial arrangement – certainly as far as her brother was concerned.

"No," he said gently, "you cannot change who you are."

"You… you must not be thinking," she faltered again, "that I am like my father because you see… well," her colour very much heightened, "I am not – *truly!*"

He had not needed her to tell him this, like her brother she was as different to her father as it was possible for an offspring to be, but he had no doubt she was right in that Christopher had not told her the full sum of her father's activities. Such knowledge would unquestionably shock her, but, like her mother, Deerham could not discount the fact that someone could quite easily make it their business to inform her and, most probably, have no compunction in doing so.

"No," he said slowly, "you are not."

"Tell me, sir," she asked with a directness which would have rendered her mamma acutely uncomfortable, "did you know my father?"

"Yes, I did," he told her quietly, "but we were not friends, you understand."

If only half of what Christopher had seen fit to tell her was true, then she could quite well understand this, and merely nodded her head. Then, as if a thought had just occurred to her, she raised her head to look at him, asking, not a little hopefully, "Please, you will not tell Mamma what I have said, will you? You see," she confessed, the impish gleam in those wide green eyes quite spoiling her contrition, "she would not think it at all seemly, indeed, she would deem it as most improper."

"No," he shook his head, not impervious to that mischievous look, "I won't tell her," he smiled, "but would *you* tell *me* something?"

"Yes, of course," she nodded.

"Does it not concern you that I am considerably older than you?" he asked calmly. "I am thirty-two years of age, Louisa," he reminded her, asking gently, "do you not mind having a husband who is thirteen years older than you."

Far from being disconcerted by such a question, her eyes gleamed impishly and, with that impulsiveness which would have made her mamma wince with embarrassment had she have been privileged to hear her reply, said, not quite able to suppress the laughter bubbling up in her throat, "Well, you must know, sir, that I can only benefit from your age and experience!"

He laughed at that. "Did your mamma tell you so?"

"Yes," she nodded, her eyes brimful of laughter.

"I see," he smiled, unexpectedly attacked by another unfamiliar stirring in the pit of his stomach. "And what else did Mamma tell you?" he enquired, wishing he had not taken a liking to this young lady whose keen sense of the ridiculous threatened to influence his judgement; but the devil was in it that he did like her – more than he had bargained for! There may not be any immediate urgency attached to him marrying, after all he was only thirty-two and still young enough to look about him for a bride and, whilst he could not deny that he had no liking for having his hand forced, right now, as he sat next to the Lady Louisa Markham, he could not, in all honesty, as had been the case prior to this morning, say that he was totally averse to the match.

"Only that I was to be on my best behaviour and not say the first thing which came into my head which could well give you a disgust of me," she confided mischievously, "and that should you indeed make me an offer, I was to count myself exceedingly fortunate and to thank you very prettily."

Deerham could almost hear her saying it, and whilst he could not entirely blame her for this, he could well imagine her horror should she ever discover that her daughter had confided her warnings to him. "I see," he nodded, not quite able to keep laughter out of his voice, "and did Mamma proffer any further advice?"

"No," Louisa shook her head, "but I do feel I should perhaps tell you that I have none of the accomplishments which are considered indispensable for young ladies!" she told him irrepressibly. He raised a questioning eyebrow at this, to which she responded in a way that was really quite delightful. "I am afraid I cannot sing or play an instrument... well," she chuckled, "not in tune, that is; and my drawing and water colouring are alike very bad; so too is my sewing and, no matter how hard I try," she told him honestly, "I cannot pronounce one whole sentence in French or Italian which is in the least intelligible."

"It is a good thing you have told me," he shook his head sadly, suppressing the twitch hovering at the corner of his mouth.

"Yes," she agreed, catching the smile lurking at the back of his eyes, "I thought it was best to be entirely truthful."

"Very wise," he nodded, rising to his feet, "after all, there is no telling when one may be taken unawares and made to look no how!" She laughed and, taking the hand he extended to her, placed hers into it and rose to her feet.

It seemed then, that he was destined to offer for her after all, although, if he were being honest he knew it had never really been a question of doing otherwise, but where, before today, he had been seized with doubts as to the wisdom of it, now, and much to his surprise, he found they were of little or no importance. It was evident that Louisa Markham had inherited none of her father's traits but it was also evident that she had inherited none of his good looks either, nor her mother's if it came to that, but of one thing Deerham felt certain, and that was life would never be dull with this young lady; a young lady, he decided, whose looks mattered not at all. Under normal circumstances, he would have acquired her brother's permission to pay his addresses to her and courted her in form then obtained his permission to offer for her, but these were not usual circumstances; his father's promise, whether legally binding or not, not to mention the urgency to set Christopher's mind at rest, rendered following normal convention out of the question.

"It is, perhaps, a little unfortunate," he said kindly, "that we have not been granted much time in which to become better acquainted, but, I think, Louisa," he told her softly, keeping hold of her hand, "you and I could deal extremely together."

"Yes, I think so too," she smiled, casting a glance up into his face.

"Then, this being so," he smiled, knowing he could not offer for her until he had confirmed it with her brother, "would you, do you think, be prepared to receive me - say tomorrow?"

"I should be pleased to, my lord," she curtsied, suddenly recalling what was due to his dignity.

He raised her to her feet, his lips lightly brushing her fingers, then, escorting her to the door, bowed her out.

Her mamma, who had been sitting on the edge of her chair in Christopher's book room, lending only half an ear to her son, felt herself to be torn between hoping Louisa had not said anything in that spontaneous way she had which could possibly give Deerham a disgust of her and a natural reluctance to relinquish her daughter in marriage to a man she had never before laid eyes on.

Similar thoughts were also going through Christopher's mind, but he was practical enough to realize that his sister's marriage to Deerham was imperative if he was to make any serious inroads at all into reclaiming his estates. He was himself far from happy to know that through his father's hedonism he had rendered it out of the question for Louisa to look about her for a husband and, like his mamma, could not help but wonder what was taking place between them in the sitting room. He had no desire to see Louisa tied to a marriage she was in no mind for but, for all that, she did not want for sense, fully realizing the predicament their father's lifestyle had placed them in, and although he knew his sister could be a little impulsive, he felt sure that, on this occasion, she would pause to consider before saying something, quite innocently of course, to make Deerham cry off.

At no point had he heard anything to Deerham's detriment and, upon the occasions they had met, he had to own he had found nothing to make him take him in dislike, but it could not be argued that beneath his unruffled affability ran a reserve which, Christopher suspected, could well be as impenetrable as the determination clearly evident in that square and firm jaw was inflexible. Should Deerham decide to honour his father's promise and make Louisa an offer after all, then a man of his age and experience would surely recognize her spontaneity for precisely what it was as well as her youth and inexperience in the ways of the world but, more importantly, that she was nothing like her father. Nevertheless, Christopher could not help the apprehension which swept through him upon hearing the door to the sitting room open quickly followed by Louisa's footsteps crossing the hall before mounting the stairs, leaving his mamma to speak to his sister while he re-joined Deerham.

The countess, like her son, was perfectly well aware of the importance attached to the marriage with Deerham and that should he decide not to offer for Louisa after all, then their situation would be dire indeed, but, at the same time, she could not help feeling as though her daughter was being most shamefully used. The betrothal agreement may have been arranged years before but it was not legally binding, thereby giving Deerham the chance to renege on it if he so wished and Louisa to refuse his proposal should he offer it, now though, there was no possibility of Louisa refusing without placing them in desperate straits, and should Deerham decide not to uphold his father's promise after all then their future looked extremely bleak. Not for the first time, she found herself deprecating her late husband's way of life and the selfish pursuit of his own pleasures which had ultimately resulted in her daughter being sold into marriage in order to alleviate the difficulties he had created, but upon entering Louisa's bedchamber in the full expectation of finding her sitting disconsolately on a chair or lying stretched out on top of the bed crying her eyes out, she was somewhat surprised to find her standing by the window eagerly looking down onto the street in order to try to catch a glimpse of Deerham as he left the house.

She had not needed Louisa to tell her what had passed between them in the small sitting room, one look at her face was enough to inform her that not only had she found favour with Deerham but that he intended to call upon the morrow, which could only mean he was going to seek Christopher's permission to formally offer for her. Whilst this was a tremendous worry off her mind, she nevertheless felt it incumbent upon her to question her daughter as to whether she had indeed liked him, because although she knew nothing against him, indeed his manners were irreproachable and just what one would expect of a man of his breeding, she did know that there was a reserve to him which had, on occasion, given the impression that he could be quite unapproachable. However, upon having this pointed out to her, Louisa said, with such genuineness that her mamma had cause to look rather closely at her, "I did not find him so, Mamma. Indeed," she confessed, "I… I like him."

"I own I am pleased to hear that," her mamma smiled, relieved, "but, my dear," she pointed out gently, laying a hand on her daughter's rose-pink cheek, "you must remember that you have only just met him."

"Yes, Mamma, I know, but, you see," she told her truthfully, "I feel as though I have known him all my life."

Her mamma, not at all sure whether to feel relief or not at this, had not only voiced her concerns to Christopher later but had anxiously turned it over in her mind during the night time hours, but when, the following morning, she informed Louisa that Deerham had arrived and was awaiting her in the sitting room having spoken to her brother, the light which had entered those green eyes left her in no doubt as to the truth of it. If only Deerham would be patient with her, she felt sure it would reap rewards, nevertheless, she felt it behoved her to warn her daughter against falling in love with him or to expect him to fall in love with her, but upon tactfully pointing out these two important facts to Louisa just before she went downstairs, the only reply she received was a quiet, "No, Mamma."

The countess, having been advised only first thing this morning by her daughter that she had mentioned Burlington House to Deerham and that he was going to see what could be arranged, caused her to close her eyes on an agonized sigh. In her opinion nothing could be more detrimental to a lady's chances than announcing such a peculiar interest, especially to her prospective husband and, not for the first time, wondered what she had to do in order to get Louisa to contain that spontaneity which could give people a rather odd opinion of her. There was not an ounce of harm or malice in her daughter, indeed she was a most affectionate and dutiful child besides being totally honest, but whilst these were qualities that did no harm in the bosom of her family once adorning society such impulsiveness and saying the first thing which entered her head, could so easily be misconstrued. Had she have known of this yesterday she would not have closed her eyes all night because there was no denying that such a confession could not aid in any way her chances of inducing Deerham to offer for her, but since it appeared that her daughter's somewhat eccentric diversion had by no means deterred him, she could only offer up heartfelt thanks. She was pleased too to know that Deerham had wholly acquiesced with Christopher's suggestion that it may perhaps be best if the betrothal was not publicly announced immediately in order to give them both time to get better acquainted.

Deerham may not adopt the extravagancies of fashion or apply powder and paint to his face, but there was no denying that the sight of him dressed in burgundy velvet and gold lacings with a heavy fall of lace at his throat, a diamond pin glinting within its folds, he looked far more imposing than he had yesterday. Louisa, after swallowing uncomfortably and dropping him a curtsey, raised doubtful eyes to his, relieved to see the smile lurking at the back of those dark grey ones, and knew she had not been mistaken in her first impression of him, and gave him a rather tremulous smile.

He was far too experienced to be taken in by guile or deceit, and although he could not argue against the sense of those who wished him well when they said that such a union could only end in disaster, as he stood looking down into those wide green eyes looking up at him with a nice mix of apprehension and expectancy, he knew he had not erred in that whatever else the Lady Louisa Markham may or may not be, she was most certainly not a replica of her father.

He had meant it when he had told her that he believed they could deal extremely together, but he had also meant it when he had told himself that he certainly had no intention of falling in love with her, but, now, as he lightly took hold of her hand and asked if she would accept of his own in marriage, he was conscious, and not for the first time since making her acquaintance, of that strange and unfamiliar stirring somewhere deep inside him. It disappeared almost at once, but upon seeing the colour deepen in her cheeks and hearing her say, rather tremulously, "Yes, I should like to very much, if you are sure you do not dislike it," it returned with some force.

Chapter Six

Deerham's early return to town may have taken his household by surprise, being under the impression he was remaining at Worleigh until the end of the week, but as far as the Honourable Letitia Rawnsley was concerned it was certainly most providential. Upon seeing that masked figure emerging from nowhere to stride up to the coach had filled her with such relief that no suspicion had crossed her mind that she could be exchanging one villain for another. She may not have been able to see his face but there had been something in those dark grey eyes and the way he spoke that told her she could trust him, and therefore she had known no hesitation in placing herself under his protection any more than she had in describing him as her knight errant, indeed she was heartily thankful for his timely intervention, coming at a moment when she had believed all to be lost. She had no idea who her masked rescuer was but even if he had turned out to be a highwayman as she had originally thought, she would have infinitely preferred his company to that of Singleton's.

Within the covers of the lurid romances she had read, smuggled into her by her dear friend Mary Boothby and which her aunt had forbidden her to read, the handsome and dashing young hero always fell madly in love with the damsel he had just rescued and, naturally, she fell in love with him too. Of course, he had to fight overwhelming odds to win her hand, including the refusal of her family and a wicked arch enemy bent on villainy, but, in the end, he had cleared all before him to finally whisk her blissfully down the aisle to live happily ever after. Tucked up warm and cosy in bed it had all seemed very romantic and, of course, she had imagined herself in all the improbable situations in which the fictional heroines had found themselves, but on a dark and sleet cold evening in mid-February, on an unknown and deserted stretch of road travelling to an unnamed destination alone with the man she detested, had been so far removed from romance that she had in fact been extremely frightened. Terrified that Singleton might try to kiss her again, she had sat as far away from him in the coach as was possible, but despite her show of defiance and that resounding slap she had inflicted on him in the private parlour of *'The Angel Inn'* she knew that such tactics would not have kept him at bay for ever, and she had lived in dread of what would happen when next they stopped.

She knew she had been foolish to trust Singleton but the thought that her brother had been seriously wounded and needed her, had been the reason she had accompanied him; never for one moment thinking that it was all a ruse to abduct her and entrap her into marriage. It was for her money, of course! She knew that well enough, especially having gleaned a little about his gaming affairs from Algernon. Why else would a man old enough to be her father contemplate marriage with her? The mere thought made her recoil, and she could only hope that her unknown rescuer would, at some point, identify himself to her because although she had not fallen in love with him like all the heroines she had read about, she would like to see him again to thank him for saving her from a fate which she had no hesitation in deeming worse than death.

She had told no one about her adventure, not even Algernon, but, the truth was, she was still very much upset by it and although her rescuer had assured her that Singleton would say nothing of what had occurred any more than he would make a further attempt to abduct her, she could not be easy in her mind. It had been an unnerving moment upon discovering she had been duped and by the very man she hated, but anger at her own stupidity had allowed her to conduct herself with some semblance of pride and dignity. Nevertheless, she could not deny that had fate not intervened by bringing a masked stranger to her rescue she would now be in the unbearable position of either having to accept Singleton's hand in marriage or returning home to Wiltshire in utter disgrace with no hope of ever finding a husband, although anything would be preferable to being married to the man she loathed above all others!

The man she loathed above all others, in marked contrast to his victim, far from looking upon Deerham's intervention with relief, he had bitterly resented it. Yet again, this man's meddlesome interference had cost him dearly and although he could only hazard a guess as to how he had got wind of his intention, having not the least idea that he had broken his journey and pulled up at *'The Angel Inn'* in order that one of his leaders could be shoed and had overheard their conversation in the private parlour, the fact remained that he had done so, taking him completely by surprise. He may have conducted himself with some semblance of dignity in front of Deerham but the truth was that Letitia Rawnsley's rescue meant that he had lost his only bargaining power, leaving him with nothing to stave off the inevitable from his creditors.

Singleton could claim no liking for the married state but just knowing that he was to become leg-shackled to a considerable heiress would have been more than enough to stay their hand, now though, it seemed that nothing stood between him and being clapped up for debt. Admittedly, he had several days' grace before his creditors as well as his landlord took action against him by which time he had to somehow come up with sufficient funds to defray at least half the debt owing but even though he never doubted his own skill with the cards, the fact remained that every gamester relied upon Providence to guide their hand. Unfortunately, however, Providence it seemed had been oddly reluctant to come to his aid of late either on the turf or the table, and unless this elusive guardian of a gamester's luck showed her hand soon then his immediate prospects looked none too rosy.

By the time he arrived back at his lodgings in Half Moon Street with barely a handful of guineas in his purse, his temper was so frayed that Grimshaw, requesting his instructions, got his nose bitten off for his pains. Considering his rather delicate position, there were those who would strenuously advise caution in his dealings with Grimshaw, but Singleton had no such qualms. His henchman may be an insubordinate rogue but he knew without any doubt that he would never dare discuss his affairs and should anything leak out about this evening's venture, Grimshaw knew his employer would know precisely where to look for the source as well as knowing exactly how to deal with such a betrayal.

His plans for abducting Letitia Rawnsley may have been brought forward ahead of schedule due to the unexpected intentions of his creditors as well as her brother innocently providing the opportunity, but even so he had detected no chink in his plan's armour. It would have worked too; that is, until Deerham had intervened in his affairs, and not for the first time! Through his meddlesome interference his plans had gone awry, and whilst Singleton conceded that no plans were ever foolproof, the fact remained that they had been foiled by a man who had never failed to rouse the very worst in him, but as he sat and pondered his financial dilemma, rendered infinitely worse through Deerham's intervention, he swore he would have his revenge.

But before this firm resolve could be planned and executed there was the pressing question of his debts to answer. His skill at the table was indisputable but it seemed the devil had been in the cards for some appreciable time, so much so that he could not help but think that Providence had turned her back on him, but although he had won a few guineas here and there, at least enough to cater for his daily needs, his winnings had by no means been enough to clear his mounting debts. He may be no stranger to skating on rather thin ice but never before had he found himself balancing so precariously on the edge of a precipice where one false step could see him clapped up for debt. No one could say of him that he was a man given over to panic but as he sat in a winged chair beside the fire, contemplating his urgent need of funds over a glass of wine, he did not mind owning, but only to himself, that unless some miracle occurred he saw nothing for it other than a bolt from the Metropolis. The few guineas he had in his purse, the cost of tonight's failed venture having taken its toll on his meagre resources, were just enough to allow him to sit down at the card table at one or other of his clubs; being the very minimum stake required to put down, and were he to do so and he lost, there was no way he could redeem any IOUs he handed over. It was just as he had begun to see a dark chasm of despair looming before him when Providence took a most unexpected, not to say timely, hand in his affairs by bringing Algernon Rawnsley to his lodgings.

Were it not for this young man's eagerness to drop his blunt at the table without so much as a blink as well as his proposed duel earlier in the day providing him with the perfect opportunity to get his sister to accompany him without arousing her suspicions, his affairs were a matter of complete indifference to him, and the thought of having to listen to his enthusiastic recital of the morning's events as to how both he and his adversary had deloped, amicably settling the matter, was something Singleton could not contemplate without utter boredom. Nevertheless, it was a relief to learn that upon Algernon visiting in Cavendish Square only an hour or so ago to apprise his sister of the outcome, Letitia being out most of the day and clearly delivered safely to her door by Deerham in time for her brother's visit, she had clearly not told him about what had taken place, a circumstance which would no doubt have seen his young friend arranging another meeting, only this time with himself. With far more important matters to think about other than listening to his visitor's excited account of his first duel, Singleton was in no frame of mind for entertaining, but when it became apparent that Algernon was in no hurry to leave he soon began to see how his unexpected visit could be turned to good account and the more he considered it the more fortuitous it seemed.

To sit down to a game of piquet with the man whose sister he had attempted to abduct that very day mattered not one jot to Singleton, on the contrary it added a certain piquancy to the play. Algernon, as he well knew, was a keen gamester as well as being an extremely fat bird who bled freely and one, moreover, whose skill was far inferior to his own. This inferiority soon began to show when Algernon made one reckless discard after another, fast beginning to lose point after point until, three hours and several glasses of wine later, he was down to the tune of two thousand guineas; handing over his IOUs without a blink to the man who had not only callously used his sister for his own devious ends but had taken full advantage of his own inexperience.

This unexpected and much-welcomed enrichment to his purse not only enabled Singleton to defray the more urgent of his debts, including his unpaid rent, but presaged a most welcome change of fortune in his play. So much so that over the next few days he found himself rising a winner time after time at his various clubs, his pockets so full of guineas that his creditors, who had shown a remarkable want of respect of late, suddenly began to sing a very different tune, even urging their long-standing client to order whatever he desired, obsequiously assuring him that they were only poor businessmen, and no personal affront had been intended.

Having staved off disaster as well as the humiliation of being clapped up for debt, he was now free to turn his mind to the man he had long since vowed to repay for his meddlesome interference in his affairs. As it was not to be expected that the man he deemed his arch enemy would apprise him of his matrimonial affairs, much less his decision concerning Edmund's daughter, he could only wait with what patience he could muster until the announcement of Deerham's betrothal to the Lady Louisa Markham had been inserted in *The London Gazette*, because there was no way a man of his honour and integrity would renege on his father's promise no matter how distasteful he may find it, in order to bring about his irrevocable downfall. For one who was eager to have Deerham's pending nuptials confirmed, it was perhaps unfortunate that at the precise moment Christopher Markham was accepting his offer for his sister's hand Singleton was on his way to Paris with a like-minded crony, had he not have been then he would have seen what the whole of London soon guessed.

*

Deerham knew perfectly well that Christopher Markham's request to delay the announcement of the betrothal for several weeks was more for Louisa's sake than his own in order for her to not only accustom herself to her changed circumstances but also to give both of them the opportunity to get to know one another better and not to give him time to reflect and withdraw his offer, indeed the very thought of perpetrating such a slight was wholly repugnant to him, and consequently he accepted this with equanimity. His courtship of the Lady Louisa Markham may not have been preceded by any proclamation but it was not to be supposed that the sight of him escorting the countess and her daughter to the opera or the theatre or requesting her hand for the next dance at some society gathering would escape notice, on the contrary it clearly signified to the interested that he had, or was about to, honour his father's promise after all. It was, of course, most infuriating to these interested onlookers, which was the whole of the ton, that neither Deerham nor the Markham ladies had the least intention of assuaging their curiosity by confirming the truth of things, but when, after nearly six weeks of wondering and intense observation, the long-awaited announcement of their betrothal in *The London Gazette* merely confirmed what they already knew.

Dutifully carrying out his instructions, William, whose misgivings over the whole affair had not abated one jot during his employer's six weeks of courtship of the lady whose father had set the town alight with gossip, had reluctantly inserted the announcement of Deerham's betrothal to the Lady Louisa Markham in *The London Gazette* as well as making arrangements to enter into delicate negotiations with Stringer regarding the all-important matter of settlements. Stringer, having been filled with renewed hope and vigour about the future welfare of the Markham estates under the new earl's patronage, had driven a hard bargain, but William, still of the opinion that his noble employer was making a grave mistake was determined that Deerham was not going to pay over the odds for a young woman whose father had, by his own reckless hand, brought a once thriving estate to its knees. The negotiations, lasting five whole days, which had seen both men losing and gaining ground in the process, had finally been brought to a satisfactory conclusion, each congratulating themselves on their skilful handling of a most delicate affair, which had been concluded to the dignity of their respective principals.

Their respective principals, the one extremely relieved and the other extremely generous, may have found nothing to their dissatisfaction in the marriage settlements, but there was one, who, even if Louisa had come free of charge, was by no means happy with the forthcoming marriage. Deerham, knowing his mother's sentiments on this very matter even though she had not voiced them, had, in view of Christopher's request for a brief interim, deemed it wise not to apprise her of his decision ahead of the announcement, but, now, knowing it would be in *The London Gazette* in the morning when every member of the ton would read it over the breakfast cups and circulating in Bath by the following day, he had no wish for her to read of the betrothal before he had told her, left London for Bath on the very afternoon William had been instructed to insert it.

It was not Louisa who engendered his mother's misgivings over the match so much as the late earl, whose behaviour and shameful conduct she had been only too well aware of as well as how her husband had been one of the first to shun that noble if erratic peer. She may not have argued against the betrothal which had been discussed between her husband and Louisa's grandfather, but she had by no means approved of it, and could only be thankful that her son, when the time came, would not be legally bound to honour it. To discover now that her son had indeed offered for the Markham girl after all, caused her to look concernedly at him. "I can, of course, understand why you have not said anything until now."

"Can you, Mamma?" he smiled.

"Yes," she smiled back at him, "I can. But, *why*, Max?" she asked earnestly, leaning towards him where he sat beside her on the sofa to cover his hand with her cold bony one. "Why the Markham chit?"

"Would you have me give the lie to my father's word?" he asked gently, taking her hand in his two warm ones and affectionately kissing it, the smile he gave her rarely seen by other eyes.

"No," she sighed, "I would not." She considered a moment. "Your father was an honourable man, Max, and so are you, but, my dear," she shook her head, "in this instance no one would blame you for…"

"I would blame myself, Mamma," he told her truthfully. "To dishonour my father's promise as well as my name would, I think, be as disreputable as anything Markmoor had ever done."

"Yes," she nodded, "it would, and, of course," removing her hand from his and patting his cheek, "I honour you for it." She sighed. "I suppose I should have known you would offer for her, but I cannot pretend to being at all comfortable about it. If only your father had not made such a promise to Halford!"

"But he did," he reminded her softly, "and you must see, Mamma," he smiled, reclaiming her hand and gently squeezing it, "that I cannot, in all honour, renege on it."

She nodded. "Yes, I do see that, but have you considered, Max?"

"Yes, Mamma," he nodded, "I have; long and hard, but in spite of my caution and doubts, I knew, in the end, I would not do so. To refuse to honour my father's promise would be to offer an unpardonable insult to Markham and his sister, both of whom," he told her fair-mindedly, "do not deserve such an insult. To offer Louisa Markham such a slight would not only render her prey to gossip but would be unforgiveable of me."

"Yes," she sighed resignedly, a slight crease furrowing her narrow forehead and her faded blue eyes clouding a little, "it would, and, of course, I have no wish to see the child hurt, but will you be happy, Max?" she urged, laying her free hand against his cheek.

He kissed its soft palm, saying at length, "I told Louisa that I believe we could deal extremely together, and," he nodded, "these past five weeks and more have done nothing to make me think otherwise. She is not, as you might think," he assured her quietly, "like her father."

"So, what is she like?" she smiled. "Is she beautiful? Her mamma, as I recall," she nodded, "was quite a notable beauty!"

An odd light suddenly entered his eyes and a faint smile touched his lips. "No," he said slowly, shaking his head, "I cannot call her beautiful," going on to give his mother a description of her. "In fact," he acknowledged, not unkindly, "compared to most young ladies on the town at this present she is by no means remarkable, indeed:" he nodded, "they all cast her very much into the shade, a circumstance she is well aware of," he smiled. "She told me herself that she could not help how she looked, and yet," he said, almost as if to himself, "she has the most spontaneous and infectious laugh imaginable and those green eyes of hers can light up in an instant," to which his mother's eyes narrowed slightly at this. "Her looks apart," recollecting himself, "she *is* a little out of the common, so much so," he nodded, a strange light entering his eyes, "that on our very first meeting she expressed a fervent wish to attend a lecture at The Royal Academy."

"*The Royal Academy!*" she cried, a little startled. His eyes laughed into hers. "Max, the child was not serious, surely!"

He nodded. "Perfectly serious, Mamma. I told her that I would see what William could do, as these are precisely the kind of entertainments he enjoys and, apparently, so does Louisa. I'm not quite sure how he managed it," he smiled ruefully, "but I think she enjoyed it just as much as she did the theatre or any of the many other entertainments I have escorted her to."

The marchioness, who remembered the late Earl of Markmoor before time and dissipation had taken their toll on a once handsome countenance, was suddenly filled with a desire to meet the daughter who, apparently, took after neither parent in looks. "What else can you tell me about her?"

"I *can* tell you that she has the most mischievous sense of the ridiculous which, I own, I find quite irresistible," he nodded.

She looked closely at him, her fingers gripping his. "Are you by chance falling in love with her, Max?"

"No, Mamma," he patted her hand reassuringly, deliberately trying to ignore that recurring tug of responsiveness which took him by surprise from time to time, "there is no fear of that, I promise you," smiling reassuringly at her before promising to bring Louisa on a visit to see her.

*

Had Louisa's mamma asked if she was falling in love with Deerham instead of merely warning her against the folly of it, her daughter would have given the same response as her betrothed had to his mamma; a definite no. Having known of the betrothal agreement from childhood was one thing, after all there was years ahead of her before she need give it consideration, besides which, anything could happen in the meantime to negate it, but as her nineteenth birthday had drawn ever nearer she could not deny that it had given her no little food for thought. Louisa knew her marriage was imperative if her brother was to try to redress his father's wastage and, whilst she had much preferred to receive a proposal of marriage from a man who loved her and whom she loved in return, she had nevertheless been quite prepared to accept Deerham's offer should he decide to make one. Although she had managed to hide her apprehension about meeting him from her mamma and brother, she could not hide it from herself, especially when she considered that she had never before laid eyes on him, but, and much to her surprise, from the moment she saw him standing in front of her in the small sitting room she liked him and, as their first meeting had progressed, she found herself growing more at ease in his company until whatever misgivings she had left her, although why this should be she had no notion.

Her mamma, who truly loved her daughter, had no need to see the look on her face to know that she had taken quite a liking to Deerham, felt it behoved her to offer some words of caution as well as giving her the benefit of her experience when it came to men and marriage. Whilst she had no reason to doubt that Deerham could be a most agreeable man, she knew it would not do for her daughter to read more into it than was in fact the case, and although she had no desire to put a damper on her forthcoming nuptials, she nevertheless felt it incumbent upon her to warn her daughter that it was not to be supposed a man of two and thirty was without experience, and therefore she was not to expect him to fall head over heels in love with her. She may still bear the emotional scars of her own husband's philandering and his total lack of discretion when conducting his many affairs, not that she could accuse Deerham of that, but whilst she had no wish to either cause her daughter pain or be the one responsible for creating a barrier between her and Deerham before they were even married, she had deemed it prudent to gently point out that it was not to be expected that marriage would see him shun the rest of her sex. Upon seeing the crease which had descended onto Louisa's forehead, she had fondly patted her cheek and told her that providing she was a dutiful wife, giving her husband no reason to either rebuke or cause her distress, then she foresaw a very happy future for her as the Marchioness of Deerham.

Louisa may have no cause to either doubt or question her mamma, after all if it were not Deerham then it would be another, but, from the very beginning, she had instinctively known that she would much rather it be Deerham than anyone else and, during the last six weeks as he had escorted her from one engagement to another, she was certain of it. So too was her mamma. She was not so carried away on the tide of relief and elation in knowing that Deerham, a man who could look as high as he chose for a wife, had ultimately honoured his father's promise and formally made her daughter an offer of marriage, to notice the subtle change in her. Deeming it prudent to stem any flights of fancy her daughter may have in the bud, she gently warned her against reading anything into Deerham's courtship other than what it really was, and therefore she must not expect him to make any protestations of love to her. Without giving her daughter time to respond to this, she further added that as far as his attentions to her comfort were concerned such behaviour was only to be expected from a man of his breeding, but, more importantly, she must not expect him to dance continual attendance on her.

Louisa had no reason to suppose her mamma could be wrong, but it was all so very disheartening, particularly as she found Deerham a most pleasant companion and one with whom she felt completely at ease and whose sense of the ridiculous corresponded so perfectly with her own. He may not have made protestations of love to her but, even so, his attentions to her comfort as well as when he raised her hand to his lips upon greeting or wishing her goodnight, whether due to good breeding or not, never failed to fill her with a warm sense of well-being, although this she wisely refrained from confiding to her mamma. Nor did she confide her disappointment when he offered his apologies for not being able to escort her to Lady Ralston's soirée, ambiguously described on the gilt-edged invitation card as 'a little get together', due to it unfortunately taking place in the evening on the very day Deerham journeyed to Bath. Louisa quite understood, but as she climbed the broad staircase beside her mamma to be introduced to their hostess, wearing a dress of warm amber satin, the perfect foil for her thick copper hair which was most fashionably and becomingly styled, and with the pearl necklace and matching earrings bestowed on her by Christopher, she could not help wishing Deerham was with her.

The countess, immensely relieved that thus far no mention had been made of her late husband's wayward career either to herself or Louisa, had gradually come to relax sufficiently to enjoy the season's hectic round of social events as well as renewing all her acquaintance, most of whom were Lady Ralston's guests this evening and all of them eager to know when they could expect an announcement. As neither Christopher nor Deerham had raised any objections to her confirming it if she were asked, she merely smiled, saying, "Yes, Deerham has done my daughter the honour of offering for her, and Louisa has accepted. The announcement will be in *The London Gazette* tomorrow." Her daughter's acceptance came as no surprise to anyone nor, for that matter, her betrothed's reason for journeying to Bath!

Lady Ralston, whose staid and rather boring husband had most conveniently succumbed to an inflammation of the lung three years ago and obligingly left her his entire fortune, there being no children of the marriage, enjoyed giving parties as much as she did attending them, remembered the late Earl of Markmoor very well, in fact, she could bring to mind his shameful behaviour with perfect clarity. She was not by nature malicious, but she did receive an inordinate amount of pleasure from listening to gossip, which kept her remarkably well informed and equally as entertained and, like everyone else, she knew of that betrothal agreement which had been made by Deerham's father and Louisa's grandfather. Like

Deerham's mother, she remembered Markmoor as being a most handsome man when young, but time and dissipation had taken their toll; as far as the countess was concerned she had been an accredited beauty in her day, indeed, she was still a remarkably beautiful woman, but, sadly, their daughter did not take after either parent.

Like the rest of society, Lady Ralston could not help but wonder whether Deerham would in fact honour the betrothal agreement or, thinking better of it, renege upon it, but since he had at no time given any indication as to what his decision was likely to be, she, like everyone else, had been left to wait with bated breath to see what he would do. Deerham was, of course, perfectly amiable and one whose manners were precisely what one would expect of a man of his breeding, indeed, no hostess could fail to be anything other than gratified to see him grace her saloons in response to her invitation, even if he did not stay very long, but for all his cordial punctilio it could not be denied that he was a rather reserved man who neither discussed his personal affairs nor welcomed any invasion of them, and he would have found it a gross intrusion, even an impertinence, had he been asked what his decision was likely to be. But having witnessed Deerham escorting Louisa Markham to any number of engagements over the past few weeks only a fool could be left in any doubt that these forays into society, with the countess in attendance, signified anything other than a perfectly correct courtship, but, unfortunately, as no confirmation had been forthcoming from any one of them she, like the rest of the ton, had to wait with what patience she could. Now though, according to Lavinia Markham, it would seem that Deerham had, indeed, offered for her daughter after all, but Lady Ralston, like her guests, could not help thinking that Deerham, who would doubtless have to pay through the nose for a girl with neither looks nor portion to recommend her and one, moreover, whose father had not been known for restraint or tact, had certainly got the wrong end of a very bad bargain.

If there were those who questioned Deerham's wisdom in offering for Markham's daughter, there was no need to question the reason for his absence to night – they only wished they could be present when he informed his mother! But Lavinia Markham, by far too aware of society's delight in scandal and gossip, knew precisely the meaning of those whispered questions and hushed voiced conversations behind the unfurled fans. She knew perfectly well that Deerham's father had shunned her late husband and, unless she was very much mistaken, despite Deerham's silence on this very point, his mother could not fail to view the forthcoming marriage with anything but doubt and misgiving and, from the looks of it, everyone else thought so too. Nor had she missed the glances cast in her daughter's direction, and not just this evening, no doubt wondering whether, though nothing like her father in looks then like him enough in every other respect, something which would no doubt become evident in the course of time.

But Louisa's passage through Lady Ralston's saloons, despite her mamma's concerns that without Deerham's shielding and commanding presence someone may just be presumptuous enough to make a comment to her, had been a success. She could not fool herself into thinking that her daughter outshone all the young ladies who had been present, on the contrary she had been cast very much into the shade by all of them, and not only tonight. But one thing she did know, and that was Louisa certainly stood out in a crowd which she knew perfectly well was due to that striking combination of rich copper curls and those huge green eyes, and although she lacked any facial pretensions to beauty she had a complexion free of any blemish which owed nothing to cosmetic aids or the application of crushed strawberries.

Louisa, totally unaware of the intense interest she had aroused in her fellow guests, indeed everyone she had come across these past five weeks or so, had, despite Deerham not being with her, thoroughly enjoyed herself, excitedly telling her mamma in the carriage on their way back to Cavendish Square about who she had met and what had been said to her, eventually rounding off her animated account by informing her that she had met a young lady who, would you believe it? – lived only the other side of the garden in Cavendish Square! Her mamma, who had seen her daughter and Letitia Rawnsley with their heads together during the course of the evening, was not at all surprised that the two of them had struck up a friendship, after all they were the same age and both embarking on their first London season, but she could not help her bosom swelling with pride when that young lady's most formidable aunt, the Dowager Countess of Pitlone, a lady she had known for many years, had given her full approval of Louisa, pronouncing, "I vow and declare it was as though I was looking at her grandmother!" Lavinia Markham was therefore by no means displeased or surprised to learn that Louisa and Letitia, who, for the past few weeks, had been visiting her mamma in Wiltshire due to that lady urgently demanding her attendance owing, she said, to a deterioration in her health, had arranged to meet again, but gently cautioned her about making too many arrangements until she knew what Deerham had in mind for her entertainment.

*

Deerham, having remained with his mother overnight, did not return to his imposing house in Grosvenor Square until late in the afternoon despite having left Bath immediately after breakfast, to find, with no real surprise, several cards of felicitations upon his betrothal together with any number of cards of invitation, laid out on the marble topped table in the hall. Clifton, who had seen Trench pull up outside, had the door open in readiness before Deerham had even alighted from his coach, relieving him of his hat, cane and gloves immediately he stepped into the lofty hall, handing these carefully over to a footman, to whom he immediately nodded dismissal, before turning back to his lordship and asking how he had found her ladyship, to which Deerham smiled.

"Very well, thank you, Clifton. She sends you her regards and all manner of wishes."

Clifton, deeply gratified, bowed, then stood discreetly to one side awaiting his instructions while his lordship cast a cursory glance at his correspondence before reminding him, without raising his eyes from the notes in his hand, that he was due to dine in Cavendish Square, to which Clifton bowed, having already acquainted the temperamental but culinary genius in the kitchens to this effect. Clifton may have offered his lordship all felicitations upon his betrothal, but, like William, he could not claim a liking for it. As with Deerham's mother, it was not the young lady herself who engendered his dislike of the marriage but the fact that her father, a known womanizer and hardened gamester, who had cared more for his own pleasures than his estates, had no reason to doubt that through his reckless spending his lordship, who had already paid out what he had no doubt was a king's ransom for her, would have his hand in his pocket nine times out of ten despite the settlements. Clifton, who knew his place and what was due to his lordship's as well as his own dignity, had never, by word or deed, communicated his feelings upon the subject, but Deerham, who had a pretty shrewd idea of his sentiments and that they ran virtually parallel to those of his secretary as well as Thomas and Trench, merely raised his head and smiled across at him, saying that he would not be needed. No one observing Deerham as he leisurely climbed the curved staircase in apparent unconcern, would have had the least guess that he was thinking of Louisa as well as wondering how she had enjoyed herself at Lady Ralston's last night, conscious of wishing he had been with her.

Dinner in Cavendish Square this evening was solely for the seventh Earl of Markmoor and his mother the countess, to celebrate privately the betrothal of the Lady Louisa Markham to the Most Noble the Marquis of Deerham prior to the betrothal celebrations in Grosvenor Square later in the month. Although Deerham had accepted Christopher's apology for the invitation to dine taking place so soon following the betrothal announcement due to affairs requiring his attention at Markmoor Manor, which may take anything up to a week or more to conclude, with unruffled calm, it had nevertheless rendered it necessary for him to cancel an engagement for this evening. Being familiar with his lordship's ways and habits, this unexpected change to his arrangements, and for such a reason, was a circumstance which made Thomas shake his head and purse his lips, unable to comprehend why it did not seem to perturb his lordship in the least. His lordship had no intention of telling him that he was by no means disinclined to seeing Louisa again any more than he was of his inner struggle to deny the fact, infuriating his lifelong valet and devotee by merely stating that he had missed his ministrations whilst in Bath.

Thomas, a tall and spindly legged man of indeterminate age with an almost skeletal face, had been with his lordship for as long as he could remember and, like Trench, had followed Deerham's career with almost slavish adulation and, again like Trench, could boast of knowing his lordship better than most, indeed, both men were certainly granted far more licence than anyone else. These two Deerham stalwarts, bosom cronies, had often discussed their noble employer's forthcoming betrothal, neither of whom could claim to being overly happy about it, but since his lordship would not discuss it they wisely kept their views until they were alone over a glass of something warm and invigorating. Although it would have afforded them some comfort to be able to impart their views as well as their caution to his lordship, they had decided against it on several grounds, not the least being that Deerham would not take it kindly, even from them.

Upon Deerham entering the large master bedroom, Thomas bowed and, after responding to his lordship's comments regarding his absence being missed, he then enquired after her ladyship, who, he had no doubt, had no more liking for the betrothal than the rest of them, before informing him that he had laid out his raiment in readiness for this evening and that his bath and shaving water were already prepared. After being assisted out of his clothes, Deerham easily shrugged himself into the dark green brocade dressing gown Thomas held out to him, then, taking a seat at his dressing table, began to pare his nails, an everyday task but, on this occasion, it was done with a calmness Thomas found particularly exasperating, especially when he considered the *mésalliance* he was about to enter into. Deerham, knowing the thoughts going on behind that impassive face, suppressed the twitch at the corner of his mouth and, without raising his eyes from the task of paring his nails, asked, quite affably,

"Well, Thomas?"

"My lord?" Thomas queried, raising an eyebrow.

"Don't play the innocent with me, Thomas," he said pleasantly, "you will catch cold at that."

"I don't understand, my lord," he shrugged, bewildered.

"You understand perfectly, Thomas," Deerham told him, his concentration still on his nails. "You and Trench are both audible by your silence."

"I'm sure I don't know to what you refer, my lord," he said blankly.

Raising his eyes to his valet's face, a smile lurking at the back of them, he said agreeably, "The devil you don't! Between you, you and Trench have convinced yourselves that I am about to become a sacrificial lamb on the altar of duty. You really must rid yourselves of such a notion."

"No such thoughts…!" he began.

"Your thoughts, Thomas," Deerham told him equably, "are deafening."

A mutinous look settled on his gaunt face, saying determinedly, "If me and Trench can't…"

"Thomas," Deerham broke in placidly, "I own you are indispensable to my comfort; you take care of my clothes and my needs admirably and, on occasion, I even allow you to shave me, *but*," he stressed, not unkindly, "you really *must* allow me to conduct my own affairs."

"Very well, my lord," he sniffed, knowing it was useless to try to get his lordship to see sense, "I shall now go and check on your bath."

"Thank you, Thomas," Deerham said meekly, returning his attention back to the important task of paring his nails.

*

Christopher, enormously relieved that Deerham had come up to scratch and the settlements had finally been agreed, had, like his mamma, been quick to observe that his sister appeared to be by no means indifferent to her betrothed. She was, of course, young and inexperienced, a fact he felt sure Deerham would not only have recognized at the outset but taken for granted, but he was convinced that his mamma had been wise to warn Louisa that her marriage to Deerham was purely a contractual one and not one based on love and that she had also cautioned her against falling in love with her future husband. He could not dispute the fact that Deerham's amatory affairs had been conducted with the utmost discretion, unlike his own father's, but Christopher felt it reasonably safe to assume that marriage would not prevent him from taking a mistress and, whilst there was nothing unusual in this, he only hoped, for his sister's sake, that she did not fall in love with him. He had complete faith in Deerham treating his wife with courtesy and all the respect which was her due, therefore giving her no cause for distress or embarrassment and humiliation, but it could not be argued that should Louisa indeed lose her heart to him, then it was a pretty foregone conclusion she would be doomed to a future of unbearable heartache, because even supposing Deerham did eventually grow to become rather fond of her Christopher doubted that her love would be reciprocated. He loved his sister dearly and wished her very happy and knew no qualms in giving her to Deerham in marriage, but he was honest enough to admit that Louisa, for all her irresistible ways and affectionate nature, was no beauty, and whilst he felt sure that Deerham would never deliberately hurt or humiliate her, the fact remained that for a man such as he, who was no stranger to the company of beautiful women, his wife's lack of this necessary attribute could well see him often out of her company.

The countess, although immensely relieved now that her daughter's future was secured, had entertained similar thoughts herself, but as the time drew near for Deerham's arrival, the only thing which occupied her mind was the horrifying thought that he would be bored rigid with only four at the table. It was therefore to her considerable surprise and enormous relief to find that far from being bored he actually seemed to enjoy the evening as well as the company, at no point standing on his dignity or proving a most awkward guest by offering little or no conversation or answering only in monosyllables, but, on the contrary, extremely easy to please. He was as content to converse as he was to listen, and Louisa, sitting directly opposite him, was given no cause to re-evaluate her opinion in that she liked him very much, and when, which was quite often, those dark grey eyes came to rest on her she detected the smile she had seen many times before lurking at the back of them; a smile that never failed to rouse that responsive chord somewhere deep inside her.

Deerham may have told his mother that there was no fear of him falling in love with Louisa, but the truth was, he knew perfectly well that he stood on the brink of doing precisely that. He was the first to acknowledge that she was no beauty and, of course, she was young and innocent and wholly unsophisticated, so very different to those women with whom he had previously spent more than one pleasurable hour. He accepted it as perfectly natural that she had no doubt formed a young girl's infatuation for some young man she had known in Gloucestershire which, like all these adolescent feelings, had eventually died a customary death, but it was patently obvious that she had never been in love before, and therefore totally unacquainted with the arts of seduction which the majority of her sex never failed to use in an effort to entice a man into doing whatever she wanted. As he had himself been subjected to every lure known to her sex and, even, been known to succumb to them, he could speak with some authority on the subject, but although he had thoroughly enjoyed his liaisons while they had lasted he, no more than the lady, had wanted more than they had shared, but one mischievous smile or impish look from out of those wide green eyes was not only more enticing than any calculated art could ever be but proved that he was by no means unsusceptible to her. He had recognized at the outset that her looks really did not matter, and during the past six weeks this opinion had undergone no change, and as he sat watching her now, her face alight with laughter as she exchanged sibling banter with her brother, he knew they never would.

Yet again, he found himself trying to not only ignore those persistent stirrings somewhere deep inside him, but strenuously struggling to suppress them, telling himself that he was far too old and experienced to succumb to one of Louisa Markham's youth and artlessness, but the plain truth was that without even trying she had, from the moment he had first met her, paved a way to his heart in a way no other woman ever had. None of his affairs had encompassed love, but this one young lady, who had neither looks nor portion to recommend her, had, when he had quite unexpected it, opened the door to an emotion he had up until now convinced himself did not exist.

But he was by far too experienced and in control of himself to let anyone suspect that a severe struggle was taking place inside him in an attempt to deny any existence of the feelings she had evoked, but, later, when they were give a few moments alone before he left and he amusingly asked her how she had enjoyed herself at Lady Ralston's party, her reaction, totally spontaneous, immediately fanned the stirrings he was strenuously trying to extinguish. Those incredible green eyes lit up and with that impulsiveness her mamma had tried hard to curb, after all it would not do to appear a little rustic innocent even when dressed in the very height of fashion, she gave him a rather animated account of her evening at Lady Ralston's, leaving out not the smallest detail, her enthusiasm setting those thick copper spirals, dressed in a way Deerham thought particularly becoming, dancing.

"I wish I had been there," he told her truthfully.

"Yes," she nodded, "so do I, because you see," she confided, "I would have enjoyed it so much more, having you to talk to, I mean."

"Are you telling me," he teased, his eyes smiling down at her, fast coming to the realization that he was losing the battle with his inner struggle, "that no gentleman engaged you in conversation or even asked you to dance?"

"Oh, yes," she nodded, "any number of gentlemen came up to me, indeed, sir," she told him seriously, "they were extremely polite and their conversation quite entertaining."

"Why do I detect a 'but'?" he asked amusingly.

Her face broke into a smile and her eyes laughed up into his, having not the least suspicion as to the effect they had on him. "Well, it *is* a little difficult to talk to someone when they are more interested in catching someone's eye or interrupting the conversation to pay you compliments."

"That certainly was too bad of them," he agreed without a tremor.

"Yes, but when one gentleman asked me to dance," she informed him, "although why he did so when he spent the entire time looking at his wig in the nearest mirror - a monstrous concoction of the palest lavender, ugh," she shuddered, "I don't know, he kept forgetting his steps."

Sternly suppressing the smile which hovered on his lips, he sighed, "I am sorry you do not approve of lavender wigs because I was rather hoping to wear mine when I escort you and your mamma to Lady Castleton's tomorrow evening."

Her eyes widened at this. *"Never* tell me you wear a wig?" she exclaimed. He looked contrite. "Oh, but, indeed, sir, you do not need to do so in the least!" she told him impulsively.

"Why, thank you," he inclined his head.

Catching the smile in his eyes when he looked up, she laughed. "Oh, you are joking me!"

"Yes," he said gently, "I am joking you. Although," he confessed, "I *do* wear a wig, but," he assured her, "only on very formal occasions, but *never* lavender."

She laughed. "Are you really escorting us to Lady Castleton's tomorrow evening?" she asked hopefully.

"Most certainly," he nodded.

"Oh, I am so glad," she smiled.

"I am relieved to hear it," he teased gently, taking hold of her hand, "because I *was* rather hoping that during this giddy round of entertainment you have embarked on you would still find a little time at least for your betrothed, as you have thus far."

The smile was still in his eyes but there was something else as well, something she could not quite define but which had a most strange effect on her, bringing the colour flooding into her cheeks and her hand to tremble slightly in his.

"I… I am always delighted to accept of your company at any time, my lord," she managed, somewhat breathlessly.

"And I of yours," he bowed, raising her hand to his lips, resisting the urge to kiss her. "But if I may be permitted to make a suggestion?" he smiled. She nodded. "Most people call me Deerham or Seer but my family and friends call me Max. Do you not think," he said softly, "that it is time you did too?"

Having come to accept, during the course of the evening, that it was useless to try to deny what he had really known from the very beginning, Deerham, fully alive to the fact that so far Louisa had behaved towards him very much in the way she would to a favourite uncle or, even, the parson at Markmoor, had nevertheless noticed the subtle change in her reaction to him by the time he had wished her goodnight. He knew full well that Louisa was of the belief that it was a marriage of convenience, certainly as far as her brother was concerned, and that for him it was merely a case honouring his father's word, which, at the outset, it was, but now, having met Louisa and spent time in her company, he knew that, for himself at least, it was most certainly more than that. Louisa's somewhat shy and breathless response to his gentle teasing filled him with the hope that she was not wholly indifferent to him, although he felt reasonably certain that because of her inexperience she was unsure of what she herself had felt. She may be prepared to accept him as her husband but he shrewdly suspected that she had no idea he had fallen in love with her, much less expected him to do so.

It had been obvious from the moment they had first met that she liked him, this being at the very root of any lack of awkwardness in her manner towards him, and as he had no wish to frighten her or to kill at a stroke the trust she clearly had in him as well as her ease in his company: bringing to an end any desire she had to confide in him, to take her in his arms and kiss her would have been unforgivable of him. He had not set out to fall in love with Louisa Markham but, having done so, he determined, even before he had descended the steps of the house in Cavendish Square, to court his betrothed in earnest.

Chapter Seven

As Deerham had rightly predicted, Lady Castleton's drum ball was a dreadful squeeze, but Louisa, not quite managing to contain her natural exuberance, looked about her in wide eyed excitement. Unlike her mamma and betrothed, she had no idea of the real meaning of the curious, not to say inquisitive, stares, cast in their direction, had been in fact from the moment she and Deerham had been seen in public together, by the interested, but Deerham, by no means fooled, merely bowed, accepting their felicitations on behalf of himself and Louisa with all his usual composure.

Louisa, quite content to saunter around Lady Castleton's saloons with her hand resting comfortably on her betrothed's arm, exchanging greetings with those whom she was already acquainted or being introduced to those of his friends who had not so far come in her way, was suddenly jolted out of her happy illusion when she caught sight of her mamma standing proudly watching them, the slight crease on her forehead and an infinitesimal shake of the head bringing to mind her warning about not letting it be seen that she was forever by Deerham's side. No gentleman, she had assured her daughter after Deerham had left the house last night, wanted either his betrothed or his wife hanging continually on his arm so, with this stricture in mind, she reluctantly excused herself saying that she had spotted Letitia and must speak to her, whereupon she made her way to where her new friend was standing against the far wall with her formidable aunt sitting next to her.

It came as no surprise to Deerham to discover that Louisa had made the acquaintance of the young lady he had rescued from Singleton's clutches and knew that, at some point during the course of the evening, his betrothed would introduce Letitia to him when, he devoutly trusted, she would not recognize him. So far, the Honourable Letitia Rawnsley had kept her word and said nothing about her abduction by Singleton and her eleventh-hour rescue by a masked stranger, had she have done so, then it would be all over town by now, but from the looks of the two of them together, denoting a firm friendship was well and truly cemented, he felt it reasonably certain that his betrothed's friend would, at some juncture, impart her adventure to her.

No one looking at that tall, loose-limbed figure strolling around Lady Castleton's saloons, flawlessly dressed in amber satin with a cream silk waistcoat with golden thread embroidery, exchanging a word and a witticism here with this man or bowing gracefully over a lady's hand there would have the least guess that he had fallen very much in love with the young lady whose father had shocked society by his behaviour, on the contrary everyone knew that his offer of marriage to Louisa Markham had been out of respect for his late father and for no other reason. With the understandable exception of Louisa, there was not a soul here this evening who did not know the full sum of the late earl's antics, including his widow who, not by a word or gesture, let it be seen that she was still deeply affected by them, or of the close friendship which had existed between her late husband and Digby Singleton, whose own mother had set the town talking with her scandalous behaviour. Every member of the ton may have a dread of personal scandal but nothing it seemed delighted them more than to enjoy the gossip circulated about others and when, within half an hour of the arrival of Deerham and the Markham ladies, Digby Singleton, dressed in peacock blue satin with his face powdered and painted and wearing a wig standing at least eight inches from the top of his head in a delicate shade of blue, sauntered into the crowded saloons, every one of Lady Castleton's guests, despite their feigned attempts at indifference, excitedly awaited events. Deerham and Singleton may exchange common bows in passing, but it was common knowledge that they were not friends, but since neither man either confirmed or endorsed the many stories abounding as to the reason for their mutual dislike, society was left with only conjecture to assuage their curiosity.

The Dowager Countess of Pitlone, telling her niece with a tartness completely belied by the look of indulgence in those alert pale blue eyes, that she was much too old to be gadding about town, by no means disapproved of the budding friendship between Letitia and Louisa Markham. She was far too sensible a woman to hang a father's mantle around the neck of his offspring without a good reason for doing so and far too astute not to recognize at a glance that no such recklessness was evident in his daughter. The dowager countess, like everyone else, knew that Singleton and Louisa's father had been bosom cronies and setting the town alight in the process with their gambling and womanizing, and although Singleton's paternal connections would ensure that some hostesses would continue to send him cards of invitation, such as Sally Castleton for example, but, for herself, she wanted nothing whatsoever to do with him.

Nothing would disabuse her mind that he was a bad influence on young men like her nephew, who had more money than sense, but although Algernon, apparently quite deaf to her warnings about the unsavoury company he appeared to be keeping, continually associated with him, as far as she was concerned nothing would induce her to be upon even polite nodding terms with the man. She had a pretty shrewd idea that at some point during the course of the evening Singleton would make himself known to Louisa, and nothing would give her greater satisfaction than to warn the child about keeping well clear of him, but as her mamma or Deerham could well have done so already, she decided to let well alone for now, knowing no compunction in whisking her niece off for refreshment the instant she saw him look in their direction.

Sally Castleton, herself an inveterate card player and one who favoured deep play, had often pitted her skill against Singleton's, was rather optimistic of engaging him in a return game this evening when, hopefully, she could recoup some of the money she had lost to him only days before he had left England for Paris. Beneath her powder and rouge, she was far older than she looked, but despite the fact that any number of attempts had been made to support the bets which had been taken and laid in the clubs as to her precise age had been to no avail, she herself vowed she was not a day above forty. She knew perfectly well that Singleton was not *persona grata* with every hostess, especially those high sticklers like the Dowager Countess of Pitlone, but, for herself, she had to confess to a liking for the man whose mother she had seen with her own eyes strip the bracelets from her wrists to cover her bet and would, therefore, consider her party to be incomplete without him.

"Lud Digby!" she exclaimed, giving him her hand. "I vow and declare that wig of yours is positively indecent!" eyeing the embellished confection in wide eyed amazement.

"Were I to respond to that in like manner, Sally," he smiled, "*I* vow and declare you would never speak to me again."

"The very height of fashion, I assure you," she laughed, indicating her elaborate coiffure with a careless hand. "'*Petite innocente*'," she inclined her head. "'Tis all the rage in Paris."

"I do not doubt it," Singleton inclined his head, "but do you not think…?"

"*M. Dupont,*" she forestalled him, her eyes alight with amusement, "tells me that no young lady ought ever to wear anything else."

"A *young* lady, no," he agreed.

"Has anyone ever told you, Digby," she said without rancour, "that you are no gentleman?"

"Frequently," he bowed.

"I wonder why I put up with you?" she sighed. "It certainly cannot be anything to do with your good manners!"

"Why, for the money I allow you to win off me at cards," he replied easily, inclining his head.

"I shall make you eat those words before the night is through, and so I warn you!" she laughed, tapping him over the arm with her furled fan.

He bowed. "You are certainly welcome to try," he smiled, "but I feel devilish lucky tonight, and so I warn you. So," he mused, raising his eyeglass to glance around him "who is here tonight?" After listening to her reeling off half a dozen or so names, he said, "You know, Sally, you really are to be congratulated on filling your rooms with so many notables this early in the season." He pulled out his snuff-box, but just as he was about to raise a pinch between his finger and thumb to one thin nostril he caught sight of Deerham's tall figure at the far end of the room, his hand stilling. "Ah!" he purred, "I see you have managed to get Deerham here." She inclined her head, secretly pleased that she had managed to do so. "The countess too!" he exclaimed, not unimpressed, raising an eyebrow at her.

"Of course," Sally Castleton nodded.

"And the chit?" he enquired, taking a pinch of snuff.

"Certainly," she smiled. "You surely did not think they would leave her behind?"

"Where is she?" he wanted to know.

"Over there," she inclined her head, "talking to Letitia Rawnsley and her aunt."

The mention of his recent victim caused him neither embarrassment nor discomfiture any more than did the sight of that young lady being hurriedly borne away by her redoubtable aunt upon seeing him glance in their direction, leaving her companion a little at a loss, totally unaware that she was being closely scrutinized. "So, that's her, is it?" Singleton said almost to himself.

Sally Castleton cast a quick glance up at him, but upon seeing nothing in his face to suggest the thoughts going around in his head, said, "Yes, that's Louisa Markham, although," she sighed, "it is a pity she does not favour her mamma or, even," she added fair-mindedly, "her father."

"A pity," he repeated in an odd voice, "my dear Sally, I could not be more delighted with our P*arfait Petite Innocente!*"

She eyed him narrowly. "What mischief are you brewing, Digby?"

He brought a shocked gaze to her face, crying, "Mischief! My dear Sally," he said taken aback, raising a surprised pencilled eyebrow, "you wrong me, truly you do!" She did not think so but allowed it to pass. "I do trust," he suggested smoothly, "that you *are* going to introduce me to her?"

"Are you sure you want me to?" she asked, her eyes darting to where Deerham was standing.

Singleton's eyes followed her. "My dear Sally," he cried in exaggerated accents, "how could I not wish to make the acquaintance of one whose father I called friend? I doubt even Deerham could find anything to object to in that!"

Having promised Letitia to introduce her to her betrothed later, Louisa watched her walk away with her aunt in the direction of a small saloon where a formidable array of refreshments had been laid out, but just as she was on the point of returning to Deerham and her mamma Sally Castleton came up to her, her painted face wreathed in smiles.

"Ah, my dear!" she cried, detaining her by bringing her furled fan to rest gently on her arm. "Please, do not go yet. There is someone I should like you to meet, an old friend of mine." Turning to Singleton, she said, "Digby, allow me to introduce Louisa Markham to you. Louisa, my dear, say hello to Digby Singleton."

Louisa may be young and inexperienced but she was nevertheless a good judge of character, and in the same way she had instinctively known she liked Deerham so too did she know she did not like Digby Singleton, but being an extremely well-mannered young lady, she bobbed a curtsey, saying politely,

"How do you do?"

"Would it be impertinent of me to say I do very much better for meeting you?" he smiled, raising her hand to his lips.

"You are most kind, sir," she said faintly, unused to such practised courtliness and not quite sure she liked it.

"Not at all," he assured her.

"You must excuse me, my dear," Sally Castleton smiled down at Louisa, not at all sure it was a good thing to leave the child with Singleton, but then she consoled herself with the knowledge that there was very little he could do to her in the middle of her crowded saloons, and certainly not with Deerham and her mamma close by, "but I have just spotted someone I positively must speak to."

"So," Singleton mused, when Sally had left, "*you* are Edmund's daughter?"

"Yes," she nodded, looking up into the thin and rather sallow face looking down at her, observing that not even such clever use of powder and paint had succeeded in hiding the lines of dissipation around his eyes and mouth.

"You do not have the look of him," he remarked, eyeing her closely, noting with satisfaction that Sally was right in that she took after neither parent in her looks, a circumstance he found particularly ironic when he considered the beautiful women who had adorned Deerham's life. How disappointed he must have been upon coming face to face with this child, and one, moreover, who held no pretensions to beauty whatsoever.

"No," she shook her head, "I believe not, sir."

"You must know that I had the pleasure of calling friends with your father - but, of course," he hastened, helplessly raising his hands, "how could you?"

"You… you knew my father?" she faltered, this fact not altering her dislike of him.

"Most certainly," he inclined his head, his painted lips parting into the semblance of a smile. "He and I were good friends for many years." He had no doubt whatsoever that the countess or, possibly, her brother, had told her something of her father's dealings or, at least, enough to make her realize how important her marriage to Deerham was. Nevertheless, he felt reasonably sure that the whole truth had been kept from her, but since his sole aim in life was to have his revenge on her betrothed, regaling her with the full sum of her father's way of life would not serve this purpose in the least, so deliberately turning her mind away from the questions he knew she must want to ask he commented politely upon her betrothal. "So," he smiled, those painted eyebrows arching, "'twould seem I am to wish you happy."

"Yes," she nodded, "thank you," following his glance in Deerham's direction.

"Deerham is to be congratulated," he inclined his head, "a most fortunate young man, in fact."

"You are most kind," Louisa replied, a little restrained, detecting the irony in his thin voice.

"Not at all, my dear," he bowed. "Indeed, I almost envy him his good fortune." He offered his snuff-box, to which she shook her head. "And how do you like being betrothed to Deerham?" he asked politely.

"Well, I…"

"But, of course," be broke in with credible forgetfulness, "how could you know when, or so I infer," he inclined his head, "he has only recently offered for you," a circumstance which could not have pleased him more. "You know," he sighed, "I had begun to think he was a hopeless case, quite the determined bachelor, but here he is betrothed at last; undoubtedly a love match," then, with a magnificent display of absent-mindedness, cried, "but, of course, I remember, the match was agreed many years ago, was it not?"

"Yes," Louisa said faintly, "it was."

"And here was I thinking," sadly shaking his head, "'twas a whirlwind romance, but, of course, I was forgetting that agreement," adding with deceptive circumspection, "a circumstance I am afraid not even Deerham could ignore!"

He may say that he could almost envy Deerham and that he was a most fortunate young man, but beneath the smoothly delivered eloquence Louisa detected a touch of ill-feeling and although she could only hazard a guess as to why, she felt compelled to ask, "Are you a friend of Deerham's?"

He paused in the act of taking snuff, raising his eyes to her face before deliberately glancing over to where he could see Deerham talking to an acquaintance. "Let us just say," he said meditatively, "that we know one another."

"So, you are not friends," she stated in that direct way her mamma had warned her against.

"I see you are a most astute young lady," he bowed, his eyes glinting, "but, alas," he sighed, mournfully shaking his head, "'twould seem your betrothed and I are destined to remain mere acquaintances."

"Why is that?" she wanted to know, looking curiously up at him, those green eyes wide and enquiring. Whilst she admitted to not knowing Deerham for very long she knew enough to be certain that no two men could be more dissimilar as well as having very little, if anything, in common, and she therefore could not help wondering what was between them, but, if nothing else, she felt reasonably certain that this man, looking down at her in a way she neither liked nor desired, was trying, if not to turn her against Deerham, then certainly to raise questions in her mind.

"Why?" he raised an eyebrow, giving an exaggerated shrug of his narrow shoulders. She nodded. Then, giving all the appearance of one who was deliberating the wisdom of something, he sighed, saying with studied reluctance, "Well, you know, my dear, it is not for me to tell tales behind a man's back and, certainly, not to his betrothed."

No, this man did not like Deerham and, unless she was very much mistaken, she gained the very strong impression that he was doing his utmost to malign him to her, but although the reason for this momentarily escaped her, she repeated politely, "No, not to his betrothed."

"Perhaps," he said delicately, laying the poison down a bit thicker, "you should ask him, although," he smiled, "I doubt he will tell you. He is not, how shall I say?" he sighed, "the most agreeable of men."

"You do not find him agreeable?" she questioned, wondering what had brought about his dislike of Deerham. A trusting little innocent she may be but a fool she was not and knew instinctively that this man was attempting to use her to get to Deerham, although for what purpose she had no idea.

"Ah," he nodded comprehendingly, "'twould seem, would it not, that I have spoken out of turn? A thousand pardons," he bowed, "I had no intention of being so maladroit. It is merely that, given the close friendship I had with your father, I felt it behoved me to…" he coughed delicately, "well, let us just say that Deerham *can* make himself most agreeable, when he chooses to do so, which," he raised a knowing eyebrow, "he clearly has with you thus far, my dear." He saw the frown crease her forehead but deeming he had laid down enough poison for her to chew on for now, raised her hand to lips, assuring her that he was delighted to make her acquaintance and had no doubt that they would renew it at the many parties and balls he felt sure she would be attending.

Louisa supposed she should welcome the opportunity of meeting someone who had been a close friend of her father, but the truth was, she was not sorry when he moved away from her and certainly in no hurry to run across him again even though she knew she would be bound to. She could recall seeing the same lines around her father's eyes and mouth on the very last occasion she had seen him, but although they were not as pronounced as Singleton's, they told her more than any words could have that her father's career when away from the family home had been every bit as eventful as Christopher had said. As she made her way to Deerham's side, she could not help but compare the two men, but as he pulled her hand through his arm to allow him to escort her into another saloon she was soon able to relegate Singleton to the back of her mind, a man who, she felt quite convinced, held a grievance against her betrothed.

Singleton, watching her closely from out the corner of his eyes, was very well pleased with his efforts, experiencing neither regrets nor qualms in using the daughter of his old friend to help him bring about Deerham's downfall. Had he have known that Louisa had read more into the reason behind his cunningly contrived innuendoes than he had realized and, more than this, that she was far from being the malleable innocent he believed her to be, he would not have felt so confident in that he had chosen the perfect pawn for his needs after all.

His cunningly contrived innuendoes were not without a fell purpose, on the contrary they had a single aim in view, the irrevocable downfall of Deerham by any means at his disposal. Nothing could have pleased him more than when he read of their betrothal in *The London Gazette* upon returning to town from his very profitable sojourn in Paris, confirming that he had honoured his father's word after all. Singleton was not claiming his letter was at the root of Deerham's decision, but whilst they could not call friends he knew perfectly well that any number of his well-wishers had cautioned him against tying himself up to the Markham chit, and since Deerham was not a man who liked having his hand forced, his anonymous warning could well have been one gentle nudge against the marriage too many; this, and the fact that Deerham was too much the gentleman to do anything else. What did surprise Singleton, however, was that Deerham must have put out positive overtures to Christopher Markham within so short a space of time of making his sister's acquaintance, were it otherwise then there was no reason he could see for Deerham, as his cronies confirmed, being seen continually in the company of Louisa Markham and her mamma. It was known amongst Deerham's circle that he had been staying with friends prior to going to Worleigh for a spell, returning to town on the very day he had spoiled his game with Letitia Rawnsley, and since he had not laid eyes on Edmund's daughter before, it could only mean that he had seen Louisa Markham almost immediately upon his return to London, his promise of honouring the betrothal following in next to no time afterwards.

No more than Deerham had Singleton laid eyes on Edmund's daughter, but Sally Castleton was right when she had said Louisa Markham did not take after either parent, in fact, were it not for that striking colour combination, no one would give her a second look in passing. Setting aside her obvious intelligence, her looks were so very far removed from those beautiful women who had adorned Deerham's life that Louisa Markham must have come as a great disappointment to him. Having had a father who had been a remarkably handsome man in his youth and a mother who could still claim to being an exceptionally beautiful woman, it had come as something of a surprise to discover that their daughter could only just be described as passably good looking, but if Singleton had been quite taken aback upon setting eyes on her, how much more so for Deerham? Sally Castleton had sadly shaken her head over it, saying it was a pity that Louisa Markham had not inherited the good looks of either parent, but his own amazement apart, the fact remained that she answered his purpose perfectly.

It would, of course, take time and careful planning to bring about the ruination of Deerham, but the moment Singleton had set eyes on his betrothed he knew that Providence was continuing to come to his aid by offering him the perfect tool with which to do it. Having given his overriding obsession some concentrated thought since his meeting with Louisa at Sally Castleton's, he had come to the conclusion that it really made not the slightest difference as to whether she had inherited her father's traits and tendencies or not, as well as it being totally irrelevant whatever Deerham may feel for her or come to feel for her in time, the fact remained that as the Marchioness of Deerham she was tailor made for his needs. Even supposing she had no taste for cards after all, it was surprising how something could be fabricated to give the impression that she did or, failing this, there was always her budding friendship with Letitia Rawnsley which could be turned to good account, an avenue which was by no means unattractive to him. In fact, the more he thought about it the more certain he became that Christopher Markham, even had he held his father's tastes, would really not serve his ends quite so satisfyingly as his sister, and therefore he began to focus all his attention on a young lady who would prove the ideal instrument to bring that noble peer to his knees.

Singleton could only hazard a guess as to the full extent of the damage done to the Markham estates through his friend's expensive and carefree lifestyle, but like everyone else he knew it to be extensive and therefore the marriage settlements would be considerable and Deerham, paying what he felt sure would be through the nose for the hedonistic earl's daughter, would not take it kindly to discover that, far from being the end of it, it was merely the beginning.

*

Over the ensuing weeks Singleton followed the future marchioness's career with avid interest and, like everyone else, she was seen to take her place at the card table, but since this was a fashionable pastime by the ton it did not automatically imply that she had inherited her father's love of gambling, in fact, from what he had been privileged to see he would go so far as to say that although she appeared to derive a certain enjoyment from playing there were no signs, at least for the moment, to show that she had a gamester's blood in her veins. Of course, whether this was due to the fact that, if Deerham did not accompany her to the numerous functions she attended her mother did, he was unable to say, but having devoted a lot of time and thought to his supreme ambition, he had come to see that whether or not she was in very truth her father's daughter, the future Marchioness of Deerham could still be used to devastating effect against the man Singleton vowed to be avenged upon.

Deerham's lineage was steeped in honour and integrity, and although it went very much against the grain with Singleton to admit it, he had to own that Deerham had upheld the name he bore with the same dignity and observance as his forebears, conducting his affairs and dealings with the utmost tact and discretion. What an exquisite revenge then to bring him toppling down from that pinnacle of pride and nobility by the daughter of a man his own father had been the first to shun, the daughter of a man he had made his wife; such a humiliation would surely be more than a fitting recompense for his meddlesome interference!

As for Letitia Rawnsley – well, that was for the future, although Singleton could only heave a sigh of relief that she had told one of her adventure, thanks no doubt to Deerham advising her against it, otherwise it would have been all over town now by now, in which case not even Sally Castleton would have welcomed him.

*

Although the sight of Louisa taking part in a game of cards at Sally Castleton's drum ball in one of the smaller saloons set aside for this pastime caused Deerham no concern, after all everyone did so, himself included, what did intrude on his thoughts however, was that she had, at no point, during the past few weeks, given any indication that her feelings for him were anything more than mere liking, and even though he had kissed her, very gently in order not to frighten her, he had never once received any kind of response from her to suggest that she had enjoyed it as much as he had. As he had for a long time come to look upon the social whirl as being nothing but a dead bore, he had nevertheless taken immense pleasure from escorting Louisa, in company with the countess, to all the ton parties, delighting in her impulsive reaction to everything she saw which, to her mamma's dismay, not all her strictures had totally eradicated. Indeed, his mother, upon making her acquaintance when he had taken her to Bath to meet her, had declared herself agreeably surprised in that Markmoor's daughter was totally unaffected, but since that evening at Sally Castleton's, he had noticed a significant change in her attitude towards him.

She was clearly not averse to his company, but there was nevertheless a reserve in her manner which had not been there in the beginning, resulting in her no longer treating him in the same way she had done, nor did she confide in him or talk to him in that animated way she had and, although she listened intently to his description of Worleigh and his other estates, not once had she ever given him reason to think that her feelings for him were ever going to be more than liking or that she was ready for his lovemaking, much less that she wanted it. The nearest he had come to receiving an affectionate response from her was the clasping of his hand in her two small ones and her eyes glowing warmly up at him when William agreed, against his better judgement, to arrange for her to sit hidden in an alcove at Burlington House in order for her to listen to the lecture she had so earnestly desired to attend.

He had witnessed that conversation between Louisa and Singleton at Sally Castleton's and although she had told him about it before he even mentioned it to her, he could not help but wonder whether Singleton had, if not then, then when he had seen her again the following evening at Lady Statton's, in some way either warned her against him or even told her that his father had been one of the first to shun her own. Louisa may have nothing whatsoever in common with her father, in fact, Deerham doubted whether she had laid eyes on him more than half a dozen times in her life, but nevertheless the blood tie was there, and it could well be that, despite the late earl's ruinous way of life, she did, in some way, feel the need to come to his defence. He knew that there was no way Louisa could avoid running into Singleton especially as he was by no means *persona non grata* with every hostess, but the less she was in his vicinity the better, because whilst Deerham had no doubt of being able to answer any barbs Singleton's malicious tongue made against himself Louisa, who may, out of curiosity, ask him about her father, could well find herself being persuaded into believing something which, in her innocence, would seem perfectly plausible. Singleton may have an unsavoury reputation where women were concerned, but it could not be argued that he had a certain charm and, whilst Deerham believed Louisa was far too intelligent to be taken in by it, the fact remained that her parentage left her wide open to Singleton's persuasive tongue as well as his machinations.

Singleton may well be laying down poison which he hoped would gradually take root in Louisa's mind thereby assisting his plans for Deerham's downfall but what he did not realize was that even if she had not read the malice behind the smooth-tongued innuendoes he had glibly offered for what they really were, it would take more than this to make her believe ill of her betrothed. As for Deerham, it was not, as he had supposed, Singleton to whom he owed his thanks for Louisa distancing herself from him, but her mamma.

The countess, a lady who, having learned from painful experience the cold hard facts that husbands were by no means reliable, much less faithful, had deemed it necessary to take her daughter to one side to further caution her against expecting too much from her marriage, as well as warning her about never allowing herself to be seen hanging on his arm. It was only to be expected that a man of Deerham's breeding should be considerate in his attentions to Louisa, but, even so, she felt it behoved her to once again repeat her warnings to her daughter in that she must not read too much, if anything, into this thereby raising false hopes in that he had fallen in love with her. Not only this, but she must not encourage either his attachment or his lovemaking as it could quite well give him a disgust of her, besides which, any intimacies he imposed upon her were merely his duty and therefore when it came to his pleasures she could leave that to his discreet connection. Louisa may have told her that she had not fallen in love with Deerham but ever since that evening at Sally Castleton's she had been given cause to doubt her daughter's assertion, because there was no denying that the look in her eyes whenever they had come to rest on him when he had not been aware of it, was enough to tell her that Louisa bore all the signs of having done precisely that.

She had no doubt that Deerham would treat her daughter just as he ought, and whilst she fervently hoped that the couple would rub along together tolerably well, she felt her daughter would be hoping for too much to expect her husband to devote himself entirely to her and not look about him for amusement in the way gentlemen did, and therefore she felt it incumbent upon her to guard her daughter against the heartache most wives experienced as well as reminding her that people of their order did not marry for love. It was not that she disliked Deerham, not at all, nor was it because she was not pleased about the marriage, she was, it was simply because she loved her daughter and did not want to see her made unhappy as she had been, and therefore if her warnings would save Louisa from being hurt and humiliated, then she would regard her motherly advice as being well worth it.

Torn between her mother's sage counsel, born out of years of experience, and her own feelings, Louisa was left somewhat confused and not a little dispirited and, as the date of their wedding drew ever nearer, rather apprehensive as to precisely what Deerham expected of her. Even though he had kissed her several times, an experience she had thoroughly enjoyed, so conscious was she of her mamma's strictures that she had been afraid to respond in case she alerted him to the fact that she was very much in love with him. She accepted it as perfectly normal that gentlemen often sought amusement outside of the marriage, but the very thought that Deerham would continue to do so when they were married caused her to shed more than one tear. She may have told her mamma that she had not fallen in love with him or that she expected him to fall in love with her, but the painful truth was she *had* fallen in love with him and she *did* hope he would fall in love her, but despite his attentions to her comfort and the sense of the ridiculous they clearly shared, he had not given any indication that he had done so or would, in fact, ever do so.

With so many of mamma's strictures going around in her head as to how she should behave, particularly towards her betrothed and future husband as well as trying to remember every one of them, the spontaneity Deerham had become accustomed to and found utterly irresistible, was gradually disappearing. As Louisa had no reason to suppose that her mamma's marital experiences were anything unusual or that they had in fact soured her entire view of men and marriage, her behaviour towards Deerham, whilst continuing to be friendly enough, nevertheless underwent a change. Deerham may have more than once gently brushed her cheek with his lips, and even, on occasion, going so far as to kiss her on the lips, delicate touches which had sent the blood rushing through her veins, she had not the least suspicion that he had fallen in love with her, and therefore she could only envisage their future together as being rather strained, and when, on the evening of their betrothal ball in Grosvenor Square she found herself alone with him for a few moments, she was given no reason to think otherwise.

Chapter Eight

When Deerham had told Louisa that he believed they could deal extremely together he had meant it, and although he had not set out to fall in love with her the fact remained he had done so, but since she had given him no sign that she felt the same he, like her, was beginning to wonder what their future together would hold. From her lack of response to his gentle kisses he gained the impression that were he to wholeheartedly kiss her she would not repulse them, but, at no time, had she let him see that she was open to receiving his kisses much less enjoy them, and, in view of this, he could not help but believe he had been right from the very beginning in that his betrothed looked upon their forthcoming marriage as merely one of convenience for both of them. Despite his gentle wooing of Louisa, apart from lightly kissing her cheek or her lips, he had deliberately refrained from taking her in his arms and unreservedly kissing her, not because he did not want to, he did, so very much, but because he had no wish to either rush or frighten her, little realizing that his self-restraint was merely endorsing her mamma's warnings in her mind.

The countess, in conjunction with Deerham's cousin the Lady Margaret Henderby, who was acting as his hostess for the evening, had, for weeks past, been busily engaged in assisting with all the arrangements necessary to ensure the betrothal ball would be a success but had, despite the many calls upon her time, not failed to notice that her daughter was looking far from her usual self. It was, of course, quite natural for Louisa to be a little apprehensive about her forthcoming marriage, but upon broaching the matter to her, the only reply she had received was a subdued, "No, Mamma," forcing a smile to her lips. "Indeed, I am looking forward to it, I promise you."

But Deerham, who was not so easily persuaded or fooled, managing to take Louisa to one side halfway through the evening, not caring one jot what their guests thought as they saw them disappear into a small anteroom, asked her the same question, to which she offered the same answer.

"I wish I could believe that, Louisa," he said gently.

"But it's true," she insisted, deliberately averting her eyes.

"No," he said slowly, shaking his head, "I don't think it is."

"Why?" she asked, the breath stilling in her lungs as she stole a glance up at him from under her lashes, the look in his eyes making her wish, and not the for the first time, that her mamma was wrong.

"Because you are not a very good liar, Louisa," he told her quietly.

"But I'm not lying," she shook her head, which was true, but oh, how she wished he felt the same about her!

He paused a moment, those dark grey eyes searching her face from under heavy lids with a look which, had he but known it, was in danger of undoing her resolve not to give him a disgust of her, the very thought of which was too unbearable for her to contemplate. "No," he said softly, "not lying, but, perhaps, a little unforthcoming with the whole truth."

"But... but, why should I be?" she faltered, knowing it to be no less than the truth.

"*That*, Louisa," he told her earnestly, "is something I wish I knew."

How could she possibly tell him that she had fallen head over heels in love with him almost from the moment she had first laid eyes on him without incurring his disgust? She could not bear to see the contempt in his eyes should she tell him so, anything would be preferable to that, but no matter how hard she tried she could find no answer which would appease him, but since there was no way of escape, her back being against the wall with Deerham standing only inches away from her, she had nothing to do but brazen it out.

"Can you deny that you have distanced yourself from me of late?" he asked quietly.

"H-have I?" she managed, keeping her eyes fixed on the top button of his cream silk waistcoat.

"You know you have," he said gently, "which," he nodded, "*is* a little surprising, especially when I consider how you and I have been dealing extremely together." When she made no answer to this, he said gently, "You must know that I would never do anything to hurt you."

"I know you would not," she said in a suffocated voice, darting a quick glance up at him.

"Then what is it?" he asked gently, leaning forward and resting his left hand on the wall behind her and taking her left one in his other. "Is this your way of telling me that you do not find me particularly attractive?" he asked a little ruefully.

She shook her head, her emotions threatening to overcome her, just about managing a barely audible, "No."

"I am relieved to hear it," he smiled, then, lowering his head, lightly and delicately brushed her lips with his own.

It was not a passionate kiss, no more than any other he had bestowed on her lips, in fact, it was over in a matter of moments, but his soft and warm caresses were enough to send the most wonderful sensations coursing deliciously through her, far beyond anything she had known existed or what she had imagined. Her whole being had wanted to respond to his kiss, but somewhere at the back of her mind her mamma's warnings hovered, and however much she had wanted to feel his arms around her and to melt into him, those cautionary words held her back. What was it Mamma had said? Oh, yes, of course; she must expect some display of affection prior to the marriage, but, she had told her firmly, this did not mean that her future husband was declaring undying love and devotion for her! No, how stupid of her to think it! How could a man like Deerham possibly find one such as herself, young and inexperienced and with no looks to recommend her, remotely attractive?

"I see my kisses do not meet with your approval!" he said sadly when he had eased himself a little away from her.

"I... I'm sorry, I..." she faltered, desperately trying to control her wayward emotions.

"There is no need, I promise you," he told her in an odd voice, straightening up, "indeed, I feel I am the one who should be sorry for forcing my attentions upon you yet again." Then, without giving her time to respond, he pulled her hand through his arm, saying calmly, "Come, let us re-join our guests."

Lady Margaret, who was three years older than Deerham, had certainly been taken aback to learn that her cousin had, in fact, offered for Louisa Markham after all and, like her husband, not only dreaded to think of the cost of the settlements but prophesied nothing but disaster ensuing from such a marriage. Were it anyone other than Markham's daughter, who really had nothing to recommend her, not even a portion to take into marriage, then she would not be quite so concerned, but since Deerham had decided to honour his father's agreement she could only hope that he would not come to regret it.

Despite that deep copper coloured hair and those expressive green eyes, which really did make a quite striking impression, she could not deny that her cousin's betrothed was no beauty, far from it, and certainly so far removed from the beautiful woman who had adorned his life that he could not be anything other than struck by it, but over the following days she was brought to acknowledge that, like Deerham before her, the more she saw of

Louisa the more her looks did not seem to matter. There was something about her which was not unattractive, besides which, it was obvious to the meanest intelligence that she was nothing like her father and, this being so, she was rather hopeful that the marriage could well answer after all, moreover, she doubted this young lady would kick up a dust because her husband had a connection elsewhere, therefore giving Deerham no cause to regret marrying her.

It seemed that the Countess of Markmoor had done her work well in preparing her daughter for marriage by instructing her on what would be expected of her as the Marchioness of Deerham as well as what her husband would expect of her, but, unless Margaret misjudged the matter, the more she saw of things the more inclined she was to think that Louisa Markham, although strictly adhering to her mamma's tuition, was by no means impervious to her future husband. She was indeed a very well brought up young lady whose behaviour was such that no one could possibly censure her or remotely liken her to her father, but although it could not be said that she wore her heart on her sleeve she was nevertheless not quite able to hide the look in her eyes every time they rested on Deerham whenever he was not looking at her and, unless Margaret had grossly erred, she would say that Louisa had most definitely fallen in love with him.

Margaret may enjoy a comfortable relationship with her cousin, but, at no point, had he taken her into his confidence about his feelings for Louisa and, certainly, nothing in his demeanour suggested that she had touched his heart, but she had witnessed their discreet exit as well as their return the evening of the betrothal ball and, unless she was very much mistaken, she would say that, from the looks of it, neither party, upon re-joining their guests, could be said to look as though they found their few minutes of privacy to be overly encouraging. If Deerham had taken her aside in order for him to kiss her, which seemed likely, then it could not be said that he had gained very much from it, because although not by a word or gesture did he allow his feelings to show, not that she really expected anything else from a man of his breeding, it was otherwise with Louisa. Her colour was considerably heightened, but if, as Margaret suspected, she was right in thinking that the Countess of Markmoor had done her work well, then Louisa, no matter how much in love with him she was, would know better than to show it, much less respond to his lovemaking. It crossed Margaret's mind to have a word in Deerham's ear, but no sooner had this occurred to her than she discarded it. She had never yet known any good come from interfering between a man and his betrothed or, indeed his wife, and therefore she could only hope that these early teething troubles would disappear in time.

Even though Deerham had certainly kissed her again prior to their wedding, under no circumstances could they be described as passionate, but if the teething troubles did not disappear, none of them were evident as the couple received the felicitations of their guests after the marriage ceremony. The countess, wreathed in smiles as she witnessed her daughter's marriage to Deerham, the child really looking quite her best in a gown of oyster coloured satin, told her son in a quiet aside that only now could she breathe more easily knowing that Louisa's future was assured, to which he nodded his wholehearted agreement. She may have suspected that Louisa was not indifferent to Deerham but she would have been astonished had she known that Louisa was actually very much in love with her new husband and was fighting the overwhelming impulse, had been in fact for quite some appreciable time, to tell him so. The countess knew that from this moment on Louisa would naturally have the advice of her husband, but, for now, she felt it prudent to exercise her right as a mother one last time by not only giving her daughter one final word of guidance about what awaited her as well as taking the opportunity to reinforce her warnings as to the folly of hanging on her husband's arm, but going on to further remind her about not expecting him to dance continual attendance on her.

"Because I assure you, my dear," she stressed, "nothing would be more embarrassing for him."

Lady Margaret, watching the countess escort her daughter upstairs in order to change her gown, shrewdly guessed what advice she would impart to Louisa, but since it was not her place to intervene she decided that it may, after all, be wise to have a brief word with Deerham, especially having unexpectedly caught a glimpse in her cousin's eyes as he watched her ascend the stairs in Cavendish Square with her mamma, which told her that he was not wholly indifferent to Louisa after all, a circumstance which caused her to take a more hopeful view of their future together.

Upon reaching his side, Deerham turned and, looking down into the wide blue eyes searching his face from under his heavy lids, a slight smile touched his lips. "And what advice are *you* about to give *me*?" he asked amusingly.

"Do you think you need any?" she asked, tucking her hand comfortably through his arm.

"I think *you* think I do," he smiled, squeezing her hand.

"And were I to proffer any," she asked, looking up at him, "would you take notice of it?"

"I might," he smiled.

"And if that advice should prove a little impertinent?" she raised an enquiring eyebrow.

"I still might," he said amusingly, taking her a little out of earshot of the last few remaining guests.

"You may think it intrusive," she cautioned.

"All advice is intrusive," he replied casually.

"Yes, I suppose it is," she conceded, "but if it is well meant…?"

"It is *still* intrusive," he pointed out gently, taking hold of her hands, "even when it comes from *you*, Margaret."

She nodded, sighing, "Very well, Max."

He kissed her hands. "You know," he said softly, a smile lurking at the back of his eyes, "you really *must* allow me to conduct my own affairs."

"It is only because I am so very fond of you, Max," she told him genuinely, "the child too."

"I know," he patted her hand, then, after seeing her husband looking in their direction, he smiled, "but I think it's time I took you back to John."

She nodded, but taking a moment to look up at him, said quietly, "She is very young, and you have so much experience, Max; be patient and gentle with her."

A confirming nod was the only answer she received to this, but when she later waved the happy couple goodbye as they started out on their honeymoon, spending the first week at Worleigh followed by three weeks in Paris, she could only hope that the countess, no doubt with the best of intentions, had said nothing which had given Louisa a fear of her husband as well as her marriage.

The dowager marchioness may live quietly in Bath, but despite her son's discretion in conducting his affairs she knew all about the beautiful women who had adorned his life and thought no less of him because of it, indeed, she regarded it as perfectly natural for a man to seek amusement, but even though she had been agreeably surprised in Louisa Markham her son had not exaggerated when he had said she was no beauty. Max may have told her that there was no fear of him falling in love with her, but, even so, she could not rid her mind of that unguarded moment when his expression had suddenly softened when he had spoken of her, leading her to believe that he was not wholly indifferent to her.

Unlike the late Earl of Markmoor, she knew her son to be an honourable man and one who would shrink from bringing his name into disrepute which, flaunting his mistresses in the eyes of his wife and the world would most assuredly do, but whilst she could not discount Max taking a mistress when he was married, she had enough faith and trust in him to know that he would be as discreet as he had always been as well as affording his wife all the respect and courtesy which was her due. Of course, should it transpire that he had indeed fallen in love with Louisa despite his assurances to the contrary, then the chances were very good that he would not seek his pleasures outside the marriage, after all he would not be the first man who had kept company with any number of beautiful women to marry one who could only just be described as passably good looking and remain faithful to her. But irrespective of her son's feelings for Louisa, there was no denying that she had been agreeably surprised with the late of Earl of Markmoor's daughter, and she had therefore gradually begun to hold out some hope that the marriage, despite her misgivings, would not turn out so very bad after all.

She could not deny that it was a tremendous relief to know that Louisa had inherited none of her father's traits and tendencies, but, at the same time, it was a great pity that she had not inherited his good looks either or, if it came to that, her mother's, but, even so, there was nothing in her manner or behaviour to suggest that she would not do justice to her position as Marchioness of Deerham despite her youth; carrying out her role with a dignity she had not dared to hope for when her son had told her of his decision to offer for her.

Unlike her niece, Margaret Henderby, she had missed that revealing expression which had entered Max's eyes only a short time ago as they had followed Louisa as she mounted the stairs in company with her mamma, but she was not unhopeful that, if nothing else, he may grow to be extremely fond of her in time. Not having seen the way Louisa looked at Max when he was not aware of it, she had no way of knowing what her true feelings were for her son, but she felt reasonably confident that whatever these were she would do her duty by her husband with all the dignity that was required of her.

As with Margaret, she had to admit that the Countess of Markmoor, who she personally thought could count herself extremely fortunate in marrying her daughter as well as she had considering her late husband's disreputable career, deserved the fullest praise for not only raising Louisa to be a well brought-up young lady but also for preparing her for marriage. Nevertheless, she too had a pretty shrewd idea as to the kind of advice she had been giving her daughter as well as her parting counsel and, whilst she could only commend her on her tuition so far, she only hoped that she had not been foolish enough to compare her son to the late Earl of Markmoor, whose behaviour, even now, was still the talk of the town, thereby giving her a fear of Max and marriage. She felt sure that her son needed neither advice nor instruction on how to deal with a nervous young bride and one, moreover, who was as unsophisticated and unworldly as Louisa, but whatever recommendation she would have liked to impart as she wished him goodbye, died on her lips.

But no one observing the Marquis and Marchioness of Deerham upon their return to Grosvenor Square following their honeymoon could detect anything in either of their demeanours to suggest that all was not well.

Deerham, who had, almost from the beginning, realized that he could not stop loving Louisa if he tried, had needed no prompting on how to deal with his new bride, and although it put a great strain on his self-control his lovemaking had been sensitive as well as restrained, even though he wanted nothing more than to show her how much he really loved her. He could not deny that Louisa had never once repulsed his lovemaking, but, to his regret, neither had she let me see that she was open to receiving it much less inciting it, in fact, whenever he took her in his arms and kissed her, none of which could be described as being remotely passionate, it was almost as though she was fulfilling her duty rather than enjoying shared intimacies with her bridegroom. The only glimmer of hope on his horizon was when Louisa, on the occasions she had forgotten her mamma's strictures in the excitement of the moment, had reacted in that impulsive and spontaneous way he loved such as when they attended a garden party at Versailles and she was introduced to the Queen, followed by a firework display. Turning round to look up at him, her eyes wide and glowing, she cried unaffectedly, "Oh, Max, isn't it exciting? I've never seen anything like it before in my life!"

Taking more pleasure from her reaction than the occasion, he had merely raised her hand to his lips, saying softly, "Knowing you are happy, Louisa, makes me doubly so." For a brief moment he thought he saw a look in her eyes which made his heart miss a beat but it was gone in an instant, although it was most probably a reflection from the fireworks.

Max, having given instructions that the bedchamber which had once been used by his mother was to be fashioned into Louisa's boudoir during their absence, a delicious confection of pale blue and oyster coloured satin, had made Louisa look about her in wonderment which, for some reason she could not fully explain, filled her with the overwhelming desire to cry her heart out. Had it not been for Mary, her dresser, who had been with her even at Markmoor, busily engaged in unpacking her trunks, she would certainly have given in to this urgent need, but, of course, she could not and, instead, forced herself to enter into Mary's excitement. Louisa was not by nature prone to fits of sullenness or bouts of melancholy, on the contrary she was lively and, as her mamma had often told her, a little too open and, even, rather more impulsive than she should be most of the time, but as she set about sorting out her belongings she could not help wishing that mamma had not counselled her quite so much. She knew that her mamma, whose experience was far wider than her own, had only her best interests at heart, giving her the benefit of her advice in an earnest desire to prevent her from being made unhappy, but as she looked round at her boudoir that first day in Grosvenor Square, specially created for her by her husband, her mamma, who surely must know best, could not, however unintentionally, have made her more unhappy if she tried.

Her mamma, whose sole aim had always been to avoid this contingency at all costs, upon paying her a visit two weeks after her return from honeymoon, having been staying at Markmoor Manor in Gloucestershire, had seen at a glance that her daughter, despite her praiseworthy attempts to hide it and her own sage advice, had done precisely what she had cautioned her against, foreseeing nothing but disaster resulting from it. From the moment Deerham had offered for Louisa, her overriding ambition had been to do everything in her power to prevent her daughter from suffering all she had herself at the hands of her late husband, but by giving her heart to a man who had married her only to honour his father's promise, she very much feared that humiliation and embarrassment would not be the only things Louisa would have to endure. She knew perfectly well that there was no fear of Deerham flaunting his mistresses in public, the very idea being quite distasteful to a man of his breeding, but the fact remained that no matter how discreetly these affairs were conducted they were never that unobtrusive that they escaped notice indefinitely.

"You are a sensible girl, Louisa," she had told her as she made ready to take her leave, "and therefore I know you will not take it amiss when I say that it really will not do to fall in love with Deerham or to let him see that you have, because I can see that is precisely what you have done! As I have told you often and often," she reminded her, *"nothing*, I promise you," she assured her, pulling on her gloves, "could be more embarrassing or uncomfortable for a husband than for him to suspect his wife holds such feelings. It would be different, of course," she conceded, "if his affections were engaged, but you know as well as I Louisa that he did not offer for you out of love, and as for wishing to be continually in his company," she nodded darkly, "well," she sighed, "that will not do at all. *Gentlemen*," she emphasized, "have such peculiar notions which we cannot possibly hope to understand, but I promise you, my dear," she patted her cheek affectionately, "one thing I *do* know, and that is that Deerham does not expect you to be always seeking his company or demanding his attention and, as for the rest," she warned her, *"that*, as I have said many times before, you can leave to his *chère ami!"* whereupon she kissed her daughter, leaving her feeling even more miserable than she had been before.

Even though Louisa regularly received Deerham in her boudoir he showed not the least sign that he was any nearer to falling in love with her than he had ever been, signifying that he was clearly spending his time with one whose company pleased him far more than her own obviously did.

Nevertheless, Louisa's mind, as it was rather prone to do of late, reminded her of all his attentions to her comfort, but, unfortunately, it also, and quite ruthlessly, reminded her of those moments in his arms when she so desperately wanted to respond to his lovemaking. She may not be able to lay claim to having any amatory experience but she instinctively sensed that even his kisses had a reserve to them, but, as restrained as he was, he nonetheless evoked the most wonderful sensations inside her, leaving her yearning for something which she knew could never be. Had Max loved her, then, surely, he would have told her, but, more than this, it would surely be reflected in his lovemaking but, however painful it was, she had to face the fact that her mamma was right in that he had married her merely to honour his father's promise and whatever intimacies he shared with her were nothing more than his duty as her husband and nothing whatsoever to do with love – *that*, she told herself sadly, would be for another! She knew that Max being the kind of man he was, would always accord her respect and courtesy, but knowing he did not love her nor ever would was enough to break her heart, but, worse than this, was knowing that somewhere out there was a woman discreetly tucked away whom he frequently visited.

The image of an exquisitely beautiful creature, entwining her arms around his neck to receive his passionate kisses had to be sternly suppressed especially when, during the night time hours, she lay awake after attending an engagement while Max had kept one of his own or visited his club, wondering whether he would come to her or continue on to his own room, having no desire to either see or make love to his wife, much preferring to be in the arms of this unknown but extremely beautiful and sophisticated woman. She longed to go to him, to tell him that she loved him but her mamma's warnings always held her back; she could bear anything but seeing disgust in his eyes at the sight of his wife seeking either his attention or his lovemaking, and therefore no one looking at her would ever have suspected how very much in love with her husband she was and the joy she felt whenever she was with him or, worse, the pain it caused her to deny him her company as often as she possibly could.

"I am, of course, happy to know that you are making friends," he had told her only the other evening, when she yet again denied him her company on the grounds of a prior engagement, "but I seem to recall, Louisa," he reminded her gently, "that you once told me you would be happy to accept of my company at any time."

Even though she knew his request for her company was merely out of courtesy and not because he desired it, the recollection brought a lump to her throat, but managed to reply with an airiness she was far from feeling, "Yes, I know and I meant it, it's just that, well you see Max…"

"You have found other company you would rather accept of than mine," he supplied a little stiffly.

"I'm sorry, Max," she apologized, turning hurriedly away from him so he would not see the effort it was costing her to forgo the pleasure of his company, "it's just that, well… I… I cannot now disappoint Letitia; she has been so looking forward to attending this party."

"There is no need for you to explain, my dear, I assure you," he told her, "I understand perfectly," whereupon he bowed himself out of her room.

Even though he fervently wished that Louisa would come to feel something for him other than what she considered was expected of her as his wife, there were nevertheless times when he had caught something in her eyes; a look, a glance which led him to hope that she did indeed feel something for him after all, but as it disappeared as quickly as it had materialized he had come to believe that he had merely imagined it. He was no callow youth in the throes of a calf love; tortured and torn apart by rejection, but an experienced man of two and thirty and yet, as he left Louisa's boudoir, he was conscious, for perhaps the very first time in his life, of suffering all the agonies and jealousies of an adolescent embarking on his first love affair. But no one looking at him some hours later as he sat with his friends playing piquet at his club could possibly have suspected him of being deeply in love with his wife, much less the torment running riot inside him at Louisa's apparent preference for company other than his own, his demeanour as calm and self-assured as it always was.

*

Despite the fact that Clifton had held the late Earl of Markmoor in contempt as well as thoroughly deprecating his disastrous way of life, resulting in Deerham no doubt paying well over the odds for his daughter to save the Markham estates, could not deny that the young Marchioness of Deerham comported herself with all the dignity one could have wished for. So far certainly, she was definitely giving the lie to those who had thought the marriage could only end in catastrophe and, even though he had himself thought along similar lines, unless his eyesight was playing tricks on him, he was fast coming to the conclusion that her ladyship felt more for her husband than he had originally thought. This impression was further confirmed when, only this afternoon, she had come downstairs to learn that Deerham had left the house some half an hour ago, because although she merely smiled and thanked him, he could have sworn he caught a glimpse of disappointment in those expressive green eyes.

As Lady Yelton's alfresco party had had to be cancelled due to a sudden change in the weather, Louisa, deciding to take the opportunity to write a long overdue letter to Reverend Berry made her way downstairs to enquire of Deerham if he would frank it for her, but upon asking Clifton, who was at that moment crossing the hall, if his lordship was in his book room, tried to hide her disappointment when told that he had found it necessary to go out. Firmly banishing the thought of what could well be his errand, Louisa sat down at the escritoire in the yellow saloon and began her letter to Reverend Berry, forgetting her wretchedness as she began telling him all about her visit to Burlington House and all her experiences since leaving

Markmoor. Not until the ormolu clock on the marble mantelpiece struck the half hour did she realize just how lengthy a letter it actually was and how long it had taken her to write, so hastily finishing it off she affixed a wafer and left it for Deerham to frank for her, hurrying up the stairs to change for dinner before attending the opera with him, something she had been looking forward to.

Mary, who was already waiting for her, bobbed a curtsey, then, immediately dispensing with formality, broke into enthusiastic chatter as she always did while assisting her mistress with her toilet, but Louisa, whose participation was unconscious at best, stopped talking altogether when she heard Max's familiar footsteps pass her door on his way to his room about twenty minutes later, wondering if he would come and see her before they went downstairs to dinner. It was just as Mary was putting the finishing touches to her hair when he quietly entered her room some three-quarters of an hour later, immaculately dressed in pale blue satin with a deep fall of lace at this throat, from which a diamond pin glinted in the light from the chandeliers, and, just visible beneath the lace at his wrists, was the gold signet ring he always wore on the little finger of his left hand. Mary, bobbing a curtsey, instantly left them alone together, but although Louisa was glad of her departure not all her efforts were having the slightest effect upon helping control her reaction at the sight of him, her only hope being that he would read the deepening colour in her cheeks as nothing more than excitement for the evening ahead.

Like her son, the Countess of Markmoor could not be anything other than relieved to know that Deerham had actually come up to scratch and offered for Louisa after all, but whilst she truly loved her daughter and wanted nothing but her happiness, at no time had she fooled herself into thinking that Louisa could lay claims to being a beauty. Unlike those other women who had previously adorned Deerham's life, all diamonds of the first water if what she had heard was true, Louisa must have come as a sad disappointment to him, and no matter which way she looked at it she failed to see how her daughter's striking colour combination, engaging ways and infectious sense of humour could possibly compensate him for the lack of this very necessary attribute. Naturally, she hoped the couple would rub along together tolerably well, but at no point had it ever so much as crossed her mind that Deerham, a connoisseur when it came to women, could possibly fall in love with a young woman who was not only unsophisticated but nothing short of a Plain Jane, and therefore when she had cautioned Louisa about the folly of falling in love with her husband as well as not looking for love in return, she had meant it for the best.

Had she but known it, Deerham had recognized at the very outset that Louisa's looks did not matter in the least, and that her infectious laugh, mischievous sense of humour as well as her spontaneity, making those green eyes light up in an instant, were far more alluring than all the calculated charms of the women who had previously adorned his life, even more so because she had not the least idea of it. She would also have been surprised to learn that at no time could it be said that he was either impervious or blind to his wife, on the contrary his love for her rendered him very much aware of her as well as acutely susceptible, and now was no exception.

As Louisa came towards him, dressed in gold lustring with her hair most fashionably dressed, all his resolve not to give in to his feelings, something which he had so far managed to do, though not without difficulty, stood in imminent danger of crumbling at the foundations, and had to sternly suppress the overwhelming desire to take her in his arms and kiss her, but, instead, smiled down at her asking how she had spent her day since the alfresco picnic had been cancelled.

"Well, I *was* disappointed, of course," she told him, "but I visited Letitia, and then occupied myself with writing a letter to Reverend Berry."

"Which," he said amusingly, "is now awaiting my frank."

"Yes, if… if you do not mind, Max," she said apprehensively.

"And why should I mind?" he asked, taking hold of her hands.

"Well," she admitted, "it… it *is* quite a long letter; covering several pages."

"No doubt you had much to tell him," Deerham said softly.

"Yes," Louisa smiled, trying to ignore the fluttering inside her which always attacked her when she was with him. "He… he and I are old friends," she told him unnecessarily.

"Then there is no more to be said on the matter," he said gently.

"Thank you," she managed. "I… I really should have written to him before."

"I am sure he will forgive you," Deerham smiled. Then, after raising first one hand and then the other to his lips, held her at arm's length, asking softly, "A new gown, Louisa?"

"Yes," she nodded, trying to ignore the warmth of his fingers as they held her own. "Do you like it?" she asked hopefully.

"Very much," he told her in an odd voice. "It is most becoming."

"Thank you," she smiled. Then, momentarily forgetting her mama's advice, said, in that impulsive way he missed, "I was rather hoping you would think so."

"Were you?" he smiled, his fingers holding hers tighter.

"Yes," she nodded, her eyes suddenly sparkling, "because you see," she confided impishly, "the other evening at the Dewhurst drum, I overheard Mrs. Wraye telling Lady Sutton that no one with red hair should ever wear this colour!"

"And you wish to prove her wrong, is that it?" he asked amusingly, drawing her a little closer to him.

She nodded. "Do you think I have?"

"Most certainly," he agreed.

"Well," she smiled, "I think I have too."

"But your hair, Louisa," he told her, holding out the frail hope that her reaction to his gentle teasing as well as his continued self-restraint presaged the remotest chance that she would grow to love him, "is not red."

The almost caressing note in his voice made her look up at him, his eyes dark and warm as they searched her face causing her to catch her breath, but just as he was about to take her in his arms and kiss her, Mary, not realizing they were still here, opened the door into her sitting room, but although she made a hasty exit, the moment was unfortunately lost.

Chapter Nine

Singleton, who had been keeping a very discreet but keen eye on the young Marchioness of Deerham, could not fail to notice that she was not venturing out with her husband as often as one would have thought, but whilst this neither surprised nor concerned him what did perturb him, however, was her blossoming friendship with Letitia Rawnsley. So far, this spirited young lady had kept a very diplomatic silence on his attempted abduction of her, had she not have done so then not only would it have been all over town long since, but doubtless he would have been called to account by that aunt of hers and probably her brother as well, but of one thing he was sure and that was, at some point, she would confide her adventure to her friend.

As far as discovering the identity of her rescuer was concerned, he doubted very much that Deerham would have revealed it to her, in fact, he would own himself astonished had he done so, although Singleton had no doubt that he had cautioned her not to mention the matter, though not for her abductor's protection but her own. For this same reason, he took for granted Deerham's continued silence on the episode, which, of course, would extend to his wife, but Singleton knew perfectly well that should Letitia Rawnsley ever tell her, then such knowledge could easily hamper, if not seriously jeopardize, her inclusion in his plans for the downfall of Deerham.

He had not totally discounted the idea of abducting Letitia Rawnsley, she was, as he so quaintly phrased it, an insurance policy in case his fortunes took a turn for the worst, but for the moment at least they seemed fairly steady and if his current run of luck continued, he held out every hope that they would remain so, but, regrettably, one could never tell when the dice may fall against one! But, for now, his finances appeared to be reasonably settled, at least for the immediate future and, this being so, he was now at last free to turn his mind to his long-cherished ambition of bringing Deerham to his knees by any means at his disposal. But the means at his disposal had been a little uncertain, because whilst he may have toyed with the idea of using Louisa Markham or, failing her, then her brother, to bring Deerham to his knees, it had not been a foregone conclusion that he would offer for her, and therefore Singleton had had to wait somewhat impatiently upon events. But Providence, in her infinite wisdom, had smiled upon him by guiding Deerham's hand and providing him with the perfect tool in the future Marchioness of Deerham; a young lady who, though she did not know it, was to feature large in her husband's ignominy.

Singleton may experience no qualms in using the daughter of a man he had called friend to assist him in his aim in bringing about the ruination of one whom he had long since deemed his enemy, but whilst she was the ideal instrument with which to do it he could not deny to having been somewhat taken aback to discover that, far from taking after either parent, she did, in fact, have no looks whatsoever to recommend her; the irony of which had not escaped him! But however much she may be deficient in looks she was by no means lacking in intelligence and, unless he had misread his instincts when he had first met her at Sally Castleton's, in spite of those good manners Louisa Markham had most definitely taken him in dislike. But these were mere irrelevances!

'Parfait Petite Innocente' was how he had described her and, having followed her very short career in society to date with avid interest, nothing so far was leading him to believe that this epithet no longer applied. He could only speculate on the reason why the young marchioness was seen in society more often than not unaccompanied by her husband, but if his conjectures were correct marriage to Louisa Markham had definitely not stimulated love in Deerham's breast. Of course, he would expect his wife to comport herself with dignity whatever his feelings for her or whether he accompanied her or not, but since it struck him that Deerham was leaving her more or less to her own devices, for reasons which surely needed no explaining, it was therefore logical to conclude that he was also leaving the Countess of Markmoor to further instruct her daughter in the ways of the ton now that she was Marchioness of Deerham. Lavinia Markham was of course more than amply qualified to instruct her daughter, but it was not to be expected that a lady of her quality and credentials would know anything about certain establishments, much less frequent them, as her late husband had done, and pass such information onto her daughter any more than she would know of this person or that who could be guaranteed to shepherd an *ingénue* like the young Marchioness of Deerham to a venue which would prove beyond any doubt that she was in very truth her father's daughter.

But whether he actually went this far to secure his ends or just far enough to give the illusion of it, made no difference to the result. Once the word had spread, and it was surprising how quickly it would, the shame and humiliation it would bring to the man he despised more than any other and by the hand of his own wife of all people; the daughter of a man his own father had been the first to shun, would be more than fitting compensation for Deerham spoiling his game; indeed, it would be a most exquisite revenge.

Singleton had, of course, met Louisa a number of times since that evening at Sally Castleton's, but although she had passed a few pleasantries with him she had certainly not been any too eager to engage him in conversation, in fact, he had gained the very strong impression that were it not for politeness's sake, she would have nothing whatsoever to do with him. He had also gained the impression that the poison he had so delicately laid down that first evening had not, as he had hoped, taken root, but whilst the reason for this momentarily escaped him, especially when he knew her marriage to Deerham was not a love match, he had decided not to waste any more time on a strategy which clearly was not working, and had therefore begun to toy with the idea of hinting that her deceased father-in-law had actually shunned her own. But this too he found would have to be discarded if, for no other reason than it could well be that Deerham had deemed it prudent to warn her against him thereby fending off this line of attack and putting Louisa on her guard. Knowing that he had found no favour with Edmund's daughter, she may, for some obscure reason, just take notice of Deerham's warning and therefore concluded that the only way forward, and as quickly as possible if he did not want Letitia Rawnsley adding her mite to Louisa's already unfriendly reception of him, was to pay a visit to a certain lady whom he knew could be relied upon to approach her without arousing her suspicions.

The young Marchioness of Deerham, in blissful ignorance of Singleton's scheming, was the first to acknowledge that she was no beauty, but as she sat beside her husband in their box at the opera, she had never been in better looks than she was this evening. Upon their return from honeymoon, Deerham had naturally presented her with the Seer sapphires, a quite impressive set comprising a rather heavy and intricately worked necklace with a matching headdress and earrings which had been worn by the Marchionesses of Deerham for over two hundred years, for her to wear on special occasions, such as when he had taken her to be presented at court. But sapphires did not become her and therefore he had bought for her to wear instead an emerald necklace with matching earrings and a bracelet, all of which could have been specifically designed to complement her colouring and that dress of gold lustring, which, as anyone with eyes in their head could see, definitely gave the lie to Mrs. Wraye's observation to Lady Sutton; it became her beautifully.

But the lustre on her face and the glow in her eyes had nothing whatever to do with her gown or her jewellery, but simply because she had not missed that look in Deerham's eyes earlier, a look which had not only made her heart soar but filled her with hope that he did in fact feel something for her after all. Not love; no, she would not ask for impossible things; but at least a warm affection which had prompted him to... but, sadly the moment had been lost; Mary's timing could not have been worse!

Digby Singleton, laying his plans on what he believed to be a secure foundation, would have been totally stunned had he known that those foundations were not as secure as he had believed them to be. Had he attended the opera this evening just one look at Louisa would have told him that she was very much in love with her husband despite all her efforts to conceal the fact, and whilst Deerham was too much in control of himself to allow his feelings to show, the fact of the matter was that their marriage, even though they did not know it themselves, was most definitely a love match.

Had Singleton the slightest suspicion that whilst he was keeping a close but discreet eye on Edmund Markham's daughter her husband was keeping an equally close eye on himself, he would not have been quite so confident in formulating plans for his downfall. As Deerham had rightly predicted, Louisa had introduced her new friend to him at Sally Castleton's, but although there had been nothing in Letitia Rawnsley's demeanour to suggest that she had recognized him, there had been no disguising the anxiety in her eyes whenever they rested on Singleton, nor had he missed the way her aunt had whisked her away out of his vicinity upon his approaching Louisa. Deerham knew perfectly well that Letitia Rawnsley had said nothing about that night, not even to her aunt, had she have done so then that formidable lady would not have allowed it to pass, but he knew too that she was by no means safe from Singleton's machinations and, unless he had grossly erred, neither was Louisa, because in his desire to do him harm he would not put it beyond Singleton to use his wife to do it. Despite her youth and inexperience, Deerham knew that Louisa was by no means unintelligent or that she had taken no liking to her father's old friend, but he doubted Singleton would allow these factors to weigh with him, and whilst he had no fear of her seeking his company at the many functions they would be certain to meet at, he would not put it beyond Singleton to use his very persuasive tongue to good effect with his old friend's daughter. It was therefore as much for his wife's sake as Letitia Rawnsley's that he kept a very close on eye on Digby Singleton.

The following evening Deerham escorted his wife to Vauxhall Gardens in company with her brother and Miss Charlotte Laid who, with her mamma, was spending a few weeks in town. Lady Sybil Laid, after giving the matter considerable thought, somewhat forcefully told Sir Michael that she saw no reason why Christopher should be made to suffer for his father's way of life any more than he had already by denying him permission to marry their daughter, because anyone but a fool could see that he was doing everything possible to redress the damage his late parent had done to his estates. Sir Michael, whose recollections of the late Earl of Markmoor were far from favourable, having considered the justice of this as well as knowing perfectly well that the son was a totally different kettle of fish altogether to the father, finally relented and gave his permission for Christopher to marry his daughter.

"I am so happy for you, Christopher," Louisa smiled up at him as they strolled down one of the lighted pathways which Vauxhall Gardens abounded with her hand tucked comfortably in his arm.

"I knew you would be," he grinned, giving her hand a squeeze. "I don't mind saying though," he confessed a little ruefully, "I thought Sir Michael would never give his consent."

"No," she shook her head, "especially as he did not like Papa!"

"I know," Christopher agreed with feeling, "but I have Lady Laid to thank for persuading him."

"I should think she had a deal of work on her hands," Louisa said thoughtfully, "because although Sir Michael is a most agreeable man, he can be a little obstinate."

"Don't I know it!" Christopher exclaimed, "because there's no denying that when he takes a stand it is seldom he backs down from it!"

"I am so glad he did," she smiled up at him.

"Yes," he sighed his relief, "so am I!"

"I have never seen Charlotte in greater beauty," she told him truthfully, pleased they were going to be sisters-in-law at last, "and no wonder; she is clearly very happy now that her father has finally relented."

Briefly glancing over his shoulder to where Charlotte strolled with Deerham a little way behind them, her arm pulled through his and his head bent in order to hear what she was saying. "Yes, she *is* in great beauty!" Christopher smiled, not quite able to hide his feelings, but the thought of his own happiness at the expense of his sister's had the effect of bringing a frown down onto his forehead, and upon being asked what was wrong he looked considerately down at her for a moment before saying, not unsympathetically, "Louisa, I know how unfair it may seem to you; I mean, here am I being allowed to marry whom I choose while you… well," he nodded, "you know what I mean."

"Yes, Christopher," she said quietly, "I know what you mean."

"I know you never kicked up a dust about it," he sighed, "but for all that I wished things could have been different for you, and even though I would rather it be Deerham than anyone else, I don't mind admitting that I felt guilty about it; at first I mean, but, I see now," he told her honestly, "that I needn't have worried; it seems to have turned out very well."

As they had by now come within sight of the big rotunda where, from the sounds of it, the orchestra had laid down their instruments signifying the first supper was about to be served, and Deerham and Charlotte had almost caught up with them, Louisa only had time to say, in a hollow voice, "Yes, very well."

Deerham, who had hired a booth and ordered a supper to tempt the most capricious appetite, had watched Louisa do no more than swallow a few morsels of the wafer-thin ham for which the gardens were famous, but although she eat the peach which he had carefully peeled and cut into segments for her, it was obvious that she had not much appetite.

This, sadly, like her newly found joy the previous evening, had unfortunately taken a somewhat painful plummet this afternoon, when, in company with Letitia and the Dowager Countess of Pitlone, she had attended that fatal alfresco gathering which Lady Yelton had found necessary to cancel yesterday due to the inclement weather.

This delightfully engaging but strong-minded widow who, according to the malicious, had more money than sense, having decided it was a shame not to make use of the blue and white calico marquee she had had erected, at enormous expense, in her garden at Richmond, she had therefore caused numerous invitations to be hurriedly written out by her fraught companion and delivered by harassed footmen and two page boys before the breakfast cups had been removed. With the exception of one or two absentees, Lady Yelton could proudly boast that her hastily re-arranged entertainment was a roaring success indeed she had not looked to see so many guests at so short a notice, and if there were those who thought it nothing but a dreadful squeeze, they were but few.

Everything had been going splendidly, in fact, Louisa had been thoroughly enjoying the afternoon, even the sun had honoured the occasion with its presence, and the dowager countess, having spotted someone whom she had not seen for some appreciable time, had been more than happy to leave the two young ladies to wander about the lantern hung and festooned gardens while she engaged her old acquaintance in conversation. It was just as they were about to leave the marquee to meander down the garden towards the river's edge, the heat inside having become just a little oppressive, when the sound of a late arrival met their ears. Louisa, like everyone else, turned slightly to see who the latecomer was, but Letitia, having excused herself at this precise moment in order to return to her aunt's side to retrieve something she had forgotten, left Louisa waiting for her standing behind two middle-aged and formidable ladies who apparently had no trouble identifying this late guest as Lady Helene Yoxall.

Louisa found herself looking at an exquisitely beautiful brunette whose thick hair was most fashionably styled allowing two deliberately trained ringlets to fall carelessly over her left shoulder. Her dark brown eyes, huge and expressive, glowed as she greeted first this acquaintance then another, her full pouting lips breaking into a smile, revealing a perfectly matched set of even white teeth, her tinkling laugh wafting melodiously across the air at some sally which had been addressed to her. To Louisa's amazement it seemed as though this incredibly beautiful woman floated rather than walked, provocatively exposing a neatly turned ankle as she slightly raised her pink skirts to make her way to the other side of the marquee to greet yet another acquaintance.

"Did you see those diamonds?" one of the two women asked the other in a whispered aside as Lady Yoxall passed them with a nod and a smile, totally oblivious to Louisa's proximity almost immediately behind them. "I vow and declare they must have cost a King's ransom!"

"Very probably," replied the other, "but I should own myself astonished if Yoxall bought them for her!"

"No," her friend nodded, "her husband is far too preoccupied with Diana Coulter!"

"Of course," the other sighed, "I suppose one really cannot blame Helene for seeking amusement elsewhere! They say that Yoxhall hardly spends two evenings a week at home!"

"'Tis all of a piece!" came the conspiratorial reply. "Although," she acknowledged fair-mindedly, "one cannot deny that Helene is very beautiful."

"Oh, without doubt," her friend replied. Then, lowering her head, whispered, "I hear there have been many who have thought so. Deerham for one!"

"Does he still, do you know?"

"As to that," she nodded, "I really could not say."

"Well," came the deep sighed reply, "I must confess to a liking for Deerham; but whether he still keeps company with her or another I have not the remotest conjecture, not that it would surprise me for a moment because I can't help but think that Markham's daughter must have come as a sad disappointment to him."

"But of course!" her friend acknowledged. "An agreeable child, the Markham chit; well-mannered too and so different to that father of hers, but, alas, that hair and those eyes, really quite breathtaking I own, but can they possibly compensate a man like Deerham for having no beauty?"

"Oh, quite!"

Had anyone chanced to glance in Louisa's direction at this moment they would have seen a young lady who looked for all the world as though she were going to faint, so pale did she look, but as if by a superhuman effort she managed to not only overcome the giddiness and nausea which swept over her but to stifle the heart-breaking sob which had leapt into her throat. Somehow though, she found the strength to go in search of her friend on legs which were far from steady, relieved that, no more than Letitia, did the dowager countess or the rest of the guests detect anything in her behaviour or demeanour to give them the least cause to suspect that she wanted nothing more than to run away and hide. It was one thing to have one's mamma say more or less the same thing, even to think it oneself, but to hear it from the lips of others was quite another.

It was not so much what they said about herself that hurt so much as seeing such an exquisite creature, one of many who had haunted her dreams day and night, an utterly desirable woman with whom Deerham must have spent some very pleasurable hours. But the truth was it made no difference whether the connection was still being conducted or not, the fact remained that if it were not Lady Yoxall it would be another equally as beautiful and desirable. How could Deerham, after spending time in the company of one who possessed everything she herself lacked, possibly love her? - and, as for her nonsensical daydreams about him holding some affection for her after all, seemed too ludicrous when faced with the harsh reality.

The rest of the afternoon resembled nothing short of a nightmare, but, eventually, she found herself seated beside Letitia in the dowager's carriage on their way back to town, hoping that sharp eyed old lady sitting opposite would detect nothing in her face or forced smile to give rise to searching questions. They did not, but by the time Louisa was set down in Grosvenor Square she felt so exhausted that were it at all possible she would have cried off from going to Vauxhall Gardens, but as this was quite out of the question there was nothing she could do but put her despondency to one side and brace herself for the evening ahead. She neither blamed her brother for the events which had overtaken them nor envied him his happiness with Charlotte, but his observation about her own marriage having turned out well after all only served to increase her wretchedness, and the forlorn hope she harboured in her breast began to resemble nothing more than a cruel cajolery.

But although Deerham's attentions to her comfort never wavered there were no indications to suggest that his behaviour towards her stemmed from love: on the contrary it was merely what one would expect from a man of his breeding. But if the young Marchioness of Deerham was suffering all the agonies and torments of unrequited love, no one looking at her as she attended one engagement after another would have had the least suspicion of it; most certainly her husband did not.

As he had no reason to suppose that her continuing detachment from him had its roots in her mamma's warnings, aggravated all the more by that fatal conversation she had overheard at Lady Yoxall's brought about by the unexpected vision of a woman he had once enjoyed a most pleasurable connection with, he had come to the conclusion that Louisa did indeed look upon their marriage as one of convenience after all. If he had hoped that by four months into the marriage Louisa would have come to love him or, if not that, then show some signs that she was not wholly indifferent to him, he was doomed to disappointment, and yet, there were times when he had unexpectedly caught her at an unguarded moment when he could have sworn he had seen a look in her eyes which gave the lie to his ever-growing belief that she had married him solely to save the Markham estates.

Louisa, trying as hard as one could who had tumbled headlong into love with her husband, a man who neither wanted it nor showed the least sign of returning it, to prove the complete opposite were true, decided that being in Deerham's company seriously jeopardized this aim. It was therefore with a complete lack of enthusiasm that she crammed almost every hour of every day with as many engagements as possible, indeed so successful was she that over the following weeks she was seldom to be found in Grosvenor Square. Had anyone asked her if she enjoyed the balls, soirées, card parties or even driving the curricle with the perfectly matched greys Deerham had bestowed upon her in the park at the fashionable hour of the promenade, she would have replied with a categorical yes. Of course, she would have been less than human if she did not, but the truth was Deerham's absence seriously impaired her enjoyment, but since this line of thought would only undo what little resolve she had, she decided not to think of it all.

Clifton, having been brought to acknowledge that her ladyship was as far removed from her father as anyone could be, began to look upon Deerham's marriage in a far more favourable light, because whilst he would not go so far as to say that it was a love match, neither of them evincing any signs of it, not that he would expect such vulgar behaviour from either of them, he had nevertheless begun to see that it may well work out after all. Even so, had anyone asked him if he had any concerns over the marriage he would have said no, particularly as he was by no means convinced that the young marchioness was totally indifferent to her husband. However, he did not mind owning to himself that, whilst it was common practice for married couples to have their own engagements and not live in each other's pockets, it was noticeable that Deerham and his wife were to be seen less and less in each other's company and, love match or not, it did seem a little odd for a couple who had been married for such a short time.

*

Louisa may not be a beauty but she very soon acquired a fashionable court of devoted young gallants about her, and Deerham, who had himself when young formed part of a court of young fashionables around some delectable exquisite, was neither jealous nor disapproving, and her mamma, as she fervently told her son, was far too relieved to see her daughter playing her part in society and not wearing the willow for her husband. Certainly no one looking at the young Marchioness of Deerham as she attended one party after another would have been given the least cause to suspect that beneath the elaborate powdered coiffure and painted and patched face was a young woman yearning most unfashionably for her husband, much less that she would have willingly given everything she possessed just to have Deerham tell her he loved her. He would not, of course, she knew that well enough, but it was a most lowering reflection, enough to depress one's spirits, but no one glancing in her direction as she took her seat at the card table at Lady Biddenham's select little gathering had the least guess that her mind was not on the cards in her hand but wondering instead how a tall, loose-limbed man was spending his time at Worleigh.

She had wanted nothing more than to go with him when he had requested her to accompany him this morning when he paid her a morning visit over her cup of hot chocolate in bed, but whilst nothing gave her greater pleasure than to be near him, it was becoming more of an agony than a joy, but just when she thought he had accepted her reasons for remaining in town due to the press of her engagements calmly enough, he had taken her hands in his, asking, in a tone of voice she had not heard before, "Are your engagements more entertaining than your husband?" How could she possibly tell him that she was deliberately filling every moment of every day in an attempt to keep as far away from him as possible because she could not bear the torment of being near him, knowing he did not love her or ever would without giving him a disgust of her? She could not of course, any more than she could cast herself into his arms and tell him how agonizingly in love with him she was and heaved a sigh of relief when he demanded no answer, but when he left her a few minutes later, her lips tingling from his gentle caress, she turned her face into the pillow and burst into tears.

But with half the polite world gathered in Lady Biddenham's saloons, now was not the time to think of her husband or how utterly miserable she was without him and how the next few days were going to seem like an eternity until he returned to town. Were she to do so then there would be nothing she could possibly do to stem the tears which were forming at the back of her eyes, but, not only that, Bella Biddenham missed very little and just one glace from out of those sharp eyes of hers would suffice to expose her secret, and the tale would be all over town by tomorrow.

Despite Bella Biddenham's winning ways, Louisa had seen the insatiable love of gossip and scandal which lay beneath the plump and amiable surface, but whilst one could be assured of a most entertaining evening under her roof, the truth was Louisa did not like her over much and were it not for the fact that Grosvenor Square was unbearably empty without Deerham she would not have come here tonight. It was also true that, by half past twelve, apart from the fact that her head throbbed painfully, she had been ready to take leave of her hostess for over an hour or more, but the thought of returning to a vacant house had decided her to remain a while longer when, hopefully, she would be so tired that she would fall asleep on the instant and not lie awake thinking of the man who had come to mean all the world to her.

Lady Biddenham, like the rest of polite society, had waited with bated breath to see if Markmoor's daughter had inherited his love of gaming, but had been forced to reluctantly acknowledge that, whilst the young Marchioness of Deerham was seen to take her place at the card tables like the rest of the ton, there was no evidence to suggest that she derived much pleasure from it, in fact, it was noticeable to the initiated that she clearly lacked the passion to be a true gamester like her father. One of the initiated, who had been closely if covertly watching her all evening, had seen nothing to dispute this, indeed, from what she could see of it the young marchioness displayed no more than a moderate interest in the cards. She was a competent but not a reckless player, never staking more than a few rouleaux at a time, which certainly proved her lack of enjoyment in what was a chief pastime of the ton, but her friend was right – she was perfect for what he had in mind.

Louisa, taking advantage of the lull in play, made her way through the uncomfortably hot and packed saloons to a small empty salon at the rear of the house where she thankfully sank down onto a sofa of straw-coloured satin and placed an unsteady hand to her forehead. Perhaps if she sat quietly for a moment the throbbing in her head would ease sufficiently for her to have her carriage called to take her home, but no sooner had she closed her eyes than the sound of tapping heels and the rustle of stiff skirts approaching made her open them. She found herself looking at a lady whose age it was impossible to calculate beneath the paint, rouge and patches, but it was evident from her elaborate coiffure, which stood at least a foot high off the top of her head, and very expensive toilet that she was clearly a woman of substance and respectability. The diamonds in her ears and around her neck and wrists glittered in the light from the chandelier and, as she took her seat beside her and laid a slender white hand, every finger bedecked with rings, on Louisa's, said kindly,

"Forgive me if I intrude, my dear, but I could not help noticing you slip quietly away. You have the headache, do you not?"

"Yes," Louisa acknowledged faintly, looking into the sympathetic face concernedly regarding her. "I cannot imagine why," she shook her head, not wishing to alert this stranger, however kind she was, as to the reason for it. "I am not usually prone to the headache."

"Well," she smiled, "neither am I, but I vow and declare I never leave Bella's without one! Oh, do not misunderstand me, my dear," she smiled, patting the cold hand beneath her own, "Bella is a dear sweet creature, but she does have a tendency to fill her drawing-rooms as full as they can hold!"

"You know Lady Biddenham?" Louisa enquired, having no recollection of encountering this woman here before, indeed, she had no recollection of ever meeting her at all.

"La, child!" she cried. "Our acquaintanceship is of long duration, which is why I can abuse her so!" she laughed.

"I didn't know," Louisa shook her head. "I have never seen you here before."

"Well," her new acquaintance smiled, not in the least perturbed by this, "you must know that I have been living quietly in the country since my husband died some years ago, and I have only recently taken a house in town and begun to renew all my acquaintance. But I forget my manners," she apologized. "My late husband was used to say that I would forget my head were it not attached to my shoulders. Allow me to introduce myself, my dear," she smiled. "My name is Caroline Marchand, but my friends call me Carrie, which…" she said with calculated hesitancy, "is what I hope you will become, particularly as I knew your grandmother, the Countess of Halford."

"You knew my grandmother?" Louisa asked, surprised.

"Yes, indeed!" she nodded, perfectly happy to overlook this blatant lie in the furtherance of her friend's cause. "We were friends for many years, and it is because of that that I cannot tell you how delighted I was to learn from Bella that you were here this evening – not that I needed her to point you out to me, of course!" she smiled, patting her hand. "That hair and those eyes, so like Elizabeth's, would have been enough to apprise me of the connection." Having done what she had set out to, setting Louisa at her ease, she exclaimed with credible remorse, "Oh, dear, here am I prattling on about this and that when you must long to be alone to nurse your headache." Louisa disclaimed, but her acquaintance, rising to her feet, said, "I will leave you now, but do not get to thinking we shall not meet again," wagging a warning forefinger. "Having found my dear friend's granddaughter, I am not about to let you slip through my fingers! Indeed, I fully intend that you and I shall be friends, and therefore I hope to see you again soon." It was just as she was about to turn away that she paused, her faded blue eyes lighting up as if a thought had just occurred to her, "But how stupid of me," she declared, "I almost forgot: such a scatter-brain that

I am, I am giving a little soirée at my home tomorrow evening, just a few friends reliving old times, nothing grand I assure you. Please say you will come, my dear."

"Well, I..." Louisa began.

"Of course," she smiled, too well practiced to force the issue outright, "I quite understand. You do not know me, after all."

Louisa blushed and stammered. "I'm sorry, I had not meant to be rude."

"You weren't," she assured her. "It is merely that it would be nice to talk to you about your grandmother, indeed," she smiled, "had I not run into you here I had promised myself the pleasure of making your acquaintance." Gently pushing her argument, she said happily, "Well, if you will not accept my invitation, at least accept my felicitations on becoming the Marchioness of Deerham. Your grandmother would have been extremely proud of you!" Taking advantage of Louisa's momentary awkwardness, said, with a nice mix of hope and understanding, "Well, should you change your mind, my direction is Wimpole Street, number 32, at eight o'clock." Then, without giving Louisa time to either accept or refuse, turned on her heel and left, neither woman hearing the soft rustle of stiffened skirts withdrawing hurriedly from a small alcove a few seconds later, listening to every word they said.

Unlike his young and inexperienced wife, Deerham knew all about her newly acquired acquaintance, but if he did not just one look would have sufficed to tell him all he needed to know about Caroline Marchand and her precise role in society as well as the kind of company she kept, but Louisa, falling asleep almost as soon as her head touched the pillow several hours later, had no such knowledge.

An advantageous marriage to a successful merchant may have taken Caroline Marchand out of obscurity into immediate respectability, but the taint of the City which enveloped her late husband would always ensure that she lived on the fringes of society and not at the heart of it. She kept a box at the opera and was often to be seen at the fashionable hour of the promenade in the park, but with the exception of certain hostesses like Bella Biddenham, whose passion for the cards happily led her to turning a blind eye to those whose obsession if not their background matched her own, no card of invitation would be sent to her by any hostess of note. But however much she may resent this as well as only being accorded a slight bow of acknowledgement in passing by those ladies who invited her to their select little card parties, it was thanks to their incautious gossip that she had gleaned a mine of information about people she had never met, nor was ever likely to, but which had been turned to very good account on more than occasion, eventually bringing her into contact with Digby Singleton.

Her friendship with Singleton was of long duration, its commencement due, in the main, to their love of cards and his frequent visits to her discreet little gaming house in Wimpole Street, an enterprise she had embarked on when finding herself widowed and penniless. The late Mr. Marchand, who had been a most generous husband, indeed he had been more than happy to indulge her every whim, had, much to her surprise and disbelief, left her only an allowance; substantial but by no means sufficient to keep her in the lifestyle to which she had become accustomed, the bulk of his money going to a nephew. She may have put her lowly origins behind her long since, but not all her husband's open-handedness had either assuaged or eradicated her natural acquisitiveness and, as she was also covetous and grasping, her select little card parties, attended by those whose love of the cards far exceeded their ability, had so far proved quite a financial success.

Her origins may be somewhat obscure but she had, during her marriage, become used to living a life of some luxury, and nothing, certainly not the death of her husband, was going to change that, and she was therefore determined it should remain so. Consequently, her association with Digby Singleton had proved fruitful; he would lure the uninitiated to her discreet little house where he would very soon part them of their money; happily splitting the proceeds between them. Indeed, so successful was their partnership that neither of them was eager for it to end, and therefore when he had approached her about the young Marchioness of Deerham she had been only too happy to oblige him. However, experience had taught her that not only was discretion the order of the day but also a motherly approach would never come amiss, particularly with someone as young and inexperienced as Deerham's young wife, and since none of their victims were in the least bit aware of how cleverly they had been manipulated until it was too late, Carrie Marchand had no reason to think that the Marchioness of Deerham would not honour her house with her presence.

Chapter Ten

As expected, by the time Deerham left for Worleigh, Louisa's acquaintanceship with Letitia Rawnsley had grown in to a firm friendship, so much so that it was not long before that young lady poured the whole of her adventure into her friend's ears. Louisa, who had never liked Digby Singleton despite his friendship with her father, was naturally shocked, never believing him capable of such infamy, but just as intriguing was Letitia's masked rescuer. Louisa, having given her solemn promise not to mention it to a soul, was nevertheless agog with curiosity to know who he was.

"But didn't you see his face?" she asked wonderingly.

"No, I mean… well, that is," Letitia faltered, "I only saw his eyes. You see, he had a cravat or some such thing pulled up over his face and a tricorn pulled low over his forehead, so you see," she shrugged helplessly, "I couldn't see him properly."

"But he was a gentleman, you say?" Louisa urged.

"Oh, yes," Letitia nodded. "I thought at first he was a highwayman, but as soon as he spoke, I knew he was no such thing."

"And he wouldn't tell you who he was?" Louisa asked incredulously.

"No," Letitia told her sadly. "I wish he had, because I feel I owe him a debt of gratitude for saving me."

"Yes, indeed," Louisa shuddered, not daring to think what would have happened to her dearest friend if she had not been rescued. She had given her word that she would not speak of it to a soul, and nor would she, not even to Deerham particularly as she knew there was no love lost between him and Letitia's would-be abductor, but to her way of thinking Singleton deserved to be exposed for such a dastardly and cowardly act.

In the meantime though, there was her visit to Wimpole Street this evening. The invitation had been left open, Caroline Marchand neither urging nor demanding her presence, but even so, Louisa had given it quite a lot of thought, not at all sure whether to go or not. She had no other engagements this evening, or at least none which she felt like attending, and felt sure that Deerham would have no objection, after all she had met Caroline Marchand at Lady Biddenham's, a woman who, dreadful gossip though she was, was a most respectable person, so after agonizing the issue for most of the day, she decided to attend, after all what could possibly happen to her? Besides, it would be good to talk to someone who had known her grandmother, a woman who bore all the hallmarks of being eminently respectable, but if nothing else, it was preferable to sitting in an empty house wondering what her husband was doing miles away at Worleigh.

And so, at ten minutes past eight o'clock, Louisa, dressed most becomingly in a gown of spangled gauze over oyster coloured satin wearing the double of row of pearls Deerham had given her and a pearl and diamond bracelet on her wrist, she climbed out of the chair Clifton had called up for her and trod up the two shallow steps of number 32, Wimpole Street. Before the clapper even had time to die away the door was opened almost immediately by a butler, not as stately nor, she guessed, as proficient as Clifton, but quite precise nonetheless, whereupon he invited her to step inside.

"Madam is expecting you, your ladyship," he nodded his head. Louisa found herself standing in a medium sized hall with rooms leading off either side and a narrow-carpeted staircase, but without giving her time to take in her surroundings he immediately requested her to follow him up the stairs. Louisa could hear voices and laughter emanating from one of the saloons on the first floor, which should have set her mind at rest, but for reasons she could not quite define she found herself devoutly wishing she had not come, and instinctively wrapped her gauze spangled wrap closer around her.

No sooner had she been announced than Caroline Marchand came forward, wreathed in smiles and holding out a heavily jewelled hand, smiling, "My dear, how good of you to come. I did not think you would."

There was nothing outwardly wrong with Caroline Marchand, indeed she appeared to be everything she purported to be, a respectable widow living in a reasonably comfortable style, but it did seem to Louisa that the bejewelled purple turban and the liberally frilled lilac dress she was wearing, embellished with numerous lace bows, gave her a very different appearance to when she had seen her last night. Around her neck she wore a sapphire necklace with diamond drops hanging from her ears, while around her wrists were draped diamond bracelets which, whether real or not, appeared rather too opulent for one of Louisa's exquisite taste.

"Come," Caroline smiled, not giving Louisa time to say anything, "you must allow me to introduce you to my friends."

The saloon, decorated in straw-coloured satin with a myriad of candles in the crystal chandeliers hanging from the ceiling, giving off a blazing light, was certainly elegant, indeed there was nothing whatever that one could take an exception to. Discreetly placed around the room card tables had been set up, all except one already in use, and on one of the carefully arranged sofas sat a man and a woman who, Louisa saw at a glance, although bearing all the hallmarks of being eminently respectable nevertheless gave her the impression that they were hardened gamesters, not at all the kind of people she had expected to meet, particularly as Caroline Marchand had led her to believe that they were all old friends, catching up on old times. To Louisa's way of thinking she gained the distinct impression that 32, Wimpole Street was not quite as respectable as she had at first thought, but giving herself a mental shake she told herself that she was being ridiculous and that it was perfectly acceptable for people to meet and play cards, but although this went some way to steadying her nerves instinctively her uneasiness grew, and by the time Caroline Marchand had gone around the room introducing her to everyone, Louisa was convinced of it and wanted nothing more than to escape, but it seemed that her hostess was not about to let her leave, inviting her to sit down and nodding to a footman to give her guest a glass of champagne. There was nothing she could do but accept it, but instead of taking a sip Louisa placed the glass down onto a small side table next to her, trying to think of something to say as she did so, but Caroline Marchand forestalled her, smiling,

"Well, now you have been introduced to everyone, I daresay you would like to take your place at the card table."

Louisa had not come here expecting to play cards but to meet Caroline Marchand's friends, all of whom it seemed were more intent on playing piquet or faro than conversing, and to talk to her about her grandmother, but upon pointing this out to her hostess, she merely flicked Louisa's cheek with a careless forefinger, saying,

"And so we shall, but later, my dear. Now," she nodded, placing a hand beneath Louisa's elbow and raising her to feet, "let me see about seeing you comfortably established at a table."

Louisa disclaimed, stating that she really had no wish to play, but was instantly overrode by a woman who knew precisely how to bring a recalcitrant young woman up to scratch, saying, not a little archly,

"That is not very kind in you, my dear. I felt sure you would not say no."

Louisa blushed and apologized that she had meant no offence, to which Caroline Marchand immediately embraced her, saying,

"Why, you silly puss! There is nothing wrong in playing cards, after all," she smiled, "your father was a keen player. Come," she invited, pulling a chair out from under the table, "you shall play with Cedric," waving to a middle-aged man who was busily engaged in casting out dice from left hand to right.

Some instinct told Louisa that it would be far better not to take her father as a role model, but Caroline Marchand, who seemed to take it for granted that she had inherited her father's love of cards, took her silence as adequate proof of this. Louisa, who had no feel or love for the cards, was a competent but not a skilled player, and certainly not enough to worry her partner, and although she rose from the table a loser to the tune of fifty guineas following the two games she had played, she told herself it was really nothing to signify, her losses being quite small and nothing she could not cover, but she was tired and very uneasy and longed to go home, promising herself that never again would she ever set foot inside 32, Wimpole Street, but her hostess, seemingly determined to keep her here for as long as possible, brooked no argument when Louisa told her it was time she was leaving.

Louisa, who had been convinced almost from the moment she had entered the house that this was not the type of establishment Deerham would like her to visit much less be on speaking terms with the company, felt quite inadequate to deal with her strong-minded hostess, and before she realized it she had allowed Caroline Marchand to bring another player to the table, saying,

"I shall leave you now with Frederick, but I warn you, my dear," she teased, "he is always devilish lucky!"

Louisa's heart sank, but she summoned up a smile as she looked at the man, who could have been any age between thirty and forty, dressed in puce satin with quite a preposterous wig balancing on his head, bowing politely over her hand before sitting perfectly at his ease opposite her, and upon him asking her if she preferred picquet or faro she shrugged, saying faintly, "Piquet."

She watched him shuffle the pack and deal her cards with her mind in a whirl. This was not the kind of evening she had expected, indeed so far removed was it from the comfortable gathering she had anticipated that for one awful moment she thought she had stepped into a dream. Not surprisingly, the game ended with her losing, not heavily, but enough to disquiet her, and when she said that it was time she was leaving, her companion insisted that she play one more game, assuring her that her luck was bound to change. She looked around her but there was no sign of her hostess, and however much she never wanted to set eyes on her again good manners decreed that it would be extremely rude to leave without saying goodbye. Her companion, leaning back in his chair idly shuffling the pack of cards with his long white fingers, said cheerfully,

"Never mind Carrie. Lord knows where she is! Never know what she's at from one minute to the next. Come ma'am, one more game."

Louisa looked every inch her indecision, searching frantically round the room for her hostess, but upon seeing no sign of her she felt like a trapped animal, leaving her with nothing else to do but nod her head, saying hesitantly, "Very well, then, just one more game," resuming her seat with the utmost reluctance.

Her mind was only half on the game, making her discards without much thought, just wanting the game to be over, longing to be gone from this dreadful house, which, despite the elegance of her surroundings, made her feel decidedly uncomfortable. Eventually though, the game came to an end, to which she was heartily relieved, but her relief was only short-lived when her companion, having totalled up her losses, jolted her out of her lethargy by claiming, "I make that three hundred and fifty guineas you owe me, your la'ship."

For one horrifying moment Louisa thought she was going to faint, staring from the scattered cards on the table to her companion as though one in a daze, hardly able to believe that she could possibly have lost so much. It was only by a super-human effort that Louisa remained standing on her feet, her small white hands gripping the back of her chair and her eyes looking somewhat blankly down at the man reclining at his ease, but somehow she finally managed to find her voice sufficiently to repeat, somewhat faintly, though with perfect calm,

"Th-three hundred and f-fifty guineas?" to which her companion nodded.

"A pound a point, ma'am," he told her cheerfully, raising his glass to his lips. "Distinctly remember agreeing to it at the start of the game."

Louisa had no such recollection, telling herself it would never have happened had she been concentrating on the game instead of wishing she could leave here, but that was a seemingly small matter when compared to wondering how on earth she was to find four hundred guineas before Deerham returned from Worleigh in three days' time. The thought of her husband brought the tears to her eyes, but managing to hold them back as well as dismissing him from her mind, she looked down at the man leaning back in his chair with a calmness she was very far from feeling. He was certainly good looking, even so, there was no disguising the faint lines around his eyes and mouth, forcibly bringing to mind the same lines, though more accentuated, that she had seen around her father's the last time she had seen him, and not for the first time she found herself at a loss to understand how anyone could take even a modicum degree of pleasure from losing thousands in a night's sitting.

Caroline Marchand, watching her closely from her vantage point, knew precisely what had happened, just as she knew it would; trust Frederick, he could always be relied upon to fleece the uninitiated and in a way that was as unobtrusive as it was ruinous, was very well satisfied with what she saw. The young Marchioness of Deerham was far too young and inexperienced to realize that she had been deliberately lured to this house for the express purpose of completing the first stage of bleeding her husband dry, and upon seeing Louisa, following her disastrous and ruinous games of piquet, wrap her gauze scarf around her, floated over to her side, and, after holding her left hand and squeezing it warmly, smiled.

"Did he fleece you dreadfully, my dear?" looking amusingly down at the man who had also risen.

"No," Louisa smiled faintly, feeling a little sick, "not at all, but... but I am afraid I shall have to ask for time to settle the debt."

This was said quite calmly, but Caroline Marchand, far too experienced, was consideration itself, stating that she must not worry her head over such a trifling matter.

"What is four hundred guineas between friends?" she smiled, putting her arm around Louisa's waist, accurately assessing the thoughts going around in her head. "You really must not tease yourself over such a trifling sum, I assure you there is not the least need."

Louisa would not call four hundred guineas a trifling sum, on the contrary it was an enormous amount and one she could not possibly raise, especially being so close to the end of the quarter. She would rather die than ask Deerham for the money, especially when she considered his unstinting generosity as well as those staggering settlements he had paid upon their marriage, which, if all Christopher had told her was true, was a small fortune.

"I do realize, of course," Caroline broke into her thoughts with spurious sympathy, "what an awkward position this places you in, especially as, correct me if I am wrong, my dear," she smiled, "but being almost at the quarter, as I have no doubt you are, it will take some little time for you to pay the debt, particularly as... well," she sighed on a little shrug of her shoulders, "I feel sure you have no wish for your husband to know how much you have lost at play." Louisa felt the colour stain her cheeks at this, and Caroline Marchand, who could not have wished for the commencement of the destruction of Deerham to have got off to a better start, said suggestively, "Of course, you could always win it back."

"Win it back!" Louisa cried, startled.

"Why of course!" Caroline Marchand smiled.

"B-but I... I don't understand!" Louisa shook her head, rather bewildered, wishing, for the umpteenth time, that she had never come here.

Caroline Marchand patted her hand, smiling, "You really are a little innocent, aren't you? But there," she cried, shrugging, "I should have known you were not at all up to snuff." Louisa shook her head and Caroline laughed, giving her hand a little shake. "It's really very simple, my dear." In answer to Louisa's puzzled stare, Caroline pinched her cheek, advising, "Do not look so concerned, it's not nearly as bad as you seem to think." Waiting only long enough for these words to go home, she smiled, "What I was about to suggest is that you remain here until you have won it back, because apart from it wanting only five minutes to midnight, the night still being young, one's luck must change sooner or later." She gave a pregnant pause before saying softly, "Of course, you could always return tomorrow evening, when, I promise you, we should be delighted to see you, but if that is not convenient to you then you could always write an IOU promising to pay the debt owed."

Had anyone asked Louisa if she had ever spent a more unhappy, and really quite dreadful, evening, she would have replied with a categorical "no", wishing herself at home long since, but as remaining here until she won her debt back, and there was no guarantee of this, or returning tomorrow evening was too horrendous to contemplate, then it seemed she had no choice other than to write an IOU. The thought was extremely distasteful to her, but unfortunately there was no alternative, but as Louisa looked at her hostess, a picture of affable sociability and understanding, it suddenly occurred to her that, despite the elegance of her surroundings, 32, Wimpole Street was nothing short of a gaming hell to which she had been deliberately lured, but why she should have been she did not know. As she was unaware of the long-standing friendship between Caroline Marchand and Digby Singleton and that they had deliberately contrived her being here merely to bring about Deerham's downfall, Louisa's only concern was preventing this from coming to his ears, but as there would be time enough later to worry about this, she hastily scribbled an IOU and, after wishing her hostess a hurried goodnight, she left the house, stepping into the chair the footman had called up for her.

By the time she entered the portals of Deerham House in Grosvenor Square it was almost half past twelve, and the hall porter, by no means unused to being up this late, wished her a rather sleepy goodnight, to which she merely nodded and hurried up the stairs to her room. As expected, Mary was waiting for her, but Louisa, apart from the odd comment, was in no frame of mind to indulge in conversation with her, merely allowed her to remove her dress and jewellery, but just as Louisa was about to take the bracelet off her wrist to give to Mary she noticed it was not there. For one horrifying moment she could do nothing but stare at her bare wrist, unable to think what could possibly have happened to it. She could have sworn that the catch was not defective and that she had not lost it, and was therefore momentarily at a loss to account for it. This, coming on top of what had been the most awful evening of her life, was almost too much, and for one awful moment she thought she was going to faint, but pulling herself together she looked at Mary through the glass of her dressing table and smiled, saying,

"Thank you, Mary. I shan't need you again this evening," hiding her relief when Mary, who strongly suspected her mistress had the headache and longed only for her bed, made no mention of the bracelet, but merely bid her goodnight before bobbing a curtsey and leaving her.

How long Louisa sat staring at her somewhat pale and drawn reflection in the mirror she had no idea, and try as she did, she could neither dismiss nor ignore the gravity of this evening's events. No matter how many times she told herself that she should have remained resolute and left 32, Wimpole Street after her game with Cedric had finished and not allowed herself to be persuaded into another two games by Caroline Marchand's coaxing, made not the slightest difference. The truth was she had been powerless to resist, resulting in her writing that infamous IOU, which, no matter how she looked at it, seemed nothing short of a crime. She played cards merely because everyone did so and not because she took pleasure from it, but never before had she lost so much money, but how on earth she was going to redeem that IOU she had no idea, and, if all that were not bad enough, she had lost her bracelet.

She remembered Deerham presenting it to her and her pleasure when he had fastened it around her wrist, saying, "Just a little something to complement those pearls." She had no idea how much it was worth, but its value must be considerable; the pearls alone, which were truly exquisite, must be worth a small fortune, and the diamond, unquestionably of the finest quality, equally so. This evening had been the first time she had worn it when out of her husband's company; in some strange way making her feel as though he was with her, but she could have sworn that there had been nothing faulty with the catch. It was then that she remembered Caroline Marchand holding her hand, gently squeezing it as she had reassured her that losing four hundred guineas was nothing but a mere trifle and she was not to worry her head over it. What could have been more natural than Caroline Marchand undoing the clasp?

Deerham may not love her, but he had been crushingly generous. Those appalling settlements apart, he had nevertheless bestowed upon her a considerable sum which he had placed in Childs for her as well as giving her a handsome quarterly allowance, which, to a young woman who had never been able to imagine the half of it, seemed enormous. And now, after all his generosity, she found herself with this horrendous debt. Had it not have been for the fact that it was almost the end of the quarter she would have paid it tomorrow, but unfortunately she was considerably short of four hundred guineas, and somehow she did not think that Caroline Marchand, despite her protestations of not letting herself worry over a trifle, would not expect to be kept waiting over long for the redemption of that IOU, and certainly not for another month when the new quarter would be here and she would be well in funds again. If Caroline Marchand would not grant her the time to redeem that IOU, then Louisa had no idea how she was to settle it, unless, of course, she drew money from Childs, but that would necessitate employing a go-between, and whilst she felt sure that William would act for her she could not help feeling that out of loyalty to Deerham he could well tell him. But even before she had turned this over in her mind her every feeling revolted to use some of that money merely to get her out of debt, not only that, but she was determined not to let it come to Deerham's ears, and as for asking him to loan her the money to pay it, she would die rather.

But it was not only that horrendous debt she had to consider but her bracelet as well. The more Louisa thought about it the more convinced she became that Caroline Marchand had cunningly removed it from her wrist, although for what aim had Louisa in a puzzle, but at no point did she believe for one moment that the catch was defective and it had simply fallen off her wrist without her being aware of it, Louisa knew it was no such thing. If Caroline Marchand had contrived to remove it without her being aware of it, and no other explanation presented itself, then it stood to reason she had a motive, but that she would return it to her was doubtful. The more Louisa thought about it the more certain she became that Caroline Marchand would offer to sell it back to her or, even, approach Deerham, then her tale would be told.

At all costs Louisa had to prevent this from happening, and loath though she was she knew she had no choice but to call in Wimpole Street tomorrow to speak to Caroline Marchand. It was not something Louisa was looking forward to, but she was left with very little choice, the thought making her face pucker, then, as though she could not stop herself, she burst into tears.

Chapter Eleven

Hardly had the breakfast cups been removed the following morning than Caroline Marchand's butler tapped on her breakfast parlour door to inform her that she had a visitor. She did not think it would be the young Marchioness of Deerham, at least not this early in the morning for it wanted only ten minutes to half past ten, but upon being told that Digby Singleton had called and was wishful of a few words with her, she nodded, telling him to show him into the drawing-room, by no means displeased by his early visit.

No evidence of the previous evening's proceedings was visible, and as she opened the door to this spacious and elegant apartment her visitor, who had been reclining at his ease pouring through a journal, no sooner saw her than he cast it aside and rose to his feet, taking her outstretched hand in his and raising it to his lips before holding her at arm's length, smiling,

"You look charmingly, my dear."

She laughed. "I am pleased you think so."

At fifty years of age Caroline Marchand still retained her looks, even if she did have to resort to using hair colour to maintain her improbably blonde curls as well as cosmetic aids to hide certain imperfections and resorting to wearing a lace collar to conceal the fact that her skin was no longer as smooth as it had once been, but Singleton, a connoisseur when it came to women, had to admit that she was still a remarkably handsome woman.

It could not be said that Caroline Marchand was a cruel or vicious woman, but she did take enormous pleasure from listening to gossip as well as deriving a great deal of enjoyment from hearing of other people's misfortunes, and she certainly delighted in intrigue, which was why she was not averse to helping her old friend in his efforts to ruin Deerham. He had never once visited her establishment, a discreet little gaming hell which she presided over and where she was only too happy to relieve those who favoured deep play or the young and gullible of their money, but he certainly knew of it, and whilst personally she had nothing against him, she admitted to a certain piquancy in relieving him of his money and sharing the proceeds with Singleton.

Digby Singleton was a rogue, indeed, Caroline Marchand would go further, he was nothing short of a reprobate, to which the lines around his eyes and mouth more than adequately testified, but she owned to having a liking for him, so much so that after removing her hands from his, her eyes alight with amusement, smiled,

"I wish I could say the same of you, however. Puce, my dear Digby, is not your colour."

He seemed to give this due consideration, looking down at his immaculate person through his eye-glass before inspecting his appearance in the mirror above the fireplace, sighing at length, "Alas, my dear Carrie, I do believe you are right."

"Of course I am," she told him.

He sighed mournfully. "But what is one to do I ask myself," shrugging helplessly, "when one's tailor persuades one to the contrary?"

"Find a new tailor," she suggested, raising amused eyebrows.

He thought this over for a moment, acknowledging resignedly, "You may, of course, be right, my dear Carrie, indeed you always are, but, alas," he sighed, shrugging his narrow shoulders, "it would pain the poor fellow dreadfully to deprive him of my patronage."

She laughed and patted his cheek. "Confess, Digby, you have no intention of doing any such thing!"

"Alas," he shrugged, "how well you know me."

"Too well to be fooled into thinking that another tailor would grant you such extended credit," she told him candidly.

"Ouch," he purred softly, his eyes glinting.

"Touched a raw spot, did I?" she asked.

It was a moment or two before he spoke, and when he did so it was noticeable that some of the amiability had left his voice. "Let us just say," he said reservedly, giving her a mocking little bow, "a little tender."

She laughed. "I vow and declare it is!"

He eyed her considering for a moment. He liked Carrie, indeed she was a good sport, especially when it came to helping one out of a fix, but that tongue of hers could, on occasion, say things that were a little too close to home for comfort, but electing to put this to one side, he raised an eyebrow, asking, "So, tell me, did our young friend accept your invitation last night?"

She did not pretend to misunderstand him, knowing precisely whom he meant, and, after disposing herself gracefully onto a chaise longue of straw-coloured satin, said, "Yes."

"And?" he urged, sitting down opposite her, watching her closely.

It was a moment or two before she answered this, her attention momentarily diverted by a loose thread she had spied on her lace sleeve, but after snapping it off with her fingers she looked up at him, saying, "She went down to the tune of four hundred guineas, and," she nodded significantly, "this," pulling out of her pocket the bracelet she had so expertly removed from Louisa's wrist.

Singleton was on his feet on the instant, almost snatching the bracelet out of her hand to have a closer look, his eyes glistening as they inspected it. "You have done well, Carrie," he told her at length, having subjected the pearls and diamond to intense scrutiny, "very well, indeed!"

"Thank you," she inclined her head. "So," she wanted to know, "what happens now?"

"Now," he smiled thinly, looking satisfyingly at her, "the enjoyment begins." He thought a moment, musing at length. "What a pity she only lost four hundred guineas."

"I must confess," Carrie told him, "I was hoping she would lose more, but it was obvious from the moment she stepped inside that she was wishing she had not come, indeed," she sighed, "I was surprised I was able to get her to play as much as I did, but I do have this," she told him, removing Louisa's IOU from her pocket and handing it to him.

A strange light entered his eyes as he scanned the single sheet of vellum, reading enthusiastically: *'I promise to pay the sum of four hundred guineas – Marchioness of Deerham.'* "Excellent, my dear Carrie," he smiled, "truly excellent."

"I am glad you think so," she told him, "but four hundred guineas will hardly break Deerham's bank."

Singleton eyed her speculatively for a few moments, his brain racing. No, four hundred guineas would most certainly not break Deerham's bank, although he had no doubt at all that to the young marchioness it would seem like a fortune, but unless he had grossly erred that bracelet could be put to very good account. He could only speculate how much it had cost Deerham, but those perfectly matched pearls alone were worth a small fortune, and as for that diamond, really quite exquisite – well, it must be worth a king's ransom at least!

"Tell me, my dear," he asked, raising a pencilled eyebrow, "how much would you say this is worth?" holding the bracelet in the air with his finger and thumb.

Caroline Marchand, who had done nothing but admire it ever since she had cunningly removed it from Louisa's wrist and had envied her the possession of it, had asked herself this question more than once since last night, and therefore had no hesitation in saying, "Several thousand pounds, at least."

"Yes," Singleton mused, "so would I."

Her eyes narrowed slightly. "What are you thinking?"

It was a moment before he spoke, his painted lips parting into a none too pleasant smile, "I was thinking of Deerham's chagrin when he learns that his young bride staked the bracelet to cover part of her debt."

"*Part* of her debt?" she queried, sitting forward a little.

"Yes," he repeated, his voice purring like a cat, "*part* of her debt."

Thanks to her late husband's city connections, a fatal taint to anyone wishing to adorn the fashionable world, she may be forced to live on the outskirts of polite society but thanks to those few hostesses whose love of the cards made her *persona grata*, she had come to know that there had never been any love lost between Singleton and Deerham. What it was that had brought about this breach between them, then she, like the rest of the ton, had no idea, but that it went deep she was certain, but that look on Digby's face, telling her more than any words could, boded well for a most exquisite revenge. Being a woman who possessed few scruples, she had no aversion in helping him to fleece Deerham dry, even if it meant using his young bride to it, and therefore knew no hesitation in agreeing to what Singleton had in mind, giving it her full approval.

"Lud, Digby!" she cried, when he had come to the end of what he had outlined, "that's positively Machiavellian!"

"I knew you would like it," he smiled. "For myself," he opined, raising a pencilled eyebrow, "I think it is nothing short of genius." Walking over to where an escritoire stood against the far wall he pulled out a chair and sat down, whereupon he dug Louisa's IOU out of his pocket and, after scrutinizing it for several moments, he pulled out a sheet of vellum upon which he practised writing several lines, then, when satisfied he had created an excellent facsimile of her handwriting, pulled out another sheet of vellum and began to write, only the scratching of the quill breaking the silence. "There!" he cried, almost exultantly when he had finished, holding the sheet in the air.

Jumping to her feet, Caroline Marchand hurried over to where he sat and virtually snatched the piece of vellum out of his fingers and eagerly read the few lines:

'I, the Marchioness of Deerham, having accrued a gaming debt of five-and-a-half thousand guineas, have, as a token of my assurance to pay, handed over my pearl and

diamond bracelet, which has been calculated as being worth two thousand pounds, with the promise that the balance of three and a half thousand guineas will be paid as soon as may be possible, or the full redeeming sum of five-and-a-half thousand guineas and the return of my bracelet. The Marchioness of Deerham.'

Her eyes flew to his and, as if she could not prevent herself, burst out laughing, exclaiming, "Why, it is perfect!"

He mockingly inclined his head. "But of course," he smiled, "what else?"

"Are you never at a loss, Digby?" Caroline Marchand enquired, raising an enquiring eyebrow.

"Seldom, my dear," he inclined his head, rising to his feet, "very seldom."

She thought a moment, asking at length, "Do you think she will pay?"

"Perhaps," he sighed, shrugging a casual shoulder, "perhaps not, but Deerham most certainly will."

A slight crease furrowed her forehead, and upon being asked if anything were amiss, she said, "Not amiss precisely, but I am fully expecting to receive a visit from her about her bracelet, if not today, then soon, after all," she shrugged, "the loss of her bracelet would not go unnoticed once she arrived home last night."

He tapped his eye-glass against his painted lips, then, after pondering a moment, he looked at her, saying softly, "You know, Carrie, I do not think it will come amiss if you disabuse her mind of accidentally losing her bracelet, nor, for that matter, correcting her misapprehension as to the amount of her losses, after all," he raised an eyebrow, "how can she possibly dispute the case when it is in black and white?" handing her the IOU he had written together with the bracelet.

She did not pretend to misunderstand him, she knew perfectly well what he meant and what he wanted her to do, and therefore took the sheet of vellum from him without a blink or qualm of conscience. "Very well," she nodded, "it will be as you wish."

He raised her hand to his lips. "How nice it is to deal with someone whose grasp of the matter corresponds precisely with my own, rendering explanation unnecessary!" to which she laughed.

*

Not surprisingly, Louisa hardly closed her eyes all night, only falling into a fitful sleep just as the dawn began to break. Her dreams, which only magnified the horror of the previous evening's events, were very far from edifying, and by the time Mary came in with her cup of hot of chocolate, Louisa, lying inertly back against the pillows, felt quite exhausted. She could hear the rain beating steadily against the window pane, keeping perfect time with the sickening thud of her heart, not at all sorry that the sudden change in the weather meant that Lady Remington's alfresco breakfast would have to be cancelled. In truth, she had never felt less like keeping her many engagements which, ordinarily, would see her out of the house for most of the day, but this morning she was in no mind to attend the many entertainments on offer, for which last night's unforgettable events and her subsequent visit to Wimpole Street today were responsible.

She could not pretend that it was a visit she was looking forward to with any degree of pleasure, on the contrary she never wanted to step foot inside the place again, but unfortunately circumstances dictated that she must, especially as she was quite convinced that the catch on her bracelet had not been faulty, therefore falling from her wrist accidentally. She could not even begin to think why Caroline Marchand should want to remove the bracelet from her wrist, but that she had done so Louisa was certain, after all she *had* held her hand for several minutes. As she lay back against the pillows sipping her hot chocolate, a deep frown creasing her forehead, she tried to think of any other way she could possibly have lost it, but no matter how hard she tried or unpleasant the thought she was left with only one conclusion – Caroline Marchand had removed it quite deliberately.

Of course, it could well be nothing short of a clever ploy to get her into her clutches, particularly if, as Louisa seemed to think, 32, Wimpole Street was nothing short of a gaming hell, but, somehow, she did not think so. If Caroline Marchand had cunningly removed her bracelet, and Louisa was absolutely convinced that she had, then she could think of no possible reason for her to do so, and knew that the only way she would discover the truth was to visit her at some point today.

But it was not only her bracelet that gave Louisa pause for thought; there was also the question of how she was to find four hundred guineas and redeem that IOU she had been forced into writing without it coming to Deerham's ears. She had, during the course of what had been a long and worrying night, considered confiding the whole to Christopher and asking him to lend her the money until she received her allowance at the new quarter when she would pay him back, but no sooner had this thought occurred to her than she immediately vetoed it if, for no other reason, than it was hardly fair to burden him with a gambling debt, the very reason he now found himself in the position of bringing his estates back into order.

She knew without being told that Deerham, being a man of honour, would redeem her IOU if she asked him to, but she only had to think of those heavy marriage settlements and his crushing generosity to make her recoil from doing so, in fact, she would rather die than present him with a gambling debt, no matter how innocently acquired. Useless to tell him that she only played because everyone else did so and not because she enjoyed it or because she was a gamester, and certainly not because she was indeed her father's daughter, mentally shrinking from the look of disgust which would cross his face. No, under no circumstances could she tell him, the very thought making her shudder, even so, it did not prevent her from wondering what her husband was doing at Worleigh and if he was missing her as much as she was missing him and how all she wanted was to go to him and pour her difficulties into his ears, something she knew she could not do.

She could only be thankful that Mary had not so far noticed her bracelet was missing, but Louisa supposed that sooner or later she would, and what she would tell her she had no idea. Mary, who knew her jewellery by heart, would know perfectly well that there was nothing wrong with the clasp, and therefore her mistress could not possibly have lost it accidentally. Louisa knew she could trust Mary, after all she had been with her long before she married Deerham, but the thought of confessing her visit to Wimpole Street and all that followed was something Louisa could not bring herself to do, and therefore she could only hope that she would return from her visit to Caroline Marchand with her bracelet.

Unfortunately, however, it was an empty hope. Alighting from the sedan chair, her heart beating rather fast and her mouth somewhat dry, Louisa knocked on the door, not daring to think what she would do if she was wrong after all and Caroline Marchand had not managed to cunningly remove her bracelet from her wrist. Having been shown into the drawing-room by a footman, where only the night before she had spent the worst few hours of her life, she waited anxiously for her hostess, pacing nervously up and down, unable to be still. She did not have long to wait. Caroline Marchand, wreathed in smiles, entered the drawing-room and walked gracefully towards her, her hand outstretched.

"My dear marchioness! What a pleasant surprise."

"I… I must apologize for the intrusion," Louisa stammered, absently taking her hand in her own.

"Intrusion!" Caroline Marchand repeated, raising a surprised eyebrow. "Why, what nonsense is this?" patting her cheek. "I am delighted to see you." Without giving Louisa time to respond to this she escorted her to a sofa and, after seating herself beside her and commenting unfavourably on the weather, to which Louisa merely nodded and smiled, asked, "Now, tell me, what is it that brings you here? Not that I am not pleased to see you."

Rehearsing what she would say was one thing, but to actually find herself on the point of having to say it to the woman who Louisa was convinced was not as sincere as she had thought when she had first met her at Lady Biddenham's, was quite another. It was therefore not without a little awkwardness that Louisa found herself saying,

"Well, you see, when I arrived home last night, I found that my... my bracelet had gone from my wrist and I... I wondered if... if you could tell me if I lost it here, but how I could have," she shrugged, "when... when the clasp was not defective, I have no idea."

Caroline Marchand, experiencing neither qualms nor remorse over the deceit she and Singleton were perpetrating, indeed she had fully expected this visit, allowed her eyes to widen to their fullest extent at hearing this, staring in disbelief at the youthful face in front of her, repeating,

"Lost it?" to which Louisa nodded.

It was several moments before Caroline Marchand spoke, looking at her guest as though she could not believe her ears, then, having heaved a deep sigh, said, "Well, I suppose in a way you did lose it, my dear."

"You know where it is?" Louisa asked hopefully.

Caroline Marchand, looking at Louisa in complete and utter astonishment, shook her head, crying, "But... but surely you have not forgotten?"

Louisa looked a little dazedly at her, momentarily at a loss to understand what she was on about, but pulling herself together managed, although rather faintly, "Forgotten? Forgotten what?"

"Why," Caroline Marchand cried, eyeing her in no little surprise, "only that you pulled the bracelet off your wrist yourself to cover part of your gambling debt."

At first, Louisa thought her hostess was merely jesting, but one look at that calm and innocent face was enough to tell her that far from teasing her a little she was in deadly earnest, and therefore she could only look in disbelief at the woman opposite her, but eventually she found her voice to repeat,

"*Part* of my gambling debt!"

Caroline Marchand nodded. "I must confess, though," she told her, "I was rather surprised you did so, indeed," she nodded, "I recall earnestly requesting you not to do so at the time." Louisa had no such recollection, but without giving her time to respond, Caroline Marchand went on with spurious sympathy, "I am afraid you were badly dipped last night, my dear." Then, making great play of scrutinizing the rings on her fingers, she looked up, saying, "I am afraid you went down to the tune of five-and-a-half thousand guineas."

For one awful moment Louisa thought she was going to faint, so unreal were the circumstances in which she found herself, but somehow managing to overcome it, said, in a voice which she knew must be her own, "*Five-and-a-half thousand guineas!*" to which Caroline Marchand nodded. "But... but that's not true," Louisa cried faintly.

"Alas, my dear," Caroline Marchand sighed, "I am afraid it is."

Louisa shook her head. "But I... I only lost four hundred guineas."

"If only that were true," Caroline Marchand sadly shook her head.

"But it *is* true," Louisa insisted. "I recall writing an IOU to that effect."

"So do I," Caroline Marchand nodded. "Perhaps you would like to see it?"

"Yes, yes I would," Louisa said, hardly above a whisper.

She watched almost mesmerized as Caroline Marchand rose to her feet and walked over to the escritoire and opened it, opening a drawer from which she retrieved a sheet of vellum. Louisa, feeling sick, rose unsteadily to her feet, taking the sheet Caroline Marchand handed to her.

"You see, my dear," she said sympathetically, "what can't speak can't lie."

Louisa took the sheet in her nerveless fingers, reading with horrified eyes:

'I, the Marchioness of Deerham, having accrued a gaming debt of five-and-a-half thousand guineas, have, as a token of my assurance to pay, handed over my pearl and diamond bracelet, which has been calculated as being worth two thousand pounds, with the promise that the balance of three-and-a-half thousand guineas will be paid as soon as may be possible, or the full redeeming sum of five-and-a-half thousand guineas and the return of my bracelet. The Marchioness of Deerham.'

"But I... I did not write this!" Louisa exclaimed, looking every inch her stupefaction.

"Are you saying that is not your handwriting?" Caroline Marchand raised an enquiring eyebrow.

"Yes, no... I mean," Louisa shook her head, bewildered, "it... it looks like it, but I never wrote it," to which her hostess merely raised a sceptical eyebrow. "I admit I did write one," Louisa confessed, "but it was for four hundred guineas, but certainly not this," indicating the sheet in her hand.

Caroline Marchand looked quite taken aback at this, stating, "But, my dear, I saw you write it with my very own eyes!"

"But y-you couldn't have!" Louisa cried, her face rather pale and her mind awash with conjecture and fear.

For some inscrutable reason, Caroline Marchand had taken quite a liking to the young Marchioness of Deerham, a young woman she had lured to her house for the specific purpose of fleecing her husband, but now, as she watched the various emotions flit across Louisa's face, not the least being panic and alarm, she knew a moment of guilt, but then she told herself that it would be foolish to throw away her half of five-and-a-half thousand guineas. Digby Singleton was nothing if not generous – when the dibs were in tune that is! Ruthlessly pushing any finer feelings to the back of her mind, Caroline Marchand sighed, then, taking the sheet from Louisa, said,

"I'm sorry, my dear, but there is not a doubt of it."

It was several moments before Louisa could find her voice sufficiently to say, "But it's a lie! You know I did not write it or lose anywhere near that much money!"

Caroline Marchand sighed and, shaking her head, said sadly. "You know, my dear, it is not good ton to deny a gambling debt." When Louisa made no reply to this, simply because she was too stunned to think of anything to say, Caroline Marchand told her, with specious empathy, "I realize, of course, that to put one's hands on five-and-a-half thousand guineas is no easy matter, but... well," she shrugged helplessly, "I feel I should warn you that the gentleman to whom you lost at play is adamant that if the debt is not paid by the end of the week there will be no alternative but to place the matter before your husband."

At the mention of her husband, Louisa physically blenched. She had no need to be told that under no circumstances must Deerham get wind of this, but how to keep it from him she had no idea. There was no possible way she could put her hands on such a sum, and as for her bracelet, she could not fool herself into thinking that he would not notice it was missing from her collection of jewellery. Tears filled her eyes, but managing to hold them back, she looked at Caroline Marchand and said, with as much dignity as she could muster, wanting nothing more than to leave this place as quickly as possible,

"Thank you for your hospitality, ma'am. I shall endeavour to redeem my IOU as soon as may be possible," whereupon she walked out of the room leaving her hostess, for once in her life, with very mixed feelings.

Chapter Twelve

Deerham meanwhile, in happy ignorance of his wife's dilemma, was spending a most satisfying time at Worleigh, and William, never happier than when immersed in work, told Deerham after dinner on the eve of their departure as they sat in the library that he could not believe just how much they had actually got through, to which Deerham smiled,

"You are a hard task master, indeed."

William coloured slightly and disclaimed, to which Deerham laughed, then, suddenly remembering the scented billet which had been handed to him by Clifton earlier in the day, he pulled it out of his pocket. William watched Deerham's long fingers break the wafer and spread open the single sheet of vellum, still reclining at his ease in the leather wing chair, but although William may be dying to know who had seen fit to write to him at Worleigh, the fact that it was scented surely could only mean one thing; Deerham had a new love in his life.

William may have been sceptical about Deerham's marriage to Markmoor's daughter, but during the four months of their marriage he had been brought to see that not only was the young marchioness nothing like her father but was by no means indifferent to her husband. As William had no way of knowing that Deerham was very much in love with his wife he was not in the least surprised that his noble employer was seeking his pleasures elsewhere, particularly as the couple were not seen together in public as much as one would have thought. Of course, this was by no means unusual, but if the marchioness was in fact in love with her husband then he could not quite understand why they were not seen in one another's company more often, and he could only conclude therefore that her feelings were completely one sided. Of course, there was no fear of Deerham flaunting his new mistress in the eyes of the ton as his late father-in-law had done, indeed he would be as discreet as he ever was, but William could not help feeling a little sorry for the marchioness because despite her lack of facial beauty there was nevertheless something very attractive about her, and therefore he could only hope that she would not get to hear of her husband's new flirt. Not that William expected her to make a scene about it, indeed he doubted very much whether she would even acknowledge such a connection, but if she did love her husband as he strongly suspected she did, then just knowing Deerham had another love in his life would be hard indeed for her.

Deerham, scanning the single sheet without so much as a blink, was nevertheless a little at a loss to know what could possibly have induced one of his past *cheri aimees* to write to him, but that she felt the need was evident:

'*My Very Dear Max,*

I know you will forgive my writing to you at Worleigh, which all the world knows you are, but I feel you will forgive me when I tell you that it is a matter of some moment.

If you would do me the honour of calling upon me in Hertford Street upon your return to town, I will explain all.

In the meantime, my very dear Max, I remain yours, as ever, Julia.'

If she was hoping to pick up where they had left off, despite his marriage, then her note did not suggest this. Up until fifteen months ago he had enjoyed a most pleasurable relationship with her, and although she was exquisitely beautiful and utterly desirable, he had no intention of resuming the connection. The last he had heard of Julia was that she had some Italian count in tow, whether she still did, remained to be seen, but her note had definitely intrigued him. Even though her late husband had left her more than adequately provided for, Deerham had nevertheless proved more than generous towards her, and therefore he did not think the reason for her missive was so she could ask him for money, but Julia was nothing if not honest and fair and unless he had grossly underestimated her, he did not think that now she was out of his protection she would ask him for financial relief. Of course, it could be that she was seeking his advice about something, which he was perfectly happy to give her, but until he had spoken to her he was left with nothing but conjecture.

Folding the single sheet back into its crease and putting it in his pocket, Deerham, knowing that behind that passive face his secretary was agog with curiosity, reading the thoughts in his head with unerring accuracy, knew too that William, who had been with him long enough to know that scented messages usually only betokened one thing, smiled, saying soothingly, a smile lighting those dark grey eyes,

"I know, William, I know."

"My lord?" William queried.

Deerham shook his head, then, as if deeming the matter closed, began to talk of other things, leaving William in little doubt that his lordship had no intention of telling him who is correspondent was or the content of that note, ending by saying that he intended to make an early start in the morning, requesting William to inform Trench that he was to have his coach at the door by half past seven.

*

Louisa, leaving 32, Wimpole Street in a kind of shocked daze, sat back in the chair the footman had called up for her with her mind too numb to comprehend the significance of her meeting with Caroline Marchand. Two things she did know though, and that was there was no way she could possibly raise five-and-a-half thousand guineas and also that under no circumstances must Deerham get wind of it.

She could not even begin to imagine what game Caroline Marchand was playing, but that she was in league with Digby Singleton never so much as crossed Louisa's mind. That he hated Deerham went without saying, although why this should be she had no idea, but that last night's unforgettable experience was all part of a clever ploy to bleed him dry never so much as entered her head. Knowing that she had unwittingly lost four hundred guineas was bad enough, but five-and-a-half thousand was insupportable and there was no way she would have stooped so low as to hand over her bracelet to cover part of the supposed debt. Louisa could only hazard a guess as to why Caroline Marchand had gone through the pretence of claiming that she had lost such a huge amount, even going so far as to show her the supposed IOU she had written, which Louisa was convinced had been altered. It had certainly borne all the appearance of being her handwriting, but Louisa was as certain as she could be that someone had forged it, but why this should be she was at a loss. According to Caroline Marchand the recipient of her IOU was prepared to give her until the end of the week to pay her debt, if not, then he would have little choice but to present it to her husband, the thought making Louisa shiver.

By the time she was set down in Grosvenor Square her mind was in turmoil and her face pale and drawn, a circumstance that thankfully went unnoticed by the footman, but Mary, far more astute, took one look at her mistress and told her to lie down until her headache had subsided. Louisa may not have the headache, but she was nevertheless only too eager to take such advice, believing that a period of quiet reflection was all that was needed to set matters to rights, and after being assisted out of her gown and into a deliciously frivolous wrap, she lay down quietly on her bed as soon as Mary had left her, but unfortunately it brought her no counsel or comfort.

It was a sad reflection, but Deerham was due back home the day after tomorrow, a circumstance that made Louisa wish his stay at Worleigh had been longer. It was not that she did not wish to see him, she did, with all her heart, even though she knew he did not love her, but how to face him as though nothing was wrong, she had no idea. Deerham was far too astute to be fooled, and she knew him well enough to say that it would not be long before he prised the truth out of her, the very thing she could not do. But even supposing she did tell him and he paid her supposed debt, he would never forgive her, not only that he would be left with no choice other than to think that she was indeed her father's daughter after all – in every sense. The thought brought a tear to her eye and, before she knew it, they were falling unheeded down her cheeks, made infinitely worse by the thought that there was nothing she could do to redeem her so-called debt.

For the next two nights she forced herself to attend her many engagements, deriving very little if any pleasure from any one of them, telling herself that it was pointless when her mind was only half on the entertainments on offer, promising herself an early night tonight. Only the thought that she had engaged to accompany Letitia to the Devonshires' masquerade ball pulled her out of the pit of despondency into which she had fallen, and before she realized it Mary was powdering her hair then dressing her in the new creation she had had specially made for this evening, her reflection in the mirror giving no indication as to her inner turmoil or preoccupied state of mind.

Letitia, who had no suspicion that her dearest friend was in such distress, was enjoying herself immensely. Dressed in a strawberry pink dress of stiff brocade with a mask of the same colour, which became her beautifully, her face glowed with pleasure, telling Louisa that she was glad her aunt was not with her because she would not have had half as much fun. Louisa commented suitably, playing her part in the evening's entertainment by engaging in several dances and behaving delightfully with those who made up her court, giving them no suspicion that she was very far from happy. One part of her missed the presence of a tall loose-limbed man, longing to see him and wondering what he was doing at Worleigh, while the other dreaded tomorrow when he would return to Grosvenor Square. It was not surprising therefore that she returned home feeling quite exhausted, wishing she had not gone to the Devonshires because she could not honestly say that she had enjoyed it, especially with her mind in chaos wondering how on earth she was to raise five-and-a-half thousand guineas. It was impossible, of course, but the matter teased her mind rendering sleep hideous, awaking the following morning feeling anything but refreshed.

Mary, seeing her mistress heavy-eyed and rather pale, shrewdly guessed that she had had very little sleep, but believing that it was her headache which persisted she placed her cup of hot chocolate on the little table beside the bed, advising that she remain where she was for a while, to which Louisa nodded. Not for the first time Louisa fervently wished that she had never stepped foot anywhere near 32, Wimpole Street, indeed her own instincts upon her arrival had told her what kind of a place she had walked into. She tried to comfort herself by saying that she had not gone there to play cards but to meet what she had believed to be Caroline Marchand's friends, but just one look at them had been enough to tell her that far from being friends they were nothing but hardened gamesters sure of finding deep play at 32, Wimpole Street. That she had been induced by gentle coercion to play herself was small comfort, but it did, if nothing else, go to justify what had become nothing short of a nightmare.

A glance at the clock told her it was almost eleven o'clock, and finishing off her hot chocolate she was just about to ring the bell pull for Mary when she heard a tap on the door followed by the immediate entrance of Deerham. Louisa was at once overjoyed and horrified to see him, not having expected him until this afternoon, but managing to clamp down on her overstretched nerves she watched as he closed the door behind him without a backward glance before walking over to the bed. She wanted nothing more than to pour her troubles into his ears, but she knew she could not, indeed it was the very last thing she could do. If he loved her, then she would be strongly tempted to do so, but as it was, she merely held out her hand to him, whereupon he bent down and raised it to his lips before sitting down on the edge of the bed in front of her. "I was informed that you had not yet left your room," he told her softly. "A late night?" he raised an amused eyebrow.

"Yes," she managed as lightly as she could, trying to school her disordered nerves into some kind of order. "I went with Letitia to the Devonshires' masquerade ball."

"Ah," he nodded knowingly, "a *very* late night then?"

"Yes," she smiled, "I am afraid it was," conscious that he was still holding her hand and how good it felt.

"I expect that is why you are looking a little pale and drawn," he remarked gently.

Louisa supposed she should have known her somewhat drained appearance would not escape his notice, but since she had no wish to alert him to her troubles, she merely smiled, saying, as casually as she could, "Yes, I expect so." Her fingers moved in his, revealing more than she knew to the man who was closely watching her. "I... I had not expected to see you until this afternoon," she told him.

"Didn't you?" he asked softly, squeezing her hand.

"No," she shook her head. "You... you must have left Worleigh very early."

"I did," he told her, raising her hand to his lips.

"Did... did you have an enjoyable time there?" she asked, trying to ignore the frisson of awareness that shot through her from the touch of his lips, her heart beating so fast from the combined effect of nervousness and excitement she could only marvel that she could speak at all.

"Mm," he mused, a crease furrowing his forehead, "I wouldn't say enjoyable precisely," to which she raised an enquiring eyebrow. "No," he shook his head, a smile lighting his eyes, "I am afraid that William kept me very much too busy for that."

"That was too bad of him," she managed.

"Yes," he sighed, "so I told him."

"Did... did you get much work done?" she asked, faintly, feeling some input on her part was required.

"According to William," he told her, "not nearly as much as he had hoped."

"Oh," she nodded, "I see."

"I really have no idea what I have done to deserve such a task master for my secretary," he sighed, a smile lighting his eyes, to which she gave a perfunctory smile. He looked at her for a moment, his thumb rhythmically stroking the palm of her hand, sending the most delicious sensations coursing through her, saying gently, and most unexpectedly, "You would tell me if something was troubling you, wouldn't you, Louisa?"

Louisa's eyes flew to his, the breath stilling in her lungs. She supposed she ought to have known that Deerham would notice when something was worrying her, but under no circumstances could she tell him the truth. She lowered her eyes, then, having somehow managed to calm her chaotic nerves, she glanced up at him, smiling,

"Of course, but indeed Max," she shook her head, "there is nothing whatever troubling me."

"You mustn't be afraid of me," he told softly.

"I... I'm not," she shook her head, "indeed, I am not."

His expression appeared inscrutable, then, after a moment or two, he smiled, nodding at her nightgown, "This, my dear, is most becoming. I don't think I have seen it before."

"N-No," she shook her head, her voice hardly above a whisper. "I... I am so glad you like it."

"I do," he told her in a deep voice, "very much indeed." Then, very slowly, he leaned forward and gently brushed her lips with his own, light and delicate caresses that made her want to melt into him, but it was just as his kisses were about to deepen when a slight sound came from the dressing room door. Mary, who had no idea that Deerham had arrived, was just on the point of entering Louisa's bedroom when the sight of him pulled her up short, but even though she made an immediate exit the moment was gone. Experiencing all the discomfort natural to a man being caught kissing his wife at this time of the morning while she was still in bed, he straightened up, his colour just a little high, saying lightly,

"And now, I think it is time I rid myself of all my dirt. By the bye, my dear," he said casually, as he rose to his feet, "I don't know what engagements you have today, but I am afraid I have to go out shortly, so I hope you will forgive me if I leave you to your own devices for a while."

Louisa, not at all sure whether to be glad Mary had entered her bedroom when she did or not, made some indistinct reply, her eyes filling with tears as she watched him close the door behind him, burying her face in the pillows to enjoy a hearty bout of crying. She had wanted to respond to his kisses, but not only did her mama's strictures come to mind preventing her from doing so but also because she had no need to be told the reason for him going out, after all it had been seven days since he last saw his inamorata, and as for him kissing her, well, that was easily explained; it was his duty to do so.

*

Deerham may not wear his heart on his sleeve, but he had nevertheless missed Louisa during his stay at Worleigh, so much so that it had taken every ounce of self-restraint he had to remain at his principal seat and go through the work William had told him needed to be done and not return to town well before he did. Having spent a week at Worleigh on their honeymoon, the only time Louisa had been there, he had nevertheless felt the place to be strangely empty without her, and if, once or twice, a frown descended onto his forehead, William merely attributed this to the fact that he was missing the new love in his life. He could, of course, only speculate as to who she was, but if Deerham ran true to form, and William had no reason to question it, then she was without doubt exquisitely beautiful. Deerham meanwhile, unaware of the thoughts going around in his secretary's head, had not failed to notice that Louisa had looked a little pale and drawn when he called upon her in her boudoir this morning, although this could well be due to an extremely late night at the Devonshires as she had claimed, even so, he could not help wishing that Louisa loved him - just a little.

Having changed his raiment then wrote a couple of letters it was just a little over an hour and a half later that he was being shown into a charmingly furnished drawing-room of strawberry pink satin in Hertford Street, memories of how he had once been a regular visitor and the pleasurable hours he had spent here coming to the front of his mind. He did not have long to wait for his hostess, a vision in oyster coloured satin eventually intruding on his thoughts. Julia was indeed very beautiful, and one who definitely cast Louisa very much in the shade, but as he watched her float towards him, he was conscious of no desire of wanting to resume their relationship, just an agreeable recognition of meeting an old friend.

"Max!" she cried, holding out her hands to him, "how lovely to see you. I wasn't sure you would come."

"How could I possibly refuse such a charming invitation?" he bowed over her hands, raising them to his lips.

"I see you haven't changed," she smiled up at him.

"Nor have you," he told her, kissing her soft scented cheek.

"A good thing too!" she pulled a horrified face. "That would be *quite* fatal."

"The last I heard of you," he smiled, releasing her hands, "you had some Italian count in tow. What happened to *him*?" raising an amused eyebrow.

"Let us just say," she told him archly, a mischievous laugh in her beautiful blue eyes, "that I *dis*counted him."

"I am sure you did it charmingly," he inclined his head.

"But of course," she exclaimed, "to have done otherwise would have been too cruel!"

"Oh, *much* too cruel!" he smiled. "You always did play fair, Julia."

"And you were always very gallant," she told him, "still are I see. I wonder why we parted?" she mused, laying a hand on his arm.

"As I recall," he reminded her, taking the delicate white hand and kissing its soft palm, "you told me that Talland had swept you off your feet; and such pretty feet they are too!"

"You should know," she smiled playfully, "you saw them often enough!"

"Very true," he acknowledged, releasing her hand, "and they are just as exquisite as the rest of you."

She gave a tinkling little laugh. "I wonder how many you have said that to?"

"No doubt as many as those who have said it to *you*," he returned.

"Yes, but not quite as beautifully," she smiled.

"What!" he exclaimed, "not even Talland?"

"Not even Talland," she shook her head sadly.

"Poor Julia," he commiserated, casting a glance around the elegantly furnished drawing-room, "what a dreadful time you must have had of it!"

She laughed again. "Yes, of course, quite dreadful!"

"You know, there really is no one *quite* like you," he told her.

"I hope not," she cried in mock horror, "I should dislike that very much!"

"So would I. So too I imagine, would everyone who knows you," he smiled, walking over to a small side table on which rested a vase holding a bouquet of huge yellow roses. Flicking the card attached, he asked, "A new admirer, Julia?" raising an amused eyebrow.

"Jealous, Max?" she teased.

"Not at all," he shrugged, "merely curious."

She laughed. "For shame Max! You surely do not expect me to tell you his name?"

"No," he shook his head, "you always were discreet, that is one of the most wonderful things about you. You never were a tale bearer."

"Heaven forbid!" she cried. "I detest tale bearers!"

"So do I," he agreed. Then, moving away from the table on which sat those yellow roses, he said cordially, "You know, Julia, delightful though it is to see you again, I must own that the reason for your most charming invitation, irresistible though it was, is somewhat eluding me; or could it be, I wonder," he smiled, "to renew our acquaintance?"

It was a moment before she spoke, then, shaking her head, said slowly, "No, although I must confess nothing would give me greater pleasure than to enjoy your company again," she told him truthfully, "but, the truth is Max, I did not ask you here for that."

"For what then?" he raised an eyebrow. "To felicitate me upon my recent nuptials?"

"Not quite, although," she smiled, "I *do* wish you happy. Do you think you will be?"

He eyed her closely from under his heavy lids, but said quite cordially, "You should know me better than to think I would discuss my marriage, much less my wife, with anyone - even with you, Julia. If that is your reason for asking me to come here..."

"It is, but not in the way you mean." She saw his eyes narrow slightly, and said, "Don't worry, I'm not out to make mischief Max, if that is what you are thinking?"

"I own I have never known you to," he acknowledged.

"Nor am I now," she assured him.

He raised an enquiring eyebrow. "So...?"

She looked thoughtfully at him for a moment or two, her beautiful alabaster brow puckered a little as though she were considering something, remarking at length, "You know, Max, I know you have always found the social whirl to be a dead bore, but I must confess to some surprise in that you neglect your young bride, especially after only four months into your marriage, for the pleasure of your clubs. A great mistake, if I may so?"

"You may not!" he told her lightly, flicking her cheek with a careless forefinger.

"Pity," she shrugged.

"I thought you said you were not out to make mischief?" he reminded her.

"I'm not," she shook her head, "but that does not mean to say others aren't."

An arrested expression entered his eyes at this. "Just what the devil are you driving at, Julia?" he asked quietly.

She took time to answer this by turning round to look at herself in the ornate mirror above the fireplace, one slim white finger twisting a blonde curl into place before casting a glance at him through its reflection. "You know Max," she smiled, "although I have always been grateful to my late husband for leaving me so comfortably established it is to be regretted that his money was trade earned, because *nothing*," she assured him, turning to face him, "is more detrimental to social success than the taint of a Cit. However," she shrugged, "that circumstance has not, I am glad to say, rendered me *persona non grata* with every hostess - Bella Biddenham for instance; at whose soirée a little less than week ago, I spent a most enjoyable evening!"

"Bella Biddenham?" he repeated, an odd inflexion creeping into his voice, looking keenly at her, knowing perfectly well that Louisa had attended her party.

"Yes," she nodded. "Naturally," she shrugged, "when I saw your wife was one of her guests, I automatically assumed you would be there too, until I remembered that you were at Worleigh."

"I almost feel as though I should be apologizing," he said mockingly.

"Which was a pity," she continued as though there had been no interruption, "because although Bella Biddenham, a quite a delightful creature, is from the highest echelons of society, she is not always, how shall I say?" she raised an eyebrow, "selective in her choice of guests."

"No?" he raised an eyebrow, his dark grey eyes looking keenly at her.

"Of course," she acknowledged, "Bella must be congratulated on filling her saloons as full as they can hold, but I had rather thought she would draw the line at such people as Carrie Marchand!"

His eyes narrowed at this and his finely chiselled lips pursed slightly whilst at the same time he was conscious of a feeling he could not quite define invading the pit of his stomach, but managed to say, quite calmly, "So, she was there too, was she?"

"Yes, I am afraid she was," Julia nodded.

He thought a moment, then, shrugging, asked with a casualness he was far from feeling, "What of it?"

"Oh, nothing," she shrugged, "except that she deliberately sought out your wife."

He was just in the act of raising a pinch of snuff to his nostrils, but at this his hand stilled, repeating slowly, "My wife?" to which she nodded. Pausing only long enough to inhale the delicate pinch of snuff held between his finger and thumb and return the box to his pocket, he invited, "Go on."

Julia had no wish to interfere between a man and his wife, but she liked Max too much not to acquaint him with the dangers that faced his young bride, not that he needed to be told of the dangers attaching to his wife should she get into Carrie Marchand's clutches, so, shrugging her creamy shoulders, said, "It seemed your wife had the headache a little, and no wonder," she told him, "with almost everyone of Bella's saloons filled as full as they could hold." When he made no response to this she went on, "So, quite naturally, she took the opportunity of sitting quietly in an empty saloon."

"Go on," Deerham urged again, knowing Carrie Marchand's reputation just as well as Julia did and that she and Digby Singleton were old friends.

Julia pulled an eloquent face. "Carrie Marchand made a point of following her," she told him.

Deerham's eyes narrowed even more. "She made herself known to her?" he asked, his voice suddenly a little taut.

"Yes," she nodded. "You see," she confessed, "suspecting some mischief, I took it upon myself to follow Carrie Marchand, and I overheard everything she said to her." In answer to Deerham's raised eyebrow, Julia assured him, "Don't worry, they neither saw nor heard me. You see," she explained, "I found a convenient little alcove close by."

"And?" he pressed.

The story which unfolded came as no surprise to Deerham. Carrie Marchand ran a nice a little gaming hell at 32, Wimpole Street where more than one young and callow youth had been parted from his money, a circumstance Louisa would have no idea of, but why she should seek out his wife had him in a puzzle. "You say she told my wife that she wished to introduce her to her friends and also that she knew her grandmother, the Countess of Halford?"

"Yes," Julia nodded, "and, unfortunately, your wife believed her, but then," she shrugged, "there was no reason why she should not. Carrie Marchand can be quite plausible when she's a mind."

"Yes," Deerham said almost to himself, "she can."

"I don't know if your wife accepted the invitation or not," Julia told him, "but I thought you should know about Carrie Marchand approaching her." She saw the frown which crossed his forehead and, laying a gentle hand on his arm, said, "Do not be vexed with her Max. She is young and far too inexperienced to know the ways of the world." She paused a moment before saying, "Indeed, I know you won't. I have never known you mishandle the ribbons, Max."

"Thank you," he mockingly inclined his head. Then, looking directly at her, asked, "Why have you told me all of this, Ju?"

"Why?" she shrugged. He nodded. She took a moment to answer this, then, after several moments, said, "We had some good times together, Max," she smiled, "but the truth is I like you too much, the child too, to see either of you get caught in the clutches of Carrie Marchand who, I fear," she nodded, "is not working alone in this."

"You mean Singleton?" he urged.

"Yes, I am afraid I do," she nodded. "He doesn't like you, Max. He would do you a mischief if he could."

"He is perfectly welcome to try," he said grimly.

"I think he already has," she told him.

He did not pretend to misunderstand her, but simply kissed her soft cheek, saying, "Thank you, Ju."

"For what?" she cocked her head.

"For being such a good friend," he told her.

She looked at him for a moment, saying at length, "You love her very much, don't you?" He made no answer to this, but the look in his eyes told her equally as well. "Yes," she sighed, "I thought so. Which is a great pity," she sighed again, "because it deprives me of all hope."

He smiled and, taking her hand in his, raised it to his lip, "You're an angel, Ju."

"No, I'm not," she told him, laughing. "You of all people should know that!"

He laughed and flicked her cheek with a careless forefinger before leaving her with her own reflections.

Chapter Thirteen

Caroline Marchand, who was blessed with little or no scruples, did not mind owning that she felt far from happy about deceiving the young Marchioness of Deerham. When Singleton had outlined his plans for her husband's downfall, Caroline Marchand had known no hesitation in doing whatever was necessary to help bring it about, but having met his young and innocent wife, she had found herself experiencing second thoughts, even a twinge of conscience. This was certainly a new come out for her. Contrary to even her own expectations, Caroline Marchand had taken no pleasure from deceiving the young marchioness by making her believe that she had lost more than four hundred guineas and had even staked her bracelet as a part payment of the five-and-a-half thousand guineas she had led her to believe she owed. Although she had approved Singleton's forging her IOU, the truth was when actually faced with presenting it to the young marchioness she had almost given in and told her the truth. Why this should be she had no idea, especially when she considered how she stood to lose at least two thousand guineas, Singleton was nothing if not generous.

She had, of course, known the young marchioness's father, the late Earl of Markmoor, very well, indeed she had more than once had the honour of seeing him at her card tables, laying out hundreds of guineas at a time, but it had been obvious from the first that his daughter was by no means like him. Unless Caroline Marchand had miscalculated, and she did not think she had, then she would say that Markmoor's daughter had neither a love nor a feel for the cards, only playing for appearances sake.

She knew that the enmity between Deerham and Singleton was not only of long duration but that it went deep, and although she had no idea what was between them, never having felt inclined to ask him, she now found herself consumed with curiosity. She knew that Singleton was a man who possessed few principles, and that his way of life, apart from being totally ruinous was really quite reprehensible, nothing like his late father at all, but Caroline Marchand owned to having a liking for him. She supposed she had not far to look for the reason; she herself had seen with her own eyes his mother pulling the bracelets off her wrists to cover her stakes, heedless of her reputation and the consequences. As for her son, his reputation certainly went before him; he was a hardened gamester and inveterate womanizer and, like his late crony the Earl of Markmoor, had set the ton alight with their doings. But this matter of Singleton and Deerham worried her, so much so that the more she thought about this scheme of Digby's to fleece Deerham dry by using his wife the more convinced she became that nothing but trouble would come of it, and she was honest enough to admit that she wanted no part of it, and if she could find a way out of it, she would. Of course, it was too late now for self-recrimination, she knew that well enough, the dye had been cast, and therefore all she could do now was to see if the young marchioness would indeed come up with the money.

Caroline Marchand may have met Deerham, though never at her tables, he was far too astute for that, not that he had condescended to speak to her, but she could not claim to having personal knowledge of him. However, she did know that unlike Digby Singleton, Deerham was not only a man of honour but extremely discreet, his affairs having been conducted with the utmost discretion. She knew too that despite his affability there was a reserve to him which made it extremely difficult for one to know what he was thinking, but she felt it reasonably safe to say that should he ever get wind of his wife's dilemma she would not put it past him to come knocking on her door. She had not long to wait for this premonition to be fulfilled.

*

Having left Hertford Street, Deerham strolled round to White's Club where he spent an agreeable hour or so before returning to Grosvenor Square. Upon being told by Clifton in answer to his enquiry that her ladyship had gone out, he merely nodded, then, spending a few minutes with William, who considered the couple of minutes Deerham bestowed upon him not long enough to go through the papers on his desk, left the house.

Julia had told him that she had no idea whether his wife had taken up Caroline Marchand's invitation or not, but when he recalled how pale and drawn she had looked this morning, which went far beyond being the effects of a late night at the Devonshires, he had the sneaking suspicion that she had. If, as he was beginning to believe, Carrie Marchand had lured her to Wimpole Street and she had lost a considerable amount of money at cards, then he could quite understand it. Deerham had seen enough of his wife to know that she was no gamester, indeed she took far more pleasure from looking at the different toilettes being paraded around the rooms than she did in gambling, which meant that either the cards had been marked or her opponent had been cheating. He could only hazard a guess as to why, but he had no reason at all to doubt why she had not told him this morning or, indeed, was ever going to.

Deciding to walk to Wimpole Street instead of calling up a chair or getting Trench to bring his curricle round to the front door, he was soon knocking on the door of number 32, where, after only what seemed to be seconds, it was opened by the butler. Handing him his card he was ushered up the stairs to the drawing-room where he was told that if would care to wait a moment madam would join him, taking the opportunity of looking around him at his surroundings, which were every bit as elegant as he known they would be. He did not have long to wait before Caroline Marchand entered, expensively dressed and elegantly coiffured, her painted face wreathed in smiles, but her eyes were wary. "My lord!" she exclaimed, walking towards him. "This is indeed a surprise."

"Not too unpleasant, I trust," he bowed over her hand.

"Not at all," she smiled, "indeed, I am honoured." She looked up into his face, reading nothing from his inscrutable expression. "Although," she shrugged, "why you should choose to honour me with a visit is more than I can tell."

Upon being informed that the Marquis of Deerham had called and was awaiting her in the drawing-room, Caroline Marchand knew a moment of uneasiness. Like everyone else, she knew he had been at Worleigh, which meant that he had either arrived back yesterday or this morning, in which case she did not think that there had been time for his wife to have told him, which, considering how she would do everything possible to prevent it from coming to Deerham's ears by striving to raise such a sum, was hardly surprising. That she would eventually do so however, had never been in question, either that or he would redeem her so-called IOU the moment he received it, after all wasn't the whole idea to bleed Deerham dry and by means whereby he would be left in no doubt that his wife was indeed her father's daughter? But that he was here now took her a little by surprise.

She had rather hoped that Singleton would grace her card tables last light, but unfortunately he had not done so, which meant that she had not seen him since he left here yesterday morning, and so there had been no opportunity for her to relate her meeting with the young marchioness to him. If she had to face Deerham, then she would much rather do so after consulting with Singleton so she would know precisely what line she should take, but as he had taken her completely by surprise there was nothing for her to do but make the best of it.

"Then allow me to enlighten you," Deerham told her.

"Certainly," she smiled, "but shall we not be seated, my lord?"

"Thank you, no," he nodded, "I do not intend making a long stay."

"Some refreshment, then?" she raised an enquiring eyebrow, to which Deerham politely declined. "So," she shrugged, helplessly, "what is it that brings you here, my lord?"

"My wife," he told her calmly.

"Your wife?" she repeated, incredulously, her eyes widening to their fullest extent.

"Yes," he nodded.

"I don't understand," she shrugged.

"Don't you?" Deerham raised an eyebrow.

"No," she assured him, "I am afraid I don't."

"Then permit me to explain it to you," Deerham told her.

"I... I assure you..." she began, "you have it quite wrong," beginning to feel the ground sink beneath her feet.

"You know I have not," he told her firmly.

"But I... "

"I understand you made her acquaintance a few evenings ago at Bella Biddenham's," Deerham broke in without preamble.

"Bella's?" she repeated.

"Yes. Berkeley Square," he reminded her.

"Yes, I know where she lives," Caroline Marchand said, "but..."

"Where, I understand," he broke in calmly, "you invited her here in order to meet your friends and to talk to her about her grandmother."

How Deerham could possibly know this Caroline Marchand had no idea, particularly as she doubted very much that his wife had spoken to him about this. She needed time to gather her thoughts, but Deerham was not giving her any, and therefore she could only shrug her innocence.

"Her grandmother?" she repeated, astonished. "How could I possibly talk to her about her grandmother when I never knew her?"

"Quite!" Deerham nodded.

"I'm sorry, my lord," she shook her head, "but you move too fast for me. Indeed, I am quite at a loss!"

"I doubt that very much," Deerham told her firmly. When she made no effort to say anything, he told her, "Be in no doubt, if you don't talk to me then you will talk to a magistrate; either way I shall arrive at the truth."

Her eyes flew to his, and what she saw in them was more than enough to tell her that he knew the truth or, if not that, then suspected it. He was not going to grant her the opportunity of playing for time, on the contrary he was in no mood for prevarication, and would not be satisfied with anything but the truth. As for talking to a magistrate, that was the last thing she wanted. So far, her establishment had evaded the notice of the authorities and she for one intended it to remain so. She knew that Singleton would be very far from pleased to know that she had revealed all to the man he was striving to bring to his knees, but Singleton was not here, and in the meantime Deerham was waiting for an answer, and he would not be fobbed off!

"Well?" he urged.

She decided to compromise. "Very well," she shrugged, "I did meet your wife at Bella's."

"And?" he urged again.

"She had the headache," she explained.

"So I understand," he told her. "Go on."

Had Caroline Marchand not been so taken up with trying to combat Deerham's questions she would have wondered how on earth he could possibly know that his wife had had the headache, but heaving a deep sigh and shrugging her shoulders, said, "I followed her into a small saloon where we got talking."

"When you invited her here," Deerham put in coldly. She nodded. "And did she come?"

It would be so easy to lie and say no, but something told Caroline Marchand that this would not answer, besides, she strongly suspected that even though she doubted his wife had told him he already knew she had. "Yes," she nodded, "she came."

"And?" he pressed. When she made no immediate effort to answer him, he said with an inflexibility she could not mistake, "Make up your mind to it ma'am, I am not leaving here until you tell me the whole truth."

Caroline Marchand knew when she was beaten. There was an implacability about Deerham that told her any further refutations would be futile and, after taking a turn around the room, deciding to leave what she would tell Singleton until later, she said, "I did tell her about knowing her grandmother, which is the reason why she came."

"Go on," he urged.

She sighed. "It was obvious from the moment she stepped foot inside that she recognized the kind of establishment it was, but I fobbed her off by telling her that I would talk to her about her grandmother later, so I persuaded her to take a seat at the card table. She didn't want to play, but I made it extremely difficult for her to say no."

To say that Deerham's face looked extremely grim was a gross understatement, but biting down on his anger he demanded coldly, "Who did you get to play with her?"

"Does it matter?" she shrugged.

"Yes," Deerham nodded, "it matters."

It was a moment before Caroline Marchand spoke. She seriously toyed with the idea of not telling him, but as if realizing the futility of it, said, "Cedric Mander, to whom she lost fifty guineas. Then I… I got Frederick Tillson to play next with her, to whom she lost three hundred and fifty guineas." She saw his face harden, but before he could say anything she offered, "If it is of any consolation at all, I doubt very much if she would have lost had she been concentrating on the game instead of wishing she had not come here, as I don't doubt she was, as well as wondering how long it would be before she could leave." She paused a moment, saying, "I told her that she could so easily win it back by either playing again or perhaps even coming here the next night or… or that she could write an IOU – which she did."

Deerham looked horrified. "Two of the most hardened gamesters on the town!" he bit out derisively. "Good God, ma'am," he cried, "in heaven's name why?"

Caroline Marchand was not a woman given over to remorse any more than she was to repining over what could not be mended, even so she did not mind owning that she had not really felt very comfortable about deceiving his wife. Why this should be she had no idea, after all it was not as though this was the first time she had duped an innocent, but there had been something about the young Marchioness of Deerham that had raised a few unexpected qualms in her breast. Her friendship with Digby Singleton went back a very long way, and not surprisingly it was not the first time she had assisted him in something as devious as this, particularly when it meant she received a very handsome reward for doing so, but then she had never before been faced with an indignant husband; a husband who was determined not only to protect his wife but to arrive at the truth, even if it meant taking her before a magistrate, something she was very anxious to avoid. She could all too easily imagine Singleton's annoyance when he learned that such a fat bird as the Marquis of Deerham had escaped his clutches, but when faced with that hard and penetrating stare she really had no choice but to tell him everything.

She swallowed, then, looking directly at him, said, "Can't you guess? To bleed you dry, of course."

His eyes narrowed at this. "To bleed me dry?"

"Yes," she nodded. "Since you seem determined on the truth, then you shall have it," going on to tell him about how she had removed the bracelet from his wife's wrist without her being aware of it and how Singleton had re-written the IOU.

Whatever Deerham had expected it was certainly not this, but so filled with anger was he that it took him several moments to bring it under control, saying ominously, "Singleton."

"Yes," Caroline Marchand sighed.

"And what do you get out of this?" Deerham demanded.

"Two thousand guineas," she told him.

He looked his disgust, but said, "Do you have the bracelet and both IOUs?"

"Yes," she nodded.

"Then I shall relieve you of them," he told her.

She seemed to hesitate, but as if thinking better of arguing she walked over to the escritoire and opened it, where upon she pulled out a drawer and slipped her fingers into it, retrieving both sheets of vellum and the bracelet. "And what of the four hundred guineas?" she wanted to know as she handed them to him.

Raising his eyes from the IOUs he had been reading, he said in a voice of finality, "You may count yourself extremely fortunate that I am not going to take you before the nearest magistrate!"

Casting a glance up into his rather stern face she knew better than to press the point, even though it went very much against the grain with her to say goodbye to four hundred guineas, but asked, "And what shall I tell Singleton?"

"Whatever you wish," Deerham replied curtly, pocketing the IOUs and the bracelet before turning on his heel and letting himself out of the drawing-room.

*

Deerham's unexpected early arrival had thrown Louisa into confusion. She had, of course, expected him home today, but not until this afternoon. At all costs she had to try to keep her distance from him, not only because she was afraid she would inadvertently let him see that she loved him, something she could not allow to happen unless she wanted to see the disgust on his face, but also until this supposed gambling debt had been dealt with, but how to raise such a sum she did not know.

Deerham had certainly seemed to be in excellent spirits this morning when he had come to see her and, if he loved her, she would have been the happiest of women, as it was, she could not allow herself to read more into his kisses other than he was merely doing what was expected of him as her husband. That he had commented upon her rather pale and drawn appearance came as no real surprise to her, after all she had not slept well despite the fact that it had been after two o'clock before she finally got to bed, but that he had actually gone so far as to tell her that she must not be afraid of him, gave her pause for much thought. Had she have known that he had visited one of his past *cheri aimees* who had told him what she had overheard pass between herself and Caroline Marchand she would not have known whether to feel glad or not, all she knew was that the reason for him going out could have been for no other reason than to visit his most pleasurable connection.

With so much weighing on her spirits she was in no mood for keeping any one of her many engagements, but since remaining at home doing nothing but wondering who the barque of frailty was her husband was keeping company with would do no good at all, she decided to attend the alfresco luncheon given by Lady Partington after all. Louisa could not claim to having derived much enjoyment from it even though she was, to all intents and purposes, thoroughly enjoying herself, but at least it was better than sitting alone in an empty house wondering what her husband was doing as well as wracking her brains as to how she could possibly raise five-and-a-half thousand guineas by the end of the week. It was an impossible sum of money to raise, and no matter how she tried she could think of no way of putting her hands on anywhere near the amount Caroline Marchand said she owed. Then there was her bracelet.

She had been shocked when Caroline Marchand had told her what had supposedly happened that night in Wimpole Street, and although Louisa knew that nothing was further from the truth, she could neither think of any reason to account for such duplicity nor how she could refute it. She had certainly written an IOU for four hundred guineas but that IOU stating that she promised to pay the sum of five-and-a-half thousand guineas, whilst it appeared to be in her handwriting, apart from being absolutely certain that it had been forged, she could think of nothing she could do to disprove it.

Yet again, she was assailed with the idea of approaching Christopher, whom she knew would not desert her, but not only had he been faced with the expense of his marriage to Charlotte Laid a little over a month ago, but also he was still trying to bring his estates into order, and therefore the sum of five-and-a-half thousand guineas would be virtually impossible for him to put his hands on. She had then toyed with the idea of visiting a money lender, but after only a very little thought she discarded the idea, not one she was overly keen to do, particularly as she feared the interest she would be expected to pay would be enormous, but she foresaw her debt as ending up as being never ending. With only a few days left to find the money before they presented that IOU to Deerham, despair was fast creeping upon her, and by the time Louisa arrived home midway through the afternoon following that alfresco luncheon she had made up her mind that she really had no choice but to tell him, besides, she could not endure living on her nerves for a moment longer thereby making it necessary for her to lie to Deerham, a circumstance she found totally repugnant. That Deerham would be furiously angry went without saying, in fact she doubted very much that he would believe her, after all it was a fantastic story to expect him to swallow, but that he would pay the debt she was in no doubt, but she could not help feeling that he would more angry to be faced with an IOU without any warning and to which she had said nothing. Either way it would certainly bode no good for future relations between them, indeed it would merely serve to convince him that she was indeed her father's daughter in every sense, something that, for some reason, made her want to cry her heart out.

Waiting only until Clifton had closed the front door behind her, she swallowed, asking, not a little nervously, "Has his lordship returned home, Clifton?"

"Yes, your ladyship," he inclined his head. "He is in his book room," to which she nodded.

Removing her hat and placing it on the table, she walked to the rear of the hall on legs that felt remarkably unsteady, tapping on the mahogany door and, in answer to his "Come in," she opened it and stepped inside.

Deerham, who was standing by the window in the process of repairing the nib of his pen, paused as he looked up and saw her, a smile lighting his eyes. "Tell me, my dear, how do you always contrive to look so charmingly?"

Well, if nothing else, this was certainly a most promising start, but it had the effect of bringing the colour flooding to Louisa's cheeks and, casting a glance down at her gown, her cares momentarily forgotten, said, "Do you really think so?"

"Most assuredly," he told her, a laugh in his voice.

"I... I am so glad you think so," she faltered.

"I do," he told her gently, laying his pen down on the desk.

She gave a little smile, then, taking a few faltering steps nearer to the desk, not at all certain how to begin telling him her tale, which was as entangled as it was unbelievable, said, in something of a rush, "Actually, Max, I... I wondered if you could spare me a moment."

"As many as you please," he smiled, knowing perfectly well what was on her mind and what had brought her here now.

Having rehearsed what she would say to him was one thing, but when actually faced with doing so was quite another. Sitting down on the chair he pulled out for her, she looked down at her folded hands on her lap, then, tentatively, stole a look at him, reclining at his ease in his chair, which, to one in her disordered state of mind did not make her task any the easier. Then, taking a deep breath, said, "I... I have something to tell you, but I...

I am very much afraid it will make you very angry."

"Will it?" he raised an amused eyebrow.

"Yes, I... I'm afraid it will," she managed, casting another look down at her hands. "Y-you see, Max," she began hesitantly, raising her eyes to his face, "I... I have done something that is really quite reprehensible."

"Have you?" he asked politely.

"Yes," she nodded, relapsing into distressed silence as she sought for the words in which to tell him that she wanted five-and-a-half thousand guineas from him in order to pay a gaming debt, but try as she did, she could find none.

"Well," he offered, when she made no immediate effort to enlarge on her explanation, "in the absence of any further information, I can only hazard a guess as to what it is you have done that you consider to be quite reprehensible."

The lightness in his voice made her look at him, and what she saw in those dark grey eyes filled her with the hope that he would understand, even so, it did not make what she had to say any the easier. She shifted a little uncomfortably on her chair, her fingers beginning to agitatedly pull at a bow on her gown, little realizing that the man patiently watching her wanted nothing more than to take her in his arms and kiss away her fears and absurdities. She raised her head, then, drawing in a deep breath, said, "The... the other night I... I went to Lady Biddenham's."

"Ah, yes," Deerham nodded, "I was wondering if you enjoyed the evening."

"Yes... yes, I did," she nodded, "but whilst I was there, I got the headache, and... well, you see, Max," she told him falteringly, "I found it necessary to sit quietly in a small saloon until it passed over."

"Quite understandable," he remarked.

"Yes, well, you see it... it was while I was there that I... I was joined by someone – a woman."

"Indeed!" he raised an eyebrow.

"Yes," she nodded. "I... I had no idea that she had seen me leave the main saloons, so I was quite surprised to find myself being addressed by her." She paused and swallowed. "Y-you see," she explained, "she told me that she recognized me immediately and that she knew my grandmother."

"Really!" he raised another eyebrow.

"Y-yes," she nodded. "So, you see, Max," she explained, "when she told me that, th-there seemed to be no reason why I should not believe her."

"No reason at all," he said calmly.

"No," she nodded, heartened by this unruffled response, "well, then she went on to tell me that she was a w-widow and that she had lately been l-living quietly in the country and had only j-just recently returned to town." She swallowed a little uncomfortably. "Then she told me that she was h-holding a little soirée at her home in Wimpole Street the following evening and that she would very m-much like me to attend so she could talk to me about my g-grandmother and I could meet her friends."

"Most thoughtful of her," he remarked.

"Yes, it was, at least," she hastily amended, "I... I thought so."

"So you went," he said quietly.

Louisa nodded. "Yes, I did, but I was very soon w-wishing I had not."

"Why was that?" he asked softly.

The mere recollection was enough to make Louisa shudder, and it was therefore several moments before she spoke. "I... I gained the very strong impression that it... it was nothing but a gaming hell."

If she expected Deerham to show surprise at this she was very much mistaken, considerably taken aback when he said calmly, "I know it is."

She stared at him in some surprise, repeating, faintly, "You know it is?"

"Yes," he nodded.

It was then she saw him lean forward slightly and open the drawer of his desk, staring in utter disbelief as he pulled out her bracelet and two sheets of vellum which he placed on top of the desk. Her eyes flew from his face to her bracelet and the two sheets of vellum lying on his desk then back to his face, shock tinged with immense relief flooding through her at the same time.

"You know!" she cried in a choked voice, to which he nodded. "B-But, Max," she managed, "how? I... I don't understand," she shook her head.

"I know because Carrie Marchand told me how she tricked you," he told her gently.

She stared at him in disbelief. "She told you! B-but when?"

"This afternoon," he nodded.

She looked at him in patent surprise, exclaiming, "Why? I mean..."

"Because I gave her a choice," he smiled.

"A... a choice?" she queried, feeling just a little bemused.

"Yes," he nodded. "I told her that she could either tell me the truth or she could do so to a magistrate."

Her eyes widened in surprise at this and, turning a startled face towards him, said, "A magistrate?"

"Yes," he smiled.

"B-but never tell me you paid five-and-a-half thousand guineas for them?" she cried, horrified.

"No," he shook his head, a smile touching his lips. "I did not even pay four hundred guineas for them."

Utterly confounded, Louisa could do no more than stare at him. "But, Max," she eventually shook her head, "I don't understand. H-how did you know? And why should she want to trick me in the first place?"

"To get back at me," he said simply.

"To get back at you?" she repeated aghast.

"Yes," he nodded. "It appears that Digby Singleton brewed this little scheme with her to make me pay."

She looked her stupefaction. She had suspected all along that Singleton had no liking for Deerham, but that he would go to such lengths shocked her. "But Max..." she shook her head.

"It's all right," he soothed, "I can more than adequately deal with Singleton."

A frown creased her forehead. "But Max, he..."

"Let us just say," he smiled, not pretending to misunderstand her, "that he is certainly welcome to try."

She nodded, then, taking a deep breath asked, "But how did you know about this?"

"Let us just say," he told her, "that I am greatly indebted to an old friend."

She looked a little wary, "An... an old friend?" she managed.

"Yes," he nodded. "She wrote me a letter while I was at Worleigh informing me that she had seen Caroline Marchand approach you at Bella Biddenham's, and thinking that I would not like my wife being associated with her, she thought I should know."

"She?" Louisa said faintly, her colour a little high, feeling her heart sink.

"Yes," Max smiled, "but she need not worry you in any way, I promise you. In the meantime," he advised, "I suggest you put your bracelet away," handing it to her, "while I shall get rid of these," indicating the IOUs on his desk. He watched her put her bracelet into her pocket, then getting to his feet he walked round the desk to stand in front of her, taking her hands in his and drawing her to her feet.

She looked a little curiously up at him, asking tentatively, "Who is this woman?"

"Someone you don't know or are ever likely to, but indeed," he nodded, "I stand very much in her debt."

Louisa sniffed. "Yes, I... I understand."

"Poor Louisa," Deerham said softly, raising her hands to his lips. "You must have had a dreadful time of it, but I am glad you told me."

She looked up at him, her eyes filling with tears. "Oh, Max, I... I was quite frantic with worry. I knew that I had not gambled away such a sum, but I had no way of refuting it. Then she... she told me that if the debt was not paid by the end of the week, she would have no alternative but to put the matter before you. I... I could not allow that to happen so I decided to tell you, even at the risk of you thinking that I was indeed..." she could get no further.

"Your father's daughter?" he supplied gently, to which she nodded. "It would take more than this to make me believe such a thing," he told her in a deep voice.

"It would?" she sniffed.

"Very much so," he told her tenderly. He looked down into her flushed face, but just as he was on the point of lowering his head to enable him to kiss her, a tap was heard on the door followed by the entrance of William.

"Oh, I beg pardon," he cried, looking from one to the other, a little discomfited.

Louisa, her nerves in shreds as well as being extremely fearful of giving herself away to the man she loved, needed time alone, and therefore took the opportunity of William's unexpected entrance to pull her hands out of Deerham's, saying, "I shall leave you with William." Then, casting a glance up at Deerham, said, "Thank you," before hurrying out of the room.

It was several moments before Deerham moved, then, turning to William, sighed, "Your timing, dear boy, is nothing if not impeccable!"

Chapter Fourteen

Digby Singleton, arriving in Wimpole Street later that evening, was in an extremely buoyant frame of mind, and, as expected, Caroline Marchand's drawing-room was as full as it could hold of guests playing cards. Casting a glance around the room through his eye-glass, his eye eventually alighted on his hostess, dressed in purple lustring and bedecked in jewellery with her hair elegantly coiffured, and as a connoisseur of women he had to admit that she really was quite a magnificent creature.

It was not many minutes before her eye fell upon him and, raising a hand, he tip-toed his way across the room to her side, dressed in a delicate shade of yellow with a diamond pin which glinted in the intricate folds of his cravat from the lights in the chandeliers, and a ruby signet ring sat on the little finger of his left hand. Making an exquisite bow, he smiled, "Your slave!" releasing her hand.

She laughed and tapped him over the knuckles with her furled fan, saying, "I seriously doubt that, but I'm glad you are here. There is something of some moment I need to discuss with you."

"Indeed!" he raised a pencilled eyebrow.

"Yes," she nodded, "but not here."

He cast another glass around the crowded drawing-room, "I am yours to command, my dear Carrie," he drawled, "but where do you suggest?"

"Come with me," she told him.

He followed her out of the drawing room and into a small sitting room at the rear of the house on the first floor, bowing his head slightly as he opened it to allow her to pass through. "But how charming!" he cried, eyeing his surroundings of pale blue satin with matching curtains with evident approval.

"I am glad you think so," she dismissed.

"I do," he said sincerely. "You have always had excellent taste, my dear

Carrie."

"Thank you," she bowed her head mockingly. She eyed him for a moment, then, as if deciding that it was no use delaying relating the bad news to him, told him about Deerham's visit that morning and what had resulted from it. Beneath his powder and rouge Singleton's face paled, and the black patch at the corner of his mouth twitched as it tautened, his eyes narrowing.

Without giving him time to say anything, she told him, "I know you don't like it, and neither do I if it comes to that, but there was nothing I could do so it's no use laying this in my dish. I have no wish to stand before a magistrate any more than you do."

"So," Singleton mused after getting his temper under control, completely disregarding her comment about a magistrate, "Deerham walks away with the bracelet and both IOUs without paying a penny!"

"You may believe me when I tell you," Caroline Marchand told him, "that his visit was most unforeseen, not at all what I expected, indeed, he took me completely by surprise, but I can tell you this," she nodded, "I was truly shocked at just how much he knew, although how he could I don't know. What was I to do?" she shrugged.

"What indeed?" Singleton purred, removing his snuff-box from his pocket and taking a pinch, his eyes narrowing as he pondered the situation. He could not really blame Carrie, even so he could not help feeling aggrieved that she had given way so easily, but he supposed that in fairness to her she had been placed in an impossible position, besides, he knew Deerham too well into thinking that he would believe her denials. But if nothing else, he certainly walked away with the honours, and not for the first time. He really was becoming a thorn in his flesh, so much so that paying him back in his own coin had become something of an obsession with Singleton, and nothing short of seeing him grovel on his knees would satisfy him.

So, how did Deerham know what was going forward in the first place? The question teased his mind for some considerable time, and not until Carrie broke into his thoughts announcing that she must not neglect her guests, did he focus his attention on her.

"A thousand pardons, my dear," he smiled.

"Are you going to play?" she asked.

He thought a moment, saying at length, "You must forgive me, my dear, but I must be taking my leave of you."

She wondered what he was going to do, but since no words of hers would either deter him or persuade him to take his seat at the card tables she merely made her way back to the drawing-room to join her guests.

*

Louisa, having made her escape from the book room, ran up the stairs to her room where she flung herself down on the bed to enjoy a hearty bout of tears. She was, of course, immensely relieved to find herself free of her dilemma and in a way that had not cost one penny to retrieve either her bracelet or those IOUs, and just as relieved to know that Deerham did not think ill of her or believed she was truly her father's daughter, but the pain around her heart in knowing that one of his past *cheri aimees*, because nothing would convince her otherwise, had written to him was like a lead weight. He had told her that this woman need not worry her, but the one currently enjoying his patronage most certainly did. She knew that Deerham had been on the point of kissing her before William had entered the book room, and although she was not at all certain whether to be glad or not at his interruption, the fact remained that Deerham did not love her. Her mamma had told her that it was only to be expected that Deerham would continue to seek his pleasures outside of the marriage, and that it was something that need not concern her, but loving him the way she did it was a like a knife cutting through her heart. It was only to be expected that Deerham would continue to conduct his affairs with the same discretion he had always done, but it did nothing to stop her from imagining some exquisitely beautiful creature entwining her arms around his neck, inviting his kisses and caresses, after all, wasn't Deerham a connoisseur when it came to women?

Not surprisingly, it was some considerable time before Louisa's tears subsided sufficiently for her to allow Mary to dress her and powder her hair in readiness for the opera this evening, to which Deerham was escorting her and Letitia. If Louisa was being honest, she would have much preferred to have stayed at home, but Letitia was looking forward to it, indeed, only today at Lady Partington's alfresco luncheon she had told her that she could not wait to attend her first opera, so there was really nothing Louisa could do but acquiesce.

If Louisa thought that dinner that evening alone with Deerham would be a severe trial she was very much mistaken. He conversed easily and placed no demands upon her, even going so far as not to mention what had taken place between them this afternoon, rendering her more comfortable and enabling her to take part in whatever conversation was inaugurated.

But Deerham was neither blind nor stupid. Just one look at her face when she arrived downstairs was enough to tell him that she had been enjoying a hearty bout of tears. He could well imagine her panic and alarm upon discovering that Caroline Marchand had deceived her, not only about knowing her grandmother the late Countess of Halford, but also into believing that she had lost five-and-a-half thousand guineas, handing over her bracelet as security, instead of the four hundred guineas she had actually lost and that there was no way she could possibly put her hands on such a sum, as well as her relief upon learning that her bracelet and IOUs had been retrieved without handing over a penny, but there was an air of despondency about Louisa that went far deeper than that; a despondency which, unless he was very much mistaken, bore all the hallmarks of unrequited love. After four months of marriage he was reluctantly brought to admit that Louisa was no more in love with him now than she had ever been. Admittedly, she had never once repulsed his advances, but she had never deliberately courted them either, and yet there had been times when he could have sworn he had seen something in her eyes to contradict this belief. Of course, it could have been nothing more than a trick of the light, but if nothing else it certainly gave him hope that there may well be a future for them after all.

Louisa was no beauty, but there was nevertheless something very attractive about her. Whether it was the way her eyes would light up on the instant or her mischievous sense of the ridiculous would bring forth that irresistible choke of laughter he did not know, all he did know was that he could not live without her. As far as Louisa taking a lover was concerned, although he tried to dismiss this out of hand as being wholly ridiculous, he could not totally discount it, after all, didn't she bear all the hallmarks of unrequited love as well as casting off his escort within weeks of returning from their honeymoon? He knew she had her regular court, which was considered de rigueur in the circles in which they moved, most of whom he knew he very well, but he did not think that her lover, if indeed she had one, would be one of them. The thought caused him acute pain, but as he was not the type of man to wear his heart on his sleeve no one setting eyes on him as he sat with Louisa and Letitia Rawnsley in their box at the opera would have had the least guess.

Unlike Louisa, whose mind was not fully on the opera being played out in front of her but on the man sitting beside her, a man who did not love her or ever would, Letitia thoroughly enjoyed herself, so much so that she told Deerham so in the interval, to which he laughed and flicked her cheek with a careless forefinger. So far, it seemed as though she had not associated Deerham with her knight errant, but as the evening wore on, it certainly obtruded on her consciousness. There was something about his voice, something quite familiar to which she could not put her finger on, that made her begin to wonder. Her rescuer had been determined to shield his face as well as his identity from her, but she remembered those dark grey eyes, reminiscent of Deerham's, and as she turned sideways to look at him, putting him under brief but intense scrutiny, she became ever more convinced that her knight errant was none other than her host. Feeling himself coming under intense scrutiny Deerham glanced across at Letitia, and upon comprehending the recognition in those pansy brown eyes, he gave her an infinitesimal shake of the head and a warning look. Clearly, he had not told Louisa, for reasons which Letitia could only guess at, but she was determined to speak to him before the evening was out. The opportunity came as they were about to leave the theatre. As Louisa had met an acquaintance and was briefly engaged in talking to her, Letitia looked up at Deerham and smiled, forestalling the words on his lips,

"I promise I shan't say a word to a soul, but I am glad to be able to thank you for what you did for me."

Since it was useless to deny it, Deerham looked down at the lovely face looking mischievously up at him, and smiled, "Well, now you know, I should be greatly obliged if you would keep it to yourself."

"Yes, of course," she said eagerly, "but at least now I can put a face to my knight errant."

He was just about to disabuse her mind of such a thing when Louisa came up to them, whereupon Deerham escorted both ladies outside to the waiting carriage.

*

The Dowager Countess of Pitlone meanwhile, whilst owning to being extremely pleased with Letitia's friendship with Louisa, a young lady who was as different to her father as anyone could be, was, unfortunately, unable to say the same of her brother, Algernon, and his continued friendship with Digby Singleton. She may not be one who believed in hanging a parent's mantle around the neck of their children, but Singleton's mother had been just such a one, clearly passing her traits on to her son, a man who had formed a firm friendship with the late Earl of Markmoor and setting the town alight with their scandals and indiscretions. Singleton was celebrated as much for his gambling as he was for his womanizing, both of which would be the ruin of him, indeed his face already bore all the signs of his hedonistic way of life, and she for one was therefore determined to wean her nephew away from his company. So far, very little damage had been done to Algernon's fortune, but she could not fool herself into thinking that continued association with Singleton would prove either healthy or profitable, indeed, prolonged association with him could only result in Algernon's ruin.

But Algernon was as headstrong as he was stubborn and just as reckless with his money, but she could not delude herself into believing that continued association with Singleton would not eventually bring an abbey to an eggshell. Algernon's father had been an extremely wealthy man, who not only left his daughters, Jane and Letitia, a considerable fortune, making them both notable heiresses, but his son rich enough to buy an abbey as the saying went. He was the proud owner of a considerable property in

Wiltshire, where his mother resided with her unmarried daughter, Jane, a sizeable mansion in Berkeley Square and a hunting box in Leicestershire, which, if all the dowager countess had heard was true, he used more for throwing parties for his friends and their barques of frailty than he did for hunting. But such a way of life could not continue!

As Deerham had rightly predicted, relations between the two households were somewhat fraught; Algernon believing that he was of an age whereby he needed neither advice nor counsel, and the dowager, believing it to be her task of bringing her nephew to a sense of his responsibilities, were destined on a collision course. The dowager made every allowance for a young man sowing his wild oats and visiting establishments which, she was glad to say, had never come in her way, but it was becoming increasingly apparent that Algernon's predilection for low company was causing her grave concern. She knew it was useless to request his mamma's intervention, her sister-in-law seemingly more concerned with her own imaginary ailments to give a moment's thought to her offspring, but the dowager could not help but think that even she would be astonished at her son's way of life. Algernon certainly did not inherit his wayward traits and inclinations from his father, but since he had come into the title she had noticed more and more of how self-willed he really was, and that any remonstrance was merely guaranteed to set his back up and encourage him to commit even more folly.

The dowager, who was ten years older than her late husband's sister, had accepted the responsibility of looking after Letitia for the season simply that her mother, or so she had claimed, was far too frail with her nerves to even consider chaperoning her daughter through the exigencies of a London season. The dowager, being of a very different school, had no time for such megrims, indeed it would give her tremendous satisfaction to speak very plainly to her sister-in-law, but since that lady could be guaranteed to withdraw to the seclusion of her bedchamber on the pretext that her health had taken a downward turn, thereby evading any confrontation, the dowager knew it was pointless. Nevertheless, she had a fondness for her niece, and therefore she had known no qualms in taking on the responsibility of chaperoning her from one party to another, but whilst she was more than ready to indulge her, this evening she had been more than happy to relinquish her into the care of the Deerhams by escorting her to the opera.

As expected, Letitia came to see her before retiring to her own room, bursting exuberantly into her bedchamber without even tapping on the door, hurrying up to the big four-poster and kissing her aunt's cheek before sitting down on the edge of the bed. Time and the ravages of ruthlessly applying cosmetic aids to her face had taken their toll on the dowager, turning a once beautiful countenance into a lined mask, making her look far older than she really was, but Letitia, who was in high spirits, cared not one jot for this, taking the bony hand in her own and raising it to her cheek. "Oh, Aunt," she cried, "I have had the most wonderful time!"

"So I see," the dowager commented, her eagle eyes raking over her niece's flushed and glowing face, "but why you must come bursting into my bedchamber like a hoyden I know not."

Letitia giggled and kissed her aunt's palm, going on to tell her about the opera and how much she had enjoyed it. "I wish you had been there," she told her fervently.

"I daresay," the dowager nodded, "but I'm far too old to be gadding about town!"

Letitia, who knew perfectly well that her aunt always fell back on this excuse when she did not want to do something, merely laughed. "Jane told me you said the same thing to her."

"Your sister," the dowager replied tartly, "was a moonling; as anyone with only half a mind would have known. She didn't take. As I told your mamma she would not." She twitched her shawl. "Two seasons I had of it with her, and for what?" she demanded. "As for you, you minx," she told her, the smile in her eyes at variance with the tartness of voice, "I have already had to see off I don't know how many gazetted fortune hunters! Been leading them astray, have you?"

"I didn't ask them to make up to me, Aunt," she told her truthfully. "Indeed, I did not."

"There's no need to tell me that," she nodded, "but if that brother of yours had anything about him he would take care whom you met when I am not there with you as well as being the one to set them straight that you are not a fat pigeon for their plucking instead of leaving me to do it for him."

Since Algernon had already proved how inadequate he was in both these departments, or, rather, more than happy to relinquish his responsibilities, believing it was all right to leave his sister in the care of a man like Digby Singleton and his aunt to send the hopeful to the right about, Letitia decided not to comment on it, but said instead, "Algernon has a great many engagements, Aunt."

"Yes," she nodded, "and we both know what they are. Now, puss," she admonished, "you may kiss me goodnight. It's way past my bedtime," to which her roguish niece dutifully did as she was told.

The following morning, within minutes of the breakfast cups being removed, Turnbridge, the dowager's very correct and stately butler, announced her nephew, standing aside to allow him to walk into the drawing-room. She was not expecting him, but as she had every intention of writing him a note asking him to call upon her, this visit would serve just as well.

"Well, nevvy," she cried as soon as the door had closed behind Turnbridge, eyeing him closely with that eagle-like stare which always rendered him acutely uncomfortable, "to what do I owe this visit? Not that I'm not pleased to see you," holding out her hand.

Algernon kissed it punctiliously, stating, "Oh," he shrugged, "just came to see how you do, ma'am."

The fifth Viscount Dustan was a tall and slender young man approaching his twenty-fifth year, whose delicately painted face did not quite hide the effects of last night's indulgences, a circumstance that did not escape that lady's eye. He was dressed in the very height of fashion, with a heavy fall of lace at his wrists and throat, out of which glistened a diamond pin, and on the little finger of his left hand he wore an emerald signet ring. Around his neck was draped a black ribbon, on the end of which was an eye-glass, and a fob hung from his heavily embroidered waistcoat, and his hair, which was neatly tied in the back of his neck with a black bow, was dark blond.

It had been some appreciable time since he visited in Cavendish Square, his many engagements keeping him pretty well occupied, but he had heard enough from Letitia to know that his aunt was not best pleased with him, and therefore decided to call upon her this morning, concluding the sooner he did his duty by her the better. He had a very shrewd idea of what he could expect, but as he considered himself to be way past the age of rendering himself accountable, especially to an aunt who delighted in taking advantage of her advancing years, he had no intention of giving an account of himself.

"It's been an age since I saw you last," she told him forthrightly, "so I suppose I should count myself fortunate that you are here now." She saw a slight frown crease his forehead, but ignoring this, asked, "How are you?"

The frown lifted, and he shrugged, "Oh, toll-loll!"

She could not deny that her nephew was an exceedingly handsome young man whose whole appearance was guaranteed to please the ladies, but what he needed was a wife; a good woman who would soon put a stop to his gadding about town and getting up to all manner of waywardness, but when she pointed this out to him the last time they had spoken, he told her in no uncertain terms that he had no wish to become leg-shackled, and he would thank her not to mention it again, and wisely decided to keep her views on this to herself for now.

He cast himself into a chair and began to play idly with his eye-glass, and said, determined not to allow her to either get the upper hand or reduce him to schoolboy status, "So, how *do* you do, ma'am?"

"I do very well," she told him.

"I must say," he remarked, "you look to be in high force."

"I can't imagine why," she told him, forthrightly.

Deeming it wise not to respond to this, he asked, "Where's Letitia?"

"Gone to Richmond Park with a group of friends," she told him. "I don't expect her back for a couple of hours at least."

As if suddenly remembering his responsibilities where his sister was concerned, he raised a questioning eyebrow, "Who are these friends?"

"The Simpson sisters and Lady Margaret Tomalty," she told him.

"Quite unexceptional, then," he commented.

"Of course they are," she nodded. "Do you think I'd let your sister go careering all over with someone I don't know?"

Deeming it wise not to respond to this, recognizing the signs that she was becoming rather quarrelsome, he asked, "How is she?"

"In high gig," she said.

He nodded. "Well, that's hardly surprising. I always knew she was a taking little thing."

"Ay, she's taking right enough," she told him candidly. "I've already had to see off several fortune hunters, which," she added bluntly, "should rightly be down to you as her legal guardian. Where have you been these past few weeks?"

He eyed her speculatively for a moment or two, not liking the way she was criticizing him, but shrugged, "Here and there."

"You don't mean to tell me, is that it?" she shot out. "Well, if all I hear about you is true that's not surprising."

He looked a little closely at her, saying warily, "I'm not sure I know what you mean, ma'am."

"Ha!" she cried. "The devil you don't!"

A crease furrowed his forehead. "If I may say so, ma'am," he rebuked, "that kind of expression is far from appropriate from one such as yourself."

"I ain't one of your namby-pamby modern misses, boy," she told him firmly, "so don't think you can ride grub over me!"

"I wasn't about to try, ma'am," he told her, affronted.

"Just as well," she nodded, "because you'd catch cold at that. Well," she demanded, "what *have* you to say for yourself in answer to the tales I hear?"

"People are far too busy," he snapped.

"Of course they are," she told him. "What else can you expect when you don't behave as you should?"

He had the grace to colour up at this, but said, "You shouldn't listen to gossip, ma'am."

"Perhaps I wouldn't," she told him, "if it came from someone other than Ponsonby and Winchelsea."

"What have they been saying?" he demanded, sitting forward a little in his chair, knowing perfectly well that they were old cronies of his aunt.

"Only that you've been going the pace a bit of late. Not that I needed them to tell me that," she nodded, to which he threw her a speaking look. "Don't think I don't know about these parties you throw at that hunting box of yours in Leicestershire!"

"Bachelor fare, ma'am," he dismissed, irritably.

"And the late night sessions at White's," she added.

"What of them?" he shrugged.

"I hear they bet heavily there," she told him.

"I can afford it," he shrugged.

"Yes," she nodded, "but how long for?"

"So," he bit out, "it's my fortune that is worrying you, is it?"

"Yes, and so it should you," she bit out. When he made no immediate answer to this, she said abruptly, "And then there's these gaming sessions you become involved in with Singleton."

"So," he mused, rising hastily to his feet, "we're back at him, are we? I might have known it!"

"I expect you might," she told him strictly.

His painted lips thinned, saying tautly, "For the last time, ma'am, there's nothing wrong with Singleton. Why, you may meet him everywhere!"

"Not everywhere," she reminded him.

"If you mean those starched-up tabbies who call friends with you, then no," he bit out.

"No, I don't," she nodded, "but you won't meet him at the Devonshires nor the Scott-Pearces, nor a dozen others such," she told him, "and with good reason. He's bad ton."

"Bad ton?" he cried astonished. "Why, his parentage is as good as any you care to mention."

"On his father's side, certainly," she agreed, "but his mother, as all the world knows, was a nobody."

"Sheer prejudice, ma'am," he told her.

"He'll ruin you," she told him inexorably.

"Nonsense!" he cried, irritated.

"Nonsense is it?" she cried, rising to her feet. "He's not only an established womanizer but a hardened gamester whose reputation is the talk of the ton! Why," she exclaimed, "he's been the downfall of more than one young man in your circumstances!"

"And why should all of this worry you?" he demanded. "I suppose you have been corresponding with m'mother!"

"Ha! Much notice she'd take if I did tell her!" she scorned. "More interested in her so-called frail state of health than her children."

"Let me remind you, ma'am," he told her, holding on to his temper with an effort, "that I am not a child accountable to you or anyone!"

"I know you're not," she snapped, "which is why it is about time you started taking your responsibilities as Viscount Dunstan a little more seriously!"

"Are you saying that I have brought my name into disrepute?" he demanded.

"Not yet, you haven't," she told him candidly.

"No, and nor will I!" he told her angrily.

"I'm relieved to hear it," she nodded, "but continued association with Singleton and his ilk will soon put paid to that!"

"Much you know about it!" he told her pettishly.

"When did you last visit your estates?" she asked abruptly.

"Let me remind you, ma'am," he told her a little tautly, touched on the raw by this unexpectedly direct question, "that you are not my mother nor my legal guardian."

"A pity for you I'm not," she told him, totally unabashed by this reminder. "Well?" she demanded.

He shrugged an impatient shoulder. "Biddersley does everything that needs to be done."

"A good thing too," she bit out, "since you seem to have neither the time nor the inclination to show your face!"

"I would advise you, ma'am," he warned her, his colour a little high beneath his powder and rouge, "to content yourself with looking after Letitia and to be a little less busy with my affairs."

"That's the one thing it seems I can't do, since you don't busy yourself with them!" she told him tartly.

"In case you had forgotten, ma'am," he pointed out impatiently, "I came here to see how you go on, not to receive a lecture!"

"Perhaps if you conducted yourself with a modicum of discernment and moderation I wouldn't have to," she told him.

The fact that there was more than an element of truth in what his aunt said did not make it any more palatable hearing, to which his rather heightened colour testified, but since arguing with her was as pointless as it was a waste of time, he merely raised a questioning eyebrow, saying, "If there is nothing else you wish to say to me, ma'am, I will take my leave of you."

"There is," she nodded, "but since you deem your engagements to be more important, I shall not detain you by telling you what they are," whereupon she held out her hand to him.

"Your servant, ma'am," he bowed over her hand, before turning on his heel and leaving her.

The dowager, whose spleen was by no means assuaged, could not fool herself into thinking that her nephew had taken notice of what she had said. If she was honest, she had to admit that Algernon was far too young and heedless to take advice from older and wiser heads, but that the path he had set his feet on was ruinous, she was convinced. She doubted very much whether any words of hers would see a termination in his friendship with Digby Singleton, a man who, like his mother before him, had neither the time nor the inclination to give a moment's thought about what people thought of him, but as the dowager resumed her seat, rapidly strumming her fingers on the arms of her chair, she strove, for the umpteenth time, to think of a way of weaning her nephew from his destructive influence.

Chapter Fifteen

It was not to be expected that Algernon would take his aunt's advice and warnings in good part, on the contrary he was considerably annoyed by them, so much so that by the time he arrived at White's his vexation was by no means abated. She was his father's only surviving sister and, as such, he held her in no little respect, but this tendency she had of taking him to task whenever she felt like it was too much to be borne, indeed, he was considerably rankled by it. He was neither answerable to her for his actions nor required her permission for whatever he may choose to do, on the contrary he was his own master, had been for three years, and therefore free to come and go as he pleased as well as choosing his own friends, but how to combat her sharp tongue or make her see that he was at liberty to live his own life without censure, had him at a loss.

As for her disparagement of Digby Singleton, it was nothing but prejudice. Clearly, she did not know him; only of his so-called reputation. Admittedly, he was an inveterate womanizer and a hardened gamester and one who seemed to live continually on the precipice of financial ruin, leaving him totally reliant on his winnings, but his skill at the cards had never been brought into question, indeed, he was a most proficient and experienced player. Algernon owned that his own skill at cards fell very far short to that of Singleton, in fact, apart from that time when he had played piquet with him the evening following his duel when he had lost two thousand guineas to him he had only lost a few hundred guineas at any number of games they had engaged in since, but what was that, after all? For a man of his fortune he could well afford it! And as for playing at White's, why, everyone did so! including the swells like Wellesley-Pole, Ponsonby, Devonshire and Deerham. Of course, the rules were fixed, but it was unexceptionable!

When it came to his other pastimes, Algernon did not mind acknowledging that he had been taken somewhat by surprise to learn that his aunt knew about those parties he gave at his hunting lodge in Leicestershire, and could only hazard a guess as to how she knew, easily discounting her informants as being either Ponsonby or Winchelsea as the only time they set foot outside White's was when they went home to change their dress. When he had told his aunt that it was nothing but bachelor fare, he had meant it, it was true; besides, the kind of female he associated with would neither cry rope nor expect matrimony. He had no intention of getting leg-shackled yet, which is what she clearly intended for him, but the trouble was that making up to a young woman from his own rank of society could lead to all manner of misinterpretation, not the least being from her mamma, who would easily set aside the fact that he was fast acquiring the reputation of being a rake and a care-for-nobody, besides, he was enjoying himself far too much to get tied down yet.

It was perhaps as well for his aunt's peace of mind that she had no idea that one of the first people her nephew would meet upon entering White's was Digby Singleton, a man he had no hesitation in describing as a right one, and it was therefore with the greatest alacrity that Algernon accepted his invitation to not only join him for luncheon but to embark on a game of cards afterwards.

*

His sister, meanwhile, returned to Cavendish Square in high gig, enthusiastically telling her aunt all about her excursion to Richmond Park and the many compliments she had received, to which that formidable lady merely flicked her cheek with a careless forefinger and calling her a pert minx, in response to which Letitia laughed and kissed her heavily powdered cheek. The dowager, who had taken on the chaperoning of her niece for the season with eagerness, a young lady whom she held in sincere affection, was nevertheless beginning to feel the effects of accompanying her all over, and had therefore not been sorry to relinquish Letitia into the care of the Simpson sisters and the young Lady Margaret Tomalty and her betrothed to Richmond Park. Nor, if she was honest, was she sorry to be able to shelve her responsibilities as chaperon this evening at the Inglebys' ball, knowing perfectly well that she would come to no harm in the care of the young Marchioness of Deerham, a young woman the dowager strongly favoured.

But if Letitia was looking forward to the evening ahead, Louisa was not so enthusiastic, indeed, if it were not for her young friend she would be strongly tempted to cry off. She had thoroughly enjoyed the opera last night, especially as she had been relieved of what had become an intolerable burden, and Deerham had been at his most amusing, but she had been hardly able to hide her disappointment when he had informed her this morning that he would not be accompanying her to the Inglebys' ball as he had a prior engagement. She tried not to think of what his prior engagement was, but it nevertheless preyed on her mind all the evening.

As Louisa had fully expected, the Inglebys' ball was nothing but a sad crush, but Letitia, wide-eyed and pink cheeked with excitement, claimed that it was a most splendid evening, did not her friend think so?

"Why yes, of course," Louisa smiled.

Letitia looked closely at her. "I am so glad, because you see," she told her, tucking a confiding hand into Louisa's, "I did think that you were not really enjoying the evening."

Louisa shook her head and disclaimed, but by the time she returned to Grosvenor Square she was not sorry the evening was over, although whether this was because Deerham had not been with her or because she could not prevent herself from wondering where he was and who he was with, she was not at all sure.

A visit from her mamma the following afternoon did very little to raise her spirits. Having taken the decision to return to Markmoor Manor for a while she called upon her daughter to apprise her of it, saying, "I don't know why it is, my love," she shook her head, "but I feel the rigours of town life to be more fatiguing than ever I remember."

"Must you leave, Mamma?" Louisa felt impelled to ask.

"Well, my love," she told her, "you must not get to thinking that either Christopher or Charlotte has said or done anything to make me unwelcome, indeed," she nodded, "they are all consideration, and really quite distraught at the thought of my leaving, but they have not long been married after all, and therefore must find my presence a little - well," she shrugged, "how shall I say? – a little *de trop!*"

"Oh, no, Mamma," Louisa cried. "I'm sure they do not!"

"Well, I can't say that I blame them if they did," she told her.

"How is Charlotte?" Louisa enquired, having taken a real liking to her sister-in-law.

"Well, my dear," her mamma told her conspiratorially, "she has not said anything, of course, it is after all early days, but I can't help feeling that she is in a most interesting situation!"

Louisa's green eyes lit up at this, and, clasping her hands, cried, "But that is wonderful news, Mamma!"

"Yes," her mamma nodded, "it is. I shan't say anything of course," she told her, "but I shall be delighted to welcome a grandchild." She paused a moment, eyeing her daughter speculatively before asking, not a little tentatively, "I don't suppose you have any news to impart?" raising a questioning eyebrow.

"News, Mamma?" Louisa repeated a little bewildered. Her mother nodded knowingly, then, as if realizing what she meant, lowered her head, and said in a small voice, "No, Mamma. No news."

Her mother sighed, then, after pursing her lips, enquired, "Not even a sign?"

"No, Mamma," Louisa said in a small voice.

Her mother heaved another sigh, asking, "You *are* doing your duty by your husband, I take it?"

It was a moment before Louisa answered this, saying, quietly, "Yes, Mamma," feeling the colour flooding into her cheeks.

"Well," her mother sighed, "I can't deny that I am not disappointed, as indeed so too must Deerham be." She paused a moment, saying at length, "You know, my dear, as I have told you often, while you can leave your husband's pleasures to his connection, that is no reason why you should not accommodate his wishes or conform to any demands he may make of you." She ran on in this vein for several minutes, during the course of which Louisa sat with her hands folded on her lap and her eyes downcast, not at all sure she welcomed her mamma's visit or not. "Now don't be such a pea goose, Louisa," her mother chided gently when she rose to her feet, signifying her visit was at an end. "There is not the least need to colour up like that."

"No, Mamma," Louisa said in a suffocated voice.

"You know, my dear," her mother told her, not unkindly, "it is by no means unusual for women to fail to conceive straightaway, even so," she nodded, "you have been married for over four months now!"

"Yes, Mamma," was all Louisa could bring herself to say.

Deeming she had said enough, her mamma took her leave, but not without recommending her daughter not to fail to visit in Cavendish Square to wish her a safe journey. "Of course I will, Mamma," Louisa assured her, kissing her soft cheek, not at all sorry when she finally bid her mamma goodbye.

If Louisa felt disconsolate before her mamma's visit she certainly did afterwards. Her reference to her condition, or the lack of it, only served to make Louisa feel even more wretched than ever, knowing that she was failing her husband by not giving him a child. Deerham may well seek his pleasures outside of the marriage, but it was not with these women he looked to have a son and heir, but with her, but not by a word or gesture did he let her know of his disappointment. Deerham's lovemaking may be considerate, even tender, nevertheless Louisa sensed that he was a very passionate man, and far from frightening her she only wished he loved her enough to want to release those passions on herself instead of those women who gave him what she did not.

Had Louisa but known it, there had been no one in Deerham's life since he met her, indeed he loved her far too much for that, and wanted nothing more than to be allowed to prove to her just how much he did love her, but it was becoming increasingly clear to him that his wife, who had early on in the marriage shelved his escort, did indeed look upon it as a marriage of convenience. At no time had it occurred to him that his wife was very much in love with him, and that it was her mamma whom he had to thank for her keeping her distance from him, a woman who, from her own painful experiences, in an urgent desire to protect her daughter from suffering the same fate as herself, had counselled Louisa to be on her guard as well as never allowing it to be seen that she was very much in love with her husband. The truth was, he missed her spontaneity and the way her eyes would light up in an instant as well as how she used to confide in him, even so, there had been times when he had caught a look in her eyes that made his heart soar, but as it had disappeared almost as quickly, he was left with nothing to do but hope that she did indeed love him after all.

Louisa meanwhile, despite her husband's courteous attentions towards her, which she put down to his good breeding, was totally unaware that he loved her more than life itself, changed her gown before going downstairs to a solitary dinner, Deerham already being engaged with a group of friends, followed by an evening spent at the theatre in company with Lady Durston and her rather lanky daughter, Frances. Had there been any way Louisa could have cried off she would have done, but Lady Durston, an old friend of her mamma, was a high stickler, and would have taken Louisa's excuses as a personal affront, and therefore she had no choice but to brace herself for an evening spent in the company of two people who, no matter how she tried, she could not like.

As expected, thanks to Lady Durston's ingratiating attitude and her daughter's rampant inquisitiveness, the evening turned out to be every bit as tedious and as uncomfortable as Louisa had anticipated. Long before the curtain came down on the final act, she was wishing she had risked Lady Durston's displeasure by crying off rather than having to endure her embarrassing fawning and her daughter's all too impertinent questions, none of which Louisa was in a mind to answer, and it was therefore with the utmost relief that she eventually wished her hostess and her daughter for the evening goodnight. By the time she finally tumbled into bed Louisa felt quite exhausted, her head throbbing painfully, so much so that it was some little time before she finally fell asleep, awaking the next morning feeling not very much refreshed and, not surprisingly, Deerham came to see her as she drank her morning cup of hot chocolate. He was dressed for a sporting engagement, but apart from enquiring how her evening at the theatre had fared followed by an amusing comment not to knock herself up with all this gadding about, he left not soon afterwards, leaving Louisa with no more than a careless flick of his forefinger against her cheek, feeling more dispirited than ever.

*

Singleton, meanwhile, who by no means liked his schemes being either obstructed or interfered with, was still furiously angry over his plans to bring Deerham to his knees by bleeding him dry going horrendously awry. He could not really blame Carrie Marchand, after all she had been placed in a most awkward situation, particularly as she had not expected a visit from Deerham, taking her completely unawares, but yet again this man had thwarted his schemes and in a way that was as surprising as it was infuriating. He could only hazard a guess as to whether the young marchioness had confided in her husband or not, but whichever way it was the fact remained that Deerham had once again walked off with the honours, but Singleton promised himself that it was for the last time.

As good luck would have it, he had seen the marchioness at the theatre last night in company with Lady Durston and her daughter, and unless he was very much mistaken, he would say that she had not enjoyed either the performance or her company. He had seriously toyed with the idea of approaching her during one of the intervals in Lady Durston's box, but experience had taught him that trying to engage one person in conversation in such circumstances usually proved a little awkward, and therefore decided against it, satisfying himself with an acknowledging nod of the head in response to her unenthusiastic recognition of him.

He was not the most patient of men, but he was nevertheless prepared to bide his time, which, considering she was not seen out with her husband as often as one would suppose, should not be too long, besides, he was convinced that the only way to get the better of Deerham was through his wife. Despite that striking colour combination, clearly inherited from her maternal grandmother, Louisa must have come as a great disappointment to him, a circumstance that Singleton could not help thinking to be somewhat ironic considering the beautiful women who had adorned his life. He could, of course, only speculate as to the true nature of affairs existing between husband and wife, but he nevertheless felt it reasonably safe to assume that Deerham, irrespective of whether he loved her or not, would not just sit back and do nothing once he knew his wife was in distress. Of course, how to bring about such an eventuality had Singleton a little at a loss, especially when he considered how his plans to extract money from her or, rather, her husband, at Carrie Marchand's had proved futile.

Needless to say, he had spent some considerable time in pondering the situation facing him, discarding the many ideas which had sprung to mind on very practical grounds. To say his thirst for revenge on Deerham had become something of an obsession was a gross understatement, so much so that he spent all his waking hours in striving to think of a way to bring him toppling to the ground, and in a way that would be as publicly humiliating for him as it would be gratifying for himself. Since Deerham had already proved that he was more than ordinarily astute, whatever Singleton devised to achieve his overwhelming ambition, it had to be something which would not only be totally unexpected but take him completely by surprise. To a lesser mind the task would seem insurmountable, but Singleton was nothing if not resourceful, and certainly not one who gave up at the first setback.

Quite when the idea came to him, he was not entirely sure, but the seed, once having been sown, refused to go away, indeed, the more he thought about it the more attractive it seemed. Of course, it would take a deal of working out, it would not do for it to go wrong, but for a man of his Machiavellian tendencies he felt sure that it would not tax his ingenuity too far. Happily for him, however, he could only be thankful that the dibs were in tune, had been for some little while, relieving him of the necessity of falling back on the idea of abducting Letitia Rawnsley with a view to compromising her reputation, therefore forcing that aunt of hers to acknowledge that marriage to him would be her niece's only salvation. In truth, marriage held no appeal for him whatsoever, and had his fortunes not been in such desperate straits he would never even have contemplated running off with her in the first place. Had his plans not been thwarted, he felt reasonably sure he would have been married by now and his wife's fortune safely in his own pocket, but he also felt it reasonably safe to assume that the novelty of bringing her to bridle would have long since worn off, leaving him to wish he were well out of the marriage. However, as Providence could not always be relied upon to guide a gamester's hand, leaving him very much out of pocket, he could not totally discount the idea of making another attempt to abduct her at some point in the future, and this time, thanks to the plans he was hatching where Deerham was concerned, there would be no one to either prevent it or come to her rescue. Despite his abhorrence of the married state and his wariness at being leg-shackled to someone who loathed him, it was nevertheless a pleasing thought to contemplate, but in the meantime, however, there was his plans to compromise the Marchioness of Deerham, and in a way that would leave her husband with very little alternative but to divorce her, something a man of his pride and breeding would not be able to stomach without revulsion.

Singleton was neither surprised nor alarmed at the growing friendship between the young marchioness and Letitia Rawnsley; for one thing, he doubted very much whether Deerham would have revealed his identity to her, or even told his wife, and even if he had, Singleton knew very well that he would have warned them both never to disclose what had happened that night, otherwise it would have been all over town long since. He knew perfectly well that Letitia hated him and could not bear to be near him, the same as he knew that her aunt, a woman who made no bones as to her feelings for him, had warned her to be extremely wary of him, but it could not be argued that her niece's predilection for the young marchioness's company was proving very useful, indeed he had already seen how their friendship could be turned to very good account.

It seemed that the only member of the Rawnsley family who did not despise him was Algernon, a young man who had more than once demonstrated his eagerness to hand over his blunt at the card tables without so much as a blink. Singleton had not forgotten the one time they had played cards together, the evening following his failed abduction attempt of his sister and Algernon's first duel, when he had calmly lost two thousand guineas to him, a most welcome windfall coming at a time when he had been desperately in need of funds. Their paths had, of course, crossed many times since, with more than one game of piquet being exchanged between them, but either Algernon had become a more cautious player overnight or he had been extremely fortunate because Singleton, though winning a number of games, had won no more than a few hundred guineas.

Having long been a member of White's, he often ran across Algernon within its hallowed portals, but he had not expected to see him today, being under the impression that he was still at his place in Leicestershire, having no idea that he was back in town. Looking up at the sound of a newcomer, he raised a painted eyebrow, a smile touching his thin tinted lips, and raised a hand in welcome, whereupon Algernon strode over to where he was sitting, the scowl on his handsome face telling Singleton that he was not in the best of humours, but he nevertheless greeted him with all his habitual bonhomie, indicating a chair, into which Algernon sank down onto it.

"What a pleasant surprise this is," Singleton purred. "I had no idea you were back in town."

"No, well," Algernon shrugged, "I have engagements which render it necessary for me to return. Also," he told him airily, "I had to do the pretty to that aunt of mine!"

"Indeed!" Singleton raised an eyebrow. "A most redoubtable woman."

The frown on Algernon's forehead deepened. "Don't I know it!" he snapped.

It was a moment or two before Singleton spoke, seemingly more interested in casting dice from his left hand to his right, then, after eyeing Algernon from under his lashes, said softly, "I… er… I take it she gave you a most uncomfortable time."

"Uncomfortable!" Algernon cried. "I should rather think she did," his brow darkening at the recollection. "Such fuss and palaver over trifles!" going on to recount his grievances, to which Singleton listened with courteous interest.

"I take it," Singleton gave a knowing glance, when Algernon had come to the end of recounting his grievances, "that you were not the only one she abused?"

Algernon coloured slightly, knowing perfectly well that Singleton meant himself. "Yes, well," he shrugged, "you know how it is with her!"

Singleton did know, and it came as no surprise to him that the dowager countess had not only taken her nephew to task for his frivolous lifestyle but also for fraternizing with one such as himself. He knew perfectly well that the dowager countess held him in utter contempt, and unless he was very much mistaken, he knew the reason why, but that he had in any way corrupted her nephew she was grossly at fault. He liked Algernon very well, indeed there was nothing to find against him as well as being no different to any other young blade on the town, but there was an instability in him which now and then drove him into doing something quite reckless and imprudent. Singleton would not say that Algernon was weak and easily led, on the contrary he could be extremely stubborn on occasion as well as taking little or no heed to older and wiser heads, but there was no denying that, especially when in his cups, he could be guaranteed to do something which set people's backs up. Clearly, his aunt had heard of those parties he gave at his hunting lodge in Leicestershire as well as how he would sit up until all hours playing cards at White's or one of his other clubs, not to mention his association with himself, and had decided, yet again, to take him to task. From the looks on Algernon's face, however, Singleton would say she would have been better advised to have refrained from raising such topics, not only because women could not possibly be expected to understand these things, which, after all, was mere bachelor fare, but also because any remonstrance would only serve to make him dig his heels in and become even more reckless.

Singleton's own lifestyle would not stand too much scrutiny, not that he cared the snap of his fingers for that, after all he had had his fair share of women as well as being a notorious gamester, but he was nevertheless a shrewd judge of human nature, and were anyone to ask him he would say that the dowager's idea of marrying her nephew off as soon as may be possible would be the worst thing that could happen to him. Algernon may be his own master, had been for three years now, but Singleton knew that he was still young enough to enjoy all the pleasures the ton had to offer, including these parties he gave at his place in Leicestershire as well as losing his blunt at the card tables. It was useless, of course, to expect the dowager to see it in the same light, and quite a waste of time in trying to tell her, but whilst Singleton had long since decided to give the dowager and her acid tongue an exceptionally wide berth, the fact remained that even if she did manage to get her nephew down the aisle it was extremely unlikely he would make a faithful husband. In Singleton's humble opinion, it would be a good few years yet before Algernon was ready for the married state, and when he did eventually decide to take the step of marrying it would be to a bride of his own choosing and not one foisted onto him by an aunt.

Needless to say, Algernon felt a whole lot better for unburdening himself of his grievances, but he was still rather rankled by the way his aunt continued to treat him like a novice or a schoolboy. However, it was not until she came to her mentioning that she had already had to see off she knew not how many fortune hunters dangling after Letitia, something which was his responsibility and not hers, that he suddenly remembered his obligations where she was concerned. It was not that he was not fond of his sister, he was, but being taken up with his own affairs he had been more than happy to let his aunt take care of her or, when she was indisposed, to let her go out and about with the Marchioness of Deerham, a young woman who had apparently become a firm friend. However, when he saw Letitia that evening at the Scott-Pearces' drum ball, he decided to take her to task for letting what he called all manner of men make up to her, an allegation she hotly denied.

It had not been Algernon's intention to attend the drum ball in Mount Street, not only because it was not the kind of gathering he liked but an evening spent with the Scott-Pearces was the most boring thing he could think of, but in view of his aunt's allegations that it was about time he took his duties as Viscount Dunstan more seriously, he thought it prudent. As expected, Letitia was looking in high gig. Dressed in amber coloured satin with her hair most becomingly styled and her face rather flushed as she danced around the floor with a young man Algernon had never laid eyes on before, a slight frown creased his forehead, but it was several minutes before he was able to speak to her. Not surprisingly, there were any number of people there who were either old friends of his mother or acquaintances of his late father, and, quite naturally, upon setting eyes on him they hailed him to their side, where he was forced to spend several minutes in conversation with them.

Letitia, upon catching sight of her brother, was naturally pleased to see him, not having expected him here tonight, and therefore left her partner's side with an impish smile and the promise that she would dance with him later that evening.

"Well, puss," Algernon teased, flicking her cheek with a careless forefinger, "who's the gallant?"

She dimpled up at him. "I have not least notion, but he is most agreeable."

"I daresay," he nodded darkly.

"He is most unexceptionable," she told him.

"Very probably," he nodded, "but I will have you know that I will not permit my sister to dance around a ballroom with a man who is quite unknown to her!"

"You sound very cross," she told him, not in the least perturbed.

"It's enough to make any man cross when he sees his sister cavorting around a room with a man she has never met before," he told her bluntly, to which Letitia giggled. "Yes," he nodded, "and that's another thing. What's this my aunt tells me about having to fend off gazetted fortune hunters?" he cocked his head.

"She told you?" Letitia asked, stealing a glance up at him.

"Yes, she did," he nodded. "And let me tell you, my girl," he told her firmly, "that if you think for one minute that I will permit my sister to make herself the talk of the ton you could not be more mistaken!" Suddenly becoming very censorious where the women of his family were concerned.

"I did not encourage them," she told him heatedly, her face very much flushed.

"Then what made them think to apply to my aunt for your hand in marriage?" he threw at her.

"How should I know?" she shrugged.

"I suppose you have been flirting again," he told her knowingly.

"Well, I have not," she told him firmly, her pansy brown eyes sparkling.

"Well, if you have not been flirting," he told her candidly, "you must have been behaving in a most indecorous fashion!"

"I have not!" she cried fervently. "How dare you! Can I help it if men take such foolish notions into their heads?"

It had been on the tip of Algernon's tongue to tell her that he been far too lax with her, and if she did not start behaving herself he would be left with little choice but to pack her off back to Wiltshire, but only a moment's thought told him he was being unfair, and her heated denials merely went to prove it. The truth was he was still smarting from his aunt's acid tongue as well as deeming it prudent to track his sister down to this insufferably dull party when he could have been otherwise, and far more happily, engaged. He had always known that Letitia was a most captivating creature, guaranteed to set men's hearts racing, but he knew too that she was totally naïve in the ways of the world as well as how her innocent artlessness could have the most devastating effect on men, but however much it went against the grain with him to give up his own pleasures, he deemed it prudent to start keeping a far closer eye on his sister than he had so far.

Unfortunately, it had not occurred to him that his sister stood in far more danger from Digby Singleton than she did from any young man who solicited her hand for a dance or so much as looked at her. To Algernon's way of thinking, Singleton was a right one, exceedingly good company and one who was guaranteed to give one a pleasant evening, apart from which he was not only a confirmed bachelor who had long since set himself against the wedded state but was not in the least degree interested in his sister. Had he have known that Singleton had already made one attempt to abduct her and was not averse to making another attempt should the need arise, he would not have been quite so complacent, indeed, he would have felt himself honour bound to call him to account.

Chapter Sixteen

Singleton knew very well that Algernon would have no alternative but to call him out should he ever get wind of his attempted abduction of his sister, but since this young lady had apparently kept quiet about what had happened it seemed there was very little chance of that happening. However, he did find the piquancy of the whole affair to be rather amusing, but although he had by no means totally shelved the idea of making another attempt to abduct her, for now his mind was firmly fixed on bringing about the downfall of Deerham, thanks to the indiscretions of his young wife.

Over the next few days Singleton kept a more than ordinarily close eye on the young marchioness, and since he was by no means *persona non grata* with every hostess, this proved to be not too difficult a matter. Apart from an acknowledging nod of the head, she gave no signs of recognition or even indicated that she was inclined to talk to him which, if what Carrie Marchand had told him was true, then he could quite well understand it. Nonetheless, it tickled his sense of humour, and could not refrain from approaching her at the earliest opportunity.

Louisa had suspected from the very first that Singleton had no love for her husband, and although Deerham never spoke of it she was nevertheless agog to know the reason why. That Singleton had found it necessary to collude with Caroline Marchand in an attempt to extort money out of her, or rather Deerham, surely went to prove the depth of animosity that existed between them. It was, of course, an immeasurable relief to be relieved of such a heavy burden, thanks to Deerham's intervention, but not only had the whole episode been extremely worrisome but it had left a rather nasty taste in her mouth, so much so that she would never forgive Singleton for such deceitfulness.

She could not believe that she had been so easily taken in by Caroline Marchand, a woman who had seemed so kind and friendly as well as being utterly plausible, but then she supposed that given her profession such deceit was only to be expected, indeed it would form her stock in trade. Then, of course, there was this woman to whom Deerham said he owed his thanks for informing him of wife's dilemma, a woman he had told her need not worry her in any way. Even though Louisa could only speculate as to whether this woman had been one of his past *cheri aimees* or not, although she strongly suspected that she was, and whilst she knew she ought to be grateful the very thought was enough to bring a lump to her throat.

It was while she was considering this that a voice, silky smooth and unwelcomingly familiar, intruded on her thoughts. "Quite a squeeze, do you not agree? But then, Dolly Hardwick's soirées always are."

Louisa had, of course, seen Singleton earlier in the evening, but apart from a brief nod of acknowledgement she had completely ignored him. He may be an old friend of her father, but she only had to think of what he had done to try to get back at Deerham through her as well as attempting to abduct her dearest friend that at the sound of his voice in her ear she immediately stiffened. She had not seen him come up to her, but whilst nothing would give her greater satisfaction than to tell him what she thought of him, the middle of Dolly Hardwick's soirée was not the place, especially with half the ton in attendance. She somehow gained the impression that he was laughing at her, but upon turning round to look into his painted face, a picture of innocence, she said politely, "Yes, quite a squeeze."

"No, no," he shook his head when she made to walk away from him, "please don't go," placing a restraining hand on her arm.

Louisa looked haughtily from his hand to his face, then, as if realizing he had offended her, something he could not afford to do, he removed his hand and bowed his head slightly, offering an apology. "I'm sorry," he smiled, "but is it so very bad you being seen talking to me? After all," he shrugged, waving a hand around the room, "I am not entirely *persona non grata,* as you can see."

No, he was not, but Louisa could not like him, and certainly not to the point where she wanted to hold a conversation with him, but since he seemed determined to inaugurate one, and to make a scene in the middle of Dolly Hardwick's soirée was unthinkable, she raised an enquiring eyebrow, to which he gave a low voiced laugh.

"You know, my dear," he purred, "I must confess to having a liking for your spirit."

"Do you, indeed?" she said dampingly.

"Most certainly," he assured her, quite unperturbed by her cool response. "And your loyalty, especially to your husband, is commendable, indeed I have often thought so."

"Am I supposed to be flattered?" she retorted.

"If such was my hope," he shrugged fatalistically, "then it appears I am sadly doomed to disappointment."

Louisa was neither moved by this mournfully expressed sentiment nor disposed to enquire further into what he meant, but said instead, with that frankness her mamma deplored and which she had tried so desperately hard to stem, "You were certainly doomed to disappointment when Deerham spoiled your game over your despicable attempts to try to extort money out of me!"

His eyes narrowed at this, still smarting over Deerham's quick intervention, although how he knew what he had planned for his wife before those IOUs had been sent to him, still had him in something of a puzzle, but biting down on his annoyance, Singleton immediately resumed his smooth urbanity, shrugging, as though it were of no importance, "C'est la vie, my dear."

She was not fooled by this blasé response, indeed, she could well imagine how angry he must have been to know that his schemes had come to nothing and, unless she was very much mistaken, he still was. "You make light of what could only have been a most severe disappointment for you," she pointed out.

"Oh," he shrugged eloquently, "one learns to take adversity in one's stride."

"Something I hear you are not unused to!" she raised an eyebrow.

His eyes narrowed slightly at this. "You should not listen to gossip, my dear," he said silkily.

"Then you should not provide it," she told him forthrightly.

His eyes narrowed even more, but, then, much to her surprise, he burst out laughing, "E'gad, but you could keep a man entertained for a twelve-month, I'll swear!"

"But not you, Singleton," she flung at him, "not you!" whereupon she walked away from him.

Needless to say, the rest of the evening passed endlessly by, and Louisa, who was not enjoying the evening, particularly as Deerham was not with her, was looking for the least excuse to go home, but it was not until two o'clock that she was finally able to tumble into bed.

She had not intended speaking to Singleton at all, but since he had rendered it impossible for her not to do so, now, in the quietness of her bedroom, she regretted saying what she had to him, but the provocation had been great, so too was placing a curb on her tongue. Singleton may well be *persona grata* with any number of hostesses as well as being a close friend of her father, but the truth was she did not like him. It was not just because there was animosity between him and Deerham, but there was something about him she could not like. She detected the same lines around his eyes and mouth as she had with her father the last time she had seen him, and whilst she may not know the full extent of their dealings, she was nevertheless astute enough to know that they had led far from virtuous lives.

Not unexpectedly, her engagements kept her reasonably well occupied over the next few days, and certainly too busy to even give Singleton a moment's thought much less the schemes he was hatching to compromise her. But whilst Louisa enjoyed most of the entertainments on offer, nothing gave her greater pleasure than Max asking her if she would like him to take her to Bath to spend a few days with his mother while he was at Worleigh conducting the business William had told him he should have concluded when he was there only a short time ago. Louisa may have no idea of the doubts which had plagued the dowager marchioness at the thought of her son marrying the daughter of a man she had no hesitation in calling a profligate, but she had come to know and like her mother-in-law and had no hesitation in telling Max that she would like it above all things.

And so, three days later, comfortably established in the luxurious travelling carriage and outriders riding behind, she found herself seated beside Max as they made their way to Bath. So happy was she to be in his company that she quite forgot all about her mama's strictures and what Deerham would expect of his wife, talking animatedly to him in a way she had not done for quite a long time. He was delighted, and quite happy to sit back looking and listening to her, filled with renewed hope that she did indeed feel something for him after all, so much so that after he had wished his mother goodbye later that afternoon he could not resist taking Louisa in his arms and kissing her. It was by no means a passionate kiss, but it was nevertheless loving and tender, more so than ever before, leaving Louisa to hope that her husband did in fact have some feelings for her after all.

*

Bath, a most genteel and popular resort, particularly as it was highly favoured by the Prince of Wales, was not only known for its inclement weather and how one could be taken unawares all of a sudden by a heavy shower of rain, but also for being well provided with entertainments to keep those members of the ton who visited extremely well entertained. Between visiting the pump room and watching her mamma-in-law heroically drink the waters, the libraries, the shops and walking in the Sydney Gardens, was just the kind of entertainment which suited the dowager very well and Louisa enjoyed enormously. The dowager, who had been comfortably established in Laura Place for some few years since the death of her husband, very much enjoyed her daughter-in-law's company and having her accompany her on her outings into the town and the pump room, enjoying listening to the orchestra which played there every morning.

Not surprisingly, the dowager had many friends in Bath, all of whom she lost no time in introducing to her daughter-in-law, so much so that very soon Louisa found herself accompanying Lady Millhampton and her daughter to the assembly rooms for a cotillion dance. Although this could not compare with those in London, Louisa nevertheless enjoyed herself very much, telling her mamma-in-law on her return to Laura Place that she had no idea that Bath was such an exciting place.

But no matter what entertainments Bath had to offer, Louisa, whether browsing through the shelves of the libraries, shopping in the South Parade or watching her mamma-in-law enjoy a good gossip with an old friend in the pump room, never very far away from her thoughts was the image of a tall, dark haired man, lean and loose-limbed with a pair of humorous dark grey eyes and wondering what he was doing with his time at Worleigh and if William was keeping him as busy as he would like. She wondered too if he was missing her as much as she was missing him, but that innate honesty which was so much a part of her compelled her to admit that, their parting kiss aside, their marriage had been one of convenience and not of love, and therefore she doubted very much whether his heart felt as though it was broken when they were apart.

Not for the first time her mind kept wondering about the women who had adorned Max's life; beautiful and sophisticated and knowing precisely how to keep him amused and entertained, and how very far short she was in possessing the qualities they clearly had in abundance. Then there was the woman for whom Max had told her he was very much indebted for apprising him of his wife's difficulties. As Louisa lay back against the pillows drinking her morning cup of hot chocolate, watching the rain as it ran freely down the windowpane, she tried to tell herself that she was being ridiculous, after all hadn't Max told her himself that this unknown woman need not trouble her? Perhaps not, but the fact remained that she, like all those others, had been a part of Max's life in a way she never would. She wished with all her heart that things were different, but she knew that she would never hold a place in Max's heart as those other women had, and despite his kindness and generosity towards her as well as his attentions to her comfort, she told herself that they were only to be expected of a man of his breeding, just like Mamma had warned her, and the sooner she accepted what could not be changed the better. As for their parting kiss... well, the sooner she forgot that as well the better it would be, and as for reading anything into it – why, it was nothing more than Max's good manners! And yet, in spite of all of this and knowing that Max did not love her, Louisa knew she would much rather be married to him than anyone else.

So lost in thought was she that Louisa entirely failed to hear the gentle tapping on her bedchamber door, and not until her mamma-in-law had quietly opened it to peek inside, did Louisa realize she was no longer alone.

"I'm sorry, my dear," the dowager said softly, "am I disturbing you?"

"No, of course not," Louisa smiled, putting down her cup of hot chocolate and making herself comfortable against the pillows.

"I am so glad," the dowager smiled, kissing Louisa's soft cheek before sitting down on the edge of the bed in front of her, taking her hands in her own bony ones, "because you see, I do so want to talk to you, but with all this gadding about there does not seem to have been much time."

"No," Louisa smiled, "we do seem to have had a rather eventful time of late."

The dowager laughed. "Yes, we do rather, but tell me, my dear," she asked, "you have enjoyed your stay here in Bath?"

"Oh, yes!" Louisa cried, squeezing her hand. "I have enjoyed it so very much."

"I am pleased to hear you say that," the dowager nodded, "because you see, I have enjoyed it so very much too."

"Even drinking the waters?" Louisa teased, visions of her mamma-in-law screwing up her face whenever she took a sip flitting into her mind's eye.

Yes, Max was right when he told her that Louisa was nothing like her father and that although she may not be a beauty there was something very attractive about her all the same, she had seen it for herself. The dowager laughed at this and, patting Louisa's hand, confessed, "Well, they *are* rather nasty," pulling a face, "but very beneficial."

"Of course they are," Louisa said as primly as she could.

The dowager laughed again and, sighing, said, "You know, my dear, I shall miss you when you leave here this afternoon. Indeed," she nodded, "I could almost ask Max to leave you with me for a while longer."

"And I should be very pleased to stay," Louisa told her sincerely.

"Yes," the dowager said slowly, nodding her head, "I believe you would, but I am afraid it will not do. Max has calls upon you that far exceed mine."

It was on the tip of Louisa's tongue to tell her mamma-in-law that she had totally the wrong impression of their marriage, but withdrawing it, deeming it wiser not to say anything, said instead, "There will be other visits."

"Of course there will," the dowager smiled, "and I cannot tell you how much I am looking forward to them already." She thought a moment, her fingers moving in Louisa's, then, heaving a deep sigh, said, "You know, my dear, one of the reasons that brings me here this morning is that… well," she shrugged, "I have a confession to make to you."

"Do you?" Louisa asked, raising a questioning eyebrow.

"Yes," the dowager sighed again, "I do. You see, my dear," she told her kindly, "when Max first told me that he fully intended to honour his father's promise to your grandfather the Earl of Halford and that he was going to offer for your hand after all, I was filled with the gravest misgivings. Indeed," she told her, "I strongly urged him not to."

Louisa felt the colour flood her cheeks at this, but after what seemed to be several minutes of not very edifying thought, managed, "W-was that because of my... my father, ma'am?"

"Yes," the dowager nodded, "it was."

"I see," Louisa said in a small voice.

"Oh, my dear," the dowager cried, "forgive me. You are nothing like your father, anyone can see that, truly you are not." She looked at the downcast face in front of her, imploring, "Oh, Louisa, my dear," squeezing her fingers, "please do not tell me you hate me for telling you because it would distress me very much if I thought for one moment that you did!"

Louisa raised her head to look at her mamma-in-law, but just one glance at those faded blue eyes filled with unshed tears and whatever resentment she had felt upon hearing her confession instantly left her. "Of course I do not hate you!" Louisa cried fervently, giving her a reassuring embrace. "How could you possibly think such a thing?"

"I... I know Max made me promise never to tell you," the dowager sniffed into her lace edged handkerchief when Louisa released her, "but we have grown into such a comfortable relationship you and I that I felt there should be no lies or deceit between us."

"Of course there should not," Louisa smiled, wiping away her own tears with the handkerchief she pulled out from beneath the pillow. "None at all."

"I am so glad you think so," the dowager said relieved, "because you see, apart from Max's... well," she shrugged, deciding the less said about them the better, not that she thought any the less of him because of his affairs, "never mind that, but there has never been any secrets between us."

Louisa knew exactly what her mamma-in-law had been about to say before she quickly retracted it, but not by a word or gesture did she give any sign of it. "And nor will there be between us," Louisa smiled, giving the cold bony hand lying limply on top of the coverlet a gentle shake, "I promise you." The dowager smiled and nodded, but it was obvious to Louisa that there was something else her mamma-in-law wished to say to her but was clearly finding it a little difficult to know how to broach the matter.

This was no less than the truth. The dowager knew perfectly well that Max was very conscious of the fact that he was the last of his name and therefore it was vital he provide an heir unless he wanted the name he bore to die out and the title pass to his eldest cousin, but for all that it could not be argued that she was nevertheless looking forward to becoming a grandmother in the foreseeable future for her own sake. But Max and Louisa had been married now for almost five months and, as far as she could tell, there were no signs to indicate that her daughter-in-law was increasing. Of course, it was by no means unusual for a woman to be married for some little time before she conceived a child, but unless the dowager was grossly mistaken, and she did not think she was, then Max, who was by no means inexperienced when it came to the fair sex, would by no means require instruction on what to do.

Louisa, despite the fact that she had been married for nearly five months, was young and inexperienced, unlike her husband, whose liaisons, at least if all the dowager had ever heard was true, were common knowledge, but, more than this, all of the ladies who had enjoyed his company had been exquisitely beautiful, something that could not be said of Louisa. The dowager did not think that Max was that callous and cruel that he would let Louisa see that her looks had come as great disappointment to him and therefore paid her attentions merely because it was his duty to do so, on the contrary he would treat her with the greatest respect and deference. But the dowager knew that her son, for all his affability, had a reserve about him which could so easily give one the wrong impression, and although he never subjected her to this side of his nature, she was all too well aware of how it could impact on a young and inexperienced wife, being extremely daunting to say the least. Yet for all this, the dowager could not rid her mind of the look in his eyes and the inflexion which had crept into his voice when he had come to see her to tell her about his intention of offering for Louisa, both of which had left her wondering if Max had fallen in love with her after all. Not surprisingly, he had categorically denied this when she had asked him if he had fallen in love with Louisa, but she knew her son too well to be deceived, and since all the signs pointed to the fact that Louisa, despite her strenuous efforts to the contrary, had fallen in love with him, then the dowager could only conclude that, for reasons which she could only speculate, relations between Max and Louisa were not as smooth as she had thought.

Louisa may be inexperienced, but she knew enough to know that even though Max kept his emotions on a very tight rein whenever he did come to see her, he was nevertheless a very passionate man. If he loved her then she would happily disregard every one of her mamma's strictures and know no hesitation in responding to his lovemaking, but as it was no use pretending that he would ever come to feel anything for her but a sincere attachment, this contingency was not likely to arise. For herself, Louisa, could think of no greater joy than informing her husband that he was going to be a father, but since Max no longer visited her in her boudoir, or at least not as often as he had done, then the chances of this were looking extremely remote.

She knew her mamma-in-law was hoping for good news, but as she appeared to be struggling to find a way of broaching the matter which she clearly considered to be extremely delicate to say the least, Louisa decided to put her out of her misery by smiling and giving her hand a little shake, saying, "I promise you, you will be first to know."

The dowager did not pretend to misunderstand her. It was disappointing, of course, but hopefully Louisa would be in a position to relate good news to her in time, especially if, as Margaret had confided to her on the day of Max's wedding, Louisa's mamma, who had clearly done her work too well, did not feel it incumbent upon her to further warn her daughter against allowing her feelings to show because the dowager was as convinced as she could be that her son and daughter-in-law were very much in love with one another, even though they did not know it.

*

Max's arrival in Bath midway through the morning to escort Louisa back to town, having left Worleigh at a very early hour, coincided with his mamma's absence from home, not having expected to see him so early, deciding to take the air while she waited for him to arrive by visiting the pump room in company with her daughter-in-law, the rain having given way to a fine sunny morning. Upon being informed by Ryman, his mamma's very stately -and inordinately expensive – butler, that her ladyship had gone to the pump room in company with the marchioness, Deerham nodded and, after enquiring about his health then about the ladies, left the house to make his way to the pump room.

It was just as the dowager had taken a cautious sip of the restorative water in her glass that she caught sight of Max and, waving a hand to him, he walked over to her where, after bowing gracefully over her hand, he took the seat beside her, his eyes smiling warmly down at her, saying teasingly,

"Courage, Mamma!"

"Max, my dear!" she cried, her faded blue eyes lighting up at the sight of him.

"You look as fine as fivepence," he smiled, taking hold of her hand in his and kissing it.

"I don't," she smiled, "but it is just like you to say so." Then, putting the glass down beside her, confided, "You know, Max, to say I have been drinking the waters here for some appreciable time, I cannot honestly say that I feel any the better for it!"

"Poor Mamma," he soothed, giving her hand a squeeze. Then, casting a glance around the room, his eyes taking in a multitude of valetudinarians with their attendants as well as the orchestra, which had currently ceased playing in order to take in some refreshment, he brought his gaze back to his mother's face, asking, "Where is Louisa?"

"Oh, she has merely gone to Druffield's for me in Milsom Street to return a book," she told him, having given up on the water in her glass. "She should be back in a moment," to which he nodded. "So, Max," she wanted to know, "how are things at Worleigh? It seems an age since I was last there!"

"Very well," he told her, "everyone always asks after you, but as for you not being there this age," he smiled, "that is entirely your own fault. I have lost count of the times I have begged you to let me take you there."

"Yes, I know," she nodded, "and perhaps one day I shall, it's just that… well, you see, Max, I always went there with your father and… well, it is…"

"I know," he said softly, giving her hand a reassuring squeeze, "you are happy here in Bath because you never came here with my father, at least not to stay, unlike Worleigh."

"Ah, Max," she cried, "you *do* understand!"

"Of course, I do," he smiled, kissing her hand. "So, tell me," he asked, "have you enjoyed Louisa's company?"

"Oh, yes, very much. Indeed, Max," she told him truthfully, "it has been delightful having her. I shall miss her very much – ah," she cried, "here she is now."

Louisa was no beauty, as Max was the first to acknowledge, but he had nevertheless long since come to recognize that her looks did not matter in the least, and as he rose to his feet as she approached them, he felt his heart begin to beat rather fast and that familiar feeling invade the pit of his stomach knowing in that moment that should she not love him after all, then his life would be desolate indeed. No one looking at him would have had the least idea that he had missed her dreadfully this past week while he was at Worleigh, just as he always did when she was not around, but as he looked at her now, looking exceedingly lovely dressed in pale green satin with a lace fichu around her neck, and her copper coloured hair spiralling down her back, on top of which she wore the most charming straw hat tied beneath her chin with a wide gauze scarf, he knew without any doubt whatsoever that he could not live without her.

"Max!" Louisa cried, her eyes lighting up at the sight of him. "What a delightful surprise. We had no idea you would arrive in Bath quite so early," holding out her hand to him.

"So Mamma told me," he smiled, kissing her fingers.

"Oh, Max!" Louisa smiled, "we have had the most agreeable time," going on to tell him all the things they had done.

"Gay to dissipation then!" he commented amusingly.

"Well, perhaps not that," Louisa told him with a smile, "but we have enjoyed it all the same."

The dowager, who had been watching this reunion between her son and daughter-in-law with a more than ordinarily close eye, was given to hope that whatever problems attached to their marriage would be speedily resolved, but if nothing else it merely went to confirm her opinion that they were more in love with one another than they knew. However, deciding to keep her own counsel for now she allowed Max to assist her to feet and escort her out of the pump room, whereupon he immediately called up a chair for her. Louisa, declining the offer of a chair, was more than content to walk behind it with her hand resting on Max's arm, spending the short time available to them before they reached Laura Place by telling him about the wonderful time they had spent.

Having partaken of some refreshment it was soon time for Max and Louisa to say goodbye. The dowager, embracing her daughter-in-law and telling her she looked forward to welcoming her again very soon, kissed her soft cheek, then, turning her attention to her son, affectionately embraced him, which was returned with fervour. "You know, Max," she told him quietly, patting his cheek, "I like Louisa very much indeed."

"I know you do, Mamma," he smiled.

"She is really quite delightful," she smiled. "I think you could have done a lot worse than marrying her."

"Yes, Mamma," he kissed her cheek, his eyes smiling down into hers, "so do I."

Chapter Seventeen

Louisa, who had been described as a well-behaved young woman who was as different to her father as anyone could be by those very people who had watched with keen interest her launch into the ton and eagerly waited to see what she would do, had become most sought after, indeed, no hostess would even dream of failing to send her a card of invitation. Upon her return to Grosvenor Square she was amazed to see the pile of invitations that awaited her on the table in the hall despite the fact that the season was almost at an end, telling Max that she had no idea how she would ever manage to attend the half of them.

"Must you attend the half of them?" he smiled.

"Oh, no," Louisa shook her head. "Indeed, I am certain that most of them will be nothing but dead bores, but only fancy, Max!" she told him, "who would have thought that I should be inundated with invitations, even this late in the season?"

Max's lips twitched at this. "I seem to recall," he smiled, taking hold of her hand and giving it a gentle little shake, "you telling me once that you could not wait to see all the sights and attend all the parties. Could it be," he asked in mock horror, "that you have become bored with all this frivolity?"

She laughed, and her fingers moved in his. "No, indeed I have not, but you know, Max," she told him, "you must own that some parties are duller than others."

"Oh, indubitably!" he told her with a perfectly straight face.

"Oh, now you are laughing at me!" she cried.

"Only a very little," he smiled, raising her hand to his lips and kissing it, to which she blushed adorably. "Don't draw the bustle too much," he said softly, flicking her cheek with his forefinger.

"No, of course I shall not," she told him a little breathlessly before pulling her hand out of his and running up the stairs to change her gown for dinner.

As Max had an engagement of his own which would see him dining at his club she did not see him again that evening, nor did he come to her later in her boudoir as she had thought he might, especially following what had passed between them on their arrival home from Bath, but although she tried very hard not to let this upset her and concentrate her mind on the pleasurable thought that very soon she and Max would be repairing to Worleigh for a short stay before going on to Brighton, it was nevertheless long before she fell asleep.

*

Letitia may have missed her dearest friend during her sojourn in Bath, but it in no way prevented her from attending her many engagements, and her aunt, who was frequently heard to bemoan the fact that she was far too old for all this gadding about, nevertheless enjoyed sitting against the wall with the rest of the dowagers and matrons acting as chaperones enjoying a good gossip. However, it had not escaped that sharp-eyed lady's notice that her niece, who by no means lacked male interest, a circumstance that by no means surprised her considering Letitia was a considerable heiress, had engaged the attention of one young man in particular, a young man who seemed markedly assiduous in his gallantries towards her. In fairness to Letitia however, she no more encouraged his attentions than she did to any other young man who flocked about her, but it nevertheless crossed the dowager's mind that a warning in her niece's ear would not come amiss.

To the dowager's recollection, until five nights ago at Lady Wellwater's drum ball she had never before laid eyes on this young man, but ever since then he seemed to be forever attending the same balls and parties as Letitia, and never very far from her side. To all intents and purposes, he seemed to be a most personable young man, not handsome mind but pleasantly good-looking in a quiet and unremarkable sort of way. He was not above average height but his figure was good, slim rather than lean, and he boasted an excellent leg. His mode of dress was unquestionably impeccable and his face, whilst only lightly dusted and rouged, bore none of the hallmarks of a man of the town, indeed it was open and honest and free of guile or deceit, but, for all that, the dowager, a woman of excellent judgement, had taken him in dislike.

Why this should be she had no idea, but she had not lived all these years without knowing a thing or two about human nature, and unless she was grossly mistaken it was her niece's money he was after and not her. Letitia would be an extremely wealthy young woman when she became of age, or if she should marry before then, and therefore the dowager was determined that her niece should not throw herself away on a ne'er-do-well because it was as plain as a pikestaff that Letitia had taken a more than ordinary liking to him despite the fact that she by no means encouraged his advances. She certainly blushed whenever he was near her, and she never once declined his offer to take his arm on the floor or to escort her down to partake of refreshment, and more than once she had allowed him to take hold of her fan in order for him to cool her heated cheeks, and whilst none of these things were in the least degree improper, the dowager could not rid her mind of the unwelcome thought that should he make her niece an offer then the chances were very good, despite the fact that she would need her brother's approval, that she would accept him even though their acquaintanceship was of very short duration. The dowager would, of course, feel much happier if she knew something of his family and background, but as none of the matrons she sat next to could tell her anything she was left with only her thoughts and speculations, neither of which made her feel any the easier, on the contrary they made her rather apprehensive.

So far, Letitia had only made a passing reference to him when speaking of him to her aunt, which, as far as that redoubtable lady was concerned, was more telling than a eulogy, but not until last night did she impart the news that his name was Roderick Vane and that he was the youngest son of Viscount Sawbridge who, sadly, on the grounds of ill-health, never left his home in Warwickshire. The dowager, of course, knew Sawbridge, but he had not been in town now for some appreciable time, for which is ill-health was clearly responsible, and nor was his wife, who obviously felt the need to remain at home with him; as for his two his eldest sons, both of whom were married and the proud fathers of a growing family, were therefore seldom seen in town, but this youngest sprig was quite unknown to her. As far as she knew, the Vanes, if not rich enough to buy an abbey as the saying went, were certainly well beforehand with the world, but since Letitia could not tell her anything more about this Roderick, the dowager deemed it prudent to delve a little deeper, and upon arriving home in Cavendish Square later that evening, after being divested of all her finery, tapped on her niece's door. Letitia, arrayed in a most becoming nightgown over which she wore a very fetching robe of ivory taffeta, cried,

"Dearest Aunt," hugging her and begging her to sit down while she herself curled up on the top of the bed coverlet.

"Well, child," the dowager nodded, having made herself comfortable, "I see you enjoyed yourself tonight."

"Oh, yes," Letitia cried, clapping her hands together, "it was a most wonderful evening. Did you not think so?"

"I've got eyes in my head," the dowager nodded, "but one ball is very much like another to me," she announced dismissively, tapping the floor with her cane. "When you get to be as old as I am, you will know that."

Without her paint and powder she looked much older, but her eyes had lost none of that sharpness, and eyeing her niece closely, mused, "Yes, you're an engaging minx, to be sure," to which Letitia giggled. "Now, Miss," she said bluntly, "tell me, about this man Roderick; and don't try to bamboozle me into believing you don't know who I'm talking about because that won't fadge; I've seen the two of you with my own eyes, don't forget! Are you fond of him?" she asked abruptly.

Letitia gave this some thought before saying, "I… I think so. I… I am not entirely sure, but I do know I like him very much."

The dowager pursed her lips at this. "He seems very particular in his attentions."

Letitia dropped her head a little at this, then, raising her eyes to her aunt's unadorned face, said, "Yes, he… he does seem to be."

"There's no 'seem' about it!" she snapped.

Letitia coloured up a little at this, but offered, somewhat faintly, "Yes, I… I suppose he is a little particular in his attentions, but I… I never encouraged him, Aunt."

"Suppose!" her aunt snapped again, ignoring this latter assertion. "I suppose he has to force you onto the floor with him or to escort you down to supper and I know not what else besides!"

"No," Letitia shook her head, "he does not have to force me." She was silent for a moment, then, as a thought occurred to her, she asked, "Have I done wrong, Aunt? Are you saying that I should not?"

"No, not wrong precisely," her aunt nodded, "but it won't do to let it be seen you are living in his pocket even before his ring is on your finger!"

A frown creased Letitia's forehead at this, saying at length, "I… I never thought of that."

"So I see," the dowager remarked, eyeing her niece's downcast face. "So, tell me," she cocked her head, "do you like him more than any other young man you have met?"

"Well," Letitia said slowly, "I like him more than I do, Fortherley."

"Ha!" her aunt exclaimed. "Who wouldn't?"

"And I certainly like him more than I do young Lord Hinchley, for all he's an earl," Letitia told her.

"Well, that ain't saying much," the dowager commented.

"And I certainly like him more than I do the Honourable Douglas Kingston," Letitia told her.

"So, what you are saying child," the dowager offered, "is that if this Roderick was to approach your brother with the intention of asking his permission to pay his addresses to you, you would not be displeased?"

Letitia stared a little perplexed at her aunt, repeating, "Pay his addresses to me?"

"That's what I said, child," the dowager nodded.

"But I... I never thought of that!" Letitia replied, horrified.

"Then it's time you did," her aunt told her bluntly.

"But, Aunt," Letitia exclaimed, "I... I never dreamed... " her voice failing her, jumping off the bed to kneel down in front of her aunt.

"Obviously!" the dowager bit out.

"But what am I to do?" Letitia asked urgently, taking hold of her aunt's left hand as it lay limply on the arm of the chair, those pansy brown eyes looking hopefully up at her.

When the dowager had taken on the responsibility of looking after Letitia it had been because her sister-in-law, too taken up with her own imaginary delicate state of health and the fragility of her nerves, had announced that the exigencies of a London season would be too much for her frail constitution to bear, and therefore much preferred to live quietly in Wiltshire with her eldest daughter Jane, who, sadly, had not taken. Not surprisingly, the dowager had her own thoughts on this rather moot point, but apart from passing the odd disparaging observation she had prudently kept her tongue but, for all that, she was nevertheless extremely fond of Letitia, indeed she was a most engaging and delightful child, but what the dowager had failed to take into account when she had offered to sponsor her niece for the season was that her age as well as the debilitating effects of arthritis would seriously hamper this. Of course, if Algernon were married then she could leave the chaperoning of her niece to his wife, but since he had so far showed no signs of settling down it seemed that the dowager could not relinquish her self-imposed task, and since it would be too cruel to pack the child off back to Wiltshire to stay with her mamma when she was clearly enjoying her first London season, the dowager had no alternative but to continue taking her out and about. Not that she minded, after all she had chaperoned her sister, Jane, but that was before her arthritis had deteriorated, but it was fast becoming borne in on that lady that the task of chaperoning her niece was more onerous than she thought it would be, particularly as she had already had occasion to send several gazetted fortune hunters to the right-about, which of course should have been Algernon's responsibility, and now it seemed that another spectre had raised its head in the form of the Honourable Roderick Vane.

According to Letitia he had just turned twenty-eight and was living in rooms in Half Moon Street. Since coming down from Cambridge he had spent time in Ireland on his uncle's estate there, but, now, having returned to England, it seemed he was determined to enjoy all the gaieties of town life, and since his parents were held in very good esteem he did not lack for invitations. The dowager could only hazard a guess as to whether or not he had made up to any other young woman, not that there was anything wrong in that, but the last thing she wanted was to see her niece tied up to someone who was more attracted to her money than the child herself, but if her feelings were correct, and she had the very strong feeling that they were, then this Roderick, once the knot was well and truly tied, would not be a faithful husband. Of course, it had to be said that not many were, but she loved Letitia enough to not to want to see her made unhappy, which, being married to a womanizer, most certainly would. The dowager could bring to mind more than one man who calmly disregarded the vows of matrimony, the late Earl of Markmoor for one, but she did not want this for her niece, but it seemed that Letitia was by no means certain that Roderick Vane was the man for her, which was perhaps just as well, but the dowager knew that the slightest inference on her part to what she believed was his true character, thereby leading her into making a hasty decision, she merely advised that whilst there was nothing wrong in accepting his invitation to dance, it would perhaps be as well for her not to permit any other form of partiality.

Letitia agreed with this, her face brightening, but upon asking her aunt what she should do if he persisted, she was merely told, "Tell him that he must apply himself to your brother!"

This made Letitia giggle, but when her aunt finally returned to her own room it could not be said that she was entirely quietened in her mind. She could, of course, write to her sister-in-law, but she instinctively knew it would be a complete and utter waste of time as that lady would no doubt say that her health, sadly, would not permit a stay in town, indeed it was something her physician would heartily deplore, and therefore she must do as she saw fit. This was all very well, but as the dowager blew out her candle and pulled the covers over her, she was very far from knowing what to do about a situation which, if not carefully handled, could cause all manner of problems.

*

Had the dowager the least idea that the Honourable Roderick Vane had no intention of offering for Letitia's hand either now or in the future, she would have experienced an overwhelming sense of relief. She may have taken him in dislike for reasons which she could not quite put her finger on, but had she known that he was a crony of Digby Singleton, whose acquaintance he had made during a sojourn in Paris when he was supposed to have been in Ireland as he had told Letitia he had been, then her dislike would have been more than justified; it would certainly have proved that her instincts had not erred.

Despite the big age gap that existed between the two men, they had very soon discovered that their tastes were very much in accord one with the other, and since it appeared that Roderick, no less than Singleton, was by no means impervious to a pretty face, as well as their predilection for cards and all games of chance, their friendship had very soon grown and blossomed. As it appeared that he was as careless of appearances as Singleton and that his spending far exceeded the generous allowance his father made him, therefore obliging him to pledge his credit all over town as well as resorting to punting on tick, leaving him wholly reliant upon his winnings, seemed to worry him not at all. He had as little to do with his two older brothers as possible, deploring their staid and boring lives, and had anyone ever asked him if he had ever seen his nieces and nephews he would have shuddered in revulsion. Since it seemed he was not blessed with the same sense of family honour and what was due to his name as his father and brothers, something that did not trouble him in the least, he deemed his position as the youngest son exonerated him of any family responsibility, and since Singleton was equally blessed with the same disregard of what was due to the name he bore, their friendship flourished apace.

As expected, it was not long before Singleton confided his attempted abduction of Letitia Rawnsley to him as well as the man to whom he owed his thanks for thwarting his schemes, and not for the first time, and Roderick, far from being shocked by such a confession, actually applauded it, being fully in sympathy with him and could well understand his friend's urgent desire to have his revenge on Deerham. Roderick had, of course, heard of Deerham, even seen him on a few occasions, but so far their paths had never crossed, not even over the card table at White's, and as it was not likely that Deerham would patronize the kind of gaming establishments, and certainly not the fancy houses, as he did himself, the chances were very good that they never would.

Singleton had not made a friend of Roderick simply to use him as a tool in his burning need to avenge himself on Deerham, on the contrary, he liked him very well, in fact, he had taken to the young man on first sight, indeed they had so much in common that he reminded him of his old crony the late Earl of Markmoor. Quite when the idea came to Singleton he had no very clear idea, but the more he thought about it the more perfect it seemed, particularly as Deerham was far too astute to be fooled into believing that his wife, who had been on the town now for nearly five months, had taken up with a young man whose extremely good looks were something to behold, particularly as there were any number of good-looking men adorning society. So far, there were none of the tell-tales signs on Roderick's face to inform the onlooker that he was in fact a most dissolute young man, indeed, his features were so far unmarked by either the passage of time or his way of life, and his manners, which could only be described as exquisite, were such that they were guaranteed to please even the most hardened dowager or chaperone.

Roderick, who was ripe for any challenge or wager, knew neither qualms nor misgivings when Singleton approached him about engaging himself in his cause, indeed, he threw himself into the enterprise with alacrity. In fact, he saw no difficulty in making himself agreeable to Letitia Rawnsley, who, Singleton had assured him, would unquestionably tell her friend the young marchioness all about him. If all Singleton had told him was true, then the young marchioness who, despite only being married a little under five months, was seldom to be seen in society with her husband; whether this stemmed from the fact that it was a marriage of convenience after all or merely because she was already bored with her husband, which, given the age gap between them would not be at all surprising, remained to be seen, but Roderick felt reasonably confident that he would have no trouble whatsoever in seducing her. From what Singleton had told him, the young marchioness, unlike Letitia Rawnsley, was no beauty, but be that as it may Roderick had yet to meet a woman who did not appreciate compliments and being made to feel as though she was something very special, and since he was an expert in such gallantries he envisaged no difficulties, indeed, he was looking forward to captivating her. If Singleton's strategies proved to be correct, then her husband, humiliated and disgraced, would feel he had no choice but to rid himself of his wayward wife; a wife who had finally proved herself to be every inch her father's daughter, a bitter blow to his pride and self-esteem. What better form of revenge than this?

*

As Singleton had rightly predicted, Letitia had told her friend all about the young man who had been proving somewhat particular in his attentions and her aunt's concerns because of it, the day following her return from Bath. Letitia may have admitted to having a liking for him, but when asked if she felt anything more than that, she shook her head, saying thoughtfully, "I… I don't think so. At least… but I'm not sure."

With this Louisa had to be satisfied, but when, later that evening at the Duchess of Devonshire's drum ball, she had the opportunity to meet him and to see for herself the young man who had been making up to her friend. No more than Letitia, did Louisa have the least idea that not only was he a hardened gamester but also an inveterate womanizer and a crony of Singleton's into the bargain, indeed, she was pleasantly surprised by what she saw, and when Letitia introduced her to him there was nothing in his manner to generate either disgust or aversion, on the contrary he was a very pleasant and affable young man and one Louisa had taken an instant liking to, little realizing that his charm of manner had been deliberately and carefully cultivated to perfection.

"Tell me," he raised an amusing eyebrow, "would it be impertinent of me if I called you Louisa instead of your ladyship?" he asked a little ruefully, his eyes smiling down into hers.

"Not at all," Louisa smiled. "Indeed, I should like it very much."

"That's settled then," he smiled. "Whilst you must call me Ricky. Everyone does so, you know."

Louisa laughed, finding his insouciant manner really quite charming, so much so that when he asked her if she would like to dance she had no hesitation in doing so, however, she did feel it incumbent upon her to ask, "Do you not think that you should be dancing with Letitia?"

"No," he smiled. "Why," he cocked his head, "do you think I should?"

"Well," Louisa mused, "it's just that I thought you and she were…"

"Just good friends," he assured her, his eyes twinkling down at her.

"My understanding is," Louisa smiled, "that you have been somewhat particular in your attentions to her."

"Mere gossip," he dismissed.

She raised her eyebrows at this, repeating, "Gossip! Is it gossip when you have her aunt thinking that you are about to come to the point?"

"Can I help what people think?" he asked disarmingly.

"No," she shook her head, but when the movement of the dance brought them back together, she said, "but I think you should perhaps refrain from giving people the wrong impression."

"Has anyone ever told you, *ma chérie*," he told her softly, totally ignoring what she had said, "that you are utterly delightful?"

Louisa may not have believed this for one moment, but it nevertheless took her a little aback, even more so when she considered that it was more how he said it rather than what he had said that made the colour flood her cheeks and her eyes fly to his, strangely discomfited by the rueful smile lurking in those dark brown eyes.

"I… I see you have a turn for flattery, sir," she told him as steadily as she could, not at all sure whether she liked it or not.

"*I?*" he exclaimed, raising a disbelieving eyebrow, but that smile still lingered in his eyes. "No, no," he shook his head, "you have it quite wrong *mon petite.*"

Louisa, thankful that the dance separated them yet again, thereby relieving her of the necessity of answering, which was perhaps just as well since she had no idea what to say in response to this, had been given a precious few moments in order to compose herself, but no sooner had the dance brought them together again and he took her hands in his to finish the last few movements of the dance, he said,

"Have I annoyed you?" looking down at her.

"No," Louisa assured him faintly, shaking her head, her spiral curls dancing, "not at all."

"I am glad of that," he smiled, "because you see," he told her softly, "I could not bear to think I had."

Louisa swallowed, then, after looking somewhat confusedly around her, firmly of the belief that they were being watched by a hundred pair of eyes, managed, "W-would it trouble you very much if you had?"

"I should be utterly desolate," he told her in a deepening voice, his fingers pressing hers, "so much so," he shrugged helplessly, "that there would be nothing for it but for me to blow my brains out!" This may have been said rather comically, but the look in his eyes remained, a circumstance Louisa was not at all sure whether to appreciate or not.

Compared to Letitia, who put her very much in the shade, as did most young ladies who adorned society at this present, Louisa knew perfectly well that she was no beauty, indeed were it not for her striking hair colour and those green eyes, an inheritance from her maternal grandmother, there would be nothing whatever remarkable about her, and certainly nothing to give rise to such comments as Roderick Vane had made to her. She told herself that he was just being courteous, as he obviously had been to Letitia, a young lady who by no means took exception to her friend being on the receiving end of his gallantries, but Louisa knew that she would be less than honest if she did not admit to liking him very well indeed.

Not surprisingly, he soon formed one of her court, a circumstance that considerably relieved the dowager's mind, telling her niece that she would do very well if she put him out of her mind. Letitia was only too pleased to do so, telling Louisa that she was not in the least bit jealous, a confession that made Louisa laugh.

"Oh, Letitia, you goose!" she exclaimed, embracing her friend. "I have no wish to make you jealous, and certainly not with Ricky."

Louisa may not have made Letitia jealous but there was no denying that the sight of him taking her for drives in the park, a drive out to Richmond or escorting her to a hundred different entertainments, would not create comment. Louisa would love Deerham until the day she died, but she was young enough and woman enough to enjoy the fulsome compliments Ricky made to her, even though she knew perfectly well that she was not the only woman he had made the object of his gallantry. To her, Ricky had become a dear friend, and one from whom she would hate to be parted, but at no time had her heart been touched by the things he said to her, accepting them in the same friendly spirit as he gave them, on the contrary her heart was solely lost to her husband, a man whom she knew would never love her.

Had Louisa the least idea that it was nothing but a carefully laid plot to ensnare her, or rather to force her husband's hand into divorcing her, she would have been genuinely and deeply shocked. Singleton, eyeing the couple closely, could not have been more pleased with the way things were turning out, indeed, so happy was he that he felt reasonably confident that it would not be long now before Deerham showed his hand, and when, later that evening, Ricky, having escorted Louisa to her door, joined him at one of the discreet gaming hells they both patronized, he told him, "You are to be congratulated, Ricky. Matters are progressing prodigiously well."

Raising his glass in salute, Ricky smiled, "Much obliged."

Singleton returned the salute. "You have exceeded all my expectations," he smiled, a bare thinning of his painted lips.

"Glad you think so," Ricky told him a little absently, his roving eye suddenly caught by the attentions of a dark-eyed brunette, all thoughts of Louisa deserting him.

"I do," Singleton almost purred, "most assuredly," his eyes following Ricky's appreciative glance.

"So," Ricky shrugged, reluctantly bringing his attention back to Singleton, "what happens now?"

"Now," Singleton sighed pleasurably, "we wait to see the outcome of your displays of gallantry."

Ricky thought a moment before saying, not a little hopefully, "You mean you want me to stop making up to the chit?"

"By no means," Singleton told him softly. "You will continue as before," not failing to notice the slight crease which furrowed his forehead, going on to tell him what he wanted him to do.

Having discarded his mistress for the simple reason that she had for some little time been giving off definite signals that she wanted more out of the relationship than Ricky was prepared to commit himself to, he had made Letitia Rawnsley the object of his gallantry, simply because there had been nothing else better to do. It was not in his nature to remain faithful to one woman, and since his two older brothers had secured the succession, he could see no necessity whatsoever for him to marry, an institution he had a complete and utter aversion to, indeed, the single life suited him very well. There was no denying that Letitia Rawnsley was a most taking little thing, really quite irresistible, but at no time was it his intention to arouse hopes in her breast of love and marriage, apart from which it was not his tendency to seduce innocent young ladies of the ton. He had not needed Louisa to tell him that Letitia's aunt was well on the way to believing that an offer of marriage was imminent, he knew it well enough, and therefore deemed it time to call a halt to his attentions, but as it appeared Letitia was by no means certain she liked his company more than that of any other man's, he felt he could abandon her with a clear conscience. Then Singleton had put his proposition to him.

As Singleton had rightly predicted, Letitia had told her friend all about him as soon as she had returned from Bath. Unlike Letitia, the young marchioness was by no means beautiful, indeed were it not for that striking copper coloured hair and those wide green eyes she was in no way remarkable, nevertheless, he had lost no time in making himself most agreeable to her as well as forming one of her court. Ricky could not deny that he had at first enjoyed making up to her, even taking her for drives around the park at the fashionable hour of the promenade and taking her for drives out to Richmond as well as escorting her to any number of parties if, for no other reason, than it afforded him amusement, but even though he was ripe for any mischief after several weeks of doing the pretty to her he soon found the task was beginning to pall, especially as his roving eye had alighted on far more beautiful ladies whose morals were questionable to say the least and who had let it be known that his attentions would not be in any way disagreeable to them. However, in view of Singleton's pronouncement as to the next step he wanted him to take regarding Louisa it necessarily meant that Ricky would not be free for some little time to tend to his own affairs, which was a pity because whilst he had no qualms about helping out a friend to bring about the downfall of a man he utterly despised, it did mean that it would be a little while yet before he would be able to give Louisa the go by.

So far, her husband had made no effort whatsoever to intervene much less demand to know what the devil he was playing at, besides, it was perfectly acceptable for a lady to gather about her a group of men whose sole ambition was to please her; after all, hadn't Deerham himself, as a young man, formed one of a lady's court?

Deerham knew Viscount Sawbridge very well, a quiet and rather reserved man who, due to ill-health, now found it necessary to absent himself from town and remain quietly on his estates in Warwickshire. When it came to his two eldest sons, Deerham could claim only the barest acquaintance with them as it seemed they both preferred the quiet of their country seats and their growing families to the entertainments on offer in town. As far as his youngest son, Roderick, was concerned, Deerham certainly knew him by reputation, and whilst this would not take too much scrutiny he had no idea that he was a friend of Singleton's and that Roderick's attentions to his wife were all part of a carefully laid scheme to ensure his downfall by making it impossible for him to do anything other than divorce his young wife, who had publicly made it known that she preferred another man's company to that of her husband. Deerham may not so far have intervened much less demanded to know what the devil was going on but he was by no means unaware of the role Roderick Vane was playing in Louisa's life. He knew his wife to be totally innocent and without guile or deceit, and therefore knew without being told that she was not playing some kind of game to make him jealous, after all it was quite de rigueur for a young man to take a lady for a drive, even a married lady, but although she still accepted his own escort now and then, the truth was Deerham *was* jealous, more than he had ever been in his life before, and it tore him apart.

He had not set out to fall in love with Louisa, on the contrary his offer of marriage had been merely to honour his father's agreement with her grandfather and for no other reason. As only to be expected, there had been any number of women in his life, all of whom had been as beautiful as they were experienced in knowing to a nicety how to please a man, but whilst Louisa was very far from being beautiful he had nevertheless, almost from the first moment he had laid eyes on her, been conscious of the fact that her looks really did not matter in the least. There was a spontaneity about Louisa that those other women had lacked, and those green eyes, which could light up in an instant, and that impish smile, both of which were really quite irresistible, had finally paved a path to his heart as no other woman ever had. Having told himself that he was by far too old and much too experienced to be taken in by a young lady who was as confiding as she was engagingly mischievous, he had therefore strenuously tried to ignore these very attractive qualities as well as the effect they had on his heart, but all to no avail. For a man of two and thirty to fall headlong into love with a young lady who had neither looks nor portion to recommend her was the height of folly, but he could no more stop loving her than he could grow wings and fly.

He knew perfectly well that Louisa was under the impression that it was nothing more than a marriage of convenience and not a love match, which is why his lovemaking had been very much in the same way he would treat a nervous filly; gentle and restrained, but if he thought that such moderation or understanding of her feelings would bring about a change of heart in Louisa he was very much mistaken. After five months into their marriage with no signs of Louisa coming to feel a fraction of what he felt for her, brought a pain around his heart the likes of which he had never before experienced, and, not for the first time, he was given to wondering if her mamma had warned Louisa against him or even, perhaps, if Singleton had said something to her, because there was no denying that when he first made her acquaintance there had been an ease of manner and an impulsiveness about her that had gradually disappeared. And yet, there were times, such as when he escorted her to Bath to stay with his mother, when she had completely forgotten herself and became once again that delightful and spontaneous young woman he had fallen in love with and this, coupled with the fact that there had been instances when Deerham had caught something in her eyes that not only made his heart leap but filled him with the hope that she did indeed love him after all.

Had Louisa known that her husband was as much in love with her as she was with him, she would have been the happiest of women, as it was she was faced with the painful fact that, although he obviously liked her, he was not in love with her, a circumstance that brought a dull ache around her heart. She could think of nothing better than having Deerham take her in his arms and telling her how much he loved her, but as this was nothing but a wishful dream she had to somehow try to make the best of things. But, and much to her surprise, her spirits were considerably uplifted when, upon arriving home in the early hours of the morning having said goodnight to her escort, she was met by her husband who, having himself arrived home early from his engagement and dismissed the night porter, opened the door to her himself.

"Max!" she cried, a little startled upon setting eyes on her husband instead of Jennings. "I had no idea you were home. I... I had not looked for you for some little time."

"Obviously," he replied, closing the door behind her.

It had not been Deerham's intention to mention the matter of Ricky Vane to his wife, but upon arriving home some three-quarters of an hour ago to find she had not yet returned, knowing perfectly well with whom she was spending her time, and even though he knew there was nothing between his wife and this seemingly personable young man, he was consumed with jealousy, the likes of which he had never before experienced.

It did not take the forbidding look on Deerham's face or the stern note in his voice to tell Louisa that he was very far from pleased, although why he should not be she had no idea. She could not begin to understand why he was looking so displeased, particularly as he must know that she and Ricky were just good friends. It was then that a startling thought occurred to her, so startling in fact that it was several moments before she could take it in. Surely, Deerham could not possibly be jealous?

"I take it you had an enjoyable evening?" Deerham broke into her chaotic thoughts.

"Yes," she managed, her heart pounding in her breast. "Most enjoyable."

"I am glad to hear it," he told her, the look on his face giving the lie to this statement. "I take it that your escort was Ricky Vane?"

Louisa looked up at the saturnine face looking down at her, but far from being hurt by such a display of disapproval she was overjoyed, so much so that it was all she could do to find the voice to say as calmly as she could, "Yes. You know it was."

"He seems most particular in his attentions," he told her a little harshly. "As I recall, it was not so long ago that he was paying court to Letitia Rawnsley!"

"I don't think it was anything serious," she said thoughtfully.

"Serious or not," he said coolly, "it was sufficient to set tongues wagging. I am not having them wag at you."

Louisa thought a moment, asking at length, "What would you do if they did?"

"Put a stop to Ricky Vane making you the object of his gallantry, what else?" he bit out.

Her heart leapt at this, but before she could question it further Deerham had turned on his heel and climbed the stairs.

Half an hour later, having dismissed Mary, Louisa, her heart racing and her stomach fluttering at the connotations she had drawn from her conversation with Deerham, tumbled into bed joyously conscious that she was happier than she had ever been in her life before.

When Louisa had first been introduced to Ricky by Letitia she knew instantly that she liked him, and she would have been less than honest not to admit that she enjoyed his company, but at no time had she set out to make Deerham jealous, on the contrary no such thought had entered her head, besides, there was no reason she could think of to make her do so, particularly as he was not in love with her. But however much she liked Ricky, a man who was accepted everywhere, she was by no means fooled by the lavish compliments he paid her, knowing them to be nothing more than what was expected of a man paying extravagant court to a woman.

It was perhaps as well for Louisa's peace of mind that she had no idea that Ricky's attentions towards her were nothing more than a cleverly designed plot by Digby Singleton to bring about the downfall of her husband, a man he heartily despised, in the most humiliating way possible. For a man of Deerham's pride to be obliged to watch his wife flagrantly conduct her illicit affair with Ricky Vane under the very noses of the ton, would be nothing short of an insult, leaving him with very little choice other than to save his honour in the best way he could by divorcing his young wife, a circumstance that would be as degrading as it would be humiliating.

Louisa could, at any time, have put a stop to Ricky Vane's attentions had she so wished, but although she had no idea how Deerham would attempt to do it for her, not that this mattered, just knowing he was jealous enough to try was sufficient to fill her with the hope that he did indeed love her after all, but as far Digby Singleton was concerned, he was overjoyed at the way things were turning out between his friend and the young marchioness. Indeed, he could not be more delighted, so much so that he now felt it to be the right time to put the final touches to his plans, particularly as the season was almost at the close, losing no time in tracking his crony down at his club.

But it seemed that Louisa's brief moment of joy was short-lived. If she thought that Deerham would behave coldly towards her or continue to show signs of disapproval about her friendship with Ricky Vane she was very much mistaken. Sitting opposite him the following morning at the breakfast table Louisa could hardly believe, listening to him conversing easily and quite affably to her on any number of topics, that she was facing the same man, who, only a few hours before had been far from happy, making his displeasure known about her relationship with Ricky Vane, expressing his strong disapproval.

Deerham, having somehow managed to bring his temper as well as his jealousy under control, had eventually come to realize that by making a display of his disapproval could so easily push Louisa over the brink from friendship to something more endurable, and this was the very last thing he wanted, but even though this reasoning went a long way to easing his resentment, it in no way eased the pain around his heart.

Chapter Eighteen

Deerham knew perfectly well that there was nothing more than friendship between his wife and Ricky Vane and, unless he had misread that young man's character, he would say that he had no more romantical thoughts towards her than she did to him, and therefore only the malicious would read more into it than was actually the case. When he had finally made up his mind to offer for Louisa after all, indeed not to have done so would not only have brought his name into disrepute but would be a gross insult to her, he had never for one moment thought that he would fall in love with her. That he had done so came as something of a surprise to him, especially when he considered that she sadly took after neither parent. Her father, who had been a very handsome man when young, had, due to the passage of time and the effects of dissipation, taken their toll; and her mother, who had been an accredited beauty in her day, in fact she was still a remarkably handsome woman, had not passed on these attributes to their daughter. Nevertheless, at their very first meeting Deerham had been conscious that her looks did not matter in the least, and as time had passed even less so, and that unaccountable stirring he had felt somewhere deep inside him had, over time, become an unbearable ache. There was something very attractive about Louisa, even alluring, which had nothing to do with her striking colour combination, and although he could not quite put his finger on why this should be, he did know that she was as spontaneous as she was unaffected, and therefore the very thought of her not loving him was too horrendous to contemplate, so much so that, even though he knew his wife looked upon Ricky Vane as an amusing acquaintance and not as a potential lover, he never believed that he could experience so much jealousy.

When Deerham had arrived home early the other night to the intelligence that Louisa had not yet returned, he tried to tell himself that he was being ridiculous, but upon seeing Ricky Vane hand her out of her chair and up the steps of the house the effect it had on him had been one of unaccountable anger, and therefore when he told his wife that he would put a stop to her friendship with Ricky Vane should the slightest tittle-tattle be voiced, he had meant it. It could not be said that Deerham was a friend of Vane's, on the contrary their acquaintanceship was confined to nothing more than a brief nod in passing, but he knew all about his gambling and womanizing, and although he acquitted him of having designs on Louisa, he would nevertheless have been extremely shocked to learn that his gallantries towards her were nothing but a cleverly devised plot of Singleton's to bring about his downfall.

*

For a Tuesday evening White's was unusually thin of company, but Singleton, strolling into the club a little after nine o'clock, spotted his crony seated at a table throwing dice from left hand to right and, sauntering over to him, said smoothly, "Ah, I knew I should find you here."

Ricky looked up, and, cocking his head, said, "Singleton! What's to do?"

Singleton pulled out a chair and sat gracefully down onto it, but not until he had taken a leisurely pinch of snuff and taken a moment to glance around him, extremely relieved to see that there was no sign of Deerham, did he say, "Unfinished business."

Ricky paused in the act of throwing his dice and, after draining the remains in his glass, looked knowingly at him. "You mean the Deerham chit?" he cocked his head.

"But of course," Singleton said smoothly, flicking a residue of snuff from off the cuff of his coat. "What else?"

Ricky thought a moment, saying at length, "Y'know, I've been thinking about that."

"So have I," Singleton smiled thinly. "Which is what brings me here now," pausing only long enough to wave a languid white hand at a passing acquaintance. "You have done well, Ricky," Singleton said smoothly. "Very well, indeed."

"Glad you think so," Ricky nodded.

"Oh, but I do," Singleton said slowly. "Indeed, I am all admiration, but I feel the time has now come to put our *pièce de résistance* into effect."

"Eh!" Ricky cried, surprised. "Do we have one?"

"But of course," Singleton nodded. "And it is so perfectly exquisite."

Ricky eyed him narrowly for a moment, asking at length, "And what is this *pièce de résistance*?"

Singleton eyed him steadily, shrugging at length, "Oh, nothing too taxing."

"Well?" Ricky urged when Singleton made no immediate effort to enlarge on his theme.

Singleton considered a moment, then, after meditatively running his finger and thumb up and down the ribbon of his quizzing glass, he gave a somewhat thin smile, saying smoothly, "The time, my dear Ricky, is now propitious for you to abduct her."

Whatever Ricky had expected it was certainly not this, and immediately the dice stilled, leaning forward in his seat, repeating slowly, "Abduct her? Good God!" he cried when his initial shock had worn off. "Are you mad?"

Singleton eyed him narrowly. "Do I detect a certain reluctance on your part?"

Ricky may be prime for any lark, which is why he had lent himself to making up to the Deerham chit in the first place, irrespective of Singleton's motives to bring her husband to his knees, but abduction was something else; and he had no stomach for it. "The devil you do," Ricky said slowly.

Those pencilled eyebrows rose. "Indeed! And what scruple makes you stop short of it?" When Ricky made no immediate effort to respond to this, Singleton sighed, saying a little mournfully, "You know, I am quite disappointed in you – really, quite disappointed."

"You'll get over it," Ricky shrugged.

Singleton's eyebrows snapped together. His plans for the downfall of Deerham, having already gone horrendously awry thanks to Carrie Marchand letting his wife escape from her clutches, he was certainly not prepared to have it happen a second time. The truth was he had not expected Ricky to get cold feet, but unless he was very much mistaken this is precisely what he had got, and he was by no means pleased, and allowed his annoyance to show.

"My dear Ricky," he said with ominous quiet, "having expended a considerable amount of time and thought on this matter, I am not about to let Deerham escape now."

Ricky, who had resumed his throwing of the dice from one hand to the other, looked up at this. "And you think that by abducting his wife it will push him into divorcing her?"

"I know it will," Singleton purred. "You see, Ricky," he told him, "I know Deerham almost as well as I know myself. He is by far too proud to have people say of him that he stood by while his wife cavorted around with another man and he did nothing about it. The shame," he shrugged eloquently, "would be more than he could bear."

Ricky put his dice back into his pocket and, after pouring out two glasses of wine and thrusting one towards Singleton, he leaned back in his chair, saying, "That's all very well, but aren't you forgetting one thing?" Singleton merely raised an eyebrow at this. "Supposing he does divorce her, what about me?" Ricky raised a questioning eyebrow. "Have you thought of that? Or are you suggesting that I marry her?"

"And here was I labouring under the impression that you were ripe for any lark," Singleton sneered.

"I may be," Ricky nodded, "but I've no taste for finding myself saddled with a wife."

"And what is it," Singleton raised a questioning eyebrow, "that leads you to believe you will be? I am not, after all," he inclined his head, "asking you to elope with her."

"What then?" Ricky demanded, cocking his head.

Singleton took a moment to answer this, then, after retrieving his snuff-box from his pocket and flicking the lid with an expert thumb, said, "Merely that I wish you to take her somewhere for, let us say, " he mused, "a couple of days."

"Take her somewhere?" Ricky repeated. "Where, for God's sake?" he demanded.

"Oh," Singleton shrugged, "anywhere you please. Then," he shrugged again, "you will bring her back to town to face her irate husband, who, I feel confident, will take all the necessary steps."

Ricky eyed him closely, saying, "You must be out of your senses! I've courted and flattered her, taken her out for drives and I know not what else besides, and," he pointed his glass at him, "so far nothing seems to have moved her husband. Either he knows there's nothing in it or he simply does not care!"

"He may not care for her," Singleton replied smoothly, "but he certainly cares about his good name."

Ricky, after thinking it over, shook his head, saying firmly, "No, I won't do it."

This was not what Singleton wanted to hear, and it considerably annoyed him, but after taking a moment to bring his temper under control, he said, "I had no idea you possessed such scruples."

Ricky grimaced. "I don't have many, I admit," he acknowledged, truthfully, "but there are certain things at which I draw a line."

"And this is one such, I take it?" Singleton raised a pencilled eyebrow.

"You seem surprised," Ricky raised an eyebrow.

"No," Singleton shook his head, "just disillusioned."

"Well, like I said," Ricky reiterated, "you'll get over it." He saw the look of frustration on Singleton's face, and said, "If you want to bring Deerham to his knees then go ahead, but you will do it without me. I've gone as far as I care to in this."

"Very well," Singleton surprised him by saying, "I will."

Ricky rose to his feet and, after tossing off the rest of his wine, looked down at Singleton, saying, "I wish you luck."

*

By the end of June, the season was drawing to a close, and already a lot of houses had had the knocker removed from the door signifying their departure from the metropolis. Louisa, looking forward to going down to Worleigh for a couple of weeks prior to going to Brighton with her husband, who had hired a house in the best part of town, was already sorting through her wardrobe. It had been almost a week since she had last seen Ricky, and although she could not help but wonder what had become of him, it was not something that occupied her mind.

Letitia, not as fortunate as Louisa, was not, sadly, going to Brighton as she longed to do, but home to Wiltshire. She confided to her friend that it was a pity her aunt could not be induced into hiring a house for the season as she longed to visit this seaside resort, but as this redoubtable lady was preparing to descend on a family relative, which was her annual custom, it seemed pointless to argue the matter. It could not be said that Letitia was looking forward to going home to Wiltshire, not only because her mamma, or so she claimed, was prostrated by the least exertion, but the most she could hope for was a trip to Salisbury Cathedral in company with her sister Jane or receiving regular visits from Reverend Topham, a man who was mightily prone to discussing at length his passion for butterflies and all things botanical. It was not to be expected that such subjects as these could appeal to a young lady who had, only a week before, met a most personable young man, and one who seemed to be as taken with her as she was with him.

The moment Letitia had laid eyes on the Honourable James Hastie all thoughts of Ricky Vane were forgotten, not that she had really been that attached to him, more flattered than anything else, but as she told her friend there was no comparison between them, indeed James was far and away a more attractive proposition, and therefore going into Wiltshire and not seeing him again until the season begun again, was more than she could bear. Louisa sympathized, telling Letitia that if this James Hastie was as sincere as he had led her to believe, then she could be assured of seeing him again, perhaps even taking it into his head to visit her in Wiltshire, a thought that sent her off to her ancestral home in a far lighter and happier frame of mind.

Louisa, meanwhile, had still one or two engagements to attend before the house in Grosvenor Square was shuttered for the summer months. The truth was she really had no mind for attending either, not simply because the saloons of her hostesses would be rather thin of company this late in the season, but they were known as being high sticklers, not to mention friends of her mother, who would be more than capable of taking offence if she did not attend. It was therefore in a rather dejected frame of mind that Louisa stepped into the carriage to take her the short distance to Lady Templeton's little soirée at her house in Curzon Street, not even having had at least five minutes alone with Max, having left the house some time before to keep an engagement of his own, to lighten her mood.

As expected, the evening, if not dull, was certainly not very enlivening, indeed, Louisa doubted that she had ever before met a set of persons more unexciting than those who graced Lady Templeton's saloons; either that, or she was more tired than she thought. But by midnight, Louisa finally managed to escape, one of the footmen calling up her carriage. By now, the rain, which had begun as a light drizzle earlier in the evening, was now coming down in earnest, so much so that when her carriage pulled up outside Lady Templeton's front door the footman had an umbrella ready, which he held low over her head as she stepped outside. Louisa, concentrating on holding up her skirts to prevent them from getting wet as well as looking down at the pavement in order to avoid the puddles, thankfully climbed inside the carriage, whereupon the steps were immediately put up and the door closed upon her, but just as Louisa realized there had been a mistake and she was not in Deerham's town carriage as she had thought, the equipage began to move forward over the wet cobbles.

For one bewildered moment she could not think how she could possibly have been stupid enough to enter the wrong carriage, but as it had never so much as crossed her mind that it was all part of a clever ploy she tried to pull down the glass top of the door to call to the driver, only to find that it would not budge. Even though she knew it was useless she nevertheless banged on the roof in the hope of attracting the driver's attention and instructing him to take her back to where she had come from, but no response was forthcoming. For some inexplicable reason disquiet began to envelop her, and in her desperation to make the driver aware of her predicament she tried again to open the windows, but when they remained secured against her she banged on the glass, only to find that it was totally ineffectual; either he could not hear her or he was deliberately ignoring her.

It was not long before they had left the cobbles behind them, the houses becoming fewer and farther between, and the driver picked up speed. Louisa had no idea who the driver was or where he was taking her, but it was not long before the streetlamps were left behind and total darkness met her frightened gaze as she stared disbelievingly through the pane of glass at the unknown landscape. For one brief moment she wondered if someone was practicing a jest of some kind, but only a very little thought was enough to tell her that no one of her acquaintance would go to such lengths for a prank, indeed there was no reason why they should. Her mind was awash with speculation, totally at a loss to account for it, even as to the reason why the glass on the doors had been secured, and the disquiet that had assailed her upon first entering the carriage to discover her error now turned into panic. Try as she did, she could not be still, her small hands trying yet again to pull down the glass windows in both the doors, only to find they held firm against her, bringing with it the inevitable feeling of utter helplessness. Refusing to allow the tears of frustration welling up at the back of her eyes to fall, she told herself that there was bound to be a reasonable explanation to account for this unprecedented, even ludicrous, situation she was in, but no matter how hard she tried she could think of none which satisfied her much less relieved her apprehension.

Trying not to think of where she would end up or in whose hands, she told herself that finding herself entering the wrong carriage was nothing more than a simple mistake, and once their destination was reached the error would be discovered and she would be returned home to Grosvenor Square, but somehow this did not satisfy her much less settle her nerves. Attempting once again to peer through the windows, which by now were liberally splashed with mud, proved totally useless; apart from the odd light coming from a farmhouse some way in the distance or remote cottage there was nothing to tell her where she was or in which direction she was travelling. Trying hard to clamp down on the panic and alarm growing inside her she told herself, for the umpteenth time, that it was nothing but an error and she was worrying unduly, but that streak of honesty which characterized her told her it was no such thing, and that whoever was behind her abduction, because she could call it nothing else, had a specific purpose in mind. What this was she was totally at a loss to even hazard a guess, but realizing there was nothing she could realistically do until her destination was reached, she wrapped her taffeta wrap closer around her shoulders and rested her head back against the squabs, trying to not only ignore the continuous jolting of the coach from the many potholes but to close her mind as to what awaited her.

She could only speculate how long they had been travelling, but it seemed like many miles had passed since she had entered this coach, but finally, after what seemed an aeon of time, the coach began to reduce speed, and upon leaning forward to peer through the windows Louisa could see they were entering a town. Which town it was she had no idea but after seeing the coach turn down into what appeared to be a side street and drive on for some little way, it eventually came to a standstill outside an inn, filling her with the hope that the landlord, upon discovering her plight, would offer her sanctuary until word could be got to Deerham to come and take her home. However, these thoughts were instantly curtailed upon seeing the driver jump down off the box to open the door for her and, refusing his proffered hand to assist her to alight, she managed to descend the steps on her own. Upon receiving no response to her demand to know where she was and why he had brought her here, she was just about to demand he answer her when the door was opened by a man she had no hesitation in recognizing as the landlord, but as she had no wish to create a disturbance in the open courtyard within hearing of she knew not how many ostlers, she merely followed him inside, hearing the carriage drive away as she did so.

It was a well-proportioned inn and, from the looks of it, one that clearly enjoyed a good deal of custom, if not by members of the ton then certainly from local residents as well as those looking to pay less than they would elsewhere, but at this early hour in the morning with the patrons all being in bed, all was quiet. Louisa, standing rigidly on the threshold, was feeling tired, confused and not a little annoyed, but as the landlord bent over double as he bowed to her, his nose almost touching his knees, welcoming her to his hostelry, she felt compelled to ask him where she was and the name of his establishment, but to her annoyance instead of answering her he merely opened a door on the right-hand side of the passageway, saying, "In here, your ladyship."

Looking from the landlord's impassive face to the door he had just opened with extreme wariness, it briefly crossed her mind to make a dash for the door, but only a moment's thought was enough to convince her that flight was useless, not only because she had no idea where she was or in which direction she should flee but from the looks on the landlord's face it was clear he was more than capable of preventing it. Holding her taffeta wrap tighter around her, Louisa stepped cautiously into the private parlour only to find, much to her surprise, a table laid for two people. It was a very comfortable apartment made more so by the fire burning in the grate, because although the days were pleasantly warm, at this time of the morning there was a definite chill in the air. Upon hearing the door close behind her Louisa quickly turned, apprehension clearly visible in her eyes, but upon hearing a voice say,

"Good evening, my dear - or should I say good morning?"

From out of startled eyes Louisa, much to her surprise, saw Digby Singleton leisurely rise from a wing chair beside the fireplace and make a most exquisite bow.

"You!" she gasped, hardly able to believe her eyes.

"I feel I must apologize for the unorthodox manner in which you were brought here, and at a most unconscionable hour," he smiled thinly, "but you see, my dear," he raised a pencilled eyebrow, "I felt quite certain that you would not come by my invitation."

Her eyes spat green fire at him. "Why am I here?" she demanded angrily. "What is it you want?"

No, the young Marchioness of Deerham was no beauty, but seeing her now, her face flushed with anger and those green eyes sparkling dangerously, he had to admit that there was something very taking in her. Of course, it was a pity he had been reduced to such a stratagem as this, but having been let down by Carrie Marchand, and Ricky Vane had unexpectedly shown a remarkable disinclination to take the matter further, Singleton had come to the conclusion that if he wanted to see this matter through then it would be left to him to make sure it was. Of course, it meant the outcome would not be quite what he had planned, but it would do just as well. He could not see Deerham divorcing his wife for something she could not have foreseen or planned, but upon reflection he was forced to admit that her abduction could well turn out far better than he had ever expected.

He had been extremely reluctant to show his hand, but when faced with the unpalatable thought that he really had no choice, he had set about making his arrangements without a twinge of conscious or feelings of remorse, using a submissive if unenthusiastic Grimshaw to transact the hiring of the carriage and the private parlour at *The Blue Boar*, a hostelry whose landlord was entirely devoted to his interests, as well as greasing Lady Templeton's footman heavily in the fist.

His feelings for Deerham could at no time be regarded as friendly, indeed, he could think of no man he hated more; so what better form of revenge then for being thwarted by him time and again than to make him pay through the nose for the safe return of his wife. And Deerham would pay! He was far too proud to let it be seen that he had been worsted by a man whose friend had been shunned by his own father!

When Singleton made no immediate effort to answer her, she said, "I have no idea what it is you want and, quite frankly, I do not care, but I demand you take me home immediately."

"You must forgive me, my dear," he inclined his head, "but, regrettably, I am afraid I cannot do that, at least," he amended, "not quite yet."

"If this is some jest," she told him heatedly, "then I am not amused."

"It is no jest," he shook his head. He smiled, advising smoothly, "Please, do not make the mistake of failing to take me seriously; believe me, I have never been in more earnest." He saw her turn her head to look at the closed door behind her, warning, "Rid your mind of any thoughts of escape; there is none."

Whatever anxieties Louisa felt she hid them admirably and, casting a glance at the laden table then back at Singleton, said, "If that is meant for me, you have wasted your time as well as your money."

"Do you think so?" he raised a pencilled eyebrow. "We shall see. But something tells me that before too long you will be glad of something to eat, especially if Deerham does not accede to my demands."

Louisa eyed him sharply. "Deerham?" she repeated, enlightenment beginning to dawn. "What demands?" she asked curiously.

After taking a leisurely pinch of snuff, he looked at her, a smile touching his thin painted lips. "Demands which, unless I am very much mistaken," he inclined his head, "he will find extremely difficult to ignore."

Louisa had known almost from the very beginning that there was no love lost between Deerham and Singleton, and although neither man had ever mentioned it, much less discussed it with her, she knew the animosity went deep, but that Singleton should succumb to such depths as this to get back at Deerham surprised even her. She could only begin to speculate what it was between them that had generated such animosity as this, but that Singleton was holding her to ransom she was in no doubt, but that he should dare to use her to achieve his despicable ends was the outside of enough. Singleton was not to know that Deerham did not love her, and she would rather die than admit it to a man she not only disliked but distrusted, but Singleton knew that Deerham would nevertheless pay for her release, something Louisa had to try to prevent happening, but how to escape had her in a puzzle. She had heard the landlord turn the key in the lock of the door to the private parlour so there was no chance of escaping that way, and just one glance at the windows was enough to tell her that these too would be locked, but even supposing she could escape she had no idea where she was or in which direction she should go, something that only served to increase her frustration, but she would rather die than show her fear to this man.

Something in Singleton's face told her that he knew precisely what thoughts were going around in her head, making her hands itch to slap that powdered and painted face. "I am glad to see that your situation has not escaped you," he told her smoothly, "and that it is quite useless to attempt anything in the way of escape."

"You can't keep me here!" she told him angrily, her green eyes flashing.

"Oh, but I can," he smiled thinly, taking a meditative pinch of snuff. "You see, my dear," he pointed out, "not only is the landlord, Hinkson, a particular friend of mine, and one who not only has my best interests at heart but who will ensure you remain here until Deerham complies with my wishes."

She looked disdainfully at him. "You seem to make a habit of abducting females, do you not?"

Beneath the powder and rouge a tinge of colour stole into his cheeks at this. "So," he mused at length, a crease furrowing his forehead at this, "you know about that!"

"Yes," she nodded, "I know. Letitia told me. She also told me how you were thwarted by a masked stranger."

Singleton was not at all surprised that Letitia Rawnsley had confided the truth to Louisa, after all they had struck up quite a friendship, but even though she had clearly not told her who the masked stranger was, simply because he doubted whether Deerham would have revealed his identity to her, the fact remained that this unpalatable truth had the effect of deepening the colour in his powdered and rouged face, but managing to clamp down on his temper, he said smoothly,

"A circumstance that will not happen again, I assure you."

"Really!" Louisa raised a sardonic eyebrow. "You seem very certain of that."

"I am," he told her. "So certain in fact," he inclined his head, "that you cannot look to be similarly saved."

Louisa eyed him steadily, no traces of the fear which was running through her visible on her face, saying, "You are despicable."

"I am anything you please," he bowed mockingly, "but it does not alter the fact that you will remain here until Deerham complies with my wishes."

"You could be waiting a very long time," she told him.

"Oh, I don't think so," he shook his head. "You see, my dear," he told her smoothly, "I know Deerham almost as well as I know myself, and therefore I feel confident enough to say that he will pay – never fear."

Louisa's eyes flashed. "You are not only despicable, but a commoner as well!"

Even though he would dearly love to bring her to heel he nevertheless realized perfectly well what she was trying to do and, under different circumstances, he would have applauded such an effort, but this home truth caught him on the raw. The truth was it would have given him tremendous satisfaction to slap her, but even though he knew that this would serve no real purpose, it nevertheless took him several moments to bring his temper under control. Not only this, but whilst he would stake his life that relations between Deerham and his wife were not at all what one would expect, Singleton wanted to give him no more provocation to bring him to account, but that he would fail to pay for the safe return of his wife was in no doubt. Deerham of all people would not want it known that his wife had been abducted and he had failed to secure her safe release, and from this standpoint if no other, Singleton felt himself to be on pretty safe ground.

But from the looks on the young marchioness's face however, she was not going to prove herself to be either an acquiescent or a compliant captive, on the contrary she looked every inch her indignation and more than prepared to do battle with him. Indeed, she had already shown her unwillingness to accommodate him, even going so far as to reject all sustenance. But Singleton, who had calculated that it would probably be a couple days before Deerham could put his hands on the money demanded for her release, she would no doubt be feeling the pangs of hunger and therefore only too ready to be more malleable.

"I am quite happy to be anything you please," Singleton bowed his head in mock politeness, "but I feel sure you will feel far more comfortable if you sat down." Completely ignoring this request, Louisa pulled her taffeta wrap closer around her, eyeing him in utter aversion. A slight laugh left his throat at this, then, after giving her a slight bow, smiled, "As you please, but I wonder if you will be of quite the same mind after spending a couple of days here."

Louisa, knowing it was useless to either make a dash for the door as it was securely locked and the windows too, besides which Singleton would be bound to prevent her, threw him a speaking glance, but as if realizing, however reluctantly, the sense of what he had said, she walked over to the table and pulled out a chair, as far away from Singleton as possible.

"Very sensible," he smiled.

"You do not surely expect Deerham to accede to your demands?" she demanded.

"Oh, but I do," he nodded. "Indeed," he raised a pencilled eyebrow, "I expect a most profitable return for my efforts."

"You surely do not expect to get away with this?" she challenged, her face very much flushed.

He thought a moment, then, looking meditatively at her, said, "I am afraid I do. You see, my dear, I somehow cannot see Deerham refusing to pay for your safe return, which, should this ever become known, would condemn him in the eyes of the world." She threw him a scorching look, which he totally ignored. "He will pay, never fear," he told her in ominous calm, "and without a word to anyone. How do I know this?" he raised an eyebrow, "because I know Deerham. He is far too proud to admit to the world that he had been worsted by the likes of me."

"You hate him that much?" she demanded.

"You will never know how much," he told her in a strangely quiet voice. "Your husband has meddled in my affairs once too often."

"With good cause I have no doubt!" she threw at him.

Singleton eyed her calculatingly for a moment, saying at length, "Let us just say that he mistakenly thought so."

"I seriously doubt that," she flung at him, her face very much flushed. "Perhaps if you conducted yourself more like a gentleman there would have been no need for him to have done so."

Singleton's eyes narrowed at this and his face took on an unhealthy tinge, and it was several moments before he could bring his temper sufficiently under control to say with a smoothness he was far from feeling, "Deerham, my dear, is not the arbiter of either my morals or my conduct."

"A pity," she threw at him, "because it seems to me that someone ought to be, particularly when I consider your actions this evening."

He eyed her steadily before saying, "What you think is of no consequence. All that matters is that Deerham will be brought to his knees."

Louisa looked sharply at him, having a very good idea what he meant by this, but as it was patently obvious he was not going to expand on it, she scorned, "I was right, you *are* despicable."

A slight inclination of the head was the only answer she received to this. "And now, my dear," he offered, "I must bid you goodnight. Do not make the error of raising a cry for help, there is no one here except myself, the landlord and his wife, and if you think the other patrons will come to your assistance, you could not be more in error. You see, my dear, I have reserved this parlour exclusively for my own use, so no one will enter, Hinkson will see to that. Your efforts, therefore, will be entirely wasted." He walked towards the door, then, as if bethinking himself of something, turned and said, "Please, help yourself to the dishes, it would be a shame to waste them," then, after retrieving a key from his pocket he unlocked the door and walked out of the room.

No sooner did Louisa hear him lock the door from the outside than she stamped her foot in utter frustration, finding an inevitable relief by bursting into tears.

Chapter Nineteen

Both the hall porter, Jennings, and Clifton, having been informed by Deerham that there was no need for them to wait up, had just climbed the back stairs to check everything was in order before retiring, when his eyes fell upon a sealed letter on the floor in the hall. He had no idea how long it had been there but he was convinced that it must have been delivered at some point over the last hour or so because he would have seen it otherwise. Bending down and picking it up he glanced at the legend written in a bold hand on the front, and upon seeing it was addressed to Deerham he laid it on the table in the hall ready for when his lordship returned from his club. To say that it was somewhat unusual for letters to be delivered at such an hour was something of an understatement, but Clifton, dismissing it with a casual shrug of his shoulders, merely extinguished all the candles in the hall except one which he left for his lordship on the table before returning to his own quarters.

Deerham, returning home an hour later, spotted the letter on the spindle legged table straightaway and debated whether to leave reading it until tomorrow, but after only a moment's thought he decided to read it now and, breaking the wafer, he held it against the beam of light from the candle, reading its contents with a darkening brow:

"Deerham,

By the time you receive this your wife will have been in my custody for some appreciable time. No harm will come to her I assure you, but should you prove yourself obstructive or fail to take me seriously, then I can make no guarantees where her safety is concerned.

In order to ensure her safe return, I feel sure you will agree that she is worth every penny of the twenty thousand guineas I know you will pay for her release. An extortionate sum you might think, but I feel sure that for a man of your affluence it should not prove too difficult a matter to lay your hands on such a sum. Having done so, you are to deliver it by noon on Thursday to the Piccadilly side of Green Park where a man called Johnson will be waiting for you. He will be sitting on the first bench on the left-hand side of the path just inside the entrance, but other than ascertaining his identity there will be no need for discourse between you.

If you want to see your wife safely returned to you then I would strongly advise you not to do anything foolish.

Once again, I urge you not to make the mistake of failing to take me seriously or to disregard the instructions in this letter as to do so would leave me with no alternative but to ensure you never see your wife again.

'Unsigned'

Having read it through a second time, Deerham stood for several moments staring straight ahead of him at nothing in particular, the sheet of vellum slowly crushed in his well-shaped hand, a deep frown creasing his forehead. The handwriting was clearly disguised, but it nevertheless belonged to an educated and cultured man and one, moreover, who clearly knew enough about him to not only know that he could more than well afford to pay such a sum but that he would pay anything to get Louisa back. Other than Digby Singleton, he knew of no one who hated him to the point where he would take his dislike to such a length as this, but even though Deerham shied away from such a thought it nevertheless had his named stamped all over it. Thanks to his own intervention, Singleton, having twice failed to run off with an heiress as well as taking advantage of Lord Finchley's youth and inexperience, Deerham could not rid his mind that he was the architect behind this latest but ignoble scheme. Considering Singleton's fluctuating pecuniary affairs, which were practically common knowledge, it would not surprise Deerham in the least to know that he was attempting to gain monetary advantage in some misguided attempt to pay him back for what he called his 'meddlesome interference' by using Louisa as a means of achieving it. Carrie Marchand herself had admitted that it was Singleton who had put her up to perpetrating the devious scheme to entrap his wife, so it was therefore logical to assume that the arrival of Ricky Vane in Louisa's life was also his doing. Of course, all of this was nothing more than conjecture, but try as he did Deerham could think of no one else who would have either the effrontery or the nerve to attempt something of this nature.

Deerham knew that Louisa had been going to Lady Templeton's this evening, one of the last routs of the season before they went to Worleigh prior to going down to Brighton, and although he had not expected to see her before midnight, he had nevertheless expected her to return home before now. The very thought of Louisa being held against her will, subjected to goodness only knew what, in a location that was quite unknown to her, was more than he could bear, and if he had needed any further proof that she meant more to him that life itself then this was surely it. He could well imagine her shock upon discovering that she had been abducted, frightened and extremely anxious about what was going to happen to her, but even though she did not know that he loved her she nevertheless knew he would pay whatever it cost to get her back. He closed his eyes on an anguished sigh, raising an unsteady hand to his forehead. He knew perfectly well that the blame was his; he should have taken better care of her and insisted she accepted his escort as well as telling her that he loved her irrespective of her feelings for him, and now, thanks to Singleton, because nothing would convince him that he was not the architect of this latest and scurrilous scheme, there stood a very good chance that he may not be given the opportunity.

Having by now emerged from his abstraction, Deerham pulled himself together and strolled into his book room with a leisureliness that totally belied his inner anxiety, pulling the bell tug for Clifton. Not having expected his lordship to ring for him at this hour of the morning, it was hardly surprising that it was some little time before he was able to scramble into his clothes before hurrying up the backstairs as quickly as his generous proportions would permit, putting in a somewhat belated appearance.

"You rang, my lord?" he enquired a little out of breath, not failing to notice the grim look on Deerham's face, casting about rapidly in his mind to try and detect some oversight on his part, not that he expected his lordship to rant at him, he was nothing if not generous and considerate.

"Yes," Deerham nodded. "Tell me, Clifton, did you see who it was who delivered this letter?"

"No, my lord," he shook his head, wondering what had brought about that grim look on his lordship's face. "I came upon it quite by chance when I checked everything was in order before I retired, not an hour before you came home."

Deerham nodded, then, looking from the letter in his hand to Clifton's face, mused, "So this could have been delivered at any time over the past two or three hours."

"Yes, my lord," Clifton nodded. The look on Deerham's face was particularly forbidding, and when he made no immediate effort to say anything, Clifton asked tentatively, "Is... is something wrong, my lord?"

Deerham eyed him meditatively before sighing, "Yes, Clifton, I am very much afraid there *is* something wrong." He paused a moment. "Prepare yourself for a shock, Clifton. Your mistress has been abducted."

Whatever it was Clifton had expected his lordship to say it was certainly not this, and it was therefore several moments before he could find his voice sufficiently to repeat, somewhat faintly, "Abducted, my lord?"

"Yes," Deerham confirmed in a voice he knew must be his own, unable to bear the thought that Louisa was in the clutches of those who would stop at nothing to achieve their aims.

"But I… I don't understand, my lord," he shook his head, bewildered. "Why should anyone want to abduct her?"

Deerham swallowed the lump that suddenly appeared in his throat, saying at length, "I don't know, but read it for yourself," handing him the screwed-up letter.

Straightening the crumpled sheet of vellum, Clifton read its contents with startled eyes before raising them to Deerham's taut face. "I… I don't know what to say, my lord!" handing the letter back to him.

Having come to know the young marchioness rather well during the past five months or so of her marriage to Deerham, Clifton had to admit that he could not help having taken a liking to her. He admitted that in the beginning he had been rather sceptical about Deerham's marriage to a young woman whose father had set the town alight with his antics as well as bringing an abbey to a nutshell as the saying went, but it had not taken him long to see that she was nothing like her father. She may not be a beauty but there was nevertheless something about her that was very appealing, and unless Clifton's old eyes had misled him he would say that his lordship was by no means impervious to her, apart from which she was kind and generous and never failed to offer a thank you for any service performed for her. As for her feelings for Deerham, Clifton had been brought to see that she was very much in love with her husband, despite her strenuous efforts to hide the fact, in truth, he would have to say that as far as he could see their marriage, far from being one of convenience, was most definitely a love match, even though neither of them realized it. But who would want to abduct her had him at a loss.

Having been in service to the Seer family all his life, he had come to know Deerham very well. Like his father, he was an honourable man and one whose integrity would make it impossible for him to bring the name he bore into disrepute; but despite that reserve of manner, giving the uninitiated the totally wrong impression of him as being a proud and aloof man, the truth was very different; indeed he could boast to having many friends, all of whom could testify to Deerham's affability and generosity. He certainly could not abide toad eaters or those whose impertinence prompted them to pry into his private affairs, but Clifton knew him as being a good and decent man and one he was proud to serve. However, when it came to Digby Singleton, Clifton had known for a long time that he and Deerham, despite politely acknowledging one another whenever they met, were not friends, for reasons he could only guess at, even so, he would have been astonished to know that the young marchioness's father's close friend and kindred spirit was at the back of her abduction.

"Would you please tell Trench and her ladyship's coachman that I wish to see them?" Deerham broke into his thoughts. "And William."

"Now, my lord?" Clifton enquired.

"Yes," Deerham nodded, "now."

"Very good, my lord," Clifton bowed, leaving the room on the words.

While Deerham waited for Trench and Louisa's groom to join him his thoughts were all of the woman he loved more than life itself. He had not set out to fall in love with Louisa, it had just happened despite all his strenuous efforts to clamp down on the emotions she evoked inside him; emotions he had eventually come to realize could not be ignored much less eradicated. Louisa could not, at any time, lay claim to being a beauty and, having spent more than one pleasurable hour in the arms of more than one beautiful woman, he should know, but he had recognized very early on that her looks did not matter in the least, indeed there was a naturalness and a spontaneity about her that not only rendered her looks totally unimportant but which he had found to be quite irresistible, so much so that he knew beyond any doubt that he could not live without her.

Upon first making her acquaintance, he had found her to be open and confiding, delighting him with her disclosures and confidences, but it had not been long before he noticed that she had gradually withdrawn into herself. Whether this was because her mamma had cautioned her against him or someone else had done so, he did not know, even so there were times when, even now, he caught glimpses of the impulsiveness she could not hide and which he loved so much. He knew that Louisa believed their marriage to be one of convenience and, if he was being honest, it had been so for him too, until he had discovered, much to his surprise, that he had fallen in love with her, which is why his kisses as well as his lovemaking had so far been rather restrained, having no wish to frighten her. And yet, despite the fact that she never repulsed his advances, nor encouraged them either, he had nevertheless gained the very strong impression that she was by no means unaffected by them, leaving him to take some comfort from the hope that she was not entirely indifferent to him after all.

And now, to think that the woman he loved was in the hands of those who would stop at nothing in an effort to extort money out of him, was more than he could bear. Twenty thousand guineas to a man of his wealth was neither here nor there, and he would willingly give every penny of it to get Louisa back, but before he calmly handed over such a sum to those who, for now at least, were totally unknown to him, he wanted to know how she came to be in their hands in the first place. Hopefully though, Louisa's coachman may be able to shed some light on the matter.

In the meantime, William, having been awoken from a deep sleep to the intelligence that his lordship wished to see him immediately, merely nodded, at a loss to know what possible reason he could have for wanting to see him at this hour, but after scrambling into his clothes he made his way to the book room, his mind awash with conjecture. But the news which met his startled ears was so far removed from what he had thought that for several moments he could do no more than look at Deerham in total astonishment. "Abducted, my lord!" he exclaimed, shocked.

"Yes," Deerham nodded, "here's the letter. Read it for yourself."

William read it in utter amazement, unable to comprehend what he was reading, but after looking up from the lines on the vellum he handed Deerham the letter back, asking, not a little shaken, "You are surely not going to pay it, my lord?"

Deerham sighed, "Not if I can help it, but tell me, William," he cocked his head, "should I find myself with no choice, would you transact with my bankers for me?"

"Certainly, my lord," William told him, "indeed, it is a pleasure to serve you at any time." Then, shrugging a little helplessly, said, "But twenty thousand guineas!"

"I know, William," Deerham sighed, raking a hand through his hair, "but rest assured I shall do everything possible to get… to get my wife back without handing over a penny."

William had not missed that faltering catch in Deerham's voice any more than he had failed to notice the somewhat haggard look which had descended onto his face, and immediately he was put in mind of that scented letter he had received at Worleigh. He remembered thinking at the time that the writer was clearly Deerham's new flirt, and although he had neither admitted nor denied it, it had left William with only one conclusion. But now, seeing Deerham so shaken, even though he tried his best to hide it, William wondered if he did indeed love his wife after all.

As if reading William's thoughts, whose face clearly echoed what he was thinking, Deerham looked at him, a smile lighting his eyes, "No, William," he shook his head, "the writer of that scented note was not my mistress but – er," he shrugged, "how shall I say?" he raised an eyebrow. "Someone I used to know."

William returned the look comprehendingly, nodding, "Yes, my lord," unable to prevent the smile which touched his lips.

"She wrote to inform me of something of some moment," Deerham informed him, "indeed," he nodded, "I am greatly indebted to her."

"Yes, my lord," William bowed, then, after a few more words with Deerham he left the book room.

Within a very few minutes of William's departure, her ladyship's coachman came to him, but when he entered the book room in Trench's wake, looking extremely dishevelled, having only minutes before scrambled into his clothes upon being informed that his lordship wanted to speak to him immediately, it was obvious from the look on his face that he had no idea why he had been so peremptorily summoned. Morgan, who had been in Deerham's service for a number of years, knew him to be a good and generous master and one who was extremely fair in his dealings with his household, even so, he could not help feeling a little apprehensive on being called upon to attend him at this time of the morning much less that his mistress had not returned home, but upon being informed that the reason for his attendance was that her ladyship had been abducted, so stunned was he that he could only stand and stare at Deerham as though he could not believe his ears.

"Abducted, my lord?" he repeated, shocked, when he could find his voice.

"I am afraid so," Deerham nodded, not failing to notice the complete and utter disbelief on Trench's face upon hearing this.

Upon being asked how he came to leave Lady Templeton's without her ladyship, Morgan told him. "Her ladyship ordered me to, my lord."

"Ordered you?" Deerham questioned.

"Yes, my lord," he confirmed.

"You spoke to her?" Deerham asked sharply.

"No, my lord," Morgan shook his head.

"What then?" Deerham urged, raising a questioning eyebrow.

Looking from Deerham to Trench with something resembling a bewildered look on his face, Morgan swallowed, saying, "I didn't speak to her ladyship, my lord. One of Lady Templeton's footmen came and told me that her ladyship would not be requiring the coach as a friend of hers would ensure she was conveyed safely home and therefore I need not wait for her." When Deerham made no immediate effort to reply to this, the coachman further informed him, swallowing a little uncomfortably at the dark look on Deerham's face, "I… I'm sorry, my lord," he faltered, "but I saw no reason to question it. I then brought her ladyship's coach back."

Deerham thought a moment, asking at length, "What time was this?"

"It was about eleven o'clock, my lord," Morgan told him.

Deerham nodded before asking, "Was there by any chance a coach there that you did not recognize?"

"No, my lord," Morgan shook his head.

"None at all?" Deerham pressed.

"No, my lord. We coachmen all know one another, you see," he explained, "and I would have known if there had been someone there who

I had not seen before."

Deerham nodded. "Do you recollect seeing a coach within the vicinity of Lady Templeton's that you thought suspicious?"

"No, my lord," he shook his head. "Apart from a few sedan chairs and the odd hackney, I saw nothing."

"This footman," Deerham queried, "would you recognize him again?"

"I think so, my lord," he was told.

"I hope so," Deerham told him, "because I shall need you to accompany me tomorrow to Lady Templeton's in order to identify him."

"Yes, my lord," Morgan nodded, whereupon he was dismissed.

As soon as the door to the book room had been closed on Morgan, Deerham sank into his chair and, after raising a somewhat unsteady hand to his forehead, turned to his old friend, sighing, "Well, Trench, I take it there is no need for me to tell you that I shall be needing your help in getting her ladyship back?"

"No, my lord," Trench replied sympathetically. "I'm sorry, my lord."

It was a moment or two before Deerham spoke, and, when he did, it was evident from the deep sigh that escaped his lips that he was extremely disturbed. "I have here," he told him, picking up the letter from where he had dropped it onto his desk, "a letter demanding I pay twenty thousand guineas for her safe return."

Trench's eyes widened in surprised at this. *"Twenty thousand guineas!"* he echoed when he could find his voice, looking aghast at Deerham.

"Yes," he replied, his voice just a little strained. "I am to take it to someone called Johnson who will be waiting for me in the Green Park on Thursday by midday." He thought a moment. "I have no doubt at all," he nodded, "that this Johnson is nothing more than a paid tool."

"But you're never going to pay it, my lord?" Trench asked incredulously, hating the thought that his lordship was being blackmailed, because that was precisely what it was.

"I would pay twice that much to get my wife back," Deerham told him firmly, "but first," he nodded, "I want to see what can be done to discover who it is that has taken her and why."

Trench, who, like Thomas, had held serious doubts as to the wisdom of his lordship's marriage to the Lady Louisa Markham, had soon been brought to see that he had wronged her and that she was by no means like her father. Being Deerham's personal groom and not her ladyship's, meant that he had very little dealings with her, nevertheless he had come to know the young marchioness rather well, and, like Clifton, had soon revised his first impression of her, but why anyone would want to abduct her had him fair baffled.

"Yes, my lord," he nodded.

"Tomorrow morning," Deerham told him, "I want you to make enquiries of all the livery stables to see if anyone hired a coach for this evening."

"Yes, my lord," Trench inclined his head. "Not that I see that being a problem, my lord."

"I hope not," Deerham sighed. "However, you never know," he smiled, "we may prove fortunate."

"I hope so, my lord," Trench sighed, raking a hand through his grizzled hair. Then, as if a thought had suddenly occurred to him, asked, "Do you really believe that Lady Templeton's footman is involved, my lord?"

"I don't know," Deerham admitted, "it could be that he was just asked to pass on a message to Morgan, but my every instinct is telling me that, if he is not hand in glove with the abductor, he knows a lot more than we do."

"That's for certain, my lord," Trench told him firmly. He thought a moment, then, after looking at Deerham considering, said, "You don't think, my lord, that Singleton could be the one who has taken her ladyship? Begging your pardon, my lord," he added, "but I'd say he was low enough to stoop to anything!"

"Yes, he is," Deerham said slowly. "But whilst I cannot say for certain that he is the one responsible, I would lay a heavy wager that he is."

"I'd lay my life he is!" Trench told him darkly. "He's no friend of yours, my lord, not after the times you have foiled his plans he's not!" he reminded him.

"Well," Deerham sighed, "we shall see. Now," he smiled, "it's time you were off to your bed."

It was some little time after Trench had left him before Deerham finally emerged from the book room, seemingly content to just sit and stare straight in front of him at nothing in particular, his features taut and pensive, being in no hurry to retire. After slowly climbing the stairs he made his way to his bedchamber, but just as he was about to take hold of the handle he bethought himself of Mary, Louisa's dresser, who would have to be told about her mistress. Retracing his steps to Louisa's boudoir, he opened the door and trod softly inside, still redolent of her perfume, a light and delicate fragrance that he particularly identified with Louisa, and one he had long since come to love. Mary, expecting her mistress to come home at any moment, had lit the candles sometime before, and Deerham, after looking around the room, saw her nightdress laid out on top of the bed in readiness for her to change into when she came home. Walking over to the bed, Deerham looked thoughtfully down at the garment, then, as if he could not stop himself, leisurely picked it up, as exquisite as it was expensive, in his strong fingers, easily discernible through the fine material, his nostrils filled with Louisa's perfume which still clung to it, and knew a moment of intense pain. As if in no hurry to let it go, he held it in his hand for a few moments, his mind re-living again those moments he had spent with her and just how much he missed her, then, after carefully laying it back down on the bed he walked over to the wall. It was just as he was about to pull the bell tug for Mary that the door to the dressing room opened and she walked in, taken completely by surprise when, instead of laying eyes on her ladyship, saw his lordship instead.

Having heard movement in the boudoir, Mary thought it was her mistress, but upon setting eyes on Deerham, she cried, quite startled, "My lord!" bobbing a nervous curtsey. "I… I thought you were her ladyship, my lord."

It was a moment before Deerham spoke, saying quietly, "No."

"Is… is something wrong, my lord?" she enquired.

"I am afraid, Mary," he told her gently, "that your mistress will not be returning home tonight."

"Not returning home, my lord!" she repeated, astonished, all manner of visions flitting across her mind.

"No," he confirmed.

"But I… I don't understand, my lord," she told him, bewildered, wringing her hands. "Y-you mean she's staying at Lady Templeton's?"

"No," he said slowly, "I mean, Mary," he told her gently, "that your mistress has been abducted."

She eyed him incredulously, unable to take in what he had said, repeating faintly, when she could finally find her voice, "Abducted, my lord?" to which he nodded.

Mary may not have fallen into hysterics as he fully expected her to, but it nevertheless took Deerham several minutes to calm her down and assure her that there was no cause for alarm, and that he would have her mistress back home before she knew it, to which she nodded. After vigorously blowing her nose into her handkerchief she sniffed, then, after telling him that she knew he would do everything he could to find her mistress, curtseyed herself out of the room.

*

To say that Deerham had hardly closed his eyes all night he was nevertheless looking remarkably refreshed and wide awake when he partook of breakfast several hours later. Having made short work of the cold roast beef and several generous slices of the Yorkshire ham, washed down by a tankard of ale, he was ready and waiting when Clifton informed him that

Morgan was waiting for him in the hall. Trench, having begun his rounds of the livery stables some time previously in accordance with his lordship's instructions, it was left to the under groom to bring Deerham's curricle round to the front of the house, more than happy to crouch behind on the small back seat, a small price to pay in his opinion for being put in charge of Deerham's cattle, while Morgan sat beside his lordship as they made their way to Curzon Street. Upon their arrival at Lady Templeton's, a tall slim building that showed no signs of neglect or dilapidation but, on the contrary, an elegant town residence that befitted a lady of her age and station, the under groom jumped down to take hold of the horses' heads, a magnificent pair of perfectly matched greys for which his lordship had several times turned down offers to sell them, while Deerham and Morgan trod up the steps leading to the house.

To say that Lady Templeton's butler was surprised to open the door to visitors at a little after half past ten in the morning was a gross understatement, telling Deerham, a man he had no difficulty in recognizing, that her ladyship had not yet left her bedchamber. Upon being told that it was not her ladyship he had come to see but her footman, the butler looked from Deerham to Morgan with something resembling a rather dazed expression on his face, shaking his head a little bewildered before explaining that her ladyship had two footmen. "Which one of them is it you are wishful of seeing, my lord?" he asked faintly.

"Both of them," Deerham told him.

"Both of them, my lord?" the butler repeated, puzzled.

"Yes," Deerham nodded.

Having been butler to her ladyship for a good many years with nothing untoward or irregular going on, Firth found himself just a little at a loss. He could not say he had a liking for either of her ladyship's footmen, too rackety by half he thought them, even so, he did not like to think that either of them had got themselves into any kind of trouble, and therefore felt impelled to ask, "May I enquire as to the reason why you are wishful of seeing them, my lord?"

"Merely a private matter," Deerham told him. "So if you will be good enough to present them to me I should be obliged."

For the first in Firth's life he looked his indecision. He supposed he ought to inform her ladyship of the unlooked-for visitors and the reason for their visit, but upon seeing that his lordship appeared to be in no mood for prevarication, he deemed it wise to neither question him further nor argue with him, much less tell him that he preferred to wait until her ladyship could be informed, merely bowed his head and showed him and Morgan into a small parlour at the rear of the house, advising them that he would bring both the footmen to them if they would care to wait. He knew that the Marchioness of Deerham had attended her ladyship's little soirée last night and therefore could not help wondering whether she had mislaid something and had asked one of the footmen to find it for her, but as he ventured down the backstairs to the servants' quarters, his mind awash with speculation, he could not help the sneaking suspicion from crossing his mind that it was something far more serious than that.

Fortunately for Deerham's patience as well as his growing concern for Louisa, he did not have long to wait before the two footmen were shown into the rear parlour, but if Firth thought he would be allowed to remain, as an interested onlooker to their discussion if nothing else, he was mistaken, receiving Deerham's thanks and dismissal with a brief nod of his head.

Having looked the two men over with an experienced and knowledgeable eye, Deerham could not help but unconsciously agree with Firth's estimation of them, too rackety by half, but it was the younger man of the two who was looking a little uncomfortable, but when he could not stand Deerham's scrutiny any longer, he asked, "You wanted to speak to us, my lord?"

"Yes, I did," Deerham replied. "What is your name?"

"Davis, my lord," he told him.

"And you?" Deerham cocked his head in the direction of the other man.

"Meadows, my lord," he told him, swallowing a little uncomfortably.

Then, turning to Morgan, Deerham raised an enquiring eyebrow, asking, "Do you recognize either of them, Morgan?"

"Yes, my lord," Morgan nodded, "it's him," nodding his head in the direction of Davis.

"Are you sure?" Deerham asked.

"Yes, my lord," Morgan nodded, "quite sure."

Having dismissed the other footman, Deerham looked at the fresh-faced young man who was warily regarding him, asking, "Tell me, Davis, do you recognize this man?" indicating Morgan standing next to him.

Unfortunately for Davis he recognized him very well, and unless his instincts had got it totally wrong he knew precisely what had brought both men here this morning, but deeming it prudent to deny any knowledge of him, besides which it would do him no good at all should it ever leak out that he had snitched, he merely shook his, saying, "No, my lord, I don't. I have never seen this man before."

"That's a lie, my lord!" Morgan cried, looking earnestly up at Deerham. "It was he who approached me, I swear it!"

Deerham did not need to hear Morgan's outspoken retort or to see the look on his face to know that he was telling the truth, just one look at Davis's face was enough to satisfy him. "I know," he soothed, laying a restricting hand on Morgan's arm as he was about to approach Davis with his fists suggestively clenched. Then, turning to look at the young footman, Deerham said, "Do you still say that you have never seen him before?"

"Yes, my lord," Davis nodded. "I've not laid eyes on him until now."

"Indeed," Deerham raised an eyebrow. "Somehow I find that hard to believe,"

"It's the truth, my lord. Why should I lie?" Davis shrugged, looking warily from one man to the other.

"I can think of several reasons," Deerham told him dryly.

"Well, if…" Davis began.

"If you are honest with me," Deerham broke in unceremoniously, "and answer my questions truthfully, no harm will come to you, but should you persist in lying then I am very much afraid I shall have no alternative but to hand you over to the law."

As soon as Firth had told Davis and his colleague that Deerham was here and wishful of speaking to them, he knew immediately what had brought him here, but if he thought he could brazen it out just one look at Deerham's face was enough to tell him that it would not answer. He of all people would know whether his wife had attended her ladyship's soirée or not, and although the douceur he had been given had seemed to make it all worthwhile now, upon hearing him mention the law, he felt all the colour drain from his face. Not only that, but the look on Deerham's face, as grim as it was determined, was more than enough to make him realize that lying would avail him nothing.

"Is that understood?" Deerham asked, breaking into his not very edifying thoughts.

"Yes, my lord," Davis said resignedly.

Deerham thought a moment, saying at length, "Last night, you informed Morgan here that my wife would not be requiring her carriage because someone was going to see her safely home. Is that correct?"

"Yes, my lord," Davis nodded.

"Who was it who told you to say this?" Deerham enquired.

Davis swallowed, not a little uncomfortably. On the one hand if he refused to answer Deerham's question truthfully, he could be guaranteed a visit to the local magistrate, something he was by no means eager to have happen, on the other hand however, should he tell him what he wanted to know then his unknown benefactor would be far from pleased, indeed his retribution would be swift as well as severe, so temporizing said, "I… I don't know his name, my lord."

Deerham raised a surprised eyebrow at this, asking, "Do you always transact business with people you don't know?" When Davis made no reply to this, Deerham said, somewhat sharply, "What was his name?"

Realizing it was futile to deny any knowledge of the man's identity, besides which not only did Deerham not believe him but from the looks on his face it would give him tremendous satisfaction to knock him senseless, he sighed, "He told me his name was Johnson, my lord."

"And what did this Johnson look like?" Deerham enquired.

Davis thought a moment. "About my height, my lord, but bigger built and broader across the shoulders. It looked as though he had sustained a broken nose at some point. Oh, yes," he remembered, "and he had a mole here," pointing to his right cheek bone.

Deerham nodded. There was no doubting that Davis had described this Johnson as being Singleton's man, Grimshaw, with unerring accuracy, being more than enough to tell Deerham that Singleton was indeed the one responsible for Louisa's abduction. Deerham had no doubt at all that this unscrupulous individual had driven Singleton's coach on the night he had abducted Letitia Rawnsley and also that he was the man who had tooled the coach last night to take Louisa to some unknown destination. He was also convinced that he was the man he was supposed to meet in the Green Park on Thursday when he was to hand over the twenty thousand guineas, well, both he and Singleton were in for something of a surprise.

"How did my wife come to mistake the coach?" Deerham demanded.

Davis licked his suddenly dry lips, confessing, "When her ladyship left here last night, my lord, it was raining heavily, so I held an umbrella low over her head so she wouldn't see she was entering the wrong coach until she was inside, as I was instructed to do."

Deerham gave him a scornful look, asking, "Did this Johnson tell you where he was taking her ladyship?"

"No, my lord," Davis shook his head, "but I…" he stopped

"But what?" Deerham urged.

"Well," Davis shrugged, "it may be nothing, my lord, but I seem to remember him mentioning Barnet, but whether this is where he was taking her ladyship I can't say."

"Barnet?" Deerham repeated.

"Yes, my lord," Davis nodded.

Deerham looked at Davis and, after nodding his head, asked, "Had you ever seen this man before he approached you?"

"No, my lord," Davis told him.

"Where did he approach you?" Deerham demanded.

"At *'The Old Tavern'*, my lord. In Fleet Street."

"How did he know you worked for Lady Templeton?" Deerham urged.

"I don't know, my lord," Davis shook his head. "He just asked me if I worked for Lady Templeton and I said yes. We just got talking and before you knew it one thing led to another and he asked me if I would like to earn some money."

"To which you said you would," Deerham disparaged.

"Yes, my lord," Davis confirmed. Then, feeling it necessary to exonerate himself of any wrong-doing, offered, "He told me it was just a jest, my lord."

"A jest!" Deerham exclaimed. "Do you call abducting my wife a jest?" When Davis made no reply to this, Deerham asked, "How much did he pay you?"

Davis shifted a little uncomfortably before replying, "Twenty guineas, my lord."

"Twenty guineas," Deerham repeated, to which Davis nodded. "You want to consider yourself extremely fortunate that you will have occasion to spend it instead of being taken up by the law."

"Yes, my lord," Davis swallowed. "Does this mean I am free to go, my lord?"

"Yes," Deerham nodded, "but I would strongly recommend you, Davis, to refrain from succumbing to such temptation in the future."

Davis did not need to be told this; he already knew it. When he had been asked if he would like to earn twenty guineas in return for ensuring that the Marchioness of Deerham entered the wrong coach, he had known a moment's hesitation, but upon being told that it was nothing but a jest he had swallowed his scruples and did exactly as he had been told. He had been most fortunate in coming out of this with a whole skin; indeed it would not have surprised him to find himself on the receiving end of a most punishing right, because if all he had ever heard about his lordship was true then he was mightily handy with his fives. He knew he could make a pretty good account of himself, but he had the sneaking suspicion that were he to engage in a bout of fisticuffs with him he would come off the worse from an encounter with his lordship, and therefore silently promised himself to be of good behaviour from here on in.

"Yes, my lord," bowing his head. "Thank you, my lord," effecting a hasty retreat from the parlour.

Chapter Twenty

Trench, returning to Grosvenor Square several hours later from his errand, was happy to report to Deerham that his search had not been for nothing. "The very last place I went to, my lord," Trench told him. "Tylers, in the Haymarket."

"And?" Deerham raised a questioning eyebrow.

"Well, my lord," Trench told him, "at first it seemed as if I'd drawn another blank as the two men who were looking through the books found nothing to show that a coach had been hired from them yesterday. Then," he nodded, "while they were arguing the toss and scratching their heads a man came out of the back room enquiring what the commotion was about. It seemed, my lord," Trench informed him, "that it was Mr. Tyler himself, then, after throwing them a withering look and telling them to be about their business, he went through the books himself, finally finding the entry to show that a vehicle had in fact been hired yesterday morning to a man who called himself Johnson, besides two horses."

"Our friend Johnson again," Deerham mused, going on to briefly explain what he had discovered from Davis the footman.

"Well, my lord," Trench pointed out, reflectively rubbing his chin, "if this Johnson and Singleton's man are one of the same, and from where I'm standing I'd say it looks mightily like it, because the night we stopped Singleton from running off with that young girl I got a good look at him and he fits the description which this so-called footman gave you, then I'd say it looks as if he's the one behind the mistress's abduction."

"I'm sure of it," Deerham nodded, his brow darkening.

"However," Trench offered, "although Mr. Tyler could tell me that it was one of their best coaches this Johnson had hired, and for several days from the looks of it, he unfortunately couldn't tell me where it was bound."

Deerham thought a moment. "Well, if this footman, Davis, was telling me the truth, and I believe he was, then it seems as though Barnet was the destination, even though he couldn't confirm it."

Trench thought a moment, then, after scratching his head, said, "But do you really think they're holding the mistress in Barnet, my lord?"

"If not Barnet," Deerham shrugged, "then perhaps somewhere in the vicinity, which would suggest why they needed only two horses, but I shall know more tomorrow when I meet up with this Johnson character."

"Beggin' your pardon, my lord," Trench offered, "but you'll never go alone to Green Park to meet him?"

"Of course I shall go alone," Deerham told him, raising his eyebrows. Upon seeing the frown which had suddenly descended onto Trench's forehead, Deerham smiled, "Are you saying that I cannot detect a trap when I see one or that I cannot take care of myself?"

"No, my lord, I'm not," Trench told him firmly. "Havin' known you from the cradle, my lord," he pointed out unnecessarily, "I know you're neither dicked in the nob nor incapable of takin' care of yourself," to which Deerham laughed, "but I wouldn't put anythin' past them!"

"Neither would I," Deerham told him, rising to his feet.

"They're devious enough to try anything, my lord," Trench told him forcefully.

"Yes," Deerham replied calmly, "I know they are."

"Then why…" Trench began.

"You know," Deerham smiled, patting him on the shoulder, "you really must have a little more faith in me."

*

The following morning dawned bright and sunny and Deerham, having hardly closed his eyes the evening Louisa had been taken, had slept heavily the night before, and Thomas, refusing to waken him too early, had been only too happy to allow him to lie abed longer than he normally did, to which he was taken to task by Deerham, though not very sternly. Partaking of a late breakfast, he was ready to set out for Green Park a little before half past eleven, rejecting all Trench's persuasions to allow him to accompany him.

Having walked from Grosvenor Square to Half Moon Street, Deerham crossed over Piccadilly towards the entrance to Green Park, which, although liberally sprinkled with passers-by as well as a milk maid selling milk to those who wanted it, was by no means full. Upon entering Green Park, he saw, much to his surprise, having fully expected to be kept waiting, sitting on the first bench to his left, a man he had no difficulty in recognizing as Grimshaw-cum-Johnson, Singleton's man, looking idly all about him, until his eye fell upon him. He had never seen Deerham before, but Grimshaw did not need to have it spelled out who he was, but from the look which had descended onto Deerham's face as he approached him, he would say that he was in no very good humour, however, as he watched him take his seat beside him, Grimshaw merely nodded his head, asking, "Deerham?"

After looking all around him in case someone was lurking in the bushes to overpower him or for other nefarious reasons and seeing no one, he looked straight at him, nodding, "Yes, I'm Deerham. and you, I take it, are this Johnson?"

"That's right, my lord," Grimshaw nodded. Then, remembering his instructions, cocked his head, asking, "Have you got the money?"

"No," Deerham told him shortly.

As this was not what Grimshaw had expected he was momentarily taken aback, then, rubbing his chin reflectively, said slowly, "Well, now, that puts me in somethin' of a quandary."

"I don't doubt it," Deerham nodded, but before he could say anything, he heard Deerham demand, "Where is my wife?"

Grimshaw may have no liking for abducting females, but he knew his master too well to either argue with him or to refuse to carry out his orders, indeed his retribution for either offence would be swift as well as severe, and therefore Deerham's calm reply in that he had not brought the money with him threw him slightly off balance. From what Grimshaw could see of it, Deerham was in no frame of mind to be conciliating, indeed he bore all the appearance of a man who was not only totally in command of the situation but determined not to budge an inch, but unfortunately it placed Grimshaw in quite a predicament. His instructions were that he was not to engage in any kind of conversation with Deerham but simply to relieve him of his money and walk away, but the fact that had he not brought the money with him meant that he had no choice but to enter into discussions with him, not that Grimshaw held out any hope that talking would move him, so deciding to prevaricate a little, he said,

"The deal was, my lord, that…"

"I have no recollection of entering into any kind of 'deal' as you put it," Deerham broke in unceremoniously.

Grimshaw may not be overly fond of Singleton but he had been his general factotum for a good few years, during the course of which he had put his hand to many things and no questions asked. He may not exactly like the idea of abducting young females, something his master seemed overly fond of doing, but as long as he was paid for his part in whatever venture Singleton embarked on then it was all one to him. Of course, he could not deny to having been extremely pleased to seeing Singleton in the embarrassing position of being thwarted that night on the Maidenhead road, and, in truth, had it been at all possible he would have shaken the girl's rescuer by the hand, but he was unfortunately in the position whereby, unless he wanted to find himself unemployed, he could not afford such luxury thereby leaving him with no choice but to remain in Singleton's service.

He had lent himself to this latest scheme, not only because Singleton had given him no choice, but also because he had offered him a substantial reward out of the twenty thousand guineas he fully expected Deerham to pay to get his wife back, but according to Grimshaw's reckoning his part in this little charade was worth far more than the three hundred guineas he had been promised. It was his unqualified opinion therefore, that if he played his cards right, he was not unhopeful of getting more out of Singleton than was originally agreed, but upon learning that Deerham was not prepared to pay a single penny, Grimshaw's hopes foundered. No less than Singleton would be, Grimshaw was not best pleased on hearing this, but how to coerce Deerham into handing over the money he was momentarily at a loss to know, but deciding to adopt a conciliatory attitude, he told him, "Thing is, my orders are to… "

"I know very well what your orders are," Deerham broke in, "and who gave them to you, but I don't take kindly to threats or demands, so you may as well make up your mind to the fact that not only are you going to tell me where my wife is being held but that I am not going to hand over one penny."

The look on Deerham's face was more than adequate testimony to this; he was looking most forbidding, but Grimshaw, torn between Singleton's retribution should he fail to return with the money and Deerham's implacable stand that he was not going to hand over one penny, he was not at all sure what to do. If he told Deerham where his wife was being held then not only could he forgo his money but could also look forward to Singleton's retaliation, neither of which he was any too eager to do, but then, if it came to it, he was none too eager to be on the receiving end of Deerham's retribution either.

Totally unconcerned by the dilemma his refusal to hand over the money had placed Grimshaw in, Deerham turned to face him, saying firmly, "Well, I am waiting. Where is my wife being held?" When Grimshaw made no immediate effort to reply to this, simply because he was not at all sure what to say let alone do, Deerham warned him, "Please do not fall into the error of thinking that our surroundings will prevent me from choking the life out of you, they will not."

It seemed to Grimshaw that Singleton, for once in his life, had grossly miscalculated. He had been pretty confident that Deerham would be faced with little choice but to calmly hand over twenty thousand guineas in exchange for his wife, in fact so convinced was he that Deerham would do as he was told that it never so much as crossed Singleton's mind that he would fail in extorting money out of him. Unfortunately for Grimshaw, he had been given no instructions on what to do should Deerham prove obstructive or fail to comply with the request to hand over the money, and even if he did engage in a bout of fisticuffs with him in order to bring about a change of mind, something told him that he would come off the worse from such an encounter. If all Grimshaw had ever heard about Deerham was true, then he was pretty handy with his fives, besides which, he was looking to be in no very good humour, and unless Grimshaw had got it wrong it would give him tremendous satisfaction to plant him a facer, their surroundings, as he had rightly pointed out, making not the slightest difference.

"Well," Deerham broke into his thoughts, "are you going to tell me where my wife is being held?" When Grimshaw made no reply to this, Deerham said coolly, "Please, do not make it necessary for me to force it out of you."

Grimshaw knew very well that Singleton would be very far from pleased at the way this morning's meeting had turned out, and he was honest enough to admit that he was extremely reluctant to report adverse tidings to him, but he was also angry on his own behalf that Deerham had not brought the money with him. Grimshaw had been looking forward to finding his pockets full of guineas and even pleasantly contemplating another future for himself entirely, but now things were turning out in a way that had not been envisaged, he was not quite sure what to do. As he looked at that implacable face sitting next to him he knew it was useless to even try to persuade him into rethinking his position about the money, knowing perfectly well that nothing would move Deerham into handing over the twenty thousand guineas, even so, he was extremely unwilling to forgo his share of such a handsome largesse, and it was just as he was thinking what his next step should be that he suddenly bethought himself of the knife tucked discreetly away in his coat pocket.

He had not prepared himself for using it this morning, indeed, there was no reason as far as he could see that would warrant him doing so, in fact, apart from using it as part of his day to day duties as Singleton's general factotum, it had never been used as a weapon much less pointed at a man. As far as he was concerned this meeting had been merely a case of taking the money from Deerham then making his way back to Barnet to hand it over to Singleton, where he would be given his share, but disappointment and frustration had slowly begun to override his judgement, momentarily divesting him of his common sense, so much so that before he had time to even consider what he was doing he dug his right hand into the pocket of his coat, his fingers closing around the handle, before pulling it quickly out.

Deerham, just catching the light from the sun as it glinted briefly on the blade, was quicker still; his right hand suddenly shooting out and gripping Grimshaw's wrist, those surprisingly strong fingers closing like a vice until the unrelenting pressure forced him into dropping the knife.

"Damn you!" Grimshaw cried, rubbing his wrist when Deerham had released it, a spasm of pain crossing his face.

"That was not very wise, my friend," Deerham sighed, shaking his head. "For one thing," he told him, "I don't think Singleton would like my death on his hands, at least," he nodded, "not at this stage." Grimshaw shot him an unfriendly look, but ignoring it, Deerham suggested, "Unless you are eager for more of the same, I would strongly recommend you to tell me what I want to know. Where is my wife being held?"

"I can't tells yer," Grimshaw cried. "It'ud be more than me life's worth."

Without giving him time to realize what was happening, Deerham stretched out his right hand and covered Grimshaw's left one in such a painful grip that he winced. "Well?" he urged.

"I... I don't know," Grimshaw gasped after tolerating such exquisite agony for as long as he could.

"I think you do," Deerham said, increasing the pressure of his fingers on Grimshaw's hand. "Where is my wife being held?"

"I... I... don't know," Grimshaw gasped again, his hand stinging from the excruciating pressure of those fingers.

"That," Deerham sighed, "is not what I want to hear. Now, for the last time," he nodded, increasing the pressure of his fingers, "where is my wife being held?"

Had anyone told Grimshaw that those white and well-manicured hands with the long slim fingers could inflict so much pain he would never have believed them, but unable to bear the stinging pain any longer, gasped, "Barnet."

"Where in Barnet?" Deerham pressed.

Grimshaw swallowed. "'*The Blue Boar*'. Tanner Street."

"Who is with her?" he demanded.

"Singleton," Grimshaw managed.

"Anyone else?" Deerham urged.

"Apart from the landlord and 'is wife, no," he shook his head. "Singleton 'ired a private parlour."

"Thank you," Deerham nodded, releasing the hand he had been holding.

"W-wot do I tell Singleton?" Grimshaw asked after the stinging had died down a little, rubbing his hand.

"Why, anything you please," Deerham shrugged, rising to his feet. Then, looking dispassionately down at Grimshaw, said, "Not that it makes any difference, you see, I shall be seeing Singleton myself very soon now, where I shall have a lot to say to my enterprising friend," whereupon he turned on his heel and walked out of the Green Park.

*

Upon returning home Deerham immediately sent for Trench to come and see him. Not unexpectedly he was agog to know what had happened in the Green Park, not at all surprised to learn that Deerham had eventually got the truth out of Grimshaw as to where her ladyship was being held, and without lining Singleton's pockets by so much as a penny.

"Tell me, Trench," Deerham cocked his head, "do you know *The Blue Boar*? I can't say that I have ever heard of it."

"Yes, my lord," he nodded, "I do. It can't of course compare with *The Red Lion*' or *'The Green Man'*, but it's nevertheless quite a respectable inn as I recall," this intelligence relieving Deerham's mind of one of his worries if nothing else.

He may have a score to settle with Singleton, but he had at least ensured that Louisa had a woman to take care of her needs at least, although whether this was more luck than judgement remained to be seen.

Deerham had known for a long time that Singleton would stop at nothing to pay him back for thwarting his game on at least three occasions, but that he would go so far as to using Louisa for his ends then he had gone his length, and Deerham swore that before the day was out he would make him pay for his effrontery.

Telling Trench that he wanted his travelling coach brought round to the front door in an hour's time, considerably disappointing his henchman when he told him that he did not need his company as this was a journey for himself alone, he went up to his bedchamber to change his dress.

Like Trench, Thomas was exceedingly shocked to learn that her ladyship had been taken, and in such a dastardly way, and by a man whose antics were guaranteed to set the town alight, just as they had when he and Markmoor had been bosom cronies. It seemed that nothing would change Singleton's reckless ways and his total lack of concern to the name he bore, a man Thomas had no hesitation in deeming to be a rogue and quite beyond the pale. He admitted that he had at first been dead set against Deerham's marriage to Markmoor's daughter, a man who had put his own pleasures before his estates, leaving his son and heir to make the best of things as well as he may, and his daughter to make a marriage of convenience with Deerham, but like the rest of the household it had not taken Thomas long to see that he had wronged her, and all he wanted now was to see her safely returned home where she belonged.

He knew Deerham was a man who did not wear his heart on his sleeve, but unless Thomas was very much mistaken, which he doubted, then her ladyship's abduction had hit him very hard. Not that he expected Deerham to discuss it with him, but Thomas had nevertheless seen the expression in his eyes when he thought no one was watching him and knew he felt more for her ladyship than he let on, but even though he knew Deerham would not discuss it with him he nevertheless felt impelled to point out when he came in to change his dress that he hoped he would return with her ladyship.

"Thank you, Thomas," Deerham replied calmly, "I fully intend to."

"Beggin' your pardon, my lord, I'm sure," Thomas offered, laying out his blue riding coat and fawn stockinette breeches, "but if you were to ask me, I'd say this Singleton needs to be taught a good lesson, ah," he nodded, "and pretty sharpish too."

"I quite agree," Deerham nodded, removing his sword before shrugging himself out of his coat, knowing perfectly well that Thomas received his information from Trench, cronies of long-standing, "and I intend to make sure that he gets it."

Taking the coat which Deerham had just shrugged off and laying it down with finicking care, Thomas then helped him out of his breeches before handing him his fawn ones, saying, "If I may be permitted to say so, my lord, it seems to me that he's taken one step too far this time."

"Much too far," Deerham replied grimly, tucking his shirt into his breeches, knowing perfectly well that it was really quite useless to prevent such old friends as Thomas and Trench from voicing their opinion.

Putting on a pair of gloves, Thomas then handed Deerham his riding boots, taking no small amount of pride from knowing that they were exquisitely polished. Kneeling down in front of Deerham as he sat in the chair Thomas helped to carefully ease the boots on, then, giving them a quick dust, he rose to his feet. Removing the gloves, he then handed Deerham his coat, who shrugged himself easily into it before Thomas brushed his hands over the shoulders to ease out whatever creases there were, then, having satisfied himself that his lordship looked as fine as fivepence, watched in silent satisfaction as he sat down at his dressing table to pare his nails. It was just as Thomas had brushed the clothes Deerham had taken off before putting them away that he saw him rise to his feet and walk over to the bed, picking up his sword and attaching it to his side. Deerham saw the sidelong look Thomas had cast at him, saying with a smile, "Just a precautionary measure, you understand."

Thomas nodded, but he was not fooled. He knew it was customary for gentlemen to wear a small sword, and whilst these were merely for decorative purposes, he knew too that they were nevertheless functional weapons, and unless he was grossly mistaken, particularly given the mood Deerham was in, he would have no hesitation in using it. Thomas eyed his lordship narrowly, but upon seeing the smile in his eyes he merely bowed, saying, "Yes, my lord."

*

Singleton, meanwhile, having left Louisa, defiant and refusing all sustenance, to retire to his bedchamber, was extremely confident that Deerham would accede to his demands. Singleton had chosen *'The Blue Boar'*, not only because he knew the landlord, Hinkson, very well, a man he knew he could rely on totally, but because it had been quite impossible for him to keep Louisa a prisoner at either *'The Green Man'* or *'The Red Lion'* simply because these were both extremely popular and busy posting inns who mainly dealt with the quality, and therefore to hire a private parlour for what could be several days would have been bound to lead to talk, something he was extremely anxious to avoid. Not only that, but it was quite possible that someone may accidentally spot her, particularly as the young marchioness was no stranger to members of the ton. It had been quite out of the question for him to hold Louisa prisoner at his lodgings in Half Moon Street not only because there was no room but his landlord, who was by no means half asleep would be bound to know that something untoward was going on, besides which, he wanted to keep his dealings with Deerham as far away as possible from the eyes and ears of the ton.

Having decided to keep Louisa locked in the private parlour rather than take the risk of providing a bedchamber for her, thereby eliminating all likely escape routes, he knew that there was no possible way Louisa could conceivably run away, even though he would not put it past her to try, she was certainly capable of it, but not only did he and Hinkson hold the only two keys to the private parlour but the windows were securely locked; not only that, but even if she did by some means manage to escape not only did she have no idea where it was she was being held but in which direction she should go. As far as Deerham was concerned, it had never so much as crossed Singleton's mind that he would not pay the twenty thousand guineas in order to get his wife back, indeed, so sure was he of this that he fully expected to see Grimshaw the day after tomorrow with the money, whereupon she would be conveyed back to town.

Had Singleton known that Grimshaw's meeting with Deerham in the Green Park would turn out to be anything other than what he had envisaged, he would have been extremely astonished. Singleton knew that Grimshaw could be an insubordinate as well as a disrespectful rogue when it suited him, but he knew too that he was as tough as old boots and therefore more than capable of dealing with Deerham. He knew that Deerham was a proficient exponent of the pugilistic art, and apart from the fact that his instructions to Grimshaw were not to engage in any kind of conversation with him but just to take the money, he doubted very much that Deerham would find it necessary to engage in a bout of fisticuffs in the middle of Green Park where any number of people could be abroad. Deerham was nothing if not a gentleman who would deem it to be far beneath him to resort to such tactics in a public place, indeed, Singleton knew without question that he would do nothing other than follow his instructions and hand over the money. At no point had it even so much as occurred to him that Deerham, for once in his life being quite happy to set aside the fact that he was a gentleman, would find out where his wife was being held by using forceful, even brutal, tactics on Grimshaw, a man Singleton knew as being one who could quite easily take care of himself.

Once in possession of the money, Singleton fully intended to leave England for a spell and make his way to Paris and then to Rome to not only enjoy his ill-gotten gains but to escape whatever retribution Deerham may propose meting out to him, although if Singleton was being honest he could not see Deerham's desire for revenge lasting forever, indeed he fully expected their relationship, once he returned to England, to continue in the same way it had always done. Over time, Singleton had become used to exchanging nothing more than a bow in passing with the man he hated above all others, and unless he had grossly underestimated the case, he could not see their future relationship being anything different.

When Deerham had first spoiled his game with young Lord Finchley, a callow and inexperienced youth whom he had lured to that gaming hell with a view to plucking him, he had been furiously angry to learn that Deerham, thanks to a mutual friend, had decided to intervene by warning Finchley of what going forward. Then there was the Dalby chit! Singleton would never know how Deerham had got wind of it, unless of course her father had discovered something and told him, after all they were old friends, but whatever the truth of it Deerham had eventually caught up with them on the Bath Road and, after a most uncomfortable episode, he had eventually taken her back to her father. Then there was Letitia Rawnsley, a most taking little thing and an heiress into the bargain. Singleton had no doubt that marriage to her would have been a most exciting challenge, indeed he would have enjoyed bringing her to bridle, but he was also equally confident that the novelty of schooling her would have very soon worn off. Nevertheless, he had been perfectly prepared to put up with being leg-shackled to a young woman whose money would automatically come to him on marriage, but yet again Deerham had spoiled his game.

It was of course a pity that Carrie Marchand had not only failed to lure the young marchioness into her gambling circle and making sure she remained tied to it by virtue of the gambling debts she would seemingly accumulate, resulting in bleeding her husband dry, but thanks again to

Deerham it had all come to nothing! Then there was Ricky Vane, a young man Singleton had believed to be ripe for any lark. And it had all started so very well. The young marchioness, taking an instant liking to him, had allowed him to drive her in the park and even out to Richmond, as well as standing up with him for numerous dances, but not only had Deerham made no effort to put a stop to it but Ricky Vane himself had unexpectedly turned short about. Whether Deerham had known there was nothing in the friendship between them or whether he just did not care, Singleton did not know, but whatever the reason he had made no effort whatsoever to take steps to divorce his wife. Had Singleton known that both of them were very much in love with one another although they did not know it, he would have known that using Ricky Vane would serve no purpose.

Singleton, tired of other people's inefficiency, had therefore decided to take matters into his own hands. He may be somewhat reluctant to show his hand, but having been given no choice he believed he had come up with the perfect scheme to have his revenge on Deerham, and what could be better than abducting his wife?

With Louisa safely locked in the parlour with no hope of escape together with the happy thought that before too long he would be in possession of twenty thousand guineas, Singleton climbed the stairs to his bedchamber with no suspicion that he was not only doomed to disappointment but that he was about to come face to face with the man who had seemingly taken on the role of his nemesis, a man he loathed above all others.

Chapter Twenty-One

Louisa would have scorned to show her fear to Singleton or to let him see just how much this evening's unlooked-for events had alarmed and distressed her, but once having heard him lock the door to the private parlour behind him, instead of setting her mind to escaping she had inevitably given way to her shock at finding herself in this unexpected position by bursting into tears, only pulling herself together and wiping her eyes with a napkin which lay on the table some appreciable time later. But however much her emotional outburst had restored her to equanimity, she was no nearer to finding the answer as to how she could have been stupid enough not to see that she was entering the wrong coach, indeed if the footman had not been holding the umbrella so low over her head she would most certainly have done so. At first, she thought that it had been nothing but a simple error, but upon finding the windows to the doors of the coach firmly locked against her, resisting her efforts to pull them open, and her banging on the roof had proved to be entirely fruitless, panic began to well up inside her.

She had no idea how long she had been travelling or in which direction she was being taken, but upon eventually finding herself being set down at an unknown inn at some equally unknown destination she had been considerably alarmed, to which not even the sight of the landlord bowing almost to his knees at the sight of her, had done very little if anything to assuage her fear. For one brief moment she had toyed with the idea of refusing to follow him inside, wondering if there was any way she could possibly escape, but something had told her that to refuse to follow him inside would have availed her very little, especially as the man on the box of the coach had just stepped down and was more than capable of preventing her from trying to escape. It was therefore with her head held high and her taffeta wrap pulled closely about her that she accompanied the landlord into the inn, but whatever it was she had expected it was certainly not to find herself coming face to face with Singleton, and for one brief moment she gasped her shock.

Beneath his painted and powdered face, the lines of dissipation were plainly visible, telling her more than any words could have as to the kind of life he led, but even though he and her father had been bosom cronies, setting the town alight with their antics if all she had ever heard was true, she had never liked him, although why this should be she had no idea. She remembered seeing the same lines on her father's face the last time she had seen him, and whilst she had been far too young to understand the meaning of them, despite the fact that there could be no possible comparison between Singleton and Deerham, she could now perhaps understand her mother's warnings.

She knew that Singleton and Deerham, despite their obvious dislike of one another, nevertheless accorded the other a polite bow in passing, and even though neither of them had ever mentioned the reason for such animosity, Louisa nonetheless knew it existed. But in view of Singleton's remarks this evening about Deerham having meddled in his affairs once too often, she began to wonder more particularly about the reason for it. Despite that aura of reserve which hung about him, she knew Deerham to be a man who was well-liked and respected and one who could boast many friends, all of whom held him in high regard, although she did know that he had no time for the so-called toad eaters and those who tried to pander to him because of who he was, but at no time had he ever struck her as being a man to interfere in the affairs of others, and therefore she could not help but question the reason for his involving himself in Singleton's affairs.

If Singleton's reputation was only half true, and Louisa had no reason to doubt it was, then she was left to wonder if he had attempted to abduct other females apart from Letitia, which, given his fluctuating financial circumstances, would not surprise her in the least, after all, wasn't her own abduction this evening merely to obtain money from Deerham? She then recalled what Letitia had told her about her own abduction and her masked rescuer coming just in the nick of time, and for one insane moment Louisa wondered whether it was Deerham who had saved her from Singleton's hands. This would certainly go a long way to explaining his hatred of Deerham, particularly if this was not the first time he had intervened by spoiling Singleton's game, but however it was, it had been obvious to Louisa from the first that he would harm Deerham if he could, but that he would seek revenge on him by abducting her was too base even for him.

But all of this was mere conjecture, the most important thing now was to consider how best she could extricate herself from the difficulties that surrounded her. There was no way if she could help it that Deerham was going to pay twenty thousand guineas for her release, because although such a sum was a mere trifle for a man of his wealth, and she never doubted he would pay the money, the very thought of enriching Singleton's purse through her was unthinkable. But the events of the evening had taken their toll, more than she had thought, and much to her surprise, before she could go any further in planning her escape, her eyelids closed of their own volition until she fell into an exhausted sleep, not waking until she heard the landlord unlock the parlour door the next morning.

Raising her head from where it had been resting on her elbows which had been leaning on the table, she drowsily opened her eyes to glance up at the portly figure looking down at her. Upon realizing that she had inadvertently fallen asleep, meaning that she would have to spend another whole day here because it was useless to even consider trying to escape during the daytime, she could have cried with vexation. Sitting slowly and somewhat stiffly up in her seat, her whole body aching from being in the same position all night, she eyed the landlord with loathing, pointedly ignoring his greeting by turning a haughty shoulder on him, but if she thought that such an action would discompose him she was quite wrong.

"I see you've not eaten anything," he remarked, quite unmoved by this snub, casting his eyes over the laden table.

"I'm not hungry," she shrugged.

Upon hearing this he merely shrugged before beginning to clear away the untouched remains of the meal on the table.

Fatigue coupled with a feeling of sheer helplessness engulfed her, rendering her fearful and extremely apprehensive, although her temper, exacerbated by shock by the unexpected turn of events, was by no means assuaged, but disdaining to show either, she demanded, "How much longer do you intend keeping me here?" When he made no effort to answer her, she rose rather stiffly to her feet, her eyes sparkling, "I demand you release me immediately."

Thankfully for the landlord, who had no real idea how to answer this, Singleton chose that moment to stroll into the private parlour, his pencilled eyebrows raised in enquiry upon hearing her demand. "You were saying, my dear?" he drawled.

She turned on him. "I demand you release me immediately!"

He strolled further into the room eyeing her closely, then, after tapping his eyeglass thoughtfully against his painted lips, he said at length, "I am afraid that is not possible."

"You can't keep me here!" she cried.

"I think you will find that I can," Singleton said smoothly.

Outside in the corridor she could hear the sound of the other patrons coming downstairs to partake of breakfast in the coffee room, and as

Singleton had not locked the door to the private parlour behind him she took the opportunity of darting past him to reach the door to draw attention to her plight, but Singleton was before for her. Grasping her by the shoulders he thrust her back into the room, sighing, "That really was most foolish, my dear."

Louisa could have stamped her foot in sheer frustration, but instead she threw him a look of utter contempt. "How dare you treat me in this fashion! I demand you return me to my home immediately."

"You will be returned to your home once Deerham has honoured his side of the bargain and not before," Singleton told her firmly, having to strenuously curb the inclination to slap her.

"You really believe he will calmly hand over twenty thousand guineas?" Louisa questioned, raising an eyebrow.

"If he wants you safely restored to him," Singleton told her, "he will."

By now the landlord had cleared the table, telling them that he would see about some breakfast, whereupon he left the room. Singleton, whose duties as host was already beginning to pall, especially with such an uncooperative and distinctly aloof captive, indeed were it not for the largesse he would soon have in his pockets, he would leave her in the capable hands of Hinkson and his wife, but as this was not possible he was therefore prepared to put up with what he could only describe as her petulance. Nevertheless, he felt it behoved him to warn her as to the futility of not taking him seriously and what would befall her should she try to make the attempt to escape, and that, providing she did as she was told he saw no reason why the next twenty-four hours should not be passed quite agreeably.

Louisa eyed him indignantly, telling him coldly, "I can think of nothing I should dislike more, indeed, to spend five minutes in your company is more that I can bear."

This brought a laugh from deep within his throat. "But something tells me you will bear it," he told her softly.

The confidence with which he said this considerably annoyed her, and immediately raised her hand to slap his painted face, but Singleton, quicker than she, grasped her small hand, saying, through clenched teeth, "It is a thousand pities that Deerham never brought you to bridle."

Her eyes flashed and, snatching her hand out of his, said, "Is that what you intended doing with Letitia, bring her to bridle?"

It took him a moment or two to bring his temper under control, but said at length, "Let us just say, she would have been brought to mind me - as you will."

She eyed him with loathing, but just as she was about to respond to this the landlord returned with their breakfast, then, after laying the table followed by a quiet word in Singleton's ear, he left them. Singleton, quite unperturbed by her refusal to partake of any of the dishes in front of her, even though she had had nothing to eat since nibbling a salmon canapé at Lady Templeton's last night, watched in contented silence as she sat bolt upright in the chair opposite his. A low rumble of laughter escaped his parted lips as he poured her a cup of coffee, and although she took several sips nothing would have pleased her more than to throw it in his painted face, but deciding this would serve no real purpose other than to afford her tremendous satisfaction, she merely turned a cold shoulder on him, totally ignoring him.

She thought of Deerham and wondered what he was doing and if he was arranging to get the twenty thousand pounds to pay Singleton for her release, or if he just did not care. The thought brought a tear to her eye, but then she told herself that even if Deerham did not love her there would be no way he would allow her to remain in Singleton's hands and therefore she could be assured that he was doing everything possible to secure her release. She knew that this situation in which she found herself would never have arisen had she not been so keen to shelve Deerham's escort, or if her mamma had not cautioned her so strenuously about allowing her feelings to show, but it was much too late now for regrets or self-recrimination, the only thing that mattered, and all that sustained her as the day wore on, was trying to effect her escape.

What Singleton had found to do when he periodically left her alone for a while Louisa neither knew nor cared, but whenever he did deem it necessary to put in an appearance she made not the slightest attempt to be conciliatory, on the contrary she was anything but a subdued hostage, nevertheless she had never known a day pass so wretchedly before. Apart from drinking a cup of coffee at breakfast she refused to partake of the luncheon Hinkson eventually brought in but she was more than grateful for the jug of hot water and bowl which was later brought into her by Hinkson's wife, a colourless creature who made no effort to enquire if there was anything else she wanted. But as the day wore endlessly on with Louisa's nerves torn to shreds, her only solace being watching the comings and goings of various travellers pulling up and driving away outside the window, her only company was her two gaolers, neither of whom she wished to spend her time with. But at long last the moment she had been waiting for arrived. Singleton, finally wishing her goodnight with a mocking bow and the promise that by this time tomorrow evening she would be safely back in Grosvenor Square, left her to her cogitations as he locked the door to the private parlour behind him.

Since the only two keys to the parlour door were in the hands of Singleton and the landlord, and she had herself heard Singleton turn the key in the lock when he left her, she knew it was quite useless even to attempt to try to escape that way, besides which, she doubted she would be able to get out of the front door, which was bound to be securely locked, before her attempted flight was discovered. But as Louisa was not one to give up on something quite so easily, she rose to her feet and walked over to the window and pulled back the curtains, realizing that this was her only way of escape. From the looks of it, it had stopped raining and the moon, although partly obscured by clouds, was nevertheless giving off enough of its silvery light to assist her in her forthcoming task, so placing her fingers in the base of the sash-cord window she pulled with all her strength, but frustratingly it held firm against her, but not one to be put off so easily she tried again. Unfortunately, her second attempt fared no better than the first, but since she was determined to effect her own release come what may, she turned and walked back to the wing chair where she had hidden a knife she had picked up from the table earlier. Armed with this tool, Louisa then placed the tip of the knife in the base of the window, pulling with all her strength, but just when she had come to frustratingly think that it was to no avail, it was to her delight as well as her surprise that she heard a slight cracking noise which sounded abnormally loud in the silence and, after pausing a moment to turn round with her ear cocked, she then pulled a little harder whereby the window finally gave way. Dropping the knife onto the floor she wasted no time, flinging up the window and, after raising her skirts, she climbed outside without a backward glance, extremely relieved that no grooms had been put on the watch in case she tried to escape.

It may be June with pleasantly warm days, but thanks to the heavy downpour it had left the air damp and chill, her taffeta wrap affording her no protection from either of these discomforts, and her silk shoes, hardly designed for these conditions let alone walking, she nevertheless left the confines of the inn undetected to begin walking down the street. She calculated the time as being about three o'clock, and therefore was by no means surprised to find the streets completely deserted of people, for which she was devoutly thankful as the sight of an unaccompanied lady at this time of the morning dressed in an evening gown of star-spangled gauze over satin and a taffeta wrap would be bound to occasion remark.

Raising her skirts, Louisa then hurried to the end of the street without pausing for breath until she came upon what appeared to be the main street of the town. She had no idea which town it was or in which direction she should go, but after only a moment's indecision she decided to turn right, walking quickly along the empty street. Not surprisingly all the premises were closed, but as she walked further on she saw two establishments situated on either side of the road, but even though no lights or activity could be discerned from either she quickly recognized them as being *The Green Man'* and *'The Red Lion',* Barnet's two hectic and popular posting inns.

She recalled stopping here one time with Max on their way to Hatfield to visit friends of his, but other than Barnet lay on the Great North Road she knew nothing more, and certainly not in which direction she should go to reach London.

Even if she did attempt to try and gain shelter for the night at either one of them it was extremely doubtful whether they would accommodate her, a woman travelling alone and totally unaccompanied by her maid or luggage and, to make matters worse, even if they did spot a member of the quality when they saw one, she had no money on her to defray their charges. Then, of course, there was always the possibility that Singleton, upon discovering her escape, would be bound to enquire at these two hostelries first in case they had seen her before he did anything else, and then she would be back where she started. Refusing to allow the tears of frustration welling up at the back of her eyes from falling, she walked on down the main street, not at all sure whether she was travelling in the right direction or not, but as the premises gradually gave way to open spaces she saw, in the light given off from the moon, a stone road sign telling her that London was fifteen miles away. Well, if nothing else, she was at least walking in the right direction.

But when, a few minutes later, it came on to rain again and the moon disappeared from the sky, her silk shoes, not made for walking, were beginning to pinch her feet, and her taffeta wrap, proving quite useless in affording her any protection, was soon soaked through. To add to her discomfort the darkness greatly reduced her visibility, causing her to stumble a couple of times, and if all this was not bad enough the eerie shadows which danced in front of her eyes made her jump out of her skin. It was therefore in sheer desperation that she knew she had no choice but retrace her steps back to the town in the hope that she could wake up the landlord at either 'The Green Man' or 'The Red Lion' and that they would believe her tale and take her in, and, if they did, that Singleton would not discover her. If they did not take her in then she had no idea what she would do, but as she slowly turned her steps back towards the town whatever joy she had received upon effecting her escape, it could not be said to have brought her any great dividends.

But good luck it seemed favoured Louisa. After her imperious banging on the door of 'The Green Man' for several minutes it was eventually opened by a sleepy landlord, who, upon setting eyes on Louisa in a near state of collapse on his doorstep, suffered a severe shock. Having been awoken by someone hammering on the front door he had been in two minds whether to get out of bed and open it or not, but his wife, telling him sharply that unless he answered it there was a very good chance of it waking up the other patrons, he finally got out of bed and scrambled into his clothes. But whatever it was he had expected to see it was certainly not a young lady, clearly dressed for an evening party, in a distressed state and on the point of collapse demanding entrance, but just one look at her was enough to tell him that she was undoubtedly quality, and since he was not in the habit of turning away the quality, no matter what hour of the day or night irrespective of whether or not they had luggage or a servant with them, he put his arm around her waist and ushered her into a private parlour, leaving her to sit quietly while he went in search of his wife.

Upon being informed by her spouse that the person demanding admittance was a young lady without either her maid or her luggage and was momentarily taking refuge in the private parlour, all her suspicions were aroused. Indeed it was on the tip of her tongue to tell him that *'The Green Man'* was a respectable hostelry and not the kind of place to take in waifs and strays, but upon being told that she was definitely a lady and, unless he grossly mistook the case, in considerable distress, indeed when he left her a moment ago she was almost on the point of collapse, she paused to consider. On the one hand if she was quality then to refuse her admittance would probably do *'The Green Man's'* reputation no good at all because it was surprising how quickly word got about, on the other hand of course, if she was a person of suspect morals merely looking for a quick hand out, then she was very much mistaken.

But when Mrs. Fleetwood, a rather redoubtable lady, as round as her husband was spare, finally went down to the private parlour to see for herself the kind of young woman seeking shelter, just one look at Louisa and her very expensive toilet was more than enough to tell her that she was undoubtedly quality and, more to the point, in considerable distress, and all her motherly instincts rose to the fore. "There dearie," she soothed, sitting beside Louisa on a sofa and putting an arm around her waist, "there's no need to take on so."

"I'm sorry," Louisa began, somewhat tearfully, raising watery eyes to her hostess's face. "You must be thinking it very strange that I am... "

"Never mind that now," she told her, patting Louisa's cold hand. "What you need is a cup of hot coffee and something to eat, yes," she nodded, "and a warm bed," nodding to her husband to see that coffee and food was brought immediately to the parlour and a room to be made up. Waiting only until he had left the parlour did she turn to Louisa, saying, "Don't tell me anything now if you don't want, but begging your pardon, my lady," instantly recognizing that Louisa, as young as she was, was a lady of considerable consequence, "it's as plain as a pikestaff that you're in some kind of trouble."

From the moment Louisa had retraced her steps back to the town she had known that she had to give some kind of an explanation to account for her knocking them up at this time of the morning, supposing of course they would take her in, and during her cold and uncomfortable walk back she had tried to come up with something other than the truth to account for it, because try as she did she could not see them believing her tale about being abducted and held to ransom by a man who was, however undeserved, a gentleman. But try as she did she could come up with nothing she felt was credible enough to be believed, but in face of Mrs. Fleetwood's motherly kindness and understanding, encouraging Louisa to unburden herself, she found herself nodding her head and sniffing, then, and after succumbing to the tears she could no longer suppress, resulting from all the emotions which had been gathering inside her, she haltingly told this kind-hearted woman her tale. It may have been a somewhat edited version of events, carefully omitting mentioning Singleton by name, but by the time she had come to the end of it not only did she feel very much better but it was clear that she had no need to ask Mrs. Fleetwood to deny her presence at *The Green Man* should anyone come asking for her. "Th-That is," she faltered, "unless it is m-my husband."

"Now don't you go worrying yourself over that, my lady," Mrs. Fleetwood assured her, rising to her feet as her husband walked in carrying a tray. Waiting only until she had taken the tray off him and arranged the plates and cup and saucer together with the coffee pot on the table, did she say, "You sit here quietly, my lady and eat your food. I'll be back presently," to which Louisa nodded.

Louisa was indeed very hungry having eaten nothing substantial since luncheon yesterday, and the cold meat and bread and butter was therefore most welcome, so much so that by the time Mrs. Fleetwood returned, having conferred with her spouse, Louisa had eaten every morsel. Mrs. Fleetwood, looking kindly at her said, "Now, my lady, it's time you were tucked up between sheets."

"Thank you," Louisa smiled wanly, "I am feeling rather tired."

Mrs. Fleetwood, like her husband, may have recognized Louisa as being a member of the quality and one moreover who was a young woman of considerable consequence, but Mrs. Fleetwood, apart from having taken an instant liking to her unexpected guest, nevertheless felt impelled to ask, "Beggin' your pardon, my lady, but who, may I ask, is your husband?"

Louisa, looking up at the kindly face, said, "The Marquis of Deerham."

Both Mrs. Fleetwood and her husband knew Deerham very well, being a familiar figure on the road, indeed they had more than once provided refreshment for him, and a more kindly gentleman you would be hard to find, but whilst it was not her place to ask Louisa what her husband was doing to let his wife get into such a tangle, she was nevertheless agog with curiosity. However, putting this to one side she soon had Louisa tucked up in bed wearing the nightgown, although many sizes too large it was nevertheless clean and warm, she had lent her, and promising to see what she could do about her dress and wrap, to which Louisa nodded and smiled before falling into a deep and exhausted sleep.

*

Singleton, having spent a most comfortable night in happy and contented repose, awoke betimes the next morning feeling extremely hungry, but not until he had powdered and painted his face and set his wig upon his head did he leave his bedchamber. He was in an extremely buoyant mood, indeed there was no reason why he should not be, particularly as he would be in possession of the twenty thousand guineas he knew Deerham would pay to get his wife back before many hours were out. Foreseeing nothing going wrong with Grimshaw's meeting with Deerham today, Singleton fully expected to see his henchman sometime during the late afternoon when he would not only pay him the money he had promised him but would also see the return of Louisa to Grosvenor Square, by which time he would be well on the way to Paris. The only problem being, however, was how to keep Louisa quiet in the meantime, particularly as she had already proved herself to be neither a subdued nor an acquiescent hostage, on the contrary she had done everything possible to be as obstructive and provocative as she could. Nevertheless, Singleton was in no doubt that between himself, the landlord and his wife they could more than adequately deal with her during the few hours remaining before she was released.

Upon unlocking the door to the private parlour, fully expecting to find Louisa still asleep in one of the wing chairs beside the fire it was something of a shock to discover that she was nowhere in sight. A quick look around the room was sufficient to confirm this, but just as he was about to set up a cry for Hinkson his eye alighted upon the open window and the knife which Louisa had dropped onto the floor, and hurrying over to it he put his head outside to see if he could see her, but upon no sign of her he was, for a brief and horrifying moment, held in the grip of panic, but managing to clamp down on this he set up a cry for Hinkson.

Singleton could only hazard a guess at what time Louisa had made her escape, most probably once she had assured herself that the whole household was asleep, and although she had no idea where she was or in which direction she should go did not make him feel any easier, on the contrary it only went to increase his fear. He tried to tell himself that despite her several hours start she could not have gone very far, not in those clothes and shoes, besides which, someone was bound to spot her, instantly recognizing her quality, perhaps even taking her in. Should that in fact be what happened then he could not see Louisa refraining from telling her story, leaving him exposed to all manner of things, but before he could go very far with these unpleasant thoughts Hinkson came hurrying into the room.

Upon discovering the flight of their hostage he looked aghast, but his main concern was not for Singleton but for himself and what it would mean for his hostelry. He had been landlord of 'The Blue Boar' for a good few years, and although it could not compare with 'The Green Man' and 'The Red Lion' he nevertheless ran an honest house with enough passing trade to make it a more than viable concern. It was true that he had known Singleton for a long time and it was also true that he had his best interests at heart, a man who had often stayed at his establishment, particularly when it was not high water with him, so when he had approached him about making use of his private parlour and the reason for it he had known no hesitation, particularly as Singleton had told him that he would more than make it worth his while. Unlike 'The Green Man' and 'The Red Lion' Hinkson was not used to providing for the real quality, but he had recognized quality in the young woman who had been kept in his private parlour, and although he had not exactly relished the thought of holding her a prisoner, he was nevertheless able to salve his conscience by the thought of the largesse he would soon have in his pocket. But upon learning that she had at some point during the night made good her escape he was extremely fearful of the consequences. It was not to be supposed that she would keep her mouth shut, indeed Hinkson envisaged her divulging everything at the earliest opportunity, and this rendered his need to find her as urgent as Singleton's, but where to start looking for her had him in something of a puzzle.

Singleton, not in the least bit concerned as to the awkward position this could possibly place Hinkson in, had been giving this matter some serious consideration, his eyes narrowing as he suddenly bethought himself of something. Bearing in mind that Louisa's escape had occurred at some point during the night and also that she would have no idea where she was or which direction she should take, not to mention it coming on to rain again, it was not beyond the realms of possibility that she could have taken shelter at either 'The Green Man' or 'The Red Lion', both establishments dealing with members of the quality. Only one look at Louisa, especially as she was wearing a very expensive ball gown and taffeta wrap, would be sufficient for them to recognize quality when they saw it, and therefore they would have no hesitation in taking her in. The fact that she had no money on her would make no difference, once they knew her identity they would know that Deerham would eventually pay her shot, and it was therefore in a mood of optimism that he told Hinkson he had to go out and he would not be long.

Unfortunately, however, Singleton's discreet enquiries at 'The Red Lion' proved entirely fruitless; the landlord telling him that they had no such woman as he described staying there. "Are you quite sure?" Singleton urged. "It really is most important that I find her."

The landlord, never having had the pleasure of providing a room or refreshments much less a change of horses for the man who was eagerly looking at him, could only repeat that it was not the custom of *'The Red Lion'* to take in young ladies without a maid and no luggage, and certainly not in the early hours of the morning. With this Singleton had to be satisfied, hoping good fortune would smile upon him at *'The Green Man'*.

Fleetwood, having been put in possession of the facts regarding their new guest by his wife, was therefore prepared for someone making enquiries about her and equally prepared to deny any knowledge of her. Like his spouse he had seen at the outset that the young lady banging on his door in the early hours and in a state of considerable distress was quality, and not just any quality, but a lady of the first consequence, and one, moreover, he had taken a liking to. Nevertheless he had been very much shocked by what his wife had confided, but although the tale the young marchioness had told them may seem quite incredible there was no doubt whatsoever that she was telling the truth, indeed there was a lack of guile about her that told them it was all too true, even though she had not named her abductor, but what had shocked him even more was knowing that she was the Marchioness of Deerham. Having played host to Deerham on many occasions he could proudly boast of knowing him very well; an honest and reasonable man who, unless Fleetwood had grossly miscalculated, would soon bring the perpetrator of his wife's abduction to book, indeed he would not be at all surprised to see him before too long, until then though Fleetwood was more than prepared to house her at *'The Green Man'*.

Singleton, having come up empty handed at *'The Red Lion'*, crossed the road to *'The Green Man'* with a leisureliness he was very far from feeling. He could see any number of vehicles and their owners waiting to be attended to by a small army of grooms and waiters, but since *'The Green Man'* like *'The Red Lion'* was an extremely popular and busy hostelry, this did not surprise him in the least. Walking into the front of the house he saw several waiters hurrying past him with laden trays and hasty apologies, only one of them promising to find the landlord, but unfortunately for his temper as well as his patience he had to wait at least ten minutes before Fleetwood joined him in the entrance hall. As it had been quite some considerable time since Singleton had taken advantage of the amenities offered by this excellent hostelry he knew there was very little chance of him being recognized by the landlord, and therefore in his desperation to get Louisa back it had briefly crossed his mind to pass himself off as Deerham, because if Louisa was seeking sanctuary under this roof and she had apprised the landlord of her predicament it could be that she had begged him not to give her away unless it was to her husband. However, only a very little thought told him that this would not answer particularly as Deerham, who was no stranger on the Great North Road, would most certainly have stopped for a change of horses or refreshment at either *'The Green Man'* or *'The Red Lion'* depending on which direction he happened to be travelling. Taking the opportunity offered while he was waiting for the landlord, Singleton hit upon the idea of pretending to be Louisa's brother, after all, what could be more natural than a sibling coming in search of his sister or that she would not show herself to him, because he felt certain that Louisa would not hide her identity to the landlord or, it could even be, that he recognized her. Thankfully, he did not have to wait many more minutes before Fleetwood joined him, and upon being asked if he could help him, Singleton replied, with a confidence he was far from feeling, "I hope so. I have come to enquire if my sister, the Marchioness of Deerham, is by chance staying here. My name is Markham, Christopher Markham."

Unfortunately for Singleton, Fleetwood recognized him straightaway. It may have been quite some time since he had taken advantage of the amenities *'The Green Man'* had to offer, but although Fleetwood could not bring to mind his name he remembered him simply because he had cut up pretty stiff when he had been kept waiting for a change of horses the last time he had patronized his establishment. But not by a word or gesture did Fleetwood let him see that he knew he was no such person as the marchioness's brother, indeed, unless his instincts were grossly at fault he would go so far as to say that the man looking eagerly at him was none other than her ladyship's abductor, but merely shook his head, apologizing,

"I'm sorry, sir, but her ladyship is not staying here. Indeed, sir," he shook his head, "I can see no reason why you should think she might be."

The frown which descended onto Singleton's forehead was not lost on Fleetwood, who merely waited for him to say something. "Please, do not think I am doubting your word, but are you quite sure my sister is not staying here?"

"Quite sure, sir," Fleetwood nodded.

"It is very important that I see her," Singleton urged. "You see," he explained, "I have come to tell her of the good news which I have received and that there is no longer the least need for her to continue her journey."

"As to that, sir, I really cannot say," Fleetwood told him, "but I as I have already said her ladyship is not staying here."

Unless Singleton had grossly erred, he was convinced that Louisa was taking sanctuary under the roof of *'The Green Man'* or *'The Red Lion'* because he would stake his life that she had not been able to walk very far, and certainly not in the dark and pouring with rain, and after considering the position he was in for a moment or two an idea, so blindingly audacious, suddenly occurred to him, it was certainly worth a try, so after eyeing the landlord thoughtfully for a few moments he said, with a careless shrug and a rueful smile,

"I can see that there is little point in my continuing to try to fool you. I can, of course," he said with spurious sympathy, "understand why you are protecting her, but my sister is, or rather she can be," he corrected himself, "well, how shall I say?" he raised a pencilled eyebrow, spreading his hands a little helplessly, "a little inventive."

Fleetwood, whose face was a mask of impassivity, merely shrugged, saying, "As to that sir, you would know better than me, but I can only repeat that her ladyship is not staying under this roof."

As the landlord was not prepared to say anything more, and Singleton did not wish to create a stir, he really had no choice but to thank Fleetwood and make his dignified exit. There had been nothing in the landlord's demeanour to indicate that he was lying, indeed to all intents and purposes he appeared to be telling the truth, but unless Singleton had got it desperately wrong he concluded that either the landlord at *The Green Man* or the landlord at *The Red Lion* was lying. Louisa may be intrepid, but Singleton found it extremely hard to believe that she would have been able to walk all the way to London, even if she did know in which direction she should go, and in total darkness, unless of course someone took her up, which he very much doubted, and therefore he refused to believe that she was not still hovering in the town somewhere. There were of course any number of smaller and out of the way inns in and around Barnet, but something was telling him that Louisa, despite what he had been told, was either at *The Green Man* or *The Red Lion*, but since a return to either of these hostelries to question the landlords again would merely create questions being asked, he had no choice but to return to *The Blue Boar*.

Furiously angry that she had put him in the intolerable position of having to waste time in trying to find her, especially as he was expecting Grimshaw later this afternoon with the money, Singleton's brow was black as thunder by the time he returned to *The Blue Boar*, and Hinkson, taking one look at his face, decided it best to say nothing, indeed there was nothing he could say which would either help find Louisa and get her back here or stave off trouble from her husband.

Singleton may have taken Hinkson into his confidence to some degree, but he saw no reason to tell him that it was Louisa's husband that was the cause of his dark humour as much as her escape. Whether Deerham handed over the money or not, Singleton knew him too well to think that he would not extract his own brand of retribution, he would, but he doubted whether he would be in any frame of mind to extend him the usual courtesies which customarily accompanied such encounters, and whilst he was not afraid of coming face to face with Deerham, indeed he had long cherished hopes of paying him back for his effrontery in daring to intervene in his affairs, right now his urgent need was to receive the money from Grimshaw and make haste to Paris as quickly as possible.

Angrily realizing that time was ticking away and that he could not just sit back and do nothing until Grimshaw arrived, Singleton had no choice but to make an exploratory tour of the town, visiting all the out of the way inns and hotels in case Louisa had taken refuge in any one of them. Unfortunately for him however, after traipsing all over Barnet for over an hour or more with no sign of her, Singleton was forced to return to *The Blue Boar*. His temper, having by now reached fever pitch, could do nothing but wait for Grimshaw to arrive with what patience he could muster, pacing irritably up and down the private parlour in a manner that reminded Hinkson very much of a caged tiger.

Deerham, who was no doubt awaiting the return of his wife in exchange for the money he had handed over, would not be best pleased to know that she had gone missing, and in a way that was as surprising as it was dramatic, in fact, it would not surprise Singleton in the least to know that he was even now carrying out a search for her. Had he have known that the meeting between Deerham and Grimshaw had not gone according to plan and that his stalwart had failed in his task to extricate the money from Deerham, who had in fact prised her whereabouts from him without handing over a single penny as well as getting the truth out of Lady Templeton's footman, Singleton would have been greatly surprised. He knew that Grimshaw, a man whose past was as colourful as it was eventful, was not easily intimidated let alone bullied, and therefore Singleton had every confidence in him carrying out his instructions to the letter, indeed he expected to see him any minute now. Had he the least idea that Deerham was at this very moment pulling up outside *'The Green Man'* he would not only have been greatly astonished but extremely apprehensive.

Chapter Twenty-Two

It was a little after half past one by the time Deerham set out from Grosvenor Square, a pair of high-bred chestnuts in hand. They were exceptionally fresh, not having been out for several days, and Trench, who had had some difficulty in harnessing them to Deerham's light travelling coach, told him that they were a rare handful, to which Deerham laughed.

It was all of six miles to the Great North Road, and by the time he had carefully steered his pair through the busy streets and out onto open road almost an hour had passed, but Deerham knew his team very well and what they were capable of and once the Great North Road had been reached he gave them their head, the miles speeding by, reaching Barnet without mishap just a little after quarter to four.

By the time he had pulled up outside *The Green Man* his horses were beginning to sweat slightly, but two grooms, who had spotted Deerham's team approaching, were already waiting for him. Deerham jumped quickly down from the box seat and after touching their foreheads and accepting the douceur he tossed at them the grooms then took hold of the reins, carefully leading them into the back yard. Waiting only long enough to see his team safely bestowed, Deerham then strode purposefully inside, looking around for Fleetwood. As expected, the inn was a hive of activity, but he did not have long to wait before Fleetwood spotted him and, bowing down to his knees, welcomed Deerham warmly.

"How are you, Fleetwood?" he asked.

"Very well, my lord, thank you," he smiled.

"Could you take care of my team for a while?" Deerham cocked his head. "I have business to attend to in the town."

"It will be a pleasure, my lord," Fleetwood told him, having a very good idea what his business was. Then, after looking all around him and clearing his throat, said, "I must say I am glad to see you, my lord," to which

Deerham cocked an eyebrow. However, before Fleetwood could explain the unusual circumstances surrounding her ladyship's occupancy of one of his bedchambers and Singleton's visit earlier that morning, his wife came walking into the hall carrying over her arm a dress Deerham had no difficulty in recognizing. His eyebrows rose in surprise, asking sharply, "Where did you get that dress?"

Fleetwood looked at his wife then back at Deerham, saying, not a little awkwardly, "Well, it's about that that I am wishful to have private speech with your lordship."

Deerham looked searchingly at him, demanding, "Are you saying my wife is here?" his heart beginning to beat rather fast.

"Yes, my lord," Fleetwood inclined his head, "she is. Woke us up about half past one this morning, she did."

"Woke you up?" Deerham queried sharply.

"Yes, my lord," Fleetwood nodded. "Quite distressed she was, and soaked through into the bargain."

Without giving Deerham time to respond to this Fleetwood then invited him to step into his private parlour, closing the door quietly behind him, then, looking a little apprehensively at Deerham, whose face was looking particularly grim, he cleared his throat and began his tale, but by the time he had finished telling him, if a little haltingly, Deerham was far too relieved to know that Louisa had managed to escape Singleton's clutches and was now safe. Nevertheless, it only took a moment for Deerham to decide that it would be wise to inform Fleetwood of the facts, simply because it was obvious that Louisa had told him just enough in order to account for her reasons for knocking him up, but to say that Fleetwood was shocked upon hearing the full sum of it was a gross understatement.

Deerham, having listened to Fleetwood in incredulous disbelief, found himself torn between wanting to give Singleton the thrashing of his life and relief to know that his wife was safe. It came as no surprise to Deerham to know that his wife, who he knew did not lack courage, had managed to escape from her prison by forcing the window, but to think of Louisa wandering the streets of a strange town, afraid and fearful and not knowing in which direction she should go, was more than he could bear. To even think of Louisa attempting to walk all the way to London, and in total darkness with it coming onto rain again, where anything may have happened to her, almost proved too much, causing him to raise an unsteady hand to his forehead, but he could only be thankful that she had eventually come to see the futility of such an action and had retraced her steps back to 'The Green Man', awaking the household and begging them to take her in.

Deerham knew he had a lot to thank Fleetwood and his wife for, indeed without their help he dreaded to think of what could possibly have happened to Louisa, but upon learning that a man fitting Singleton's description had come here early this morning making enquiries about Louisa and pretending to be her brother into the bargain, filled Deerham with a white hot anger. Louisa's escape had clearly placed Singleton in a most awkward position, rendering it necessary for him to search all over for her, indeed so desperate must he have felt that he had even been prepared to pretend to being Christopher. It was a moment before Deerham, who seldom lost his temper, could bring it under control sufficiently to thank Fleetwood for all he and his wife had done to assist her ladyship and also to thank him for not letting Singleton know that he knew the deception he was perpetrating, and enquire in which room he would find his wife.

"Well, my lord," Fleetwood told him, "I don't mind saying it was something of a shock to be awoken in the early hours by someone banging on the front door like as though they were fit to burst it open, but just one look at her ladyship and seeing how distressed she was we could not have done anything else but take her in. The wife I know," he nodded, "has taken quite a fancy to her, but I'm afraid the only bedchamber we could put her in, my lord," Fleetwood told him, almost apologetically, "was the small back room at the rear of the house. It's not at all what her ladyship is used to," he nodded, "but it's warm and comfortable. You will find it, my lord, on the first landing."

Deerham nodded, then, after climbing the stairs two at a time, he arrived at Louisa's bedchamber, and following his light tap on the door entered the room without waiting to be told to come in.

*

Having spent a night in dreamless sleep, Louisa drowsily opened her eyes the following morning just as the clock in her room struck eleven. For one bewildered moment she could not think where she was or whose nightdress she was wearing, but then the mists slowly began to clear and the events of the past twenty-four hours and more came flooding back with horrendous clarity. She remembered being tricked into getting into the wrong coach when she had left Lady Templeton's and being taken to an unknown destination, where, to her horror, she had eventually come face to face with her abductor, a man she not only disliked but thoroughly distrusted. She remembered Singleton, painted and powdered and dressed in puce satin, shamelessly telling her of the ransom he had demanded from Deerham to get her back and how she would remain locked up in that private parlour until he had adhered to his ultimatum. Despite her imperative demands that she be released at once, she had nevertheless been extremely fearful, and as one long hour followed another with no respite, she knew her only chance lay in escaping, and therefore she was absolutely determined to make the attempt. It had seemed like a long time before

Singleton had decided to retire, but once he had she had prosecuted her escape with vigour, but, having done so, it had left her alone at night in a strange and deserted town with no idea where she should go or in which direction.

A tiny choking sound left her throat, and covering her face with hands that visibly shook she burst into tears. Even now, she could not quite believe that the landlord had taken her in, because even in her own ears her tale had sounded somewhat lame to say the least, but whatever the reason she would never forget their kindness and generosity nor the way Mrs. Fleetwood had looked after her, ensuring she had everything she needed. But by the time she had breakfasted, Mrs. Fleetwood insisting she eat her breakfast in bed, she felt more like herself, even so, the remnants of sleep which enveloped her refused to release her, and when Mrs. Fleetwood came upstairs to remove her breakfast tray it was to find she had fallen into a deep sleep.

Opening her eyes several hours later to the startling discovery that it had just gone fifteen minutes past four o'clock, Louisa was just about to get out of bed and ring for Mrs. Fleetwood to bring her clothes when she heard a tapping on her door, but even before she could tell whoever it was to come in, she saw the door open and Deerham walk in. For one bewildering moment she thought she was dreaming, but upon seeing him walk over to the bed and smile tenderly down at her, she knew it was no dream. She felt the bed depress under his weight and as she sat up to lean back against the pillows, he took her left hand in his and held it tightly for a moment before raising it to his lips, saying softly,

"My poor Louisa. You've had a dreadful time of it, haven't you?"

She felt the tears spring to the back of her eyes at hearing this, but as words failed her, her emotions over spilling, she could do nothing other than nod her head, then, as if she could no longer hold them back, the tears fell unheeded down her cheeks, whereupon Deerham took her in his arms and held her close against him.

"My poor darling," he soothed. "My poor, poor darling."

"Oh, Max!" she cried into his shoulder, too distraught to take notice of this affectionate term, "I am so sorry; please forgive me."

"There is nothing you have to be sorry for," he told her tenderly, easing himself a little away from her to allow him to look down into her tear stained face, "and there is certainly nothing to forgive. In fact," he confessed, not a little ruefully, brushing away her tears with a gentle forefinger, "I should be the one begging your forgiveness for not being there when you needed me." Then, as if he could not stop himself, he lowered his head and very gently kissed her, saying when his lips finally left hers, looking warmly down at her, "Fleetwood told me all about it."

"H-He did?" she hiccupped, her lips tingling from his delicate caresses.

"Yes," he said lovingly.

"W-what did h-he tell you?" she faltered.

"He told about how you managed to escape from where you were being held as well as how you thought you could walk it all the way to London until you realized it was just not possible. He also told me how you knocked him up," he felt her shudder at the recollection and held her even tighter against him. "My little love," he said tenderly, "how on earth did you even think you could possibly begin to walk it all the way to London?"

"I... I don't know," she sniffed, "all I knew was that I had to try. Then," she told him a little unsteadily, easing herself a little way out of his arms so she could look up at him, "I found I couldn't walk any further. You see," she sniffed again, "my shoes were pinching me and... and then my gown and wrap got wet and... and I knew I could go no further, but I didn't know what to do, and I had no money, so I began walking back and decided to ask the landlord if he w-would take m-me in and then I c-could pay him later." An agonized groan left Deerham's lips at this, taking her back in his arms and tightening his hold. "They have been so kind, Max," she told him into his shoulder. "I... I dread to think what they must have thought upon opening the door to find me standing there."

"It's all right," he soothed into her hair. "I know Fleetwood very well. He's a good man. Indeed, I am very much in his debt."

"Oh, Max!" she cried, moving her head slightly so she could see his face, "I had n-no idea I was g-getting into the w-wrong coach," she faltered.

"I know," he told her lovingly. "I got the truth out of Lady Templeton's footman and that man of Singleton's."

She eyed him horrifyingly for a moment, her fingers gripping his arm. "Max, never tell me you have paid him twenty thousand guineas!" she cried.

"No," he shook his head, "not one penny, although," he told her softly, "I would have paid twice that much to get you back."

"Y-you would?" she faltered, her heart somersaulting and her colour just a little high upon hearing this.

"You must know I would," he told her tenderly, taking a moment to gently kiss her.

The look in his eyes made her heart soar, and although his kiss was by no means passionate, it was nevertheless more heartfelt than at any other time, but his next words, delivered in a voice which was almost raw, gave her hope that he did indeed love her after all.

"I have been out of my mind with worry," holding her tight against him, "not knowing if you were safe or not. Wondering what was happening to you."

"Oh, Max!" she cried, her body trembling from reaction and what his words signified, a happiness she had never known before engulfing her. "I am so glad you are here."

He heaved a heartfelt sigh. "So am I," he told her lovingly, his fingers entwining themselves in her hair. "As soon as I learned the truth from that man of Singleton's I had the horses put to and came straight here."

"Oh, Max!" she exclaimed, moving a little way out of his arms and looking up at him. "Please take me home."

Cupping her flushed face in his two hands, he smiled down at her, saying, "You may be sure I will, but first," he told her, "I must leave you for a little while. I shall be back very shortly. There is something I have to do first."

Louisa instinctively knew what it was he had to do, but gripping his arm, said urgently, "Max, I know you are going to see Singleton, but you… you won't kill him, will you?"

He looked down into her flushed face, his thumb gently stroking it. "No," he shook his head, "I won't kill him; just punish him a little - for his impudence." Then, looking down at her he smiled, saying softly, "You must not worry over me, indeed, there is not the least need, I promise you."

"I can't help it," she shook her head. "I don't like or trust Singleton."

"Neither do I," he nodded, then, giving her no time to say anything further he merely cupped her face in his hands and lovingly kissed her, leaving her feeling happier than she had ever been in her life before.

*

Singleton, awaiting the arrival of Grimshaw with what patience he could muster, began pacing frustratedly up and down the private parlour, refusing all Hinkson's suggestions to partake of some refreshment. He was not a man given over to panic, but as the minutes ticked by with no sign of Grimshaw the more anxious he became, especially as he could not rid his mind of the unpalatable thought that Deerham could well have refused to hand over the twenty thousand guineas after all, perhaps even prised the truth of Louisa's whereabouts out of him. Then there was the concern over where Louisa could possibly be, an added worry he could well do without, because should Deerham hand over the money after all there was no way he could return Louisa to Grosvenor Square, and Deerham could most certainly be relied upon to act upon it.

For the very first time Singleton began to wonder about the nature of the relationship that existed between Deerham and his wife, and although he had always doubted that there was love on either side, taking it for granted that it was a marriage of convenience for both of them, particularly when he considered how seldom they were seen out together, he was now brought to wondering if there was a far closer relationship existing between them than he had ever suspected. Carrie Marchand, a woman who had never yet failed him, had assured him that the young marchioness was as good as ensnared in her clutches, with no possibility of being let off the hook lightly, but then, when Singleton had least expected it, Deerham had somehow or other got wind of it, because he would swear that Louisa had not said anything to him about it, and paid a visit to Carrie Marchand, not only walking away with his wife's bracelet but those two IOUs, and without so much as paying one penny for them. Then there was his failure to take steps to either intervene or divorce his wife when he could plainly see that she had been enjoying Ricky Vane's company for some little time. Singleton had placed all his hopes on the young marchioness succumbing to Ricky's engaging and scintillating company, but, and much to his surprise, although she had very much enjoyed dancing and being taken for drives by him, he had not turned her head, and, more than this, Deerham had not taken steps to divorce her, clearly indicating that he not only trusted his wife but was assured of her affections.

A frown descended onto Singleton's forehead as he pondered it, but no matter how disagreeable the thought he was forced to concede that the couple, much against his hopes as well as his expectations, were clearly in love with one another. If this was indeed the case, and he failed to see how it could be otherwise, then Deerham would certainly be in no frame of mind to either forgive or forget his audacity in daring to abduct his wife. Singleton would certainly not have done so if Carrie Marchand or Ricky Vane had not played him false, forcing him to take an action which, in hindsight, was the perfect means to bring Deerham toppling to his knees, but which, in the cold light of day, could not be said to have run as smoothly as he had hoped it would. For one thing, he had no idea where Louisa was, for all he knew she could have been picked up somewhere on the road and conveyed to London by a perfect stranger or, which he thought most probable, she was hiding out at either *'The Green Man'* or *'The Red Lion'*, then, to add to his concerns, he could not rid himself of the feeling that Grimshaw had failed in his errand and would return without the money, in which case he could expect to see Deerham any time now.

Suddenly his flight to Paris seemed in doubt. It was perhaps unfortunate for him that he did not have sufficient funds to allow for this, and certainly not to remain there for an indefinite period, or at least until Deerham had cooled down, as no concierge would be prepared to accept a guest without seeing the colour of their money first. He could, of course, rely upon his winnings, after all he was no stranger to the gaming hells which abounded in Paris, but even though Providence had continued to bestow good fortune upon him there was no telling when she would withdraw her guiding hand. Should Grimshaw return with the money after all then all well and good, but should he return empty handed then Singleton felt it would behove him to make himself scarce for a while, or at least leave London for a spell, because even though he could not see Deerham making a public display of himself by calling him to account in the middle of some soirée or other, the fact remained that some point or other he would.

It was in the middle of these cogitations that Singleton heard the sound of a new arrival, and striding over to the window in the hope of seeing Grimshaw pulling up, he was disappointed to discover that whoever the visitor was it was certainly not his stalwart, but as *'The Blue Boar'* was patronized by customers who came more often than not on foot he took no notice of it. It was just as he turned away from the window when the parlour door was suddenly thrust open, and thinking it was Hinkson it was therefore in some considerable surprise to find himself coming face to face with the very last man he wanted to see even though he knew this meeting to be inevitable at some point.

As Deerham stood on threshold, one hand still holding the handle of the door and totally ignoring Hinkson's harassed pleadings that the private parlour was being used by a guest, just one look at his face, which was particularly grim, was enough to inform Singleton that he was in no very good humour. Walking slowly away from the window and looking from one man to the other he then waved a languid hand, saying,

"It's all right, Hinkson. I know this gentleman."

For several moments Hinkson looked every inch his indecision. From the looks of it this man, who had unexpectedly barged his way into his premises without so much as a by your leave and who was clearly in no frame of mind to listen to his pleadings, he was not at all sure whether to feel relieved or not to be told by Singleton that he knew him. However, as long as no bout of fisticuffs was to be enacted on his premises, although from the looks of it he was by no means certain of this, he slowly bowed himself out, whereupon Deerham closed the door behind him.

Singleton eyed him speculatively for a moment, then, resuming his habitual urbanity, said at length, "I suppose I should have known that I would receive a visit from you sooner or later."

"I should imagine you might," Deerham told him coldly, stepping a little further into the room.

Pouring himself a glass of much-needed wine, Singleton raised an enquiring eyebrow, saying, "I take it that you are not here to hand over the twenty thousand guineas?"

Deerham eyed him closely, shaking his head, "Not the twenty thousand guineas, no."

"I thought not," Singleton sighed. "So, am I to take it that you are here to give me my reckoning instead?" Singleton raised a painted eyebrow.

"You take it right," Deerham bit out.

Singleton thought a moment before saying, "Useless I suppose to tell you that your wife took no hurt?"

"Quite useless," Deerham replied coldly.

"Yes," Singleton sighed, "I thought so." After finishing off his wine, he looked at Deerham over the rim of his glass, saying, "You may be aware of this already, but she managed to free herself."

"Yes," Deerham nodded, "I know."

"May I ask how?" Singleton enquired, his eyes narrowing slightly.

"I came upon her taking shelter at *'The Green Man',*" Deerham told him.

"Ah," Singleton purred, "so she was there, after all." Since it seemed that Deerham was not about to expand any further on this, Singleton considered a moment, asking at length, "Would it be impertinent of me to ask what happened to Grimshaw?"

"Either he's still making his way here," Deerham shrugged dismissively, beginning to move the table to one side, "or he's gone to ground."

Singleton eyed his movements imperturbably. It was not in his nature to refuse a challenge either sporting or in any other respect, and as he had long since promised himself the pleasure of coming up against this man, indeed it had become almost an obsession with him, so much so that he was looking forward with real pleasure to their imminent encounter, he generously assisted Deerham to move the table to the other side of the room. Although he was no stranger to the art of swordplay, indeed he had been known to give a very good account of himself, he nevertheless knew that Deerham, apart from being in no mood to observe the niceties, was a past master of the art and knew that he would have to be on his mettle.

The table being moved to the satisfaction of both parties, Singleton then walked over to the door and, pulling the key out of his pocket, locked it, then, turning to Deerham, enquired, "I take it you prised your wife's whereabouts out of Grimshaw?"

"Yes," Deerham nodded, removing his coat, "and also out of Lady Templeton's footman."

"You always were thorough, Deerham," Singleton smiled, a bare thinning of the lips, beginning to remove his coat.

"I can say the same of you," Deerham told him, removing his waistcoat. "What a pity though Carrie Marchand did not come up to scratch."

"A mere setback," Singleton shrugged, removing his own waistcoat.

"And then there was Ricky Vane," Deerham pointed out, pulling off his boots.

"Yes," Singleton sighed, "I had great hopes of that," having by now removed his own waistcoat and made a start of removing his shoes.

"It must have come as a great disappointment to you to know that your efforts to try to bring about my divorcing my wife had failed," Deerham commented.

"So," Singleton mused, "you realized that, did you?"

"Of course," Deerham nodded, rolling up his sleeves. "But when you dare to go as far as abducting my wife," Deerham told him, straightening up, "you have gone your length."

Removing his sword from its belt Singleton flourished it in the air for several moments, then, coming to stand in front of Deerham, told him, in a voice that almost sounded like a cat purring, "You know, Deerham, I have always disliked you, indeed," he cocked an eyebrow, "I have been looking forward to this for a very long time."

"And I," Deerham told him, removing his own sword from its belt and giving it a little flourish, "have always disliked you."

The moment for talk was finally over. A deadly silence filled the air as the two men stood in front of each other, the one tall and lean and the other of slim build and no more than medium height, but both exuding a calm determination and strength of purpose. Punctiliously going through the salute, both men then took up their guard, their blades glinting in the light given off by the small fire that burned in the grate.

At first, it seemed that both men were toying with one another, as if testing the other's strengths and weaknesses, then Singleton, taking the opportunity which Deerham had deliberately led him to believe was open to him, lunged forward, but Deerham deftly parried the thrust with a counter attack, the unexpectedness of him parrying and attacking at the same time taking Singleton completely by surprise and forcing him to back away. For the next few minutes the only sound to break the deadly silence was the hissing of the blades ringing off each other and the padding of their feet as they glided across the floor, until Singleton, spotting his chance, once again attempted a thrust in tierce, but yet again Deerham parried with a circle parry enabling his sword to move in a circle and catch Singleton's tip, deflecting it away. Again and again Singleton attempted thrust after thrust but all to no avail, finding each lunge parried with a calmness he himself was fast losing sight of, having to pause several times to wipe the perspiration which had formed on his forehead. Somewhere on the periphery of Singleton's consciousness he became aware of just how sinewy Deerham's arms really were as well as acknowledging that he was by far the better swordsman, but trying to ignore both these unpalatable realities he attempted a feint, but Deerham would not be drawn. By now both men were breathing hard, but Singleton, more hard pressed of the two, attempted a flick, but even though his blade curved over it failed to strike

Deerham who deftly parried. Knowing that Singleton was almost spent, Deerham, having waited for just the right moment, saw his chance and passed his sword over Singleton's blade, piercing his right shoulder.

The move, totally unexpected and finding its point with unerring accuracy, Singleton clapped his left hand to his shoulder, his sword dropping from his hand, before staggering back into a chair, and Deerham, having done what he had set out to do, dropped his sword and hurried over to where Singleton lay slumped in the chair.

"I don't know… why, but… I always… did… hate you!" Singleton managed.

"Don't try to talk," Deerham told him, beginning to tear the tablecloth into strips.

By now the commotion emanating from the private parlour had brought Hinkson to the door, banging on it and demanding to know what was going on. Upon receiving no response to this he pulled the key out of his pocket and unlocked the door, hardly able to believe the sight which met his eyes. Looking from Singleton slumped in a chair with the blood gently oozing from his shoulder and Deerham tearing his tablecloth made him stare from one to the other, but just as he had found his voice to expostulate, Deerham forestalled him, ordering, "Bring some brandy, and then go and get a physician!"

"But my lord…" Hinkson began, wringing his hands, looking helplessly from one to the other "this will do my house no good at all."

Ignoring this, Deerham bit out, "Don't just stand there, man, do as I say."

When Hinkson made no immediate move to carry out these demands, simply because he felt momentarily incapable of thinking much less what he should do, Singleton looked sideways at him, saying, "Do as… he… says, Hinkson."

Hinkson, after looking a little dazedly at him, pulled himself together, saying, "Yes, sir. At once, sir," departing on the instant.

By now Deerham had torn the tablecloth into strips, and ripping apart his shirt laid bare Singleton's wound, to which he half smiled, saying with a touch of mockery as he looked up into Deerham's rather stern face, "Don't worry, I… shan't die… this time," moving a little awkwardly in his seat.

"Keep still," Deerham ordered, beginning to apply the strips of cloth.

"I must… confess that… your generosity is… quite… overwhelming and… most unlooked-for."

Deerham was spared having to reply to this by the entrance of Hinkson carrying a tray with a decanter of brandy and two glasses, which he laid down onto the table, then, backing away towards the door, said, "I will go and fetch a physician now, sir," to which Singleton merely nodded.

"Add to... your... goodness," Singleton said faintly when Deerham had finished attending to his wound, "by pouring... me out... a glass... of brandy."

Having poured out some of the brandy into one of the glasses, Deerham then held the back of Singleton's head and raised it to his lips; the fiery liquid seeming to put new heart into him and, after draining his glass, said, with something of a return to his habitual urbanity, "The honours... 'twould seem... go to... you my... dear Deerham."

"You would be well advised," Deerham told him, "not to talk."

A mocking smile touched Singleton's lips at this, watching as Deerham sat down to pull on his boots from under his heavy lids, saying, "I would... that... our positions... were... reversed."

Ignoring this, Deerham, having by now pulled on his boots, rose to his feet and, walking over to the table, poured Singleton another glass of brandy, which he held to his lips, a few drops of the amber liquid spilling from out the corner of his mouth. Deerham, having wiped them away with napkin, looked down at him, saying, "Save your strength. The physician should not be long."

Singleton was just about to say something in reply to this when the door to the private parlour was suddenly thrust open and Grimshaw strode into the room.

Chapter Twenty-Three

Grimshaw may not have associated Deerham with Letitia Rawnsley's masked rescuer, but he knew a man of determination and strength of purpose when he saw one, even so, he had certainly expected him to hand over the money in exchange for his wife. That he had not done so had left Grimshaw in something of a quandary. When he had told Deerham that it was more than his life was worth to return to Singleton empty handed he had not exaggerated; he knew his master's temper only too well, and he did not mind owning that he was extremely reluctant to tell him the bad news; not only that, but he was looking forward to finding himself three hundred guineas to the good.

He had seen at the outset that Deerham was no fool but that he would prove obstructive had taken him completely by surprise, and not all his entreaties had moved him. He had not intended pulling that knife out of his pocket in order to threaten Deerham, and the only excuse he could offer was that he had momentarily lost sight of what common sense he had, but he had certainly not expected Deerham to react so quickly. The grip on his wrist had been excruciatingly painful, leaving him with no choice but to let the knife fall. Had any one ever told Grimshaw that Deerham's long slim fingers were deceptively strong, inflicting the utmost pain until he told him where his wife was being held, he would not have believed them, finding himself with little choice other than to tell him.

Grimshaw may admit that he had no liking for Singleton's tendency for abducting women, but he had been in service to him for far too long to know that remonstrating, much less arguing, with him, would serve no purpose, other than to finding himself unemployed. Singleton was a hard master, and not one easy to please, but Grimshaw knew him well enough to know that informing him of the failed outcome of the meeting with Deerham would only serve to put him in the worst possible mood, and he was honest enough to admit that he had no liking for conveying the bad news to him. Nevertheless, Singleton would have to be told, and it was therefore with a sinking heart that Grimshaw, having left the coach he had hired from Tylers in the Haymarket at *The Blue Boar* in readiness to convey her ladyship home, boarded the stagecoach from *The White Horse Inn* in Fetter Lane, and made his way to Barnet to apprise his master of something which he knew full well he would not want to hear.

By the time the stagecoach pulled up outside *The Green Man* in Barnet, Grimshaw's nerves, which had been steadily growing to such a pitch that he could so easily have turned tail and run, alighted somewhat stiffly onto the flagway and, after receiving his valise from the driver, slowly began to make his way to *The Blue Boar* in Tanner Street.

Upon entering the inn to find himself immediately faced with a garbled account of the doings in the private parlour from the landlord's wife, having heard him enter by way of the front door, and with no sign of Hinkson, Grimshaw looked every inch his astonishment. Having fully expected her ladyship to be still in possession of the private parlour and Singleton waiting eagerly for the money, it was to his complete and utter amazement to find himself looking upon Deerham shrugging himself into his coat and Singleton lying limply back in a chair with a wound in his shoulder. He knew Deerham had told him that he would be seeing Singleton himself shortly, but it had never so much as entered Grimshaw's head that he would be before him and, from the looks of it, the one responsible for inflicting that wound on Singleton. Staring from one man to the other as though he could not believe his eyes, words momentarily failing him, he saw Singleton looking sideways at him, saying,

"Oh, it's... you... is it?" Without giving Grimshaw time to reply to this, Singleton said, "Well, now that... you... are here... you can make... yourself useful. Pour me another brandy."

As it was patently obvious to the meanest intelligence that Singleton and Deerham had engaged in a duelling match and his master had come off the worst in the encounter, was something that pleased Grimshaw no end, indeed so thrilled was he that he was able to forgive Deerham the pain he had inflicted on him earlier today, and were it at all possible he would have gladly shaken him by the hand. However, as it was blatantly clear that Deerham had told Singleton himself that he was not prepared to hand over one penny, which had clearly brought about the duel they had just fought, having no idea of the ill feeling which existed between the two men and that this had been building up for some appreciable time, Grimshaw was so relieved that the task had not fallen to him to tell his master that Deerham had not come up to scratch, that he readily poured him out a glass of brandy, carefully holding the glass to his lips.

Of course, where her ladyship was now was anyone's guess, but since it appeared that neither man was prepared to enlighten him, he merely put Singleton's empty glass down onto the table, awaiting further instructions.

Deerham, wiping his sword and returning it to its scabbard, eyed Grimshaw thoughtfully, saying at length, "When the landlord returns with the physician, I suggest that the two of you help Singleton to his bedchamber."

"Yes, my lord," Grimshaw nodded. Then, after looking from one man to the other, said, not a little hesitantly, "Y-you're not staying, my lord?"

"Certainly not," Deerham told him evenly. "Besides, I think your master has had enough of me for one day." Then, turning to Singleton, said, "You may abduct any one you choose, Singleton, but my wife remains my wife."

"I wish you well of her," Singleton told him faintly, a smile touching his thin lips. "For myself, I hope she gives you the deuce of a time!"

Deerham smiled, then, after shaking Singleton's left hand, said, "Is there anything you wish me to do for you?"

"Yes," he shrugged, "you can go to the devil!" to which Deerham laughed, then, leaving Singleton in the care of Grimshaw, left.

*

Louisa, having watched Deerham close the door behind him, lay back against the pillows and hugged her knees, feeling happier than she had ever been in her life before. Reliving those moments in his arms brought a contented little sigh from deep within her throat, feeling again the warm strength of his body as he had held her tightly against him. He may not have told her he loved her, but he *had* called her 'My poor darling' and 'My little love' as well as telling her that he would have paid twice the amount to get her back, and his kisses, although not passionate, had nevertheless been more demonstrative than she could ever remember. Instinctively she touched her lips, still burning from the touch of his, with a trembling forefinger, closing her eyes to savour again those gentle and delicate caresses which had set her whole body alight, and it was therefore a good fifteen minutes before she could sufficiently banish such pleasurable recollections from her mind to ring the bell pull for Mrs. Fleetwood to bring her clothes.

It was while Mrs. Fleetwood was helping her to dress, stating in a dismayed voice that it was a pity the hem of the skirt had got damaged due to her walk as well as the shock she had received upon seeing her on the doorstep in the early hours, that Louisa suddenly thought of Deerham's meeting with Singleton. Needless to say, her responses to Mrs. Fleetwood's comments were somewhat mechanical, being quite unable to prevent herself from wondering what was happening between the two men. She knew without being told that Deerham could more than adequately take care of himself, but Singleton, a man she could neither like nor trust, was capable of anything, in fact she would not put anything past him. She remembered what Deerham had told her in response to her plea not to kill Singleton, "I won't kill him; just punish him a little – for his impudence," her stomach lurched, and as she made her way downstairs to the private parlour in Mrs. Fleetwood's wake, she could only hope against hope that he would come back to her safe and unharmed.

But after almost two hours of anxiously awaiting his return her fears were finally laid to rest when he eventually walked into the private parlour, looking none the worse for his encounter, a circumstance that considerably relieved her mind. But if she expected him to go into detail about what had happened, she was mistaken, indeed the only reply he made in answer to her enquiry about what had occurred between them, and if Singleton had been injured, was, "Let us just say," he smiled, taking her hand in his and raising it to his lips, "that he will be off his legs for a spell. Now," he told her softly, gently squeezing her hand, "I am going to take you home."

It was just as she was about to respond to this when the sound of an altercation coming from the entrance hall met their ears, and upon leaving the private parlour the unexpected sight of Algernon Rawnsley, looking tired, frustrated and extremely angry, in a heated discussion with Fleetwood, met their startled eyes.

*

Having recklessly committed himself to go down into Wiltshire to his ancestral home to join his sisters and mamma at the end of week for a protracted stay, Algernon soon found himself regretting the insane impulse which had prompted him to make such a promise. He could think of nothing more tedious than listening to his sisters prattling on about this and that and expecting him to escort them to some historical site or cathedral or something equally as boring; then there was his mamma, whose sole pleasure in life seemed to be bemoaning her imaginary poor state of nerves and how the slightest thing prostrated her, and with nothing more exciting to do in the evenings than playing whist, he was within an ames ace of not going. The only thing which rendered his visit home tolerable was riding around his estates, but even this pleasure was short-lived as he thought of Biddersley, his pernickety man of business, who, like his aunt, the Dowager Countess of Pitlone, never failed to reduce him to schoolboy status, would no doubt insist on accompanying him, and as Algernon considered himself to be way past the age of receiving instruction from a man who never failed to irritate him, nothing could please him less. It was therefore in a mood bordering on sullenness that he resigned himself to facing several weeks tucked away in the heart of Wiltshire, but between now and Friday when he left town, he enthusiastically spent the time left to him by looking around him seeking amusement.

Having called in Half Moon Street in the expectation of inviting his friend to a game of cards, he was told by the retired gentleman's gentleman who looked after the premises that Mr. Singleton was out of town. Algernon looked a little surprised at this, and upon asking where out of town, he was apologetically told that he had no idea, but that he had left two days ago. Since nothing else could be gleaned from him, Algernon descended the steps and, after considering a moment, decided to stroll round to St. James's Street. As expected this late in the season, White's was extremely thin of company, but sitting down at a table and ordering a bottle of wine from a passing waiter, he pondered his friend's sudden departure from the Metropolis. When they had last met three days ago Singleton had not even hinted that he may have to go out of town for a few days, and therefore Algernon could not even begin to think why he should have done so or for what purpose. Of course, Singleton did not have keep him advised of his movements, all the same Algernon found it just a little odd, especially when he considered that Singleton was committed to Ridgely-Price this evening.

It was while Algernon was pondering his friend's unexpected departure from town when he felt someone clap him on the shoulder from behind, and looking up from the wine in his glass, Algernon saw it was Ricky Vane. Considering they were both friends of Singleton's it was only to be expected that Algernon would run across him in his company at some get-together or other, and considering their like tastes it had not been long before a firm friendship had been formed between the two younger men. As far as Algernon was concerned seeing his friend was a welcome sight, especially as White's resembled nothing but a mausoleum, and greeted him cheerfully, "Hello Ricky. Am I glad to see you!"

"Algernon," Ricky nodded his head. "Didn't expect to see you here!"

"No," Algernon shook his head, "just thought I'd take a look in for a while. See who's here."

"Thought you were ruralizing in Wiltshire," Ricky remarked, taking his seat opposite Algernon and stretching out his long legs in front him.

"Not until Friday," Algernon told him, barely able to suppress a shudder at the mere thought of it. "And what about you? Are you going into – Warwickshire, is it?" he cocked an eyebrow.

"Lord, no!" Ricky cried, horrified. "Apart from the fact that I can't stand the place, m'father would most probably go off in an apoplexy if I showed my face!"

"So, what's to do?" Algernon asked, signalling a waiter to bring another glass.

Ricky shrugged, "Oh, like you, I just thought I'd take a look in. See who's here, y'know."

HER FATHER'S DAUGHTER

As it was obvious that Ricky Vane was just as disappointed as Algernon to find White's so thin of company, it was hardly surprising that both men bemoaned the end of the season, necessitating an exodus to their country estates by the vast majority of the ton, but over several glasses of wine and a game of piquet, they soon forgot their grievances. It was not until a chance reference made by Ricky about Singleton, that Algernon asked him if he knew where Singleton had gone. "Called round to his place earlier," he told him, "but that man of his said he had gone out of town a couple of days ago."

"Out of town!" Ricky cried, surprised.

"Yes," Algernon nodded. "Don't happen to know where, do you?"

A frown descended onto Ricky's forehead at this, shrugging, "No idea at all. He said nothing to me about going out of town."

The Dowager Countess of Pitlone may have taken Ricky in dislike for no reason she could put her finger on, but she nevertheless had to admit that he presented himself as a most charming young man with excellent address. So far, there were no lines of dissipation visible beneath his powder and paint, but it did not take much for her to guess the kind of life he led, which she could only describe as being ruinous, and it was therefore with relief that her niece had no partiality for him, because she doubted very much that he would be a faithful husband. But had she known that her nephew had added another reprobate to his collection of friends she would have been seriously alarmed.

Algernon however, had no such qualms. To his way of thinking Ricky, like Singleton, was a right one, prime for any lark, indeed he was excellent company and certainly one who could be relied on to help pass the time, such as now when London was extremely thin on the ground for likeminded company. Having just lost his second game of piquet to Ricky, Algernon, having just re-filled their glasses, leaned back in his chair, eyeing his friend thoughtfully before saying, "Y'know, it seems mightily odd to me that Singleton should go out of town like that, without a word to anyone."

"I shouldn't worry about it," Ricky shrugged, "he'll be back when he is ready."

It was not until Algernon told him about Singleton's surprising bolt from the Metropolis that Ricky recalled their last conversation, under this very roof in fact, when he had told him that he was not prepared to take matters further by abducting the young Marchioness of Deerham, and that if Singleton wanted the job then he was quite welcome to it. Ricky liked Singleton, yes, he did, very much, in fact he could be counted on to give one a good evening's entertainment, but Ricky would have to be blind not to see that Singleton, for all his urbanity and bonhomie, was really quite ruthless but, surely, he would not go so far as to abducting Louisa himself?

The more Ricky thought about it the more certain he became that Singleton, if not going so far as to abduct her, then in view of his parting words that he would have to take matters into his own hands, was certainly planning something which was equally as scurrilous, because nothing else could surely explain away his sudden absence from town. For once in his life Ricky could own to no regrets about failing to fulfill his side of a bargain, because whilst he may be a care for nobody with little or no scruples, he most definitely drew the line at abduction.

He knew from Singleton's confidences that he was no stranger to abducting young females, and had in fact attempted to abduct Algernon's sister, Letitia, until he had been thwarted by Deerham, and not for the first time. Ricky knew that Letitia Rawnsley was a most taking little thing, after all, hadn't he enjoyed his flirtation with her? - but unless he had missed his mark, he would say that it was her fortune Singleton had been interested in and not Letitia herself. Ricky's acquaintanceship with Deerham may be slight, nothing more than a bow in passing in fact, but despite being a rather reserved man Ricky knew enough about him to say that he was a decent and honest man, and although it was common knowledge, despite his discretion, that he had enjoyed more than one pleasurable relationship, Ricky had never heard it said of him that he was a man who condoned the kind of behaviour Singleton regularly indulged in.

Ricky had never mentioned Letitia Rawnsley's abduction to anyone, and certainly not to her brother, because despite his careless ways he was not so lost to all sense of what was due to his sister as well as his name that he would allow something like that to pass unanswered. But Ricky, having partaken somewhat freely of the wine kindly provided by his friend followed by several glasses of brandy, he was well under their mellowing influence, and his tongue, like his discretion, had, regrettably, gradually grown more loosened. It was during their third game of piquet that Ricky, unconcernedly having lost the first two games and finding himself two hundred guineas down, in a somewhat slurred voice, voiced his curiosity as to where Singleton could possibly have gone, and Algernon, shrugging his shoulders, merely commented that he could be anywhere, but fully expected to see his friend in town again very shortly.

Ricky agreed with this, then, after long if not very profound thought, suddenly chuckled to himself, and after being asked what he found so amusing, said, "I've been thinking," to which Algernon raised an eyebrow. "Y'know, you have to hand it to Digby, he's up to every rig and row in town. In fact," he slurred, "wouldn't surprise me in the least if he is not now up to some mischief. Mind you," he pointed his glass at Algernon, "I told him I wanted nothing to do with it."

"To do with what?" Algernon asked disinterestedly, pouring his friend another glass of brandy.

As Ricky was by now well and truly under the influence of the warming effects of his fifth glass of brandy, his habitual discretion had gradually deserted him, and leaning forward a little in his chair, his long fingers turning over the cards on the table in front of him, said, "The Deerham chit."

"What about her?" Algernon asked, by far the sober of the two men, being only on his third glass of brandy.

"Precisely what I asked Digby," Ricky told him.

"Well?" Algernon urged.

"Seems he wanted to get back at Deerham," Ricky shrugged.

"Get back at Deerham!" Algernon exclaimed. "What the devil for?" Ricky, who seemed more interested in looking at his cards, was jolted out of his abstraction by Algernon demanding, "Well?"

Leaning back in his chair, Ricky, waiting only until he had taken another mouthful of brandy, said, "Seems he spoiled Digby's game."

Algernon looked a little surprised at this, eyeing his friend with a questioning eye, repeating, a little faintly, "Spoiled his game?"

"That's it," Ricky nodded. "And not for the first time."

Algernon could claim only the slightest acquaintanceship with Deerham, a mere bow in passing, but he knew that the young marchioness and his sister had become close friends, but what the devil her husband had to do with Digby had him at a loss, although it was most probably Ricky's condition which had befuddled his brain, and taking a look at him across the table to see him slumped in his chair, Algernon said irritably. "I wish you'd take a damper!"

"No, no, it's true, I swear!" Ricky avowed, making a not very good attempt to straighten up in his chair. "In fact," he offered, his voice becoming more slurred, "helped him to try to do it!"

Algernon stared across at his friend, not at all sure he had heard him aright, but upon asking Ricky to repeat what he thought he had just heard him say, confirmed it. "'Pon my honour I did," Ricky nodded.

Even taking into account his friend's inebriated state, there seemed to be a lot of truth in what he was saying, and Algernon, his curiosity now well and truly stirred, could not resist asking how he had tried to help Digby get back at Deerham, Ricky retained just enough understanding to keep his flirtation with his sister to himself, but although his version of his part in Singleton's schemes regarding his attempted seduction of the young marchioness may have been interspersed with slurred hiccups and long pauses, it was enough to make Algernon sit back in shocked disbelief, exclaiming, "Good God!"

"Y'know," Ricky nodded, emptying his glass, "you have to hand it to Deerham, a regular knowin' one, well, what I mean is," he pointed his empty glass at Algernon, "knew all along there was nothin' in it and that I was just kickin' up a lark with her la'ship," his voice becoming more and more slurred, "but it made Digby as mad as fire I can tell you when Deerham made no effort to step in or divorce her." Putting his empty glass back down onto the table, he looked across at Algernon, saying, "Well, what I mean is, just think how he got wind of Digby attemptin' to abduct your sister."

Algernon, declining to partake of another brandy, was in the process of gathering up the scattered cards on the table when his hand stilled at hearing Ricky mention his sister and, after staring long and hard at his friend, his brow suddenly black as thunder, demanded he repeat what he had just said, his voice ominously quiet. Ricky, not at all sure what he had said, the fumes of the brandy having clouded his brain, looked a little vacantly at Algernon, but upon having the demanded repeated, Ricky shrugged,

"What about your sister?"

"About Digby attempting to abduct her," Algernon bit out.

"Well," Ricky shrugged again, "so he did."

"When was this?" Algernon demanded.

Ricky took time to answer this, saying at length, "Don't know as I recall precisely."

Upon seeing Algernon suddenly rise hurriedly to his feet, his chair almost stumbling over with the force, his brow black and his face rather grim, took Ricky a little by surprise, but when he felt Algernon's hand grip his cravat and almost pull him out of his chair he was genuinely flabbergasted, eyeing his friend with a dazed eye. He could not begin to think what had got into his friend to bring on this display of wrath, and tried, though not very successfully, to remove that slim white hand from his cravat.

"When did Digby attempt to abduct my sister?" Algernon repeated through gritted teeth, his hand still holding that cravat. "And why?"

Ricky may still be under the mellowing influence from the fumes of the brandy, but the shock of seeing his friend suddenly fly up into the boughs had the immediate effect of sobering him up a little, but with that hand pressed up against his throat, he could only manage, "Here, what the devil are you at?"

"I'll tell you what I'm at," Algernon ground out, "about my sister. When did Digby attempt to abduct her, and why? Well?" he demanded when Ricky made no immediate effort to reply.

In fairness to Ricky however, it was extremely difficult for him to say anything with that hand pressed against his throat, but upon hoarsely mentioning this to Algernon the grip slackened sufficiently for him to tell him that it was the day he was engaged to fight that duel with Moreton.

"Are you saying he tricked her?" Algernon asked heatedly.

"Yes," Ricky nodded, glad to see Algernon remove his hand from his cravat, rubbing his throat a little gingerly. "Digby told me that he told her you had been seriously injured and was desirous of seeing her, and that he would escort her to you."

Algernon's brown darkened even more. "Why?" he demanded.

"Her money, of course!" Ricky choked. "Digby was badly dipped. Not knowing where the next guinea was to come from. Thought he'd be clapped up for debt if he didn't do something."

Algernon thought a moment. "About Deerham, where does he come into this? You say he thwarted Digby?" Ricky nodded, which was all he felt able to do. "How? Where?" Algernon demanded.

Ricky swallowed. "Digby doesn't know how he got wind of it, but it was on the Maidenhead road."

"The Maidenhead road," Algernon mused. "Then Deerham must have been on his way back to town from Worleigh."

"Digby told me that he took her to *The Angel Inn*'," Ricky offered helpfully, feeling it behoved him to make some kind of belated amends for his lack of discretion, seriously alarmed at his friend's ominous face.

"*The Angel Inn*'," Algernon repeated. His eyes narrowed in thought for a moment, musing at length, "I wonder if Deerham had stopped for refreshment there and overheard something?"

"Possibly," Ricky managed faintly, his neck still feeling rather tender.

Algernon brought his gaze back to rest on Ricky's face, saying harshly, "I don't know about Digby wanting to pay him back, but for myself," he nodded, "I'd like to shake him by the hand," whereupon he walked out of the room, leaving his friend to rub his throat, hazily calling to mind that it was his own careless words, said without thinking while in his altitudes, that had brought about that furious eruption from Algernon.

Algernon, meanwhile, leaving White's in a towering rage, strode purposefully back to Berkeley Square, conscious of wanting to inflict the direst punishment on the man he had always believed to be his friend, a man who had callously attempted to abduct his sister, but not for herself but her fortune. It annoyed him to think that he had allowed himself to become associated with this man, a man he had had no hesitation in deeming a right one, a man who could give one a most pleasant evening over the cards, but the scales had finally been lifted from his eyes enabling him to see Singleton for precisely what he was; a cynical and ruthless man who would stop at nothing to achieve his own ends.

He knew that Singleton seemed to live constantly on the brink of financial ruin, but his skill at the cards, which had never been brought into question, continually saved him from falling into the abyss of insolvency and being clapped up for debt. But that he should dare to attempt to abduct his sister was intolerable, and if it was the last thing Algernon ever did, he would bring Singleton to book.

It was a pity Singleton had gone out of town, whether to attempt mischief against the young Marchioness of Deerham or not Algernon had no idea, but it was just as he was approaching Berkeley Square that he suddenly bethought himself of Deerham. Algernon knew that he and Singleton were not friends, and if only half of what Ricky had told him was true then he could well believe it, but Deerham may just have some idea as to Singleton's whereabouts; and if there was the slightest chance that he knew something then it was worth a try. Passing through Berkeley Square, his potations having by now worn off, Algernon walked on towards Grosvenor Square, hoping that Deerham would be at home and not yet retired to Worleigh, but when he approached the house he could see that the knocker was still on the door, and it was therefore in a hopeful frame of mind that he struck it against the plate. He had to wait several moments before Clifton answered it, having been busy downstairs checking the wine cellar, but upon enquiring what the visitor wanted he was handed Algernon's card. He knew of Viscount Dunstan but this was the first time he had ever met him, but upon hearing the reason for his visit, Clifton sadly shook his head, saying,

"I am sorry, my lord, but his lordship went out of town earlier today, and I have no idea when he is likely to return."

This was not what Algernon wanted to hear, but upon asking if he knew where Deerham was Clifton merely shrugged, saying, "No, my lord. I'm sorry, my lord."

Algernon knew very well that butlers were always in their master's confidence, certainly to the extent that they knew their comings and goings, and it was therefore most unlikely that Clifton had no idea where Deerham was. "It is really most important that I speak to his lordship," Algernon urged.

"I'm sorry, my lord," Clifton shook his head, "but… "

"Just tell me his direction," Algernon urged.

"But, my lord I… " Clifton began.

"I would not be here now unless it was of the utmost importance that I speak to him," Algernon told him firmly.

It was just on the tip of Clifton's tongue to deny this request when he wondered if it was something to do with her ladyship, and after pondering the matter for a moment or two, said, "All I know, my lord, is that his lordship was heading for Barnet."

"Barnet!" Algernon cried, wondering what on earth Deerham would be doing in such a place.

"Yes, my lord," Clifton bowed, to which Algernon thanked him and left.

As Algernon made his way back to Berkeley Square, he pondered the information Clifton had given him in more detail. Of course, there was absolutely no reason he could think of to prevent Deerham going to Barnet, after all it was a regular stopping off point on the Great North Road, but unless Algernon had misheard Clifton he definitely said he was heading for Barnet, clearly indicating he was not merely stopping off for a change of horses before going on farther, which meant that his business had to be in Barnet. This then led Algernon to wondering if Singleton too was in Barnet, which would not surprise him considering what Ricky had let fall in White's, because if Singleton was planning something to do with the marchioness and Deerham had got wind of it then Algernon would not put it past Deerham to confront him. The more Algernon thought about it the more certain he became that he would find both men in Barnet, and although he would very much like the opportunity of thanking Deerham for going to his sister's aid he would also like the opportunity of punishing Singleton for daring to manipulate his sister by compromising her into marriage for the sake of her fortune.

It was almost half past three when Algernon arrived home by which time he was utterly convinced his conjectures would be found to be correct, and immediately issued instructions to his startled butler to inform his groom that he wanted his curricle brought round to the front door with the new pair of greys he had only recently purchased harnessed to it in ten minutes. Simpson, not having expected his lordship to return home at this hour, was just a little startled upon seeing him, but upon hearing this peremptory order he was patently shocked, and Algernon, running up the stairs two at a time to change his clothes totally ignored the shocked expression of his retainer as he went to carry out his orders.

Chapter Twenty-Four

Accomplishing the fifteen mile drive to Barnet in a little under an hour and a half, by the time Algernon eventually pulled up outside *'The Green Man'*, a hive of activity, his horses, which he had not spared as he sped them along the Great North Road, were sweating. Taking only a moment to see them safely handed over to a groom he then tossed him a coin before striding into the inn, setting up a cry for the landlord.

Fleetwood, who was at that moment in the middle of conveying a tray of coffee to the coffee room, looked up as Algernon strode in, but apart from briefly nodding his head with a brief apology, stating that he would not keep him waiting many minutes, disappeared into this cozy apartment. With nothing else to do but kick his heels until Fleetwood returned, Algernon paced up and down the lobby pulling his gloves through his hands, but upon seeing him leave the coffee room Algernon pounced him.

"Tell me, Fleetwood," he cocked his head, "do you have a man staying here by the name of Singleton?"

"No, my lord," Fleetwood shook his head, eyeing Algernon with a wary eye, a man he had many times had the pleasure of providing refreshment for and a change of horses, but, right now, he appeared to be in no very good humour. "I have no one of that name staying here at this present, my lord."

"Are you sure?" Algernon demanded.

"Yes, my lord," Fleetwood nodded, "quite sure."

Algernon heaved a deep and frustrated sigh, then, looking rather closely at Fleetwood, said, "You would do best to tell me the truth."

"But I have told you the truth, my lord," Fleetwood assured him, "I have no one of that name putting up here."

It was just as Algernon was about to argue with him when the parlour door opened and Deerham and Louisa walked out, and Algernon, spinning round when he heard the door open, was suddenly pulled up short at the sight of them. Fleetwood, in response to Deerham's raised eyebrow, having heard Algernon's rather incensed voice raised above the customary noise generated by an inn full of people, and Fleetwood's denials,

"I am sorry, my lord, but my lord here," indicating Algernon with a nod of his head, "is asking if I have a certain person staying under my roof."

"And do you?" Deerham asked calmly.

"No, my lord," Fleetwood bowed, "I do not."

Turning to Algernon, Deerham looked at him through his eye-glass, asking at length, "Dear me, are you by chance Letitia's brother?"

"I have that pleasure, yes, my lord," Algernon inclined his head a little stiffly, then, as if remembering his manners, he turned to face Louisa and, taking her hand in his, raised it punctiliously to his lips, saying civilly, "Servant, your ladyship," to which Louisa dropped a small curtsey.

"And who, may I ask," Deerham politely enquired, "is the person you are looking for? Perhaps I can be of some assistance to you," having a pretty shrewd idea what had brought Algernon into Barnet.

Algernon thought a moment. If Deerham was here with the young marchioness then it could only mean one of two things, the first being that they had merely stopped here in order to refresh themselves or Deerham, having discovered Singleton's whereabouts and possibly his intentions towards the young marchioness, had put a spoke into his wheel. From the looks on Deerham's face however, it was impossible for Algernon to tell which, but in response to his questioning eyebrow, said, not a little cautiously, "I am here Deerham, on a private errand."

"Ah," Deerham mused, "a private errand," to which Algernon inclined his head. "And would this private errand have something to do with Singleton and – er – your sister?"

If Louisa needed her conjectures as to the identity of Letitia's masked rescuer being her husband confirmed, then this was surely it.

"It would, my lord," Algernon said rather stiffly.

"Yes," Deerham nodded, "I thought it might."

Algernon, clearing his throat, said, "I feel, my lord, that I am very much in your debt over that."

"Not at all," Deerham smiled, shaking his head. "However, I cannot help but wonder whether your timing is not – well, how shall I say? – not quite propitious?"

Algernon looked a little curiously at him, saying, "What do you mean, not quite propitious."

Smiling down at Louisa, Deerham removed her hand from his arm, then, taking several steps towards Algernon, said, "If, as I suspect, you have come into Barnet to bring Singleton to account for what happened to your sister... "

"Demmed right, it is!" Algernon broke in vehemently.

"Then I am very much afraid," Deerham told him calmly, as though there had been no interruption, "that you will find him in no condition to receive visitors."

"Eh!" Algernon ejaculated, somewhat taken aback at this. "What the devil do you mean? Not receiving visitors?"

Deerham sighed and, shaking his head, said, "He is, how shall I say?" he pondered, "just a little incapacitated."

Algernon's eyes stared at Deerham, exclaiming, "Incapacitated? What the devil do you mean?"

"I mean," Deerham told him quietly, "that he had the misfortune to come up against an opponent who knew one trick more than he did."

Algernon looked knowingly at Deerham, a slow smile springing to his lips. "Pinked him, did you?"

"I am afraid so," Deerham nodded. "In the shoulder," sternly suppressing the twitch at the corner of his mouth.

"Well, it's no more than the fellow deserves." He thought a moment. "Are you saying it was because of what he attempted to do to my sister?"

"Alas, no," Deerham sighed, shaking his head. "It was because of what he did to my wife," turning round to face Louisa, who, in answer to his outstretched hand, walked towards him and placed hers into it.

Algernon looked from Deerham to Louisa and then back again, but the look on Deerham's face was enough to tell him that he did not wish to expand on it. "Well," he nodded mutinously, "if he thinks he can get away with abducting my sister he is very much mistaken."

"You will, of course, do what seems best to you," Deerham told him, "but I fear that it will be some little time before he will be at your service."

Algernon thought a moment, saying at length, "I take it the fellow is hiding out here somewhere in the town?"

"I think that is a very good way of putting it," Deerham smiled.

"Just tell me where the fellow is," Algernon said grimly.

Deerham thought a moment. "So you can do what, precisely?"

"Teach the scoundrelly fellow a lesson!" Algernon told him forthrightly.

"Yes," Deerham sighed, "I thought so. Now, you listen to me, you young hot head, teach Singleton a lesson if you must, but you will be well advised to wait until he returns to Half Moon Street before calling him out."

Having given this some little thought Algernon was reluctantly brought to agree to the sense of this, then, after consulting his watch, decided to remain the night at *The Green Man*, whereupon Fleetwood said he would be happy to accommodate him.

Deerham, having settled with Fleetwood and thanked him again for all his offices, then escorted Louisa outside to their waiting carriage.

*

Casting a knowledgeable eye over the fresh pair of horses poled up to his light travelling coach, Deerham could see at a glance that they were sweet steppers, then, following a word with the groom, telling him that his man Trench would be along in a couple of days to bring his chestnuts home, he handed Louisa into its luxurious confines, kissing her hand and smiling, "We shall soon be home," to which she smiled and nodded.

She saw Deerham climb up onto the box then after tossing a coin to the groom gave the horses the office to move off, whereupon she rested her head back against the comfortable squabs to spend her time during the journey back to town in agreeable contemplation.

Singleton had told her how he had written to Deerham informing him that he had her held, and that if he wanted her safely restored to him then he would have to pay twenty thousand guineas, a sum that seemed extortionate to Louisa. She knew that such a sum was nothing to Deerham, for a man of his wealth it would be an easy enough matter for him to lay his hands on such a sum, but something inside Louisa had rebelled at the thought of him paying such an exorbitant price for her release, and so had determined to rescue herself. That she had done so had really been more luck than judgement, but, somehow, she had managed to escape from *The Blue Boar* and her captors, leaving the precincts of her prison without a backward glance.

She could only speculate how Singleton had managed to reconcile the landlord and his wife into agreeing to such a diabolical scheme, until she remembered him telling her that they were totally devoted to his interests. They may be, but Louisa had the sneaking suspicion that he would nevertheless have had to pay them handsomely in order for him to hire their private parlour in order to keep her imprisoned there. Then there was Lady Templeton's footman. How on earth Singleton had managed to bribe him into acceding to his request to make sure her coachman returned her coach to Grosvenor Square on the pretext that someone had promised to safely escort her home as well as making sure she entered the wrong carriage she would never know, but that he had done so clearly implied that he possessed no scruples whatsoever. Then there was Singleton's man, Grimshaw, at least that was the name she remembered Deerham calling him, agreeing to go along with such a despicable venture by driving her through the night to some unknown destination, a man who, she had no doubt at all had been directed to collect the money from Deerham. Of course, how Deerham had managed to get information from either Lady Templeton's footman or this man of Singleton's, Grimshaw, Louisa had no idea, but that he had done so had been enough to bring him all the way to Barnet to not only ensure her release but also to bring Singleton to account.

Deerham had not told her how he had managed to get these two men to tell him what he wanted to know, indeed, it was not until she heard him tell Algernon that he had pinked Singleton in the shoulder did she learn precisely how he had brought him to account. She had had no idea that Deerham had engaged in a sword fight with Singleton, had she have done then she would not have relaxed for so much as a moment, but it was not until she saw him return to *'The Green Man'* unharmed that she could breathe more easily.

During her stay at *'The Blue Boar'*, although she had slept her first night there her sleep had been somewhat fitful, awaking the next morning feeling not very much refreshed. But even though she had spent the rest of the day feeling just a little lethargic, she certainly retained enough spirit to make Singleton wish her at the devil, but apart from a cup of coffee she could not have eaten a morsel, waiting only for the time when Singleton and the household had retired for the night in order to make her escape. To find herself in a strange town at dead of night with no idea in which direction she should go, wearing clothes that were far from suitable for such conditions, had been a most terrifying experience, and even though she had been determined to try to make her way back to London it had been with tearful resignation that she had come to see that it was impossible. She knew she had been extremely fortunate that Fleetwood and his wife had taken her in and given her a room, for which she would never be able to thank them enough, but she had certainly not intended to go back to sleep after she had breakfasted in her room this morning, but all the excitements of the past twelve hours or more had taken their toll, her eyes closing of their own volition almost as soon as Mrs. Fleetwood had closed the door behind her, sinking into the depths of a deep and very soothing sleep.

When she had heard that tap on her door, she had thought it was Mrs. Fleetwood bringing her clothes, but upon seeing Max walk in, looking at her with such tenderness in his eyes, had filled her with a happiness she had never known before. To find herself being held in his arms, and more fervently than he had ever held her before, had been a most pleasurable experience, so too was when she felt his forefinger gently wiping away her tears, but they were nothing to the joy she felt when he had gently kissed her or heard his words of endearment. She quivered at the recollection, her skin still tingling from the touch of his forefinger as they had brushed away her tears and her lips still burning from the delicate caresses of his own, happily closing her eyes as she rested back against the squabs, hoping against hope that his display of emotion and words of endearment betokened that he did indeed love her just a little after all, and not merely a natural reaction resulting from Singleton's machinations.

*

By the time Deerham pulled up outside his imposing house in Grosvenor Square it was almost half past seven, but to Louisa it seemed no time at all since they left *The Green Man*, the miles seeming to have sped by. Deerham, who had no sooner climbed down from the box, had opened the door of the coach and, after letting down the steps, he offered her his hand to assist her to alight, into which she placed her own cold and trembling one. Clifton, who had been on the watch for their arrival for some little time, no sooner saw the coach pull up than he opened the door in readiness, and Louisa, casting a look from Deerham to Clifton's familiar and friendly features, swallowed the lump that formed in her throat, feeling very much as though she had come home.

"It's good to have you home again, your ladyship," he bowed.

"It's good to be home again, Clifton," she smiled.

"We have all been so worried, my lady," he told her.

The tears stung her eyes at this, but managing to thank him without embarrassing either of them, she then turned to Deerham, who had just entered the house, to ask him if he would pardon her, but she really did need to get out of these clothes. He bowed his head in response to this, then, after watching her climb the stairs, turned to Clifton to give instructions to Trench to see that the coach was safely bestowed and the horses attended to.

Mary, relieved but very tearful at the sight of her mistress, helped Louisa to bathe, telling her between hiccups and blowing her nose how very worried she had been, but how she had had every faith in his lordship bringing her back safe and sound. Wrapping a huge towel around Louisa as she stepped out of the bath, Mary rubbed her dry, telling her weepily as she did so that she daresn't think on what would have happened if his lordship had failed to bring her back home.

"Well, he did," Louisa smiled, reassuringly patting Mary on the shoulder before allowing her to tie her corset.

"When I think of what could have happened, my lady," she sniffed, "it don't bear thinkin' on."

"Then don't think of it. As you can see," she smiled, stepping into the dress Mary had ready, "I am back safely."

Nevertheless, it took time and patience to restore Mary back to her habitual equilibrium, but eventually Louisa calmed her sufficiently, assuring herself that a good cry was all Mary needed to settle her nerves, before going downstairs to join Deerham for dinner.

Jules, that artistic but temperamental genius who held full sway in the kitchen, and paid an extortionate salary by Deerham for his culinary talents, for once had no qualms when told by Clifton that dinner was to be put back an hour, indeed so pleased was he to know that her ladyship was back home that he was quite happy to delay dinner for however long was considered necessary. Having carefully and cunningly crafted an epicurean delight to tempt the most capricious appetite, Louisa, who had hardly eaten anything for thirty-six hours, did full justice to the succulent dishes he had prepared; partaking of two slices of the chicken slowly braised in a light and fluffy sauce of cranberries and another two slices of the chyne of mutton followed by a stewed pear with peaches and Chantilly cream. Throughout dinner Deerham kept up an amusing flow of conversation, which kept Louisa well entertained, leaving her feeling more happy and contented than she had ever been before.

It was just as Deerham was about to say something in response to her amusing reply to a comment he had made, when Clifton unobtrusively re-entered the dining room, and upon receiving a raised eyebrow in enquiry from Deerham, he told him that Trench would like a word with his lordship.

"What, now?" Deerham asked.

"If it is convenient, my lord, yes," Clifton bowed his head.

"It is most certainly not convenient," Deerham told him, "but I suppose I had better see him."

"Yes, my lord," Clifton bowed again, departing as quietly as he had entered.

Deerham looked down at Louisa, saying, not a little ruefully, "I am sorry," raising her hand to his lips. "Will you excuse me, my dear?"

"Yes, of course," she nodded, rising to her feet. "In fact," she told him, "if you should not dislike it, Max, I think I should like to retire."

He nodded, then opening the door to the dining room for her to pass through, watched as she climbed the stairs to her boudoir before making his way to the book room.

Mary, having by now been restored to her usual calm, no sooner saw her mistress enter her boudoir than she asked about what she wanted done with the dress and wrap she had discarded.

"Oh, I never want to see either of them again," Louisa told her with deep feeling. "Besides, the hem of the dress is quite ruined," to which Mary nodded, although she could not help thinking it was a shame such beautiful items of clothing were destined never to see the light of day again.

"If I may say so, my lady," Mary offered hesitantly, "the wrap is still perfectly wearable."

"Yes, I daresay," Louisa said warily, eyeing the wrap Mary was holding over her arm with distaste, conjuring up the most hateful memories, "but I really could not bring myself to wear either again."

Mary supposed she really could not blame her for this, but dropping the wrap down onto a chair, she then began to help her mistress prepare for bed. After easing her nightgown over her head, she then began to unpin her hair, commenting, and not for the first time, how she envied her for not needing hot irons or curling tongues to make her hair spiral. Louisa looked at Mary through the reflection of her dressing table mirror, laughing, "Well, yes, I know I am most fortunate, but indeed I am so used to it I take no notice of it."

"Oh, my lady, if only I could get away without using either!" Mary exclaimed wistfully. She ran on this fashion until Louisa's hair had been freed of its pins then brushed out, but when this had been done Louisa kindly dismissed her, saying she would ring for her in the morning when she was ready for her, to which Mary dropped a curtsey and wished her goodnight.

By now it was a little after half past ten, but for some reason Louisa was disinclined to get into bed just yet. She had no idea whether Deerham would come to see her or not. She hoped he would, indeed she prayed he would, but as she sat down at her dressing table, her hand unconsciously picking up her brush and running it through her hair, she tried not to dwell on the thought that he did not love her, or at least not in the same way she loved him, or of how disappointed she would feel if he did not come. The clock on the mantlepiece was just striking eleven o'clock, and it was as she was on the point of getting into bed when she heard a light tap on her door and, turning hopefully towards it, saw Deerham walk in; the sight of him wearing a royal blue brocade dressing gown over his nightshirt, emphasizing his height and broad shoulders to admiration, made her stomach turn over and her heart to skip a beat.

"Max!" she cried, rising to her feet, unable to prevent the smile which touched her lips.

"I trust I am not disturbing you," he enquired softly, closing the door behind him and walking further into the room.

"No," she shook her head, "of course you are not."

"I am pleased to hear it," he told her gently.

"In fact, Max," she told him, taking a few steps towards him, "I am so very glad you are here, because… well, you see," she shrugged a little helplessly, "in all the excitement this afternoon, I forgot to thank you for… well, for coming to my rescue," pausing before saying, not a little hesitantly, "the same as you went to Letitia's rescue."

"Ah," he mused, "I thought you would pick up on that."

"Yes," she nodded, "I did, and, of course, I am very pleased that you did so, but it's not about Letitia's rescue that I wanted to thank you, but my own."

He looked at her for a moment, then, taking her one hand in his and raising it to his lips, said softly, "There is not the least need to thank me, I assure you."

The touch of his lips on her hand made her skin tingle, but not averting her eyes from the warmth in his, which had inevitably brought the colour creeping into her cheeks and her heart to beat rather fast, faltered, "I... I can't tell you how... how glad I was to see you."

"You don't have to," he told her gently, hoping that her heightened colour and the glow in her eyes signified that she had come to feel something for him at last, "I know."

The warm and tender look in his eyes, reminiscent of this afternoon, gave her to hope that he did actually feel something for her after all, and that his expressions of affection were indeed as heartfelt and sincere as she had hoped they were and not merely the result of reaction in finding her safe. But as she stood looking up at him, her eyes searching his face and her hand still resting in his, it was as though all restraint suddenly left her, indeed it was as though she was fighting for her very life, because Max was her life, without his love she knew she could no longer go on, and without even pausing to consider how she appeared to him, said earnestly, "Oh, Max! I... I know I am not beautiful, and that I must have come as a great disappointment to you; I know too that I have none of the accomplishments which are expected of a lady in my position, but in view of what passed between us this afternoon, I have dared to hope that... well, what I mean is... oh, Max," she pleaded urgently, "please tell me, does it mean that you come to love me - just a little, after all?"

For one unbelievable moment Max stared down at her as though he could not believe what he had just heard, then, briefly closing his eyes on an anguished sigh, cried, as though the words were ripped from his throat, *"Just a little!* Oh, God, Louisa!" he told her agonizingly, looking earnestly down at her, his fingers gripping hers, "I love you more than just a little."

For one dazed and joyous moment Louisa could do nothing but stare incredulously up at the man she had been in love with almost from the moment she had first met him as though she could not believe she had heard him aright, then, as her momentary paralysis gradually began to recede, she shook her head, as though she could hardly believe it, saying wonderingly, "Y-you *love* me?"

"With all my heart," he told her lovingly, his eyes reflecting the truth of this.

Having waited so long to hear him say he loved her, tears of relief and happiness welled up at back of her eyes, exclaiming, "Oh, Max!" crying and laughing at the same time, hardly daring to believe that he really did love her, "I can't tell you how happy that makes me, because you see," she shrugged helplessly, "I have been agonizingly in love with you almost from the moment I first met you."

He looked down into her glowing face and sparkling eyes, telling him more than any words could as to how much she loved him, but as there were no words adequate to describe how he felt, he let go of her hand and pulled her into his arms, not at all gently, and thoroughly kissed her. How long she remained locked in his arms Louisa had no idea, not that it mattered, all she knew was that she was where she wanted to be, now and always, but as she received his kisses with the same amount of pleasure and eagerness he was giving them, coherent thought took second place.

It seemed a very long time before his lips eventually released hers, leaving her feeling quite bereft, but looking up into his face, his cheeks as delicately tinted as her own, she managed a little huskily, "Y-you have never kissed me like that before."

"No," he said slowly, shaking his head, "I know, but I have wanted to; so help me I have wanted to. But if it comes to that," he smiled, removing his arms from around her and taking hold of her hands, giving them a little shake, "you have never responded like that before either."

"I know," she nodded, "but I too have wanted to, so very much. But you see," she explained, "Mamma said…"

"What did Mamma say?" he asked gently.

She felt the colour flood her cheeks, but since it seemed that now was the time when nothing but the truth would do, she told him, with a helpless little shrug, "Mamma said that… well, she told me that I was not to fall in love with you or expect you to fall in love with me, and that I could naturally expect some display of affection from you but I was not to read anything into that because it was only what I could expect from a man of your breeding, and that any intimacies you imposed on me was you merely doing your duty." She swallowed. "She… she said that I was not to let you see that I was forever wanting to be in your company or hanging on your arm or… or let you see that I was affected by your kisses and lovemaking which would only give you a disgust of me," she paused, "she also said that… that when it came to… to your pleasures, I could leave that to your… your connection."

Max needed no further explanation to account for Louisa distancing herself from him, in fact, he could almost hear her mamma warning her against him or, if not that, then doing everything possible to guard her daughter from going through what she had obviously had to suffer at the hands of her wayward husband, but it had the effect of bringing a sardonic reply from him, "I'm obliged to Mamma. What else did she say?" raising an enquiring eyebrow.

"Oh," Louisa shook her head, having a very good idea of what was going through his mind, not that she could blame him, "more of the same, but that's not important now," she told him, her fingers gripping his.

"No," he said slowly, looking lovingly down at her for a moment, "that's not important now."

"Oh, Max!" she cried, "whenever you made love to me or kissed me, I did so want to respond, truly I did, you must believe that, but Mamma's warnings always held me back. I could not bear to see disgust in your eyes."

She felt him heave a deep sigh, then, taking her in his arms he held her close, saying into her neck, "You could never disgust me; nor were you a disappointment to me, but the blame is mine," he said raggedly, "I should have known that your mamma would have said something of the kind to you."

"She meant it for the best, but oh, Max!" she cried, "she could not have made me more unhappy if she had tried."

"Then that makes two of us," he told her softly, "because I have been very unhappy too."

"Y-You have?" she faltered.

"Very much so," he nodded. "You see," he told her lovingly, his arms tightening around her, "what had begun as a marriage of convenience soon turned into one of love, so much so that I knew I could not stop loving you if I tried." He kissed her forehead. "I kept hoping and praying that one day you would come to love me as I loved you, but as time passed I was beginning to think you never would, even so, there were times," he told her softly, "when I thought I caught something in your eyes to give me hope, but it had gone so quickly that I had begun to think I had imagined it."

"Oh, Max!" she cried, "I… "

Silencing the words on her tongue, he kissed her, deep and passionate kisses that made her feel rather helpless and weak and quite incapable of standing on her own two feet without the support of his arms, not to mention feeling as though her lips would be bruised for days as well as a possible cracked rib, but as these were mere irrelevancies, she eagerly gave herself up to his kisses.

"I'm not going to lie to you, Louisa," he told her gently when he eventually released her, his forefinger delicately stroking her chin, "there have been other women in my life, but there has been no one since I met you, there never will be. You are the only woman I want, now and for always."

"Oh, Max!" she managed, a stray tear falling down her cheek. "I do love you, so very much."

"You had better," he groaned, lowering his head, "because I most certainly love you," then spent the next few minutes proving just how much he did love her by kissing her with long and loving kisses that she happily melted into him.

"Oh, Max," she cried when she had recovered her breath, "is it too much to ask… well, what I mean is," she shook her head, "can't we start all over again and pretend that tonight is our wedding night?"

He looked lovingly down at her, his thumb gently caressing her lips. "And that we were only married today?" he smiled, raising an amusing eyebrow, to which she nodded. "I think that that is a very good idea. In fact," he told her warmly, "I have been thinking very much the same myself."

"You have?" she breathed.

He nodded, then, as if words were superfluous, he kissed her, deep drugging kisses that made her melt into him. "You know," he smiled, when he finally released her lips, "this garment," indicating her nightdress with a nod of his head, "is most becoming, and far be it from me to dissuade you from wearing such a garment, it is rather in the way."

She cast a quick look down at it. "You mean you… you want me to take it off?" she asked, her eyes smiling up into his.

"No," he said lovingly, slowly shaking his head, "I mean I want to take it off."

"Oh," she nodded, "well, that's all right then."

He laughed, a deep and happy sound that came from deep within his throat, then, after taking a moment to kiss her, he slowly raised his head, his eyes looking lovingly down at her glowing face before travelling down to her nightdress, allowing his fingers to unhurriedly, and quite deliberately, untie the three bows of ribbon, gently spreading open the edges to gradually expose the soft swell of her breasts. Whenever Max had made love to her before she had never removed her nightdress or he his nightshirt, but as Louisa stood before him, she felt no embarrassment, on the contrary it seemed the most natural thing in the world. She heard his sharp intake of breath before slowly slipping it off her shoulders to fall in a silent heap to the floor, saying hoarsely, "You are so beautiful; so very beautiful," before passionately kissing her. Then, as if he could contain himself no longer, he picked her effortlessly up in his arms and carried her over to the bed, gently laying her down, then, after removing his dressing gown and nightshirt slid into bed beside her, taking her in his arms to begin a wonderful and irresistible assault on her defences, an assault she happily welcomed and eagerly returned.

The past two days had without any doubt been the worst of her entire life, and ones she would never be quite able to forget; the only thing which had rendered it less harrowing was when she had seen Max enter her room at *'The Green Man'*, the sight of him and his words of endearment filling her with unalloyed happiness. That Singleton had felt it necessary to take such a drastic step as holding her to ransom proved not only just how desperate he was but just how much he hated Max, and the lengths he was prepared to go to pay him back for what he called his meddlesome interference. He may have been a friend of her father, but that in no way made him any more acceptable to her.

Her father had irresponsibly gone headlong down his hedonistic path without a thought for anything or anyone but his own pleasures, wreaking a terrible cost on his estates and leaving his son and heir to do the best he could with what was left as well as leaving his daughter with no choice but to contract the marriage of convenience which had been arranged years before. Even though Louisa had known almost from the first moment she had met Max that she loved him, she had believed that that was all it was to him, a marriage of convenience, but neither this nor her mother's warnings had changed her feelings for him. But, now, knowing he had married her for love and not convenience after all, Louisa felt a contentment she had never known before, and as she basked under Max's impassioned lovemaking, returning his kisses and caresses with the same eagerness he was giving them, all that mattered was that he loved her just as much as she loved him.

ABOUT THE AUTHOR

Patricia E. Walker was born in Coseley, Staffordshire (now West Midlands). After being educated at local schools and colleges she then went on to work in the legal field in a secretarial and administration capacity. From solicitors' offices she then went into The West Midlands Police Administration Courts Department before transferring into the Criminal Investigation Department until eventually entering the Probation Service.

Patricia enjoys the ballet, growing roses, watching old black and white movies and travelling, particularly visiting historical venues and battlefields with her husband Andrew. Her trips have included St. Petersburg and the Romanovs, The Hoffburg Palace and Schonbrunn in Vienna as part of her studies about Crown Prince Rudolph, the battlefields of the American Civil War, Monte Cassino in Italy and many more.

Patricia has also given historical talks for charity, particularly Children in Need.

Patricia's love of history and writing has been merged to form her historical novels, including *Impeccable Credentials, Civil Hostilities, The Ferrers Connection, Spawn's Brat* and her new book *Her Father's Daughter*.

Printed in Great Britain
by Amazon